BEHIND STONE WALLS

ANAM CARA
BOOK 2

SILK AUBREY

PROLOGUE
SHADE

I SPLAYED MY FINGERS WIDE IN THE DIRT AND WRENCHED magic from the beating heart of the fae wilds. The neon red grass and bright blue trees dimmed as I bent their power to my will. Clouds of billowing, blue-black magic injected the fading souls of the dead who had fallen in this fight. Innocent and warrior alike rose at my call. As one, my army turned toward the battle that still raged.

My Cara *pulsed* with my pack's strategies, but I filtered them out with practiced ease. Woven magic leant its wavering quality to the world around me, and I swayed with a wild grin.

A new Tech, fifty feet of cables, metal, and mutilated human ingenuity, loomed over the battlefield. Broken and bleeding corpses littered the ground around the mechanical legs that held the new Tech's metal body twenty feet off the ground. Tech of all sorts seethed around it, killing anything that breathed.

A crackle of my twin brother's golden lightning sparked at the edge of my vision. Fireballs, probably Teyr's, rocketed toward the horror's rectangular metal torso, then bounced off a clear shield and exploded midair, showering the battlefield in sparks. Zelimir's massive, two-handed purple sword flew through the air and lodged in the Tech's defenses, looking like a toothpick sticking out of a roast. I alone could destroy the untouchable monstrosity.

The reanimated body of a little gnome girl with a wooden toy still tucked under her arm lurched past me. EarthTech didn't care who they slaughtered. I sent a wispy thread of magic her way, a little extra power to make sure she had the chance to destroy what had destroyed her.

Two of the new Tech's massive, angled legs froze under Bash's control, but the abomination only dragged them along in its march across the battlefield. The elements of the world raged as fae pitted every aspect of Thrae's magic against the invading horde.

I took up the magic's song. The wild rhythm grew louder and louder. Everything but the massive monstrosity disappeared from my reality. Power gathered in my chest. The music of Thrae rose in my ears, and I swiveled my hips in time. As I reached the climax, the buildup of magic and tension released with orgasmic pleasure.

A surge of blue-black power shot from me into my nearest thrall. The magic took whatever energy the dead had left and folded it over itself before jumping to the next, and the next. As the magic left them, my thralls tumbled to the ground.

I trembled. Before my last thrall, the gnomish girl, fell, I took direct control of her body and pushed my vision into her eyes in order to behold my genius.

The condensed magic streaked toward the suddenly still monstrosity in the middle of the battlefield. My twin, Light, hovered beneath its body. Light's brilliant, golden magic spread out from his back like wings and held the massive Tech in place. Shimmering blood dripped from his chin, and he shook with effort.

"I love you." Light lifted his arms, trusting I could hear him.

My heart stuttered. The world's song fell silent. I caught myself as the gnomish girl faltered forward.

The spell hit Light, enveloping his golden magic in deep, dark blue. My magic used his as a focus. My face, his face, all the goodness in my world, contorted in pain. His arms trembled as magic ripped through him and raced upward. Pain filled my Cara. Swirling dark and light tore into the monstrosity's underbelly. With a shower of sparks and a metallic tearing sound, oil and metal exploded across the battlefield.

I fought to stay in my thrall as the gnome's dead body absorbed the impact. The Tech's legs shook under the uneven weight of its ruined carapace. For a moment, I thought the Tech would crush Light, but the thing went ruinously still. Celebration shouts and battle cries exploded over the clash of fighting.

My twin found my thrall's gaze, my gaze, as his knees gave way and he sank to the ground. Deep blue veins covered his skin and pulsed in time with my frantic heartbeat. His grimace twisted into something resembling a smile.

A total, desolate silence sank its teeth into our Cara.

I slammed back into my own body, screaming from a throat already raw. Light. I had to get to Light. I sprinted forward, dodging blasts of energy and wildly swinging swords.

At the feet of the monstrosity, I found a ring of clear burned dirt with Light at the center. My thrall's eyes had not lied. His face had gone blue, leached of all its gold, all the good.

My deadened legs wouldn't carry me. I dropped to my knees and crawled the final few feet to him. Maybe by the time I covered the short distance he would remember how to heal. Maybe then I could remember how to breathe.

Light lay motionless in a patch of darkly scorched soil. I'd been stabbed, burned, and briefly disemboweled in other battles. A pain beyond any of those wounds ripped through my chest.

My soft wolf paw pads met the ruined dirt at his side. My wolf ensnared my mind, quieting the roar of hurt. I curled around my brother's cooling body with a weak howl, my only accompaniment to the day's victory.

1

———

ZELIMIR

I GLANCED TO MY LEFT AND SLIGHTLY BEHIND ME AT SHADE as I led my Cara mates through the door and into the Lower Council's audience chamber. We four loosely surrounded Declan with me in front, Bash and Teyr behind and slightly to each side of him, and Shade, as always, at Declan's side. I detected something indefinable in Shade. His Cara? I couldn't be sure.

From the corner of my eye, I glimpsed Declan trying mightily to hide how he favored his wounded ankle. I faced forward and prayed the Council didn't notice.

The massive, round door rolled into place behind us, sealing us in the windowless room. Hundreds of fifs lit the cavernous space, reflecting light off the polished, bare stone that looked black at first glance, but showed rainbows of dark colors in the light. Bickering over what decorations should exist in this neutral chamber had long ago resulted in a ban on all ornamentation except for an intricately carved arch of the same stone over the dais ahead of us where the Lower Council sat. The effect quailed most fae who entered the room for the first time, but I took strength from the austerity. In this place, we had nothing to hide behind. We could only trust the Cara to be strong enough, as we had the first time we took the vows.

I stopped a scant five feet in front of the Lower Council's raised stone dais. *Presumptuous*, my father's voice nagged in my mind. Politeness meant little to me with Declan's red blood still damp on my tunic. I straightened and *pulsed* to my mates. We parted from the circle to create a line. Bash, my dragon second, stood to my right, lilac head held high. Teyr moved to Bash's right, with fire flickering in his golden, slit-pupiled eyes. Declan's dark, curly hair bounced as I nudged him to my left. Shade, happy once again in dire wolf form, plopped his ass down straight on Declan's booted feet.

"As requested, we present the part-fae, Declan." My voice echoed off the bare walls. "We do not believe a mistake has been made and would like to finalize the Anam Cara."

Silence filled the room. The five fae who held our fate in their hands stared down at us from chairs carved of the same dark stone as the walls. Councilor Ambrocio sat front and center, his diaphanous, rainbow Lower Council robes draped over an antique, formal Cara uniform that only accentuated the way the tall elf's frame bent with age. His long, white beard brushed the floor. I didn't know if I should put any stock in the rumors about his ailing mind, but I knew he wouldn't stand with us. As ambassador to the Upper Council, he stood on no side but theirs.

To his left sat Councilor Gnuq, Headmaster of the Academy, wearing only his open Council robes. The satyr's pot belly had grown in the six years since we'd last been here, probably full of convenient deals and edicts that supported his reign over the training of Caras and Seccas alike. He rested his hands on the curly, golden hair that crested the midsection where his human and animal halves met and offered me a satisfied smile. I repressed a grimace. The Lower Council had earned my loyalty time and again, but I didn't know if I could count on Councilor Gnuq alone.

Councilor Odhrán sat bolt-upright in the far-left chair, though he barely cleared the armrests, wearing Council robes buttoned up to his chin. The short elf brought his trademark exuberance to the Lower Council, often swaying votes, and he managed our understanding of Tech as Liaison to the Jalan. His warm smile, as open as Councilor

Ambrocio's suspicion, eased the foul taste Councilor Gnuq left in my mouth.

To the farthest right, sat Councilor Drax, our former mentor and friend. His deep purple skin, swirling with hot-pink magic, glowed under his robe around worn leathers decorated only by a tiny, yellow lava flower. Before our demotion to border patrol, the Master Tactician managed our movements, as he did the movements of all Caras and Seccas. I had been counting on his support, but he would not meet my eye.

Lastly, I faced Councilor Xerxes. The spymaster looked much like the bhelrian he could shift into, all sharp features and cropped, brownish-yellow hair. He wore a suit of unassuming cream linen under his robe, but I knew better than to underestimate him. I could only hope his love of information would urge him to keep Declan close.

Councilor Xerxes laced his long fingers together in front of his face as he leaned forward. "The human—or mostly human, as you claim—is only a piece of the problem. Shade remains a wolf, and a replacement for a dead mate remains unheard of." The spymaster locked eyes with me. "Your Cara is in shambles, Commander Zelimir."

Declan spluttered. I stood even straighter. We'd never corrected Teyr's early lie about new fifths being common, but the Council couldn't know that.

My father's voice echoed in my ears, and I resisted the urge to clench my jaw in defiance. "My Anam Cara is in better shape with Declan than it's been since the Battle of Light."

Councilor Drax nodded sharply. "Shade shifted. We read the reports."

The tension in my shoulders eased slightly. Councilor Drax might not have looked at us, but he at least he hadn't spoken against us either.

Councilor Ambrocio waved dismissively. "The same report stated this useless human got captured at a rift that opened closer to our academy than any since the school was established."

"There have been three reports of rifts opening near the human"—Councilor Drax frowned—"four, if we include the one near the Waltzing Willow." He balled his fists. "The quantity of EarthTech that came through the rift a few hours ago implies Earth was waiting for the rift to open."

I swallowed. Bash had *pulsed* a similar suspicion, and I hadn't missed his purple-and-white scales shifting to belie his worry on the ride here. I couldn't deny I found the Tech's behavior strange, as well—if Tech could be said to have behavior. But surely, the best place to solve the problem of the escalation in rifts and what the Tech were up to would be at the Academy with the brightest minds of a generation within walking distance.

Councilor Ambrocio narrowed his eyes. "Whatever Tech happens to be patrolling on the other side is what comes through."

Fear leaked into Declan's Cara, and I sent him a wave of calm. Confusion replaced the fear, and I gritted my teeth.

Councilor Xerxes hummed. "With the escalation of late, perhaps it was only a matter of time before a rift appeared so close to the Academy."

Councilor Ambrocio fluffed his beard. "Four extra rifts is odd, but not unreasonable. Don't create conspiracies out of coincidences."

"Should we consider the Battle of Light?" With a sparkle of magic in his palm, Councilor Odhrán conjured a sheaf of papers and studied them. "The battle predates the human, but Commander Zelimir and his Cara were, obviously, instrumental."

Teyr sent me a spike of frustration. I ignored the hotheaded ember. The facts of our world couldn't be avoided to spare our feelings.

Councilor Drax shook his head. "We established the Battle of Light was bad luck. The big Tech—ChargeTech, I believe—stumbled through the rift and the others followed."

Curiosity spun through Declan's Cara. I had come to know him piece by piece, and I wanted more. My mates wanted more. Declan wanted more, I thought. But it took true emotional vulnerability to live with the soul bond the four of us shared, and our human simply didn't have the practice. He needed the training we'd all received.

Councilor Gnuq clopped a cloven hoof against the stone floor. "The rifts may be concerning, but they're not why we're here."

I eyed the satyr. His balding head reflected the light of the fifs as he studied Declan and licked his lips. Only years of diplomatic training kept me from sliding over to shield Declan from his gaze.

"I welcome the Anam Cara for retraining." Councilor Gnuq grinned. "If they can work together and repass their trials, who are we to interfere?"

I took a measured breath. Many fae called Councilor Gnuq the most powerful satyr alive. The Council relied heavily on his ability to control crowds in the Academy. He would make an invaluable ally, if he really wanted the same thing we did.

Councilor Odhrán hopped to his feet on his chair. "You can't expect to treat a veteran Cara like trainees."

Councilor Drax sighed. "They are a promising Anam Cara, but they don't have their first century together yet. They're hardly veterans."

Councilor Xerxes cocked his head to one side. "I don't like the idea that, after six hundred years, our magic is making mistakes." He ran a thumb along his thin lower lip. "To brush Declan off may be short-sighted."

"Not you too." Councilor Ambrocio sneered. "This *human* makes a mockery of our traditions."

Councilor Xerxes narrowed his eyes at Declan. "Rifts appearing around Declan isn't enough to draw conclusions. We require more information. He may have fae in him somewhere." He pursed his lips. "Come closer, human."

Declan slid his feet out from under Shade and clasped his hands behind his back like I'd shown him. Despite the fear trembling through his Cara, he took three confident steps forward.

Bash snarled and lunged after him. I twitched my hands behind my back and shot out a thin layer of purple force to grab his collar. My second growled but didn't struggle. His newly awoken dragon still strained against his iron control. We needed as much retraining as we could get. It wasn't until Declan began pulling us back together that I noticed how out-of-sync my mates had gotten. Since we lost Light, we'd all fallen back toward the fae we had been before the bond.

Declan held his head high as Councilor Drax stepped down from the dais and circled him. After a few slow circuits, he returned to his seat, and Councilor Xerxes stepped down. The spymaster lacked our old mentor's discretion and began prodding Declan. When he discovered the ears, the seated Councilors murmured amongst themselves.

Councilor Xerxes eventually retook his chair and looked at Councilor Ambrocio, who scoffed. Councilor Gnuq slid down happily. Declan's fear spiked, and our human batted Councilor Gnuq's hand away from his chest when the satyr tried to touch him. Bash growled again. I committed the intrusion to memory and tightened my grip on my second, as much to keep myself rooted in place as the dragon.

Between the Council's orders and our own prejudices, I hadn't thought to balance our bond as we traveled. To manage a true Cara, we needed to trust and love each other equally. My mates needed a commander, not the romantic Declan brought out in me.

The Councilors finished their inspection, and Declan returned to stand to my left. Shade circled him and rubbed against his hips. Declan's fear eased, and Bash relaxed. I released my magic. My hand ached from how hard I'd had to maintain my grip on the dragon.

"If you intend to fly in the face of all tradition, I have no choice but to reveal what I have seen." Councilor Ambrocio stood, and his beard shifted to expose the navy skin of his throat, the only clue to his heritage as an auspex.

I took a deep breath. In addition to more mundane magic, the old Councilor received visions like others of his clan. Most of the rumors about him suggested his visions could no longer be trusted, but that said nothing of what his fellow Councilors might believe.

"If we accept this human, I see our academy destroyed." Ambrocio braced his thin arms on the sides of his chair like the vision still wracked him. "Our towers drained of color to an Earthen white, and many of us dying in pools of our own blood."

Councilor Odhrán offered him a tense grin. "Ambrocio, I think—"

Councilor Xerxes tugged on his ear, and Councilor Ambrocio sat. The Councilors fell into a discussion as a soft haze of nonexistent room noise blotted out their words. Teyr crossed his arms. Bash rolled his neck out. Declan fidgeted with the charm on his belt. My heart pounded in my ears. Councilor Xerxes might affect our ability to hear their conversation, but I doubted he'd stop his fellow Councilors from observing us.

Councilor Ambrocio turned back to us as the sensory magic faded away. "We shall take a vote."

The air in front of each Councilor glowed a soft green as they voted. Moments later, the glow condensed into a bright circle visible to all five of them.

Councilor Drax raised an eyebrow. "Two in favor, one against, two abstentions." He met my gaze. "Commander Zelimir's Anam Cara will be given the opportunity to prove the magic is correct with retraining." He looked at Declan. "You understand what this means?"

Declan bit his lip. Councilor Drax's gaze softened. Perhaps our old mentor still remained under the surface.

"Your Cara is fresh," he said. "Your minds still walk their own paths. By training, you merge those paths, tangling them together and solidifying what connections grow, until you become a single, streamlined unit. Everything but a true hive mind." Five strings of pink magic grew out of the pink lines on Councilor Drax's forehead, tangled together to form a knot, then turned into a solid, glowing ball. "If you don't merge correctly or if you fail one of your trials, your connections will shatter." The ball burst, leaving behind scraps of broken, pink magic.

Declan flinched.

Councilor Drax turned back to me. "Will the Anam Cara submit?"

Declan shifted and tugged on my arm. If we'd been anywhere else, I would've been charmed. Here, I gritted my teeth. He'd just shown the Council he couldn't understand our *pulses*.

"You don't have to do this," he whispered. "I don't want to be the reason you lose nearly a century of work."

I addressed the Council as if Declan hadn't spoken. "We will submit."

Shade howled. Councilor Ambrocio glared as the sound bounced around the chamber.

"So be it," Councilor Drax said. "I strip you of your rank as Anam Cara. Report to Bodmier for equipping. You will undergo the five trials—"

I stepped forward, perilously close to the base of the dais. "We request our first trial."

Caras completed trials in the order we arrived at the Academy, which put me first. Declan would be last.

Councilor Ambrocio stomped. "You haven't even begun training yet."

Teyr stepped up beside me. "Our rank doesn't change our experience." He gestured to Councilor Gnuq. "The rules state an Anam Cara may request their trials as they feel ready, don't they, Headmaster? That's what separate us from mere Anam Seccas, who are tested at regular intervals."

Councilor Gnuq grinned. "Why, yes, you're right. And as headmaster, I think it only fair our newest recruits follow the same rules as all the others."

"Three days hence." A deep voice boomed around us.

The Upper Council. I'd never heard them directly before. I took a step back and poured calm through my Cara, as much for myself as my mates. Only sheer will kept me from pulling Declan to my chest. Councilor Ambrocio existed to ferry messages between the Upper Council and the rest of us, but only they would reach into this chamber and make pronouncements. A tense silence fell as the whole room held its breath in anticipation of more.

Councilor Ambrocio stood. "The Upper Council has spoken."

Councilor Drax cleared his throat, his eyes fixed on Declan. "Three days hence. I hope for your sakes that your confidence matches your skills."

Declan grabbed my arm again, and I batted his hand away. The Upper Council, the remains of Varsina's Cara, fae so powerful they no longer considered our world their home, had taken an interest in us. I couldn't remember a time in the last century when they'd interfered with how the Lower Council ran the Academy or anything else. We had to excel now more than ever.

2

———

KINNIA

We left the round, windowless room in silence. My mind spun with questions. There had to be an Upper Council to match their Lower Council, but I had no idea who or what they were, other than a booming voice that had clearly shocked even the councilors.

I gritted my teeth against the pain in my ankle and fiddled with the fading golden charm on my belt. The fact that even higher authorities already had their eyes on us couldn't be good. I couldn't mess this up. Shade's heat against my hip reminded me how fragile our growing Cara really was. My heart squeezed. I knew almost nothing of the dark-haired fae inside my wolf.

A three-foot-tall pile of brown hair popped into existence right in my path, and I skidded to a halt. Bash skipped to the side to avoid crashing into me. The pile floated up the wall, spinning like a top. Its long hair brushed the colorful cloth draped across the hallway ceiling. The pile floated back down to the floor, leaving the cloth spotless.

I dropped to one knee on the smooth stone floor and peered underneath the hair. "It doesn't have feet. How does it spin? What is it doing?"

"Magic." Zelimir grasped my arm and hauled me up.

"Gee, really?" I yanked free of his grip and turned back to the creature.

Zelimir had brushed me off twice during the meeting with the Councilors. I didn't know why, but he was acting like he had when we'd left the *Cross Roads*.

"It's called an ittle." Teyr began walking again. "Fae are magic, even when we're not using it. We shed a little, and these hairy guys eat it, which happens to also keep things clean. It's a win-win."

I raised an eyebrow and followed him. "They aren't being exploited?"

Zel put a heavy hand on my shoulder and squeezed a warning. I scowled but fell silent. Only he got to speak to the Councilors for some reason. Maybe that applied in the hallways as well?

We turned into a round room filled with wooden tables of various shapes and sizes. Two round tables near the wall held groups of five fae in all green or all red picking at plates of cheese and bread that matched a spread on a long, bright-red cherrystone counter attached to the wall on my left. Except for the roundness and the colorful drapes along the ceiling, the room looked much like the few human cafeterias where I'd eaten. Bash slipped away, pulling out a bag as he approached the table laden with bread and cheese.

Zelimir studied a stretch of dark stone wall shot through with golden veins. "Councilor Odhrán, Councilor Drax, and Commander Geminai are lecturing today."

"Geminai, really?" Teyr wrinkled his nose and looked at the same part of the wall. "At least it's a bit late in the day to attend."

I couldn't imagine what the shithead troll we'd met on the road would have to teach me. "Wait, how do you know?"

Teyr gestured to the wall where Zelimir still stared. "Rune casters can inscribe runes on any object to make it show messages, even changing ones."

I squinted at the wall. The golden veins writhed before my eyes until they settled into a recognizable order. Words! There, clear as day, I could read the schedule on the wall.

"As best we can tell, runes are the language of magic. Magic made everything, so the runes excel at granting objects properties they normally wouldn't have," Teyr said.

I grinned, stepped forward, and touched the wall. the veins shifted beneath my fingers.

"Declan." Zelimir's sharp rebuke caught my attention. "You are now a fae warrior. Behave like one."

He stepped closer and pressed a hand to my lower back, straightening my spine. I tingled with a heat that didn't match his rebuke and clenched my fists.

"The Upper Council has eyes and ears everywhere," he murmured. "You can no longer behave like we're alone on the road."

I kept my shoulders back as he removed his hand and stepped away. Disappointment filled my gut, but I bit the inside of my cheek. I wouldn't let down my mates or give the mysterious Upper Council any ammunition. If there was one thing Declan knew how to do, it was behave like a warrior. With another *pulse* I couldn't understand, my Cara snapped back into that loose formation around me, and I fell into step behind my commander. Shade panted as he padded alongside us.

We left the room and marched in silence down the halls. Swaths of brightly colored, translucent fabric hung from the center of the ceiling, painting the dark space with color and texture. The occasional round, red or green or pale wood door interrupted the picture.

A few fae in light green tunics and dark green pants cut like my mates' Cara uniforms passed us, shooting suspicious glares and whispering behind cupped hands. My stomach churned. Even surrounded by my mates and doing my best to stay stoic, I stuck out like a sore thumb. My patience evaporated.

I glanced back at Teyr. "Are the lectures bad? You said you hated it here."

Teyr raked his fingers through the sheet of longer golden hair on one side of his head. "I said I didn't want to be here. I still don't. The only thing that made any of this bearable was the sudden swarm of female attention. I hated the Anam Cara at first." His eyes darkened.

I studied him. "Thinking about Light?"

Teyr chuckled, but it sounded forced. "Not going to focus on the female attention part?"

"Bigger problems." I snorted. "I don't think a human will have the same experience as you."

He winked.

Zelimir stopped suddenly in front of a green door on the right wall, and I smacked into his back. He glanced over his shoulder and scowled at Teyr and me. I bit back a grin. At least I had someone to get into trouble with, like when Alex and I used to whisper everything David said back to each other in higher and higher voices.

With a huff, my commander placed one palm against the green wood. The door rolled silently to the side. The simple, circular room looked barren and small after our journey under the stars and the luxury of Stoneheim. Multicolored fabric draped down from the ceiling, like in the waiting room and hallway. Rays of dying light streamed in through a small window, and floating warm-toned fifs illuminated the room. Five semi-circular beds with green quilts nestled against the walls, next to little dressers that I guessed could hold a few changes of clothes and double as nightstands. A ruby leather couch and a few matching armchairs encircled a low coffee table in the middle of the room.

My throat tightened as I noticed the same green outfits I'd seen on the fae in the hallways lying on each bed. Those had to be the students' uniform, at least for Caras.

"Wait until tomorrow to put those on," Zelimir said. "Training begins in the morning."

A little chorus of *pulses* followed his words. The worn leather seats around the table looked inviting, and I had so many questions, but my mates each stepped to their own beds.

I glanced at my commander. His head nearly scraped the ceiling of the small room, and he frowned down at his trainee uniform. I couldn't remember the last time I'd looked at him and not found him already looking at me. The ease we'd found at his castle had vanished the moment we crossed the Academy's threshold.

My heart sank. How had everything changed so fast?

3

———

BASH

The next morning, I sat across from my commander at the enchanted oval table I'd lugged into the suite from a nearby common room. The three-dimensional gameboard of League lay open on the table between us. Dense magical forests gave way to two main paths along the edges of the map, and smaller trails hidden in the trees connected the two. Zelimir's side of the board remained dark, but the round tower of his home base, which held the power core I needed to win, poked up over the trees.

Shade whined unhappily from the floor in front of our suite door, which he'd refused to leave since Dee asked Teyr to give her a better look at the Academy this morning. Our first lecture would be after lunch, so Zelimir had just *pulsed* the ember a warning to not be late.

"Declan is fine with Teyr," my commander told Shade.

I grunted. Zelimir kept saying that. He'd only agreed to play League in order keep himself from pulling his copper twists out of his head in worry. He rarely enjoyed the games Teyr and I favored.

I left two pawns at my tower to protect my own core and used my telekinetic power to send the other two in search of gaps in his defense. One of his pieces crossed the border into my side of the forest, and I sent one of mine to intercept.

My scales swirled with the tension that had plagued me since we left the Council's audience chamber yesterday, but I hadn't yet located the source of my anxiety. Perhaps I missed Dee's endless stream of questions about the wilds. Perhaps I just missed Dee.

League rewarded big moves, so as I intercepted Zelimir's piece, I sent the two defending my base along the left path to join my third for an assault on his home base.

Two of my commander's pieces slipped into my home base, and I cursed. I should have guessed he'd sneak around. He grabbed my power core and sent his pieces down the left path. Glowing blue bars appeared above the pawns' heads to track how many attacks they could withstand, and his side of the board blazed to life.

I allowed myself a small smile and rocketed the one piece I'd engaged with him to join my other three, then hooked back down the left path. Our forces clashed in the middle, and I wiped him off the map. My power core reappeared in my base, and his pieces in his. Zelimir's half of the map went dark once more.

My commander scowled. "Brute force. I should have known you'd overload the left path. You play Teyr too often."

We shared a grin. I broke first, looking back to the game board.

He studied the board with a frown. "Is it your dragon?"

I grunted and cracked my tattooed knuckles. The beast in the back of my mind circled. I wished my dragon was my only problem. I feared for Declan. None of my mates understood how vulnerable she truly was.

Negative forces bonded Caras like nothing else, so Councilor Gnuq rewarded hazing and bullying. Even if I didn't want to keep Dee's secret for her sake—and my own, my dragon reminded me—she would be safer if no one knew. Declan's human heritage had already drawn enough attention. I couldn't imagine how the Council would react if they knew she was a woman. How lonely she must be, pretending to be someone else. Countless years alone with my experiences had nearly driven me mad. Only the Cara had freed me from that isolation. I wanted Dee to have that joy.

Zelimir sighed, and I realized I hadn't answered his question. I wish

I could tell him my worries were about my dragon, but that would be a lie. So, I said nothing.

The first time I walked these halls hadn't been easy, between Teyr's antics and the twins' quirks, but falling under Zelimir's leadership had been as easy as breathing. He filled the missing pieces in my heart, served as the brains to my brawn, and never asked questions I didn't want to answer. Keeping Dee's secret was the closest I'd ever come to disobeying him.

I took a deep breath and focused. Since his attempt at stealth failed, Zelimir would try something more direct. I sent two pieces sneaking down the right path and hoped I could reach his base before he attacked.

"Zel—"

My dragon closed my mouth just as two of my commander's pieces slipped into my base from the left. I slammed my hand down on the table as they shot to the right with my power core. The board lit. Another of his pieces joined them briefly before splitting for the left path. I only had two pieces in range that could catch up, and the power core could be on either side of the board. If my mind were clearer, I would have pursued the two on the righthand path with full force.

With confession boiling on my tongue, I split my forces. Zelimir's two pieces demolished mine easily and raced toward home. I sent the two I had on his side of the board toward his base in case he didn't have the core. Before the one-on-one battle on the left path had even ended, fireworks exploded from his end of the board. My gut twisted, not from the loss, but from what I'd almost done. Dee didn't want anyone to know her secret. I shouldn't know. My dragon nodded, curling back up inside me. She was mine, and mine alone. I grabbed my head. We needed to earn her trust, not own her.

My commander caught my gaze. His purple eyes burned into mine. "Bash, you can lean on me."

My dragon twisted and hissed disagreement. I dropped my hands to the board before I could pull the skin off my head. My dragon seethed with the desire to go after Dee.

I gritted my teeth and forced him to trust my commander at least far enough to remain in the suite. "Another."

4

KINNIA

I LIMPED DOWN A SLOPING HALL WITH TEYR AT MY SIDE. THE washroom in our suite only contained a sink and a toilet. He said the shared baths were down this hallway, and I wanted to scope them out before my smell situation became drastic.

The smooth floor of the Academy gave way to something more natural, and Teyr waved me forward with a grin. "This is the lowest part of the Academy anybody actually goes to. Below this, it's just storage closets and the crystals that make this part of the world so powerful. But only the Councilors are allowed in there."

My ankle throbbed. After yesterday's meeting, nobody bothered to tell me if this place had healers, and I'd quickly learned that if I stopped every conversation to ask my questions, none of my mates would ever get through a sentence. Bath first. The rest, I'd learn in time.

We walked across a thin line of runes that glowed faint rainbow colors and entered a massive, stepped cave. I stopped short at sight of the naked fae that lounged, bathed, and did...other things.

I forced my gaze to the edges of the cave walls, which were decorated with stalagmite. The walls were made of the same dark, rainbowed stone as the rest of the Academy, stalactites hung from a shadowed ceiling, and a series of carved pools sparkled in the middle of the space. At the farthest end, a steaming waterfall dumped milky blue mineral water into a deep, round pool just large enough for the dozen fae lounging there.

The water flowed down and toward us into a shallower pool nearly twice as large. A third pool lay closest to us, twice again as large and so shallow that the water at the edge of the pool barely covered the ankles of the fae there. A few rods and hooks of cherrystone ending in umbrella shapes—showers, maybe—lined the wall at the shallowest edge.

The roar of the waterfall muffled the voices bouncing around the cavern. I ducked behind a stalagmite as a group of fae exited the lowest pool and walked past me. I glanced at their erections, then yanked my gaze up to their faces. One of them pressed another to a wall with a hungry kiss, and a third wrapped his hands around each of their stiff cocks.

"Enjoying the show?" Teyr's warm breath bathed my ear.

I jumped and swung a punch. He sidestepped the blow as my fist whizzed within a hair's distance of his nose.

"I wasn't looking," I blurted.

"It's okay to watch. If they didn't want others to see, they would keep it in their suite." He licked his lips. "Mm. They say Cara and Secca trainees are the same when the clothes come off, but you can still tell who's soul bonded."

I pressed a hand to my racing heart. "I wasn't watching."

Zel's low voice echoed in my memory. *What we share goes deeper than physical pleasure.* Hopefully, whatever the Cara bond shared didn't go into specifics, because heat blossomed between my legs. The vivid dreams I'd been having about my mates since Stoneheim hadn't abated with the weirdness here, and my imagination started filling us into the other Cara's places.

Teyr grinned. "We could try something similar to that." He nodded toward the fae. "Their technique's functional, but I bring a finesse to a hand job that I doubt you've ever experienced."

Something between a laugh and a cough bubbled out of my throat. My heart began racing for a new reason. Teyr looked me up and down, reminding me of a different mineral pool, in a different time.

I grabbed the ember's arm and pulled him back toward the hall. "I've never seen you do that with any of our mates." The word *mates* still rolled oddly off my tongue.

"Every Cara's different." Teyr wrapped an arm around my waist, taking most of my weight off my injured ankle, and continued forward. "Some aren't sexual at all, while others become too enamored with themselves to do anything outside of the bond. We're still individuals with our own needs and desires. All a Cara needs is balance."

"Balance?" I vaguely remembered one of them saying something about that when they first explained Caras.

Teyr shrugged, knocking my next step slightly off-kilter.

"If I started spending all my time with Bash, my magic with Zelimir would suffer." He clucked his tongue. "Jealousy, anger, frustration, they all hurt the bond. We need to find a way to communicate and grow together."

I nodded. "How do we do that?"

"That's a good question."

We rounded a bend, and I had to drop behind him to let a group of green-uniformed trainees pass in the narrow hall. He waited for me and pulled me close again.

"Shade's wolf form made everything worse, but even before that...." Teyr paused, then smirked. "Bash is Bash. He's only into women, but he's open to sharing when he's not moody. Shade and Light shared everything, but Shade's had some rocky patches figuring out who he is. Our fearless leader has a stick so far up his butt even a treant couldn't find it." Teyr rubbed his chest, his gaze going distant. "Honestly, I've not felt a true balance for a long time. Maybe not ever."

A purple rodent scampered past us in the hall.

I bit my bottom lip, trying not to picture what *sharing* might entail. "What about you?"

Teyr tripped on the flat floor before catching himself. "Me?" He grinned. "I'm a sex god. I shared just as much as Shade and Light." He tapped his chest. "I'm the reason Bash learned to share."

Declan would laugh. Kinnia, however, didn't much like the idea of her mates being with other women.

I forced a chuckle. "So, where does that leave us?"

"I honestly don't know." Teyr jerked his head left at an intersection. "It's kind of Zel's problem to fix. Commander and all. He should already be working on it."

We turned and came face-to-face with Councilor Ambrocio. He scowled and waved his hand. My attempt to skitter to the side got a helping hand from some invisible spell, and I collided with the far wall. My ankle crashed against the stone. I collapsed as pain seared up my leg.

"Apologies." The old fae only made eye contact with Teyr before he swept on through the halls.

I cradled my ankle, fighting back tears and the sinking feeling I didn't belong here, no matter what my mates said.

Teyr stared after the Councilor. "Shithead."

He looked back at me, then raced to my side and dropped to one knee. He wrapped an arm around my shoulders. "Zel will tell you. Ambrocio's a traditionalist, but that just means stick-in-the-mud asshole. We don't need him anyway."

Despite the warmth of his skin on mine, my heart started to race with fear. My boot soaked through with blood from my reopened ankle wound, and pain dimmed my ability to reason. My last foster mother kicked me out for not being human enough. Here, I was too human to stay.

"Hey." Teyr leaned into my line of sight and grasped my chin. "Look at me."

I dragged my gaze to his. Golden eyes burned into mine.

"We're all still together. Ambrocio being bitchy doesn't mean anything, and if it did, we'd leave the Academy with you, okay?"

My breath caught. I didn't want these fae, my fae, to lose what had taken them a whole human lifetime to earn. I didn't want to ruin anything.

He grimaced. "Okay, that didn't help." Teyr scanned the hallway as if the blank walls held secrets. "I'm gonna teach you a breathing exercise all embers learn. Fire is emotion, and this helps us control that. Can you breathe with me?"

I nodded.

"In for five." He inhaled.

I sucked in a breath with him.

"Hold for one, two, three, four, five," he said in a stilted, airless voice.

I would have giggled if I could.

"Out for five." We both released all the air in our lungs.

We repeated the exercise, and on the third round, my head cleared except for the pain. He ran me through the breaths a few more times anyway. Maybe Councilor Ambrocio was just a stick in the mud I didn't have to worry about. Maybe my mates wouldn't lose anything. I just had to be tough enough to deal with all the looks and jabs in the meantime.

I took Teyr's hand and squeezed. "Thank you."

He grinned. "Any time. Can also help you slow down an orgasm, if you don't want the good times to end."

I smacked him, then let him help me up, and we continued hobbling back to the suite. Finally, finally, we reached the completely unidentifiable green door to our room. At this rate, I'd get to classes faster if I made a map by hand.

"Press here"—Teyr placed his palm against a rune I could barely make out on the dark green wood—"and the door will roll back into the wall. It only responds to the frequency of our Anam Cara. The pale doors are general use. Don't try the red ones at all. Those are for Secca trainees."

The door rolled back, and we entered the suite. Zelimir looked up. He wore only the pants of his new uniform. The midday sun snarled in his copper chest hair and sparkled off his mostly bare abs.

I swallowed and tried not to dwell on what I'd seen in the pools. Teyr's toothy grin told me I hadn't quite succeeded. I stuck my tongue out at him, and even that movement made my ankle ache. I needed to find out what damage the fall had done. I slipped into the washroom.

I sat on the closed toilet, then removed Bash's bandage and cleaned off the blood. The pain roared, but I squashed the whimper in my chest. Maybe now I could think about sharing without my nosy mates feeling anything through the pain.

My initial chemistry with Zel had been so strong. Teyr might be a near perfect example of the male form, but I couldn't stop thinking about the titan. And until we got here, it seemed like he'd been willing to pursue me.

I stared down at my ankle. I'd busted a few of Bash's stitches, but not so many I couldn't fix them. Blood dripped down my foot. I wet a washcloth, grabbed a needle and thread I kept in a pocket of my weapons belt, and got to work.

Memory of Bash's touch when he'd stitched my wounds filled my stomach with butterflies. I yearned for his comfort the most, but he hadn't demonstrated a scrap of romantic interest. He'd been more willing to touch me since the rift in the Mud Pits, but that could just be the Cara bonding.

Shade's two forms filled me with fear and joy equally. And, while Teyr brimmed with passion in a way that sometimes kept me up at night, he seemed to maintain that passion for anything that moved. Even if it wouldn't blow my secret, hooking up with any of them would change the group's balance. Worse, the Cara itself could be destroyed.

I ran my hands under the sink and raked warm water through my hair. I hadn't even had friends in years. I could just be friends with all of them.

With aching fingers, I bandaged my ankle and donned my new uniform. The forest-green pants slid over my tanned skin like silk, but the moment I buttoned the waistband, the pants conformed to my legs and hardened like armor. Just like the pants I'd worn in Stoneheim. I breathed a sigh of relief that I wouldn't have to worry about my mates expecting erections from me, on top of everything else. The mint-colored tunic remained a loose, long-sleeved garment with a single empty brown circle on the shoulder. Zel said I shouldn't wear anything here that I'd gotten in Stoneheim, as that might send the wrong message, so I sighed and tightened my bindings. My breath caught, and I prayed I'd find a way to loosen them before the real training began. Surrounded by fae, I would need my whole lung capacity to keep up.

I limped back into the suite. Zel sat on the leather sofa with a heavy book in hand. Across the room, Bash and Teyr bent over an ovular table between their beds with a three-dimensional map spread out before them. Shade thumped his tail against the floor where he lay curled against the wall. Zelimir growled, and the wolf remained in his ball.

A tiny fireworks display shot up from the side of the board closest to Bash, and he grinned at me before schooling his features. Teyr smacked the table. I took a deep breath. Things had become stranger and more complicated, but at least we had each other.

I smiled. "Lunch?"

I PAUSED IN THE DOORWAY TO THE CAFETERIA, LOOKING AT the sea of fae dressed in green or red. Food covered every counter, and bodies filled every seat. Laughter and conversation bounced around the large, well-lit cafeteria we—I—had discovered yesterday. My mates knew every corner of this place.

A hush rippled through our peers. Their peers. I gritted my teeth.

"Brace yourself," Teyr hissed.

Slowly, the blanket of noise fell back over the space. Zelimir's name bubbled through the conversation. I squared my shoulders, and we walked in. Teyr fit in perfectly with the rest of the laughing trainees, but Bash's cold expression looked carved from stone. Crow's feet danced at the corners of Zelimir's eyes, and the occasional fine line aged his features. My mates shouldn't be here. They'd moved past mingling with raw recruits nearly a century ago.

Bash found a long table near one of the walls and encouraged a few trainees to scoot down so we could fit. My mates glanced around as if expecting trouble. I followed their gazes, but I only saw curious young fae.

Teyr clapped me on the shoulder. "I don't know what brought your mood down, but food makes everything better."

My stomach rumbled in agreement, and I forced a smile. The ember led me to a buffet spread along one wall. A large bowl of yellow sauce over rice smelled delicious and tasted just as good when I brought a portion back to the table.

After I finished eating, I relaxed a bit. Despite my mate's worries, no one had bothered us. The din of voices reminded me of a tavern. A real smile tugged at my lips. I was in the fae wilds, training to be a part of something.

The trainees around us didn't look as young as I'd first assumed, though I didn't have a reference point for blobs of water or people covered in bright orange fur. Despite the uniforms, skin and hair of every color filled the space. I recognized tall, slender elves and their short, squat counterparts. The branches of a treant rustled as someone who looked like mist walked through them. Nearby, another ember, his long hair pulled back in a ponytail, scowled at me.

I fought to contain my questions, but they danced in my eyes. Teyr smiled at me, then froze. The chatter died down. A chill ran up my spine, and I realized I'd put my back to a portion of the room. Rookie mistake.

"How the mighty have fallen." A voice like a rockslide came from well above my head.

I didn't turn. Bash and Teyr stared steadily above me. The heat of Zelimir's body pressed into my side as he scooted closer.

Teyr scowled. "If you think that, you're as blind as your boulder of a father, Leonai."

Boulder. Could this be Geminai's son? Did I have a troll towering over me?

Leonai laughed maliciously. "Level zero trainees sit in the middle and eat last."

Teyr scoffed, but he glanced at the circle on the shoulder of my tunic. "C'mon. With our experience, you want to call us level zero?"

"No trials, no levels. The human will never pass a single one." I heard the grin in Leonai's voice. "Move."

Bash's eyes flashed dangerously. A soft, warm feeling I'd come to associate with peace and calm radiated from Zelimir's Cara.

"No violence. I'm level four," Leonai said.

"Right." Teyr's voice became condescending. "What's the plan? You move us to the middle table, which is luckily emptying out as we speak, and pelt us with something nasty?" He laughed. "I know it's hard for you, but you could at least try to be clever."

I peeked behind me. As Teyr said, the middle table had indeed suddenly cleared. Leonai had to be Geminai's son. Gray skin stretched over his lumpy muscles and weird, double-layered ears hid behind his frizzy, orange hair. Four full, brown circles decorated the shoulder of his tunic. That had to be the level everybody kept talking about.

Leonai caught my gaze and sneered. "What are you looking at, leech?"

I bit my lip. A laugh bubbled in my chest at a troll being disgusted by me, but caution overpowered the impulse.

"Leave us alone." Zelimir's voice held a warning the brought goose-flesh to my arms.

Leonai clamped a massive hand down on my shoulder. What little humor I'd found vanished, and my skin prickled. His thick fingers dug into my collarbone. Shade growled while my Cara blazed with rage from Teyr and Bash. I subtly shook my head and tried to increase Zelimir's calm. A wave of warmth washed out of me, and I couldn't hold back a small smile. I might not yet know how to keep my emotions out of the bond but putting them in seemed easy.

The calm washed back through me. I knew Leonai, or guys like him. I knew what he wanted. This wasn't any different than breaking Tweek's nose that first night before we headed to the *Cross Roads*. I glanced around at the sea of alien faces pointed at me. Well, maybe a little different.

"You can't be my protectors and my equals," I muttered.

Zelimir stiffened. Bash looked ready to murder Leonai. I tried to force my decision through our bond.

Please. I need to do this.

I didn't know what traveled across the knot in my gut, but Bash nodded sharply. Zelimir scruffed Shade as I stood.

"I'm a level zero," I said evenly. "I'll sit in the middle."

"C'mon, lunch doesn't last forever." Leonai laughed as he pushed me toward the middle table.

Shoulders back. Breath steady. Chin high. They wanted a target, and I couldn't give it to them. I sat as gracefully as I could manage. As predicted, the moment I touched the bench, rotten food flew at me from all sides.

"Filthy human," one fae shouted.

Insults filled the room. Food rained in from every direction. At last, a final rotten apple hit my forehead, bounced off, and squished onto the table in front of me. I took a deep breath in the silence that followed and squeezed my eyes shut. Something sticky and horrible smelling dripped down my face. I couldn't look at my mates. Rotten food and insults meant nothing to me, but I didn't want to see their humiliation.

With confidence I didn't feel, I opened my eyes and shifted to face Leonai. The troll's arrogant grin faltered. A waterfall of clinks and crashes from clay plates and cherrystone cutlery slamming onto wood tables as Bash released his telekinetic hold on the items. I flinched but didn't break eye contact with the troll. I stood, my expression steady, and shook like a dog to dislodge the biggest chunks. A piece of something gooey landed on Leonai's tunic. I bit back the smile and stepped away from my table.

Shoulders back. Breath steady. Chin high.

The skitter of paws on stone followed me out of the room. I'd barely gotten two steps past the door before Shade caught up to me and began madly licking my food-covered arms. I choked on a laugh, and the sound came out halfway to a sob.

"At least I know you'll love me no matter what I'm covered in," I said.

Shade stopped licking me and barked twice, his multicolored eyes glowing.

5

———

SHADE

I followed my Kitty back to our suite, licking every morsel of food off her. She fell onto her bed, and I leapt up to lick her face. She had to know how much I loved her, especially covered in food.

Salty tears mixed with her natural taste of honey and woman. I stopped licking and barked, then sank to my chest on the bed and wagged my tail. If I could get her to play, she'd be less sad.

"You shouldn't be forced to start over because of me." My Kitty threw a pillow at me.

I froze. She grabbed her second pillow and curled around it.

Her pain ripped through me and the fur on my paws began to recede in a blue-black cloud. I howled, then tore out of our suite and raced through the halls. A door spit me outside, and the smell of wet dirt greeted my nose, along with the faint, gamey stink of duck, my favorite transplant from Earth.

I put my snout to the ground intending to chase the fowl, but my fae mind fought to the surface. I blinked and found myself lying on the muddy bank of the canal, staring up at the midday sky through a cloud of my own lingering magic. The hazy blue-black over the firmament gripped my heart with pain. The night always overtook the day, like my magic overtook—

I reached for the safety of my wolf, and the ache in my chest dulled.

Duck scent filled my nose again. I rolled in the mud until my hands were once more paws, then bolted. Through the trees, I spotted the birds drifting on a canal, close to shore and beside a canoe with two fae holding fishing poles. I sprinted downwind just within the trees. When I neared the canoe, I burst from the trees and launched myself into the boat.

The vibrant green and blue speckled ducks scattered skyward in a flurry of quacks. Something clipped my haunches, and I whirled to find the two fae cursing at me and wielding their poles. I bared my teeth, and their eyes widened in fear. Just like the fear my Kitty felt when I first touched her.

The fur on my paw began to recede again, and I sprang out of the boat. I landed in the cold water as a loud splash sounded behind me. I swam the few feet to shore, then bolted into the forest. My skin ached with the itch of the shift, my fae mind pushing back on my wolf, and I tumbled to the moist ground on my hands and knees. The glowing leaves overhead lost their intensity, but gained a shade of purple I hadn't seen in a long time.

I couldn't look anywhere without seeing my brother at the Academy or around the Academy's town. He'd scaled that particular wall. He'd eaten at that table. He'd mocked those drapes. Mere seconds separated our births. Anywhere I'd been, I'd been with him. When our mother threw us out, we built a tower at the edge of the wilds with a roof of sunlight for him and a blanket of death for me. We'd grown our crafts in the quiet together. The call to the Cara had been exhilarating and terrifying, but our training brought us closer in ways I'd never imagined. We met Teyr, our mates.

I fell face-down in the dirt.

Light smiled. Light defended me. Light walked always at the center of our pack. Light burned in pain as my power snuffed the golden glow of his wings. I inhaled the bitter soil of the Academy grounds, and my Kitty's Cara filled with frustration.

6

———

KINNIA

I WOKE THE FOLLOWING MORNING CURLED AROUND A GRUBBY wolf. No one was awake to see me, but I hid my smile, nonetheless. I wished we didn't have to leave this room. Here, I was safe amongst my mates. They had eventually followed me to the suite last night and found me scrubbing food stains off my new trainee greens with tears in my eyes. Bash sat at my side while Teyr raved about how he was going to burn Leonai so badly it echoed up his family line and torched Geminai's ass.

Zelimir had stood in the doorway for a long moment, then declared we'd start lectures the next day. My complaints that I was here to learn fell on deaf ears, and we'd spent the rest of the day in the suite. In the evening, Zelimir led us outside and through a few training exercises, but my inability to see through the dim twilit stopped us quickly. In the middle of the night, I'd crept to the baths and showered in the silent night, thinking of the way Elaine had quieted her steps to pick pockets.

I sat up abruptly, but Shade just whined in his sleep and rolled over. The rest of my mates lay in their beds. They hadn't disappeared overnight, so either they really wanted me with them, or they had been locked in. Either way, all I could do was better.

I slid out of bed, scrubbed as best I could in the washroom sink, and pulled on trainee greens the ittles had cleaned overnight, as Teyr had explained they did for everyone. Even the stink of rot had disappeared. Still, I wished I could just get a new set. I didn't need another reminder no one wanted me here.

Bash had woken by the time I exited the bathroom. He tried to dress quickly and come with me, but I waved him off. I needed to clear my head. I limped along the path I'd taken yesterday to one of the training yards. The Academy remained a maze to me, but I had a few important locations down. The baths. The door out.

The sunrise shone down on the burnt orange grass. The tall brown leather boots that came with the uniform helped keep the bandages around my ankle in place, but despite Zel mentioning a trainee healer, his imposed suite exile meant I still hadn't been able to get fixed up.

The gash ached as I wobbled through my stretches. Every time I turned, I caught a new fae gaze pointed in my direction. Every time I turned away, new whispers started up. I needed to grow accustomed to the attention. My mates needed me to get good enough that we could leave this place quickly.

My morning routine passed slowly. I trained myself not to wince when my ankle burned or when somebody whistled at me. I slowly realized that the red uniforms outnumbered the green by a lot. Even at the Academy, Caras seemed rare. When I returned to the suite, Zelimir had already brought food up from the cafeteria, and I inhaled it. He looked at Bash and nodded.

Without a word, the dragon took me to get kitted out by the weapons master, Bodmier. Apparently, Cara mentors normally handled this, but no one would mentor us. I grinned up at the golden centaur Bash introduced to me as the weapons master, but Bodmier stared down at me with disdain.

"Your choice to include the human"— he stamped a hoof—"is too controversial."

My heart dropped. I couldn't just be a tavern curiosity anymore. I needed to prove my worth.

Bash crossed his arms. "He still needs gear."

Bodmier's scowl deepened, but he shrugged. "You sign the right paperwork, I'll get you what you need."

Bash nodded, and I tried to keep embarrassment from overwhelming me.

I pushed, shoved, and squeezed through a whirlwind of fittings. One of my mates always lingered by my side, but I caught glimpses of the others training alongside fellow fae in the wide fields beyond. I ached to join them, but apparently none of my gear met fae standards.

By the time lunch rolled around, I had another new cuirass, green leather this time, new matching gauntlets, new cherrystone arrows and blades, new scabbards, and even a new bag to carry it all in. I immediately traded out the fae blades for my katana and daggers and loosened my bindings under the cuirass. The rune-drenched scabbards shaped themselves to my old weapons.

My mates joined me to eat sandwiches on the orange grass of the training yard. We'd eat in the cafeteria again soon, Zel promised, but he wanted to give the rest of the trainees a day or two to grow accustomed to me. I bit back a retort. A lot of becoming a proper fae warrior seemed to be shutting up and knuckling down.

After lunch, my mates led me through yet another identical set of halls in another tower and into a large, round room with a podium in the middle and a circle of stepped benches with attached desks ascending toward the low ceiling. A dozen groups of five in trainee greens dotted the benches, chatting amongst themselves. Councilor Ambrocio stood at the podium. He looked up from some papers, spotted me, and frowned.

"Where are the Secca trainees?" I whispered.

Teyr shook his head. "Different classes. You'll really only see them in the training yards, cafeteria, and baths."

Zelimir led us up the steps to a high, central bench. He *pulsed*, and my mates sat in unison. Teyr and Zel on either side of me, Bash in the row behind, and Shade perched on my feet. I sighed but took my seat in the middle.

The Councilor cleared his throat. "Class will begin a few minutes late."

A murmur of voices swept through the room.

"I am well aware Farquin was on your schedule, but the Jalan finds himself otherwise occupied." He scowled at my mates. "Another Councilor will be along shortly."

I bit my lower lip, fought down the suspicion the class had changed because of me, and whispered to Teyr, "Jalan teach here?"

He shrugged. "A Jalan teaches here. Farquin. He's the liaison, works with the Lower Council. Got the position after we graduated. I knew the last one, but I've never talked to Farquin directly." Teyr grimaced. "His head thingy creeps me out."

Zelimir stared at Councilor Ambrocio, who'd begun whispering to a bright pink, naked, winged woman about the size of my index finger.

"There's a small Jalan community in the wilds," he said. "In exchange for cleaning up after the battles around rifts, they get to keep some of the spare parts. The Lower Council made the arrangement centuries ago."

I flinched. I couldn't imagine anyone wanting to keep Tech.

"There's only a handful of them, maybe a few dozen." Bash placed a hand on my shoulder and squeezed. "Farquin works with the Council so we can keep an eye on them as much as maintain a relationship."

I forced my breathing to slow.

Teyr pursed his lips. "Fae don't like Jalan, but they're better than humans, and they trade." He made a drinking motion. "Remember the punaky liquor? Goblins and Jalan work together a lot."

There hadn't been anything bad in the cellar, I reminded myself. But learning from someone who'd willingly put Tech in their body? Nothing good came from those metal monstrosities. The taste of Alex's blood coated the back of my throat as I thought about them.

"Ah," Councilor Ambrocio said, then turned and strode from the room.

My stomach sank. Gnuq, the handsy satyr Councilor, grinned up at me as he entered. The flying woman fluttered over to him. Most of the Councilors had been respectful, if cruel. Only Gnuq had transgressed any reasonable boundary. Whatever Zelimir said about respecting the

Lower Council and needing them on our side, I would never consider the satyr anything other than an enemy.

"Good afternoon, students. As *most* of you know, I am Headmaster Gnuq."

Titters raced through the classroom, and I scowled. He knew I knew he was headmaster.

"Although I'm sorry your scheduled lecture has been postponed," he said, "I'm very excited to announce a new afternoon series. All Caras in training will be required to participate in this wonderful opportunity."

I glanced at my mates to see if this was normal for Cara lectures. Skepticism painted each of their faces, so I leaned back with my arms crossed.

"I can feel your excitement." Gnuq gestured.

The tiny pink woman flew off his shoulder and tapped the wall. Golden writing appeared across the stone, like the schedule in the cafeteria.

"Pixie," Teyr whispered.

Gnuq stared at us. "You'll be working in partnerships outside of your Cara. After the event at lunch yesterday, we felt some…camaraderie would be beneficial."

My heart sank. Great. My suspicions had been dead-on.

Bash growled and tightened his grip on my shoulder. Teyr scoffed. Zelimir tensed.

"This learning series will take the place of your first afternoon lecture until we're sure there's not going to be a repeat of such behavior." Gnuq clapped his hands. "Partners are on the wall behind me. Pair up, and let's get started."

Guilt ate at my stomach, but I couldn't change anything. Zelimir warned me nothing would be simple. Time to face test number one.

Our peers stood and filed down the stairs to find their assigned partner. I squeezed Bash's hand on my shoulder before standing to do the same. Zelimir grabbed my wrist.

"The Upper Council are always watching, right?" I asked.

My commander froze, indecision written on his face. If he stepped forward, if he disagreed with Gnuq's ruling, if he said anything, I'd sit back down. Instead, he dropped my wrist and nodded.

Councilor Drax had been very clear that we needed to grow together, and this seemed like growing apart. But what did I know? I was just the stupid human everyone needed to get used to. I descended the stairs, Shade at my heels, and squeezed between a fae I wasn't sure was corporeal and a fae made of gray stone.

Before I could find my name on the list, someone touched my arm. Long-honed instincts kicked in, and I dug my fingers into my attackers' forearm and spun, twisting his arm up. Shade shoved between us, barking.

"Whoa there, little killer," The fae raised his other hand. "I'm Chrysophylax. Your partner."

I released his scaled arm and pulled Shade to me before he could bite the guy. The fae in front of me was unmistakably dragon. Spiky white hair accented two red and blue horns spiraling out of the top of his head. Scales the same color as his horns gathered around his eyes and spread down his graceful neck. Elegant, fanned ears, almost twice the size of Bash's, disappeared into his hair.

"Sorry," I muttered.

"A beauty like you?" Chrysophylax gestured to the students around us. "In this owlbear trap? I don't blame you. Never fear, the great dragon Chrysophylax is here." He leaned in. "You can call me Chry."

Obvious flattery, but I couldn't imagine what he expected to get out of it. "Declan," I said.

"I know who you are." Chry gave me a dazzling smile. "Councilor Gnuq asked me if I was willing to work with you, as you might be lacking some…fundamentals. I would be lying if I said I didn't jump at the chance."

I frowned. "I should be working with my mates."

Chry winked. "Lucky for me, that's not the assignment." His gaze flicked behind me. "Ah. Zelimir."

The dragonkin leaned back, and I suddenly realized he'd been mere inches from my face. When had he gotten so close?

"Commander Chrysophylax, I assume." Zelimir's voice oozed, low and threatening, over my shoulder.

I stepped back, siding with my commander. I expected Zel to pull me to his side, like he did in Stoneheim, but he didn't move. Right. Fae warrior.

"The very same." Chry swept into a low bow. "And you're here just in time."

"For what?" Zel crossed his arms.

"For the apology." He looked at me, the picture of regret. "I didn't eat lunch with my mates yesterday. I actually had to meet with Councilor Gnuq concerning one mate's actions. In my absence, my mate, Leonai, behaved abominably." He put a hand to his chest. "I hope you can find it in your heart to forgive both of us."

Zelimir snorted. My mind whirled. I didn't want anything more to do with Leonai after yesterday, but even with all the fluff, Chry's apology was the second I'd gotten since entering the wilds. I didn't want to dismiss it out of hand. I nodded, and Zel straightened abruptly at my side.

"Wonderful!" Chry clapped. "We'll be in the Bird Room. Your mates are welcome to come check on us any time."

"We will." Zelimir folded his hands behind his back like he had in the Council's audience chamber. "Shade, with Declan."

Chry frowned but gestured toward the door. "Shall we?"

I looked up at Zel, but he'd already turned away. I followed the dragonkin out of the room with Shade pressed against my hip the entire time.

7

———

TEYR

That afternoon, I lay back in the hottest bath and listened to the voices bouncing around the cavern. Moans mixed with laughter and gossip. Life and love surrounded me. I'd intimidated my assigned partner in a matter of minutes, leaving me with a free afternoon. Luxuriating in the enjoyment of others seemed as good a way to spend the time as any. Nothing quite like the Academy baths at prime hours.

Zelimir *pulsed* to let us know Declan had once again returned from his one-on-one with the dragonkin uninjured and in a reasonable state of mind. A bead of relief laced through his report. When we attended the Academy the first time, I could count on one hand the days I spent away from my Cara. Not seeing Declan for hours at a time grated on me. I took a deep breath. Shade always went with him, and Zelly said we had to play by Academy rules.

Well, mostly. We'd busted in on our human today. We'd probably do it again when we resumed lectures after our trial. But a few moments hardly counted. Every time we interrupted, the dragonkin seemed to be teaching Declan the basics of magic and the origins of power. Harmless stuff. But I didn't like the slimy way he smiled.

I sank deeper into the scalding water. I didn't like the thought of anyone else teaching Declan. We should be watching his eyes light up when he learned something new. I should.

The fae around me all seemed to be having the time of their lives, but in the seventy-five years since our last stint, I'd gotten wiser. If I looked away from the moaning knots of limbs, I spotted whispered conversation, cold-shouldered brush-offs, and anti-eavesdropping runes. This place overflowed with fae jockeying for popularity and power.

I sighed. Whatever grand designs Varsina's Cara had when they started this place had been consumed by the nature of the fae. Not that I'd helped, last time around. Fire, I'd been mad. All that time battling to the top of ember society, only to have to restart in this place. I'd run, fought, and set more fires than a toddler.

I snorted. Sometimes, I couldn't believe we survived. But in the warm water of the pools, listening to the laughter and moans, I couldn't quite forget just how lonely I'd been that first year.

Fuck memory lane. I came here for a good time. The town that had sprung up around the Academy had a tunnel leading to these baths, though a runic gate kept them from entering the rest of the building, and I'd picked a spot that gave me a view of everyone who entered, like the pair of female tinggi elves approaching my pool.

The shorter one dropped her towel and ran her hands down her bare, curvy hips. I followed the movement with my gaze, but my mind wandered to Declan's hips. Would they curve like his shoulders? Fall straight like my own? I couldn't tell with the arsenal he kept strapped around his waist.

The tinggi elves rolled their eyes and moved on. I sighed and returned my attention to the pool. An androgynous sprite winked at me, then dipped into the water and shot back up, their torso turning transparent except for their dripping, dark blue nipples. I'd run into Zel exiting the showers down here yesterday in nothing but a towel. Beads of water had snaked down his dark chest, snagged in the coiled copper hair. My cock sprang to life.

I rubbed a hand down my emerging erection. "Right, the mood is male. We'll just forget Zelly started it."

A chorus of low moans drew me toward the middle pool. I floated to the edge and looked down to discover a muscular, green-skinned fae had pinned a thin, fluffy shifter to the wall below. Their tongues danced for the world to see.

I licked my lips, expecting another reaction from my cock, but I got nothing. When I imagined the green-skinned fae as Bash and the shifter as Declan, however, blood rocketed down from my brain.

I sank under the water, frustrated with my Cara and its single-minded focus. I just wanted to get laid, a little simple stress relief. When I popped up, the moans had turned to little grunts. No reaction from my cock. I huffed. Nothing to do but wait a day or two for the newness of our Cara bond to wear off. I'd be back to my old self in no time.

8

KINNIA

THE LATE AFTERNOON SUN BEAT DOWN ON MY SHOULDERS AS I pounded down the packed dirt of the obstacle course. There had to be some kind of magical moisture-wicking in the uniforms because my tunic remained light and dry. We'd been training for three hours now after another session with Chry, and I'd long ago compartmentalized the dull ache of my unhealed ankle. The limp slowed me down, but I kept pushing. Ahead of me, Teyr slid to a halt in front of a three-story wall next to Bash and Zelimir. I slowed. Any quick stop would tear my ankle up.

"There are several ways to get over this one." Zelimir pressed his hand against the magic-slick wood surface. "We can always use magic, but our goal here is teamwork, thinking together. Magic should be an option, not our first instinct."

I wrinkled my nose. "Why? It seems like using the tools you have is always the best option."

"If you always use the same tool, eventually it wears out." He motioned toward Shade. The black wolf lay half in a canal with his tongue out to battle the heat. "Shade as a divar, is an exception. Or was." My commander's eyes clouded for a moment, but he blinked and said, "Remember the Mud Pits? Magic is unlimited, but the amount we can hold at one time isn't. We had to rely on ourselves to get Teyr to the horses, then horses to pull us back to Thrae. The magic only helped those physical goals."

I dropped my gaze. Learning new things had always been what drove me, but my mates had to spend so much time teaching me, I felt like I knew nothing. My *energy* could run out, but so slowly I'd never thought twice about using it unless I'd been going all day. Or if someone might see. I glanced at the sky. I didn't know where the Upper Council would be looking from, or if they were looking at all, but I knew we'd be screwed if they discovered my *energy*. Damn Zel for being right so often.

Zelimir and Bash stood across from each other at the base of the wall and dropped into squats, then laced their hands together. Teyr stepped into their hands and bent at the knees, then Bash and Zelimir drove up in unison. Teyr leapt upward. He soared through the air and landed at the top of the wall, then threw his arms up like a gymnast. My heart raced. I jumped well. I could do this.

"Your turn," Zelimir said.

He and Bash lowered their laced fingers, and I stepped onto their hands good foot first. Despite their strong grip, flesh felt nothing like flat ground, and I wobbled.

"Don't forget, you still need to jump at the top." Zel adjusted his grip to stabilize me.

I nodded and bent my knees while Zelimir counted us down. On three, they drove upward. I jumped way too early, and with more power on my uninjured ankle. Instead of going up, I fell left.

Bash caught me. "Good first try."

He cradled me to his chest, one hand dangerously close to my ass. I blinked, and my breath caught. He set me down, but he lingered with his hands on my hips for a long moment before he released me and stepped back. My heart raced, the shame of failure mixing with a pleasurable heat. What the hell?

"Don't aim for height yet," Zel said. "Tighten your core, make sure you push up with equal weight on both legs, and wait until we're most of the way through our throw."

"I know." I clenched my fists. "I messed up. Do it again."

Zelimir nodded, and we reset. Three more times, I fell. My second try went almost the same, and the next two, I jumped at the wrong time, though I managed to go straight by babying my hurt ankle.

I landed in Bash's arms after the fourth try. He cupped my inner thigh. Fear and desire tore through me.

He set me down quickly. The scales on his face swirled. "Better."

"You're still jumping early," Teyr called down. He sat on the wall, feet dangling over the edge. Maybe I'd grab a foot to haul myself up next time.

Zelimir spun me away from Bash with a hand on my shoulder. "You need to trust us, feel our muscles through your feet, and jump just as we release."

My ankle throbbed. I clenched my fists. I wanted to scream, or at least dip into my *energy* to help me out.

I glared at my commander. "Again."

Three more failures. My mates' frustration mounted to match my own.

Bash and Zel reset. I climbed into their hands. They drove up. My injured ankle buckled with a spike of pain.

I tumbled out of their grasp to the dirt below. Air rushed out of my lungs, and tears sprang to my eyes. I beat a fist against the ground. At least when people had been launching rotten food at me, I could blame them. This fell squarely on my shoulders.

Bash rushed forward and extended a hand for me to grab, but I shook my head. If I couldn't get up without help, I should leave the Academy now and spare my mates the trouble.

Shade streaked forward and sank his teeth into Bash's arm. Bash bellowed in pain. I screamed. Shade released his grasp and stood over me, growling.

"Enough!" Zelimir darted forward and smashed a purple-covered fist into Shade's head.

A loud *crack* split the air, and the wolf flew backward. I sat up. On one side of me, Bash sank to the ground to cradle his shredded arm, gray blood leaked from jagged wounds. On the other, Shade lay crumpled with his tail between his legs.

I'd always known Zelimir was big, but as he stepped toward Shade, I felt his size for the first time. The mountain of a titan filled the training yard.

"Declan belongs to the Cara." He knelt next to the wolf. "Bash is not going to hurt him."

My stomach twisted. Just another thing I'd ruined. Shade whined and tried to bury his face in the dirt. Zelimir let out a breath. The wolf didn't look up, but as his commander reached out and ran a hand through his fur, he thumped his tail against the ground.

Zel's gaze softened. "Declan will train with us, bleed with us, and fight at our side." He pulled his hand back and frowned. "That's more than you've done as a wolf."

Teyr landed next to Bash with a soft *thud* and began tearing strips off his uniform tunic to stem the bleeding from Bash's arm. They healed naturally faster than any human, but a little first aid still sped the process. My head throbbed from that last fall, and the bandages on my ankle sagged with new blood, but Bash needed him more.

I'd never felt so...human. My *energy* always made me above average, if not exceptional. It had gotten me very little in the way of companionship or good times, but I'd always been able to fall back on my physical abilities.

My Cara *pulsed*, but even I could tell the message was strange and buzzy. Bash and Teyr turned as one to face our other mates.

"Shade?" Teyr asked softly.

Shade let out a strangled bark and thumped his tail, though he remained still under Zelimir's gaze. Teyr shook his head, then scrambled to my side and ran his hand down my leg. I flinched away when I reached my ankle.

"Declan's done for the day." The ember's molten gold gaze bore into mine.

I wanted to cry and rage and try again. I certainly didn't want to be done. But I didn't know I could walk to the suite under my own power, much less leap thirty feet.

"My trial—" Zel said.

Teyr scowled. "His ankle's bleeding again. We might've reinjured it, and your trial's tomorrow."

Zelimir grunted. "We'll take Bash to the trainee healer and see what kind of reception we get. We can't have Declan handicapped any further. If I need to ride back to Stoneheim tonight, I will."

I went cold. Handicapped any further? I already started ruining our chances before I got injured.

"I'll handle it." I tried to keep the pain out of my voice. I could talk someone into helping me, or ride back to Stoneheim alone. Zel should be focusing on the trial.

Zelimir spoke over me. "And Shade can no longer sleep in your bed."

I ripped a blade of orange grass out of the ground. Shade had been my one companion when the rest of them treated me like dirt. I didn't want him to leave my bed.

"The only way to enforce that is to have one of us join you instead." Zelimir crossed his arms. "I'll start tonight, and we'll figure it out after that."

If I thought he wanted to be with me, I'd have jumped for joy, even with my ruined ankle. But the sharp lines of his posture and drawn, disappointed expression told me this was nothing more than an assignment. He hadn't even looked away from Shade as he handed down the order.

I took a deep breath. Declan didn't cry. Declan signed up to be molded into a fae warrior, to become part of something new. My breasts ached at the thought of being bound overnight, because I didn't have a single shirt thick enough to hide them if I didn't, but like all the other little pains, I would figure out how to suck it up.

9

———————

ZELIMIR

The morning before my trial passed in a blur. The healers willingly tended to Bash and, less willingly, fixed up our human. Despite personal prejudices, Declan officially counted as a member of an Anam Cara and a trainee.

We strode across the training ground, trying to look like a unit. When we arrived, I folded my arms across my chest and looked at Declan as he stared at the portal to the colosseum. A pocket of pink and blue trees intersected by one of the canals served as the backdrop for the vibrant green marble archway. Rainbows of power swirled together, creating a screen of sparkling colors that would teleport us to the pocket of magic at the center of Thrae where the colosseum sat.

Declan gasped and brought a hand to his chest. The motion drew my gaze to the neck of his tunic. I closed my eyes, fighting the feeling of waking with him in my arms.

His delicate head had rested on my chest. The warmth of his body against mine had roused my cock with a speed that ached. He'd awoken with a start and shimmied away from me. Through slitted eyes, I glimpsed the pink blush on his cheeks. I'd kept my breathing steady, pretending to be asleep so as not to ruin the moment, but he crept from the room without a word, taking my heart with him.

The male form had never been attractive to me before, but when Declan whispered, "What is this place?" I had a hard time keeping my body from reacting.

I opened my eyes just as he traced his fingers across the rainbows of magic, leaving ripples in their wake. I shivered as if he had touched me.

"It's a doorway to a piece of the world that floats beneath Thrae's surface." Teyr grinned, copied Declan's motions, and made another set of ripples.

The top of the archway turned white in the late morning light, and my blood began to rush. That was the signal to enter.

"Pretty neat, huh?" Teyr grabbed Declan's hand and pulled him through.

With a howl, Shade barreled after them while Bash and I brought up the rear.

Like stepping through a door, we appeared in the middle of a green marble colosseum filled with a roaring crowd. The teleportation magic flickered out of the archway that stood in the middle with us just before the archway itself melted away. Despite the years, the stadium hadn't changed. A few doors dotted the oval arena, behind which I knew lay the network of portals that made Cara and Secca movements faster and easier across the wilds. Above those, levels of steps climbed up and up. At the open top of the colosseum, the bright reds and hot oranges of the lava surrounding colosseum's pocket dimension swirled.

Declan wiped sweat off his brow with the back of his hand. "Where are we?"

"The colosseum." Teyr threw his hands in the air. "The home of our trials, and a floating bubble of magic that bends only to the will of the Councils, submerged in lava at the heart of the world."

Declan bit his lip and squatted to brush his fingers against the chalky, green sand beneath our feet. The crowd roared. Teyr jumped, looking for someone to high-five, but Declan turned away from him, eyes wide as he took in the hordes of spectators. I sucked in a breath, and the familiar burn made my eyes water as the smell of sulfur filled my heart with our past victories.

"Today's challenge is League!" Councilor Drax's voice boomed across the colosseum.

The crowd erupted into cheers. I grinned. Our old mentor still got to announce our trials. Fae rushed around us, herding my Anam Cara to our side of the arena.

"Brute force left," my second said.

I chuckled. My heart leapt as League strategies sprang to life in my mind. Shade barked and ran figure-eights through the attendants. Illusion and manipulation magic twisted the colosseum floor into a solid, life-sized version of the League map. A gray stone tower sprouted out of the ground behind us. We stood in the matching stone courtyard below the tower with the fountain that held our glowing power core.

Teyr bumped Declan's shoulder. "No more questions?"

Declan glanced at me and straightened. "It's magic."

I nodded with a small smile. The human learned quickly. "As is this game of League."

Declan scrunched up his face. "This is that board game, right? But I thought you needed magic to move the pieces."

Teyr grinned. "We *are* the pieces."

He pointed skyward, and Declan looked up. A shimmering blue line floated above each of their heads, but not mine. That meant I would be playing. Our opponents probably stood in their own courtyard, but we couldn't see them through the trees. A full Cara, no doubt. The Council knew us too well to send trainees, or even a full Secca.

Councilor Drax's voice boomed again. "You have five minutes to prepare. Standard rules. The trial is forfeit if either commander leaves their tower."

My mind raced. The colosseum spanned thousands of feet, far too long for me to shout instructions, even from the top of the tower. I wrapped my hand around a simple ball of force and tossed it at Bash. The ball bounced off an invisible shield around him, just like the ones that surrounded the pieces in League until they met in battle, or someone captured a power core. We'd have to communicate through our Caras. Which Declan still didn't understand. My stomach sank. If a week and a half hadn't given him the ability to understand us, five minutes certainly wouldn't. I simply had to plan around him.

"Bash and Declan, take the left track," I said. "Shade and Teyr, go up the right and wait at the river. It's the only chokepoint." I eyed my mates. "The enemy knows us, but we don't know them yet. Play it safe. Declan, do not leave Bash's or Teyr's side. You can return to our home base by turning in a circle three times."

My mates nodded. I charged up the stairs outside the tower. As I crested the top, all the territory on my side of the oval spread out before me while my opponents' territory remained in shadow, as it would until someone stole their power core. I leaned against the waist-high wall encircling the platform as my mates stepped out of the courtyard, all armed to the teeth. Bash's axe and Declan's bow shone dully in the light of the fireball already in Teyr's palm. The crowd roared.

"Begin!" Councilor Drax shouted.

Shade bolted down his assigned path. A soft haze enclosed my mates, and Shade's lope slowed to a crawl. The playing field would be level until they met in combat, just like the game pieces. Shade whipped his head back with an unhappy howl. He sniffed the ground and danced in place, looking between the direction Teyr went and Declan.

I *pulsed* my orders again, praying the hint of his fae mind we'd glimpsed yesterday would obey. Shade howled and sat. The bottom fell out of my gut. Declan couldn't hear me. If we didn't have Shade, we didn't stand a chance. I let my need trickle through my Cara with Shade and turned my attention to the game.

Movement in the trees caught my eye. Cream tunics and standard-issue brown pants. Brettrus' minotaur horns had gotten stuck on a low-hanging branch, and Exilis freed him with his tiny hands. Geminai's Cara. I growled.

Exilis, Brettrus, and Gorar snuck down one of the smaller paths which connected the two main ones toward Bash and Declan. I *pulsed* the information to Bash and told him to do as much damage as possible while falling back.

Praying the wolf understood me, I ordered Shade to back up Bash. He howled miserably again. I smacked my hand against the wall and searched for Teyr. Geminai, a traditionalist as of our last game, would have left one piece at his base to guard the power core, so Teyr had almost total freedom to creep through the trees. He agreed to see how far into Geminai's territory he could push without support from Shade.

Fear shot through my bond with Declan, and I whipped my head back to his location. His bubble disappeared as Geminai's trio surprised him and combat began. Exilis shot two arrows into Declan's chest, and he stumbled. His health bar dropped to zero. Before the human's body hit the ground, he reappeared in our base. I could almost feel his wild heartbeat as he fumbled around his chest, feeling for injuries his body hadn't actually sustained.

The crowd roared a mixture of excitement and frustration. In the chaos, Bash managed to slip into the trees. Although Shade wandered nearby, he sniffed the ground and loped back toward our base when Declan appeared, clearly still following his wolf mind. I *pulsed* my orders more forcefully, underpinned with the certainty Declan would be all right.

To my surprise, Shade turned and bounded back in Bash's direction. I clenched my fist in victory and turned my attention back to Teyr. The ember had snuck most of the way into my opponents' shrouded territory. We had a chance.

Motion below me drew my attention. Declan jumped and waved his arms. His mouth moved, but no sound came out.

"Join Bash," I shouted.

Declan pointed at his ears, then shook his head. My stomach curdled. The Councils' box loomed high above the colosseum. The Lower Councilors would be there, lounging on padded chairs and taking notes. Testing a Cara's command of their *pulses* made sense for a trial. Making it impossible to communicate any other way verged on setting us up to fail. Did they remember Declan whispering to me in the audience chamber? Had they deafened him on purpose?

I shook my head. That would be ridiculous. I'd gain more by passing my trial than by indulging paranoid fantasy. I didn't know where Geminai's mates had gone, but I pointed toward the path Bash had taken and *pulsed* my instructions. Declan scrunched up his face but bolted in the direction of my gesture. Good enough, I supposed.

Near the river, Bash and Shade had tracked down Brettrus and Gorar. Instead of fighting back, however, Geminai's mates withdrew into the darkness of his territory. I blinked. They could have slain my mates.

Declan pounded down the path toward them. His shield dropped, and his Cara abruptly pinched with pain. He crumpled, then reappeared in the base. I scanned the trees where Declan had fallen. In the shadow of a few branches, Exilis' tiny wings beat a hundred beats per second, holding his round fairy body off the ground. He saluted my tower with his bow, then vanished back into the trees. I slammed my fist down on the wall as the crowd went wild again.

I sent out a flurry of emotionless *pulses*. I had never struggled this much and not lost, in League or anything. In defeat, we could learn. But this....

Declan's heart rate spiked again as Terris found him and tossed him into the air like a ragdoll. Declan tumbled back toward the ground, and the air elemental summoned a blade of wind into his empty hilt to cleanly sever Declan's head. Terris spun toward his base with a grin.

The crowd had stopped yelling. Now, only a few jeers greeted Declan's death.

The human reappeared below me. His mouth moved so violently that I could guess the colorful words echoing off the stone around him. Pieces died in League, but most players considered ten deaths excessive for any single team. This brought Declan to fifteen.

I *pulsed* for Teyr to expect company and take cover. He'd been able to sneak all the way to Geminai's base and hid just outside, but I had no support in place if he made a grab for the core. Bash and Shade had a death or two each, but they moved as a steady team, trying to find and counter Geminai's Cara.

The troll's strategy made no sense. Our old nemesis moved his Cara almost randomly, killing Declan every chance he could. League had centuries of careful strategy, but Geminai hadn't used a single known play. Could Geminai truly be arrogant—and petty—enough to only focus on killing Declan?

I grabbed one of my twists and pulled. Leaders create optimal circumstances. They don't wait for them to occur. I needed to get out ahead of Geminai. When our human looked up at me for direction, I pointed him to left path, where I could see Geminai's death squad racing back to their base, then gestured for him to move slowly. He nodded and obeyed.

The moment Geminai's mates spotted him, they changed direction and obliterated Declan once more.

So, Geminai played to humiliate. To show how useless Declan made us. Who had planned this trial? Who permitted such petty opponents to engage in such a sacred tradition? I grabbed the stone wall and schooled myself. The Council designed our trials to point out a particular weakness. Perhaps I had to learn humility. Perhaps they already knew how shamefully attached I'd grown to Declan.

I'd learned my pieces could hear each other if they stood close enough. At my *pulse*, Bash sprinted back to base to communicate with our human what I'd discovered. Through our Cara, Declan's frustration turned to surprise, then steely resolve. He looked up at me and gave one sharp nod. With a few more *pulses*, our plan fell into place.

I beamed as Declan darted to the right with his bow out, keeping to the side paths and doing his best to both hide in the shadows and show himself on the road. Perfect bait. Bash snuck up the left path. He doubled back and crawled through visible spaces to hide his progress. Shade wandered aimlessly, as if I'd lost control of him completely.

As expected, three of Geminai's Cara charged toward Declan. Only Brettrus, Geminai's second, hung back to protect the core. My breath caught in my throat as Declan's bubble popped, signaling battle had begun. Any damage would be temporary. I hadn't truly decided to play with his life. Declan rolled gracefully, bow at the ready, and fired off two arrows. One missed, but the other hit Terris in the shoulder.

I would've whooped, but Gorar slithered into view and spat his paralytic poison at Declan seconds before Terris' air blade pierced his heart. The crowd laughed. Declan reappeared and immediately headed to the right again, *accidentally* showing himself on the main path before darting onto one of the smaller ones. Geminai's death squad veered from their return to base to give chase once more.

After another short battle that ended in Declan's demise and more laughter, he appeared in our base and sprinted out again. Geminai's mates smirked and stopped again to slaughter him. Twice more, Declan repeated the process, until he'd led the trio of enemies far from their base, and the rest of my Cara had taken position.

Shade trotted into the base of my tower. Our too-brave-for-his-own-good human engaged Geminai's three a final time. I *pulsed* to Bash and Teyr, deep in enemy shadow. If this didn't work, we didn't stand a chance. Teyr and Bash rushed each door of the enemy base. My second's Cara filled with rage before satisfaction bloomed. The pain of Declan's death pinched my Cara. Geminai's mates madly turned their circles, desperate to get home before Teyr and Bash stole their core.

"Grab it and get out!" I shouted and *pulsed*.

The colosseum held its breath. Terris winked out of existence, followed by Exilis. Gorar struggled on his final loop, his snake body bending poorly into the tight curves. Every corner of the map lit. Bash and Teyr shot out the right side of Geminai's base and down the main path. They each clutched one of Teyr's fireballs with a glowing chunk of stone in the center, one the power core and the other a decoy. Even I didn't know which was which.

The colosseum erupted in cheers. Below me, Declan reappeared and vaulted onto Shade's back. The two raced down the right path. I whooped, sending my mates every bit of hope and encouragement I had. Wind whipped behind Geminai's Cara as they sprinted out of their base. With Terris boosting their speed, they'd catch up to Bash and Teyr in a heartbeat. My stomach sank.

All four of Geminai's mates bore down on Teyr. My hot-headed mate whirled, then enveloped Gorar in a whip of fire and threw him against Exilis. The two fae collided, and the crowd screamed as Exilis' bow skittered into the trees. Teyr blasted another fireball in their direction, but Terris flung it back with a gust of air. Teyr dove to avoid the flames and crashed into Brettrus' horns-first charge. A sickening crunch made even the audience groan. Pain lanced through our Cara, then nothing.

Teyr's first death. Now, he wouldn't reappear until both cores had been returned to their original fountain or shared one. The fireball rolled out of his limp grip, and I held my breath. The flames dissipated to reveal a dark stone the size of a power core. The crowd surged to their feet in a mad frenzy.

"GO!" I screamed.

Bash hadn't stopped to fight, and his wild dash allowed him to reach the river mid-map by the time his flames died out to show the real silver-and-gold glowing power core in his grasp. Geminai's Cara whipped around, the wind driving them unnaturally fast as they once again gave chase.

Declan and Shade finally reached Bash. My second tossed our human the power core and turned to face the oncoming horde. Declan caught the core and clutched it to his stomach before leaning low on Shade's back to reduce wind resistance as Shade, tongue out, whirled and raced back to base.

All four of Geminai's Cara charged my second. Bash roared, and his four opponents came to a screeching halt, pinned in place by his magic. A ball of poison hit my second's leg, forcing him to his knees. Wind tore at his clothes, but Geminai's Cara couldn't move.

Shade's long strides ate up the distance to our base. The crowd screamed as the wolf slid to a halt in front of our fountain. I grinned, banging on the wall in front of me. Declan leapt off Shade with the power core in his hands and held it above his head, his mouth open in a yell. The crowd's cheering turned to tittering confusion.

Pain lanced through my Cara with Bash, then nothing. Despite his strength and magic, not even our dragon could win four to one. Three bodies lay still in front of him. Terris, his wind behind him, sprinted toward our base like his life depended on it.

Declan looked up at me, big blue eyes wide, and shook the power core. I blanched and started *pulsing* that he had to put the core down before I realized he wouldn't understand. The noise in the arena rose to deafening levels. I leaned so far over the wall I almost fell and pointed at our fountain. We couldn't win until he placed the core there.

Spectators screamed insults and encouragement. We could still lose.

Terris could not only take his power core back but ours in the process. My heart raced as I beat my fist against the wall. If I could just go down —but I couldn't forfeit the trial, not after we'd come this far. Declan had to figure this out.

I screamed, "Fountain!"

Blue-black magic gathered around Shade. My breath caught. Where once stood a wolf, a divar in a rotting Cara uniform rose. Uncontrolled necromancy whirled around him and dripped like tears out of his mismatched eyes. He reached out and placed his long, thin fingers over Declan's hand on the power core.

"Here, my Kitty." I heard the words in Shade's mind as he pressed his other hand against the small of Declan's back, guiding him to our fountain.

Declan dropped the silver-and-gold swirling ball into the water just as Terris attempted to flatten him with a blast of magic. The gust of wind rolled harmlessly over them, and Terris vanished, banished back to his side of the League board in the face of our victory. I jumped and roared. Fireworks filled the top of the colosseum, adding color to the churning lava above us.

The League board began to melt away. Bash and Teyr reappeared and each grabbed Shade and Declan in massive hugs. I rode the dissolving tower to the floor, using the distance to calm myself. Though I yearned to pull our human to my chest, as much to prove his safety to myself as anything else, I settled for a nod of approval.

We'd passed our first trial.

10

———

KINNIA

I STUMBLED INTO OUR SUITE IN A FOG, SCRUBBING AT nonexistent blood. Blood that had never been on my uniform or body. My mates trailed somewhere behind me, but I couldn't tear my mind from injuries I hadn't really received. The phantom feeling of Terris' blade severing flesh and bone lanced through my neck, and I flinched. Rationally, I knew getting my head cut off had to be more painful than the intense, short flash I'd felt each time I died. But rationally, I'd never had my head cut off before.

Bash stepped into his customary spot behind me and placed a hand on my shoulder.

I shrugged him off. "I don't want your pity."

"You did good." He followed me.

"I don't want your empty praise either." I stepped back. "I died twenty-one times. How can that be good?"

My breasts ached from being bound for almost twenty-four hours. Once I'd heard there would be an audience, I decided I couldn't risk being caught—good thing, too, given all the arrows I'd taken to the heart. I took a shuddering breath.

Bash closed the distance between us and grasped my shoulders. "We passed. We worked together, and well. You didn't let us down."

"Yes, I did." I clenched my hands into fists. "Good bait does not equal a good teammate."

I stepped back once more, aching for some kind of space to think, to feel. My calves hit the side of my bed. I wobbled and sat down hard, which sent a shock of phantom pain up my never-shattered spine. I wished I had an injury to point to, some bloody mess that explained how awful I felt.

Purple and white scales gathered on Bash's face, then receded. His eyes swirled with emotion. "You can talk to—us."

My bottom lip trembled. I caught it between my teeth and bit down so hard I tasted blood. What did he expect me to say? I'd been set up to look like a fool, and I'd played the part well. Who should I be angrier at, the people who set me up, or myself for falling into the role so easily?

"Have you ever died twenty-one times?" I demanded.

Bash shook his head.

"Then you don't get it." I pushed farther up onto my bed.

He frowned, then knelt so he could meet my gaze. Thankfully, for once, he didn't come closer.

"I might understand more than you think," he murmured. "But you have to let me in."

With that, he stood and walked to his bed. I scowled as he stripped off his shirt. Chiseled pectorals melted into sharp lines of ab muscle speckled with white and purple scales that guided my gaze lower. He settled, cross-legged, on his own bed and put his palms on his knees. He began meditating or maybe reviewing the trial. Either meant our conversation had ended.

I wanted to believe him. I wanted to tell all and move forward as an actual unit, but as I looked away from Bash, at my commander with his head buried in another book before he even changed, at Teyr juggling fireballs on the couch for his own amusement, even at Shade, padding expectantly toward my bed, I knew I couldn't.

They could've won today's challenge without me. Maybe even more easily. The only thing that kept me here was the web of lies I'd constructed to make them think I had something to offer, and the hope I could one day make the lies come true.

Shade threw his front paws onto my lap, and I wrapped my arms around his neck. "You turned into a fae again today."

He thumped his tail against the floor.

I squeezed his neck. "If you hadn't changed, we would've lost."

He barked softly, wiggling farther onto my lap so I could pet his stomach.

His long fingers had been cold over mine. The mismatched eyes in his wan face had been wild but intelligent. Shade the fae had saved me twice now. And after, he got to turn back into his wolf like nothing had changed.

Frustration grew in my chest. "But you're never you until shit hits the fan."

He cocked his head to the side.

He'd been a wolf for six years before me. The rest of them barely counted wolf-Shade as a mate. They couldn't communicate with him, couldn't rely on him.

"At least I'm trying," I hissed. "Failing, sure, but trying."

I pushed Shade off my lap. His back paws on the ground kept him from falling,

but he tilted unsteadily before regaining himself and staring at me.

"No. Zelimir's right." My voice rose out of my control. "I've been letting you walk all over me from day one, and you haven't been putting in the effort to do any better." I jabbed a finger at his face. "You bit Bash."

He tried to scramble back onto my bed. I braced my foot against his chest and pushed. His nails skittered on the smooth floor, and he slid until he bumped into Bash's bed next to mine. He whined. I glared at him, pushing my frustration through my Cara. Bash winced. Shade stuck his tail between his legs and slunk to his own bed.

"There are times I want to bite Bash too." Teyr up over the back of the couch. "Like right now. I could nibble those abs all night. Nothing says victory like sex."

I turned my scowl onto him.

"All right." Teyr slid over the back of the couch, out of sight. "Don't let yourself enjoy the show." A red fireball soared straight up in the air and back down, then up again.

My bottom lip trembled, and I reached down to unlace my boots. I didn't belong here. I wasn't fae. I wasn't even really Declan.

At least at Stoneheim, I could draw the curtains around myself for privacy. I tugged my boots off and burrowed under the blankets. Once, David and I found a pile of musty pillows and spent all day making a house out of them. I channeled his skills now. One pillow at the headboard. Another against the wall.

Feet shuffled around the edges of my bed. More pillows landed on top of me. I snatched them up, inhaled the smells of my mates, and expanded my blanket fort until I could call it a kingdom.

Finally, I undid the chest bindings I wore with the eyes of the Academy on me and let my silent tears fall. Someone's weight made the other side of my bed sag—Zelimir, I thought—but they didn't cross the border I'd set up. The quiet support kept me company until sleep found me.

11

―――――――

ZELIMIR

I woke the next morning to find Declan's pillow fort deflated. My chest tightened as I swept my hand over the last vestiges of his heat still clinging to the sheets. I allowed myself to linger a moment longer than I usually did in the morning, until the odd pressure in my chest eased.

Teyr snored loudly, echoed by a smaller, softer snore. Bash never snored. I sat bolt upright. As usual, Teyr sprawled across his bed. My second's bed lay empty. But Shade's....

Green blankets covered most of a dozing fae in a rotting Cara uniform with a dense thicket of untrimmed dark hair. My heart stuttered as I laid back down. Once upon a time, waking up to his and Light's twin snores had been part of my daily routine. His last few shifts into a fae had sparked hope in my mates, but I'd doubted we would ever see him for longer than five minutes and, even then, only in moments of extreme danger. I almost wished I could run a hand through his hair, as I did his wolf. I'd wanted to give him what space he needed, but his absence left a gap in our Cara that I feared we could never recover from.

Perhaps he needed the tough love Declan offered last night. I smiled. I nearly commanded a whole Cara once more. My smile turned into a dopey grin as I imagined Declan's excitement. Hopefully, Shade's return would spur him out of last night's sulk. My trial might not have been pretty, but Declan had passed a Cara trial after only three days' training. Most Caras waited months, if not years, to compete.

I hopped out of bed, ready to get a start on what seemed to be a promising day. Declan's and Bash's Caras ended somewhere to the south, probably one of the training yards. I could bring them coffee. I'd done that on the road, more to get us moving than anything else.

Based on Teyr's snores, he might be in greater need of the coffee. I pulled off my silken sleep cap, let my twists fall free around my shoulders, and turned to drop the cap on my bed. A single rolled piece of parchment with the oscillating rainbow seal that marked all Lower Council communications lay on the blanket. Ittles must have delivered it while I slept, like they did any internal mail.

I crossed the room quickly, trying to keep my steps light. I wanted to handle this without my mates looking over my shoulder. Morning sunlight streamed through the window as I cracked the seal and read quickly. An invitation to meet before lunch. No topic. I bit back a groan and rerolled the parchment. Any meeting without a topic set my teeth on edge. Maybe they wanted to apologize for their choice of opponents and Geminai's hostile tactics, but I sincerely doubted it.

Coffee for everyone, then.

Slipping into the smooth trainee greens still felt surreal, like a trip back in time. One full, dark circle shone on the shoulder. Level one, as of yesterday. I'd caught myself waiting for Light's laughter more than once since we'd received our new uniforms, but nostalgia wouldn't help Declan survive this place. I padded out of the suite with my boots in my hand, then pulled them on in the hall.

Halfway back from the cafeteria with a full carafe of coffee in hand, I dodged two trainees in the busy hallway and turned a corner to come face-to-face with Councilor Xerxes. He gestured me out of the flow of traffic. I caught a passing ittle and gave it the carafe to deliver to the suite. Declan and Bash would be all right.

I bowed slightly, halfway between the courtly dip my father taught me and a fae salute. "It's an honor, Councilor."

The spymaster narrowed his already sharp eyes. "Is it?"

I straightened. "Is there a reason it would not be?"

Councilor Xerxes looked sharply left and right. "Your human doesn't speak or listen through his Cara."

"He does both." I slipped a familiar mask of political ease over my features. "We've simply only had time to teach him the basics."

"Of course," Councilor Xerxes said smoothly. "And how was your visit to your family?"

"Enjoyable." I rubbed my chest, hoping the gesture looked like love rather than annoyance. "I'd not seen my sister in years. We are so rarely in the same place."

He inclined his head. "What is your father up to these days?"

My mask slipped into a grimace, something I would never have allowed in my younger days. Living in the wilds required a certain dance. With so many creatures and belief systems packed together, and so few rules, all of us learned respect or died. Growing up with a mantle of power on my shoulders only meant I had to learn faster. My every facial expression carried weight with the whole of Stoneheim and often beyond. I'd lost my touch during our years in the borderlands.

"I honestly don't know." I offered the Councilor a genuine smile to cover my fumble. "I'm a Cara commander, stripped of my inheritance. My loyalty is to my mates and Thrae."

Councilor Xerxes smiled. "And the Councils, of course."

I slipped the mask back on with a nod. "Of course."

Councilor Xerxes grew distant for a moment, then gestured down the hall. "Your meeting with the Lower Council has been moved up."

Long ago, I'd mastered the trick of clenching my jaw without showing the effects on my face. I ground my teeth together. "Whatever the Council needs."

I *pulsed* to my mates and received various sleepy and irritated responses. Teyr insisted the Council did this on purpose to see us at our worst. I sent him a wave of calm certainty and turned to follow the Councilor.

In all likelihood, an earlier meeting had been canceled, and they wanted to meet with us as quickly as possible. That didn't exactly settle my nerves about why they wanted to see us in the first place, but it made more sense than sheer malevolence.

I sent a prayer to my titan ancestors that Teyr had enough brains to keep his mouth shut.

Councilor Xerxes walked ahead of me into the harshly bright, windowless audience chamber and joined his fellow councilors on their dais. I stopped in the middle of the room and folded my hands behind my back to await my mates. Councilor Drax nodded at me, but the gesture looked a little crooked. I followed the line of his chin to find the Jalan liaison, Farquin, standing against the wall behind the dais. I'd never seen him in this chamber before.

My mates arrived in pairs. Declan and Bash wandered in, sweat-drenched and grubby, and took positions on each side of me. Teyr and Shade took a bit longer but finally entered in the wake of a bright-pink, stark naked pixie who had clearly given them no time to dress. Teyr wore a soft purple tunic I recognized as my own, knee-length on him. Shade had switched his rotting Cara uniform for only a pair of loose undergarments. However, while Teyr fidgeted as he walked to Bash's side, Shade stood tall and glided next to Declan. I could almost picture the layers of robes he used to favor.

We faced the Lower Council in a single line. The pixie fluttered past us to Councilor Gnuq. She paused at his ear, then disappeared from the chamber entirely. Declan trembled next to me, panic lancing through his Cara. I glanced down and found goose bumps peppering his arms where he'd shoved the sleeves of his tunic up past his elbows. When I tried to meet his eye, he was staring at the Jalan. To my surprise, Farquin was staring at him just as intently.

I hadn't seen Farquin since before Light's death, but he hadn't changed much. His thick blonde hair gave way to a smooth metal plate covering half his skull. Thin cables wound from the plate down into his black turtleneck, where I knew they met his spine to power the litany of other tools and gadgets he'd integrated into his body. At the elbow, his left arm became a silvery blaster. None of that made me like how he looked at our human.

Councilor Drax broke the silence first. "Shade, welcome back."

I filled Shade's Cara with calm as he widened eyes, then narrowed them to slits. He trembled. His Cara split wide open to reveal confusion and panic. A soft haze of blue-black magic surrounded him, began to take on the shape of his wolf, then drifted apart once more.

When it became clear Shade wouldn't answer, Councilor Odhrán said, "Congratulations on passing your first trial."

"Thank you for your support." I dipped my chin. "I'm glad we didn't disappoint."

"Oh, much the opposite." Councilor Gnuq stomped one of his cloven hooves and grinned. "Declan was brilliant. I can't wait for your next trial." He cocked his head, his rectangular pupils burning into me. "Though your teamwork was…unorthodox."

"More like nonexistent." Councilor Drax tapped his armrest.

I met my old mentor's pink gaze and found it full of frustration. Childish heat burned across the back of my neck.

"They're still a young Cara." Councilor Odhrán stood on the seat of his chair. "Even without Declan, they don't yet have a century between them."

Councilor Ambrocio scoffed. "They're an abomination. Humans, even partial humans, cannot withstand the power of a Cara." He jabbed a finger at me, his long, white beard swaying. "You cheated your way through the first trial, but mark my words, the second will see you fail."

"Why would human blood stop magic?" Farquin's low voice sounded flat compared to the fae around him.

Councilor Ambrocio sucked in a breath to answer, but Councilor Drax put a hand up. "Ask your questions of the trainees," he said. "This is not an open forum, liaison."

Farquin nodded and fell silent. At the Councilors' prompting, my mates stepped forward one by one. Although the questions varied, we all discussed the trial. The Councilors poked at our teamwork, prodded Declan's poor communication, and critiqued my slow response to Geminai's obvious tactic. Although Teyr's inability to string a sentence together told me the coffee had not arrived in time, and Shade answered most of his questions by closing his eyes and trying not to turn into a wolf, the Councilors eventually seemed satisfied with the information they got.

Declan's turn came last. As he stepped forward, a steely resolve stole through his Cara that made my stomach sink.

Councilor Odhrán folded his hands. "Zelimir tells us you are coming along with your *pulses*. Is that true?"

"Actually, I have a question for you." Declan clenched his fists. "Who designed that shitshow? Was it just to humiliate us?"

All the Councilors and the Jalan leaned forward. I *pulsed* to him to stand down, but of course, he had no idea.

"Interesting." Councilor Xerxes scratched his chin. "You believe one of us is out to get you. Do you deny all responsibility for your actions?"

Declan blanched. "I'm not denying responsibility, but Councilor Ambrocio basically just threatened us—"

Councilor Ambrocio stood, his beard quivering. "How *dare*—"

My blood boiled as Declan crossed his arms and the other Councilors tried to rein in Councilor Ambrocio. I didn't know who to be angry at anymore. The Council had every right to talk through a trial with trainees who barely passed, but inviting the Jalan made the event feel nearly public. Declan should never have said such a thing, and he knew it. I should never have allowed my mates to show up to a meeting with the Lower Council in such a state.

Councilor Ambrocio scowled and clapped sharply. "The Upper Council has spoken. Your next trial will be in a week's time."

I started to nod, but anger took control of my tongue. Trainees had to bow to the whims of whosoever chose to inflict them, but I didn't feel like a trainee. I felt like the commander of a full-fledged Anam Cara.

"We would prefer the trial be sooner," I said.

"Do you have somewhere else to be?" Councilor Xerxes cocked his head to one side.

Teyr threw his hands up. "Anywhere that's not here and has coffee."

I growled and *pulsed* for him to keep his mouth shut before he got us into trouble. He replied that I started it.

Councilor Odhrán chuckled. "I understand your excitement, but a few extra days will not hurt you."

With my hands still behind my back, I fingered the hem of my trainee tunic. A good leader only flexed power when he knew he outranked his opponent by orders of magnitude, but we were trainees. We had to behave like trainees if we wanted to become a full-fledged Cara again.

"A week then." I inclined my head. "We thank you all for your support."

Councilor Drax waved, and a line of pink magic rolled the pale wood door behind us aside. I *pulsed* to take up a diamond formation, but Shade bobbed in and out of place at the front, and Declan seemed to curl in on himself.

We walked for a few minutes in silence as I struggled to regain myself. The Council has been right, of course. Our teamwork had been abysmal at best, and as commander, I needed to fix that.

"Declan, Bash, Teyr," I said. "Pack for a trip. You're going to the mountains to train away from prying eyes and academic interruptions for the next few days."

Shade grabbed my arm. I could feel his question through our Cara.

"Shade and I will stay here." I looked at the mostly naked necromancer. "You need time without Declan. You know why."

Power billowed around Shade, and his face elongated before pulling back into his fae bone structure. We both glanced at Declan. A mix of curiosity and fear churned through his Cara.

"You need control," I murmured into Shade's ear. "Please don't fight me."

He didn't acknowledge my words, but he stayed by my side, like his wolf had Declan.

12

TEYR

A few hours later, I found myself in the stables, fully dressed, with equal parts blood and caffeine flowing through my veins as I double-checked the girth and saddlebags on Declan's faithful roan.

Zelly had to have some kind of mind control magic to put all the paperwork together for this trip so quickly. We had a whole packhorse, a tent, and a week's worth of provisions for our three-day trip split across each of our mounts. No wonder he'd outmaneuvered the younger me in our training days.

Bash already sat tall on his Friesian, staring out the stable door. I swung up into my saddle and leaned on the smooth pommel. Declan, Zel, and Shade stood outside the stables.

Shade remained fae, like a piece clicking back into a puzzle. Even half-asleep while being interrogated by the Lower Council, I kept stealing glances at him just to make sure he was still there. When we got back to the room, after I swallowed nearly the whole carafe of cold coffee, I'd helped shave his face and the sides of his wild hair in the same fashion I maintained my own. He'd preened under my touch like his wolf being pet, and I half-wished he hadn't decided to leave the middle of his hair long so I could have spent more time on him. Of course, the mane of dark hair had instantly fallen into his eyes. Both of us were surprised when Declan offered to braid it.

Shade flicked the sleek, simple tail over his shoulder, a constant reminder of the swiftness and dexterity of Declan's fingers. I licked my lips.

Zelimir looked in the door at us and crossed his arms. "Bash is in charge."

I sighed. I never got to be in charge of anything.

Shade opened his arms to Declan, and when the human stepped in, Shade wrapped around the man with more care than I'd seen him use in seventy-five years together. Did he think Declan needed gentleness?

I didn't know. Shade's emotions had been oddly opaque since his return to fae form, except that one blast in the audience chamber, like he was keeping something from us. Or maybe just from me. I'd caught his mismatched gaze once, and the gulf of grief in them knocked me back on my heels. I'd seen that look enough in the mirror in the weeks after Light's death, but I couldn't imagine carrying that weight for years. If I felt like that, I'd keep people out too.

Declan stepped away from Shade. Not to be outdone, Zelimir leaned in and whispered something, his eyes burning with focus. The human nodded resolutely. I rolled my eyes. If Zelly didn't have such a stick up his ass, they could have fucked it out already, and I wouldn't be stuck dealing with this melodrama.

Finally, Declan escaped the clutches of our other mates and mounted up. Bash took the lead with Declan, trailing the packhorse behind him. I brought up the rear. Normally, I wouldn't mind, but between the narrow, volcanic trails and the packhorse, I wouldn't be able to hear a word they said.

I sighed. Our ride would take several hours, and the time couldn't pass fast enough. I hated silent riding. Plus, I'd packed a few extras to help loosen Declan up. We'd be doing more than training if I had anything to say about it.

Halfway into our journey, a spike of rage and determination shot through Shade's Cara before the connection closed again. Declan twisted in his saddle and shot me an expression of total confusion. The dragon didn't even flinch.

"Shade's fine. He's probably in a deep meditation." I tapped my chest. "He needs to figure himself out. He had balance problems before he spent all those years as a wolf. Mages usually don't live this long, because the magic eats away at them, and nobody really knows what's goes on in a divar's mind."

Declan rubbed his stomach, then faced forward again. "Why did Shade live? Not that I'm complaining."

"Always gotta know why." I wanted to be annoyed, but I couldn't quite summon the feeling. "We don't know, really, but I think it's because of the Anam Cara." I allowed my hand holding the reins to rest on my pommel. My horse knew enough not to slow. "Zelimir gives him rules and limits. When I first met Shade, he would do things just because he could. Dead itzal in the wall? Why not bring it back to life to make a nest in Bash's undergarments?"

I barely heard Declan's giggle.

"You only know him as a wolf, but"—I smiled—"he's one of the few divar left in the world."

Declan cocked his head to one side. "You've said that word before, but you haven't explained."

I groaned. "You know so little, human,"

My little human snorted. "Too bad this path isn't wide enough for me to come back there and kick you."

"Too bad, indeed." I smirked. "I'd love to be under your boot."

Declan glanced over his shoulder at me, and satisfaction shot through me at the blush of pink in his cheeks.

He opened his mouth to say something, but I waved my hand at him. "Save it for camp."

He spluttered, and Bash made a sound that could have been a chuckle or a growl. I waited for a *pulse* from the dragon to clarify, but nothing came.

Declan faced forward again, and I said, "Shade's mother was blessed by Thrae, marked for power. We call those fae *divar*." I shrugged. "Divar are wild, often short-lived, and some of the only fae that don't need intermediaries to access the whole well of Thrae's power. Shade just needs his mates to ground him. You'll see."

Declan's spirits lifted. We rounded a corner, and the steep, narrow switchback cut off any conversation. As we crept up the mountainside, past where fae normally crossed the range to get to the Academy and up to its volcanic peaks, the air thinned. Eventually, the sparse red and orange trees disappeared, leaving only low yellow scrub and dark, jagged volcanic rock that reflected the same rainbows as the Academy. A few clusters of lava flowers dotted the crevices, sparkling in the sun. The cold, crisp air contrasted the whiffs of sulfur and the warmth radiating from the ground.

A brilliant sunset bled into the sky as Bash called a halt. Thrae's magic always collected at volcanoes, pulsating up from the center of the world, and that magic hung thick in the air here. Almost certainly enough to hide our training and Declan's weird *energy*.

As we set up camp, our human poked and prodded the sharp-edged lava flowers. Bash got a hearty stew bubbling over a small fire next to our tent, and I pulled out the small keg of whisperberry cider I'd pilfered from the kitchen.

The sky darkened as we ate. Both of them accepted cherrystone mugs of my contraband. The three of us sat side-by-side on the rocky ground with Declan in the middle, our bright-red cups catching shreds of the dying light. When the sky filled with stars, Declan's curiosity shifted back into the melancholy I felt too often from our human.

I refilled his cup. "I can't believe how fast your emotions change."

"Sometimes it's worse than others." He drained his cider frighteningly fast and held out the empty cup again.

I refilled it again before taking a sip of my own. The tangy lightness chased away some of my worries.

"Is that a human thing?" Bash asked.

Declan laughed, though I detected no humor in his Cara. "Hell, if I know." He took a deep breath. "Believe it or not, this is the first time my body's been filled with magic. I'm not sure if I've ever really spent time analyzing what I'm feeling. Usually, I just feel it and move on."

I chuckled, and Bash nodded. Declan laid down, and the stars shone in his blue eyes. My heart thumped as I stretched out beside him.

He closed his eyes and turned his head, pressing his cheek to the volcanic stone we sat on. "I can't believe the ground's so warm."

"We're on top of the world's heart." Bash took a sip of cider. "Where magic is formed."

Declan opened his eyes and turned his face back to the sky. My heart raced again.

"The world's heart." His Cara turned thoughtful. "There's so much more to learn."

I didn't come up here for quiet lessons. I rolled on top of my human mate and held myself up on my arms. "I've got a few things I can teach you,"

Declan's blush spread down his neck, bright even in the dark. I liked to tease all my mates, but something about him sharpened the pleasure. He squirmed beneath me.

I pressed myself closer, so our noses almost touched. "I don't know about human men, but for me, it's the build-up." I trailed a finger up the outside of his arm. "I like it when my partner squirms under my fingers, when I can push the pleasure to the edge of overstimulation and hold it there."

A wave of pure lust washed through his Cara, but Declan put a hand on my chest and pushed me back. I let him, but only went as far as he pushed. Could he feel my racing heart? I gazed into his eyes, looking for a sign, permission, anything to feel those plush lips on my own.

Declan pulled his hand back with a shy smile. I loved that smile. It invited pressure, asked to be teased. Just a little more, and I'd have our human right where I wanted him. I pressed forward again.

Bash clapped a hand on my shoulder. "That's enough, Teyr."

I flung myself back onto the stone with a grunt of frustration, my erection straining against the front of my pants. "I can feel your body's response. Why do you always push me away?"

"You just come on really strong." Declan bit his bottom lip. "I'm, um, not used to the attention."

I trailed a finger up his arm. "You have my attention. You've had it since day one."

Bash pulsed an echo to my sentiment, tinged with his own arousal. I glanced at the dragon, looking for a less subtle hint that he'd be happy to share. He glared back at me, his jaw clenched like he would take me out if I even touched Declan again. His scales shifted on his face, and I took my hand back quickly.

"Humans," Declan said, "or at least *I* think about these things differently. Sex isn't as open. I'm still acclimating to, ah, new ideas."

"Humans hide their sick natures behind closed doors," Bash said quietly.

I glanced at the dragon. Nobody knew what happened to him before the civil war, just that his past made him hate humans. He'd never addressed it head-on. Before now.

Declan frowned. "Some. But a lot of humans believe you have a soulmate, one person who you find and make a life with."

I snorted. "And how would you know if you found this person? Don't you have to test the waters first?"

Declan looked at me, disappointment taking the place of the stars in his eyes. "It's not all about sex, Teyr."

A twinge of guilt stabbed my chest, and I covered the response with a snort. "Can it be more than one person? Like a dragon mutt and an ember?"

Bash lay down on the other side of Declan and ran his finger along the side of his face. Our human shivered. I narrowed my eyes. The dragon had been uncharacteristically tender with our newest mate. I knew he still felt guilty about forcing his memories onto Declan, but I didn't think he'd try to make up for any mistake in this fashion.

"Did we take you from your soulmate?" Bash asked quietly.

My blood chilled. That possibility hadn't even occurred to me. The twinge of guilt grew.

"No." Declan chuckled, but the sound had an edge. "I had a few lovers, mostly in the distant past."

"It can't be that distant." I snorted. "What are you, sixteen?"

He laughed. "Do I look that young?"

"I'm a hundred and seventy-five, I think. I lost track in the nineties for a while." I scratched my head. "Every human looks young to me."

"Shit." Declan peered at me through the dark before giving Bash the same once-over. "How old are you?"

Bash studied Declan's face. "Two hundred and thirty-four."

Declan whistled as he returned his attention to the stars. "Maybe humans burn hot and fast." He stuffed one of his arms behind his head. "We live into our sixties, seventies if we're lucky." He squeezed his big, blue eyes closed, then opened them to look at me. A dizzying mixture of emotions swirled through his Cara. "Sex is easy, Teyr. Anyone can stick their dick in something. But love is hard."

He laughed. "Don't get me wrong, I enjoy a good roll in the sheets. But I want—I *deserve* something deeper." He held one hand in front of his face and wiggled his fingers as if testing what he could see in the darkness. "I don't necessarily think love is confined by numbers, though I hadn't really thought about it." He pursed his lips and released a breath.

He'd held something back. I burned with curiosity, but I didn't want to ruin the moment. Our human relaxed against the warm stone, and the stars once again took up residence in his eyes. A longing filled my Cara, but I couldn't tell if it came from Declan or myself.

"Have you been working on the exercises we taught you for controlling the Cara?" Bash looked away from the human.

Declan sighed. "I don't understand why they won't work for me. I calm myself. I picture the strings of the knot. I can feel each of you in them. I can feel them between my fingers like they're real pieces of string." He brushed something in the air.

Something in my Cara hummed. Not the comfortable, magical buzz I'd grown accustomed to, but as if somebody reached a hand into my guts and strummed. I glanced at Bash. The dragon gave me the barest of nods. He'd felt the same thing. That made no sense. The Cara was pure magic. He shouldn't be feeling anything, and neither should I.

I shivered. I'd never felt anything like that before.

Declan fisted his hand. "But when I try to manipulate them, to change anything about them, they turn into water and slip through my fingers."

The phantom sensation of water slid down my back.

Bash grunted. "It takes time."

I snorted. Normal advice would be useless to Declan. "How did you block the Cara on the road?"

Declan sat up and took a sip of his cider. Bash and I followed his lead.

"I wrapped the entire knot in my *energy*. But I don't really understand what I'm doing, or how I'm doing it." He lay back down. "And before you ask, I don't know how I got my *energy*. I don't remember a time without it. When I really need to do something, *energy* just comes out and helps me."

Another swirl of emotions rushed through his Cara, but I caught shame at the forefront this time.

He laughed. "I sound conceited and insane."

Bash shook his head. "You don't. My magic was unknown to me. Then...." He grunted and lay down. "When I had nothing left, it flooded me, destroyed everything in its path."

I frowned. Twice tonight, he alluded to his oh-so-secret past without even being asked.

"That must have been horrible." Declan tangled his fingers with Bash's.

My world tilted. I'd stumbled upon a private moment, except we were three fully clothed mates talking under the stars. I swallowed and shifted so that I could lay my head on Declan's stomach.

He didn't push me away. Something hard jutted into the back of my head, and I pulled a fading, gold-painted rune on a leather string out from under me. Human garbage. I pushed it aside and nestled into Declan's warmth.

Bash growled. I stuck my tongue out at him. Possessive dragon bullshit.

"What about you, Teyr?" Declan asked.

It took me a moment to realize he wanted to know about my magic. "I'm an ember," I said. "We're a clan of elementals, fire manipulators. I don't remember my magic ever not being a part of me." I flung my arms out. "I might not have Zel's lifelong education, but all embers learn control at a young age. Otherwise, our city would constantly be on fire."

Declan laughed, making my head bounce.

I poked him in the ribs to get him to keep still. "What's funny?"

He batted away my hand. "I'm picturing a tiny Teyr running around the city, learning what can and cannot be set on fire."

"You are not." I prepared to poke him with both hands. "You don't even know what Emberhold looks like."

Before I could begin my assault, Declan leaned up on his elbows and caught my gaze. "Then you'll have to show me."

My heart raced. The fight drained out of me. I could feel Bash's fingers, still twined with Declan's. I didn't want to be kept outside. I snagged the human's other hand but held it loosely in case he wanted to pull away. When he didn't, my racing heart fluttered.

"Do you know your stars?" I asked to cover my nerves.

Declan strummed the air. *No.*

His whole Cara vibrated with the word, but the feeling wasn't a *pulse.* It felt like the beginning of something new.

With my free hand, I pointed out constellations. Bash's occasional grunt kept me from missing any. Declan ate up my words, and my star chart melted into a history of the fae. Events I knew but never put much thought into made him laugh or gasp or scowl. My world came to life through Declan's eyes.

13

BASH

The sun reflected off the lava rock beneath our feet and made the empty caldera appear to ripple as we trained our bodies and magic. I'd removed my shirt hours ago. Sweat beaded my scales.

A screech echoed off the stone. We all fell silent and flattened ourselves to the walls. A purple itzal scampered into hiding next to me. The caldera itself was safe, but a handfuls of rocs made their homes in the volcanic mountains. The massive birds only fought to protect their young and their territory, but the three of us together couldn't hold off a single one if they decided to attack. Rumor claimed a single roc talon to be as long as most fae and as wide around as a young tree, with a vicious point.

When the sound died out, I called for a break. Teyr and Dee collapsed to the rocky ground with waterskins in their hands.

Dee grinned. "Can we practice more of the tossing stuff?"

She tipped her waterskin back. Her throat bobbed. My cock stirred, and my dragon snarled. She splashed the final few drops on her sweaty face and the back of her neck.

Teyr grinned and poked her in the side. "You just like to be thrown into the air."

"I do." She batted her eyelashes at me. Dee's grin could have lit up the darkest of nights.

Teyr added his hopeful look to Dee's, and my heart melted. I gulped my own water and tried to center myself. Keeping her gender a secret killed me. I kept waiting for someone else to discover it, like Teyr last night. The touchy ember I'd spent nearly a century with wouldn't resist trying to cop a feel. Perhaps he, too, was changing because of her.

I closed my eyes. Neither my cock nor my dragon had control right now. We came here for a reason. Zelimir needed us to train.

"When Dee has completed five dodges from the back without getting hit, then we can return to the throwing." I opened my eyes. "But tomorrow, we must focus on strategy. It's one thing to react. Another, to understand our abilities and intentions well enough to use them during battle."

Ugh, another lecture, Teyr thought.

I shut my eyes again and massaged my temples. Dragons were known for their mental abilities. I'd never displayed any beyond my telekinesis. Now, the beast Dee woke inside of me threw me new surprises every day. My dragon challenged me for dominance and offered new magic I couldn't yet control.

I opened my eyes. Before I could say anything, my Cara tingled. Shade's emotions sprang to life in our bond for the first time since our ride up. Dee jumped and looked around as if Shade would sprint over the rim of the caldera. I contained my amusement to a smile.

Teyr lacked my self-control and laughed loudly. "Shade's on the mend."

Shade closed his Cara, but the simple knowledge of him warmed me. I'd been more worried about the wolf than I realized.

Dee cocked her head to one side. "Why does he feel frustrated?"

Teyr sat up. "He's sharing emotions with you?"

"I guess." Dee pressed her stomach. "Is this how I feel to you all the time?"

I frowned. Dee had no control. Everything she felt, we felt. Shade, on the other hand, had control. If she felt something from him, he wanted her to.

"Time to train," I barked.

Teyr rolled his eyes at me and winked at Dee. The two trotted to their places, Dee's back turned to me. Without warning, I *pulsed* left and pelted a small rock at Dee's shoulder. She rolled, dodging the rock, and came up ready to fight.

I let my approval travel through our bond. "Again."

AS OUR LAST DAY DREW TO A CLOSE, THE THREE OF US LAID together while studying the sky once more. Our training had been productive but exhausting. We couldn't do much more than stare at the stars after dinner.

"Teyr, you have to leave it be." Dee laughed. "You can't force me to be comfortable with something, especially something personal like sex."

Teyr poked her, and she squirmed closer to my side. Her honey and leather scent filled my nose, and my dragon roared. The mineral pools in the area were far too hot to use, so none of us had bathed in days. Teyr hadn't complained once.

"I'm not forcing anything." He poked her again. "I'm telling you how you feel."

Dee groaned. "You can't tell someone how they feel."

"Fine." Teyr rested his head on her stomach. "I'm telling you what I felt from you across the Cara."

Like the first night, she didn't push him off, but I could feel her eyes roll.

"You're telling me what emotions I'm going through," Dee said. "Not how my brain's handling them. The day you understand me is the day I shit bricks."

Teyr snorted. "Do you know any swear words other than 'shit'?" He sat up and finished off the last of his cider. "I've heard you use that one for almost everything at this point."

Dee shifted so her head rested on my stomach like Teyr's had on hers. My dragon celebrated. I froze. If I acknowledged her, she might realize what she'd done and move.

"It's the best one," she said.

My dragon taunted me with visions of her until my cock started to harden. I closed my eyes and released a breath. Teyr's recitation of swear words in more tongues than I knew existed helped.

Dee nestled into me. "I don't want this to be our last night."

Teyr scooted to my other side and put his head on my stomach as well. I draped an arm across each of their middles. My dragon purred.

"How do you feel about Shade and Zelimir now?" I asked.

My jealous dragon applauded. Teyr looked at me.

"For balance." I traced the black veins in the stone of my mug.

"I miss them." Dee ran a hand through her curls. "I know the four of you are different people, uh, fae, and this might sound weird, but even from that first day riding together...." She rubbed the inside of her wrist, a nervous tic she'd picked up during our travels.

I grabbed one of her hands, interrupting the motion. Her fingers looked so thin in mine. My dragon urged me forward. I pressed her palm to my lips before twining our fingers together. I could blame the cider in the morning.

Dee looked up at me with a knowing smile. "I feel like I belong with you. All of you. I miss Shade and Zel, but I feel closer to the two of you now. Maybe this is what we needed." She bit her lip. "Maybe I don't miss them as much as I should."

Teyr tsked. "You just told me you can't tell someone how they should feel."

I kissed the back of her hand. A shred of lust crept into our bond, and my dragon roared. I inhaled deeply. I loved the softness of her skin on my lips, but that had to be all.

"You think too much,' I said. "Just feel what you feel. Want what you want. No guilt, no pressure."

"The dragon's right," Teyr said. "Speaking of emotions, what's that lust I'm feeling from you about?"

"The alcohol." Dee sat up and finished her cider.

My blood boiled at the blush staining her cheeks.

THE FOLLOWING MORNING, I WOKE IN THE WARM, SUNLIT tent. Dee snored softly from her spot sandwiched between us. I smiled and pushed a few curls out of her face. Her singed eyebrows and the impressive black eye I'd given her made her face lumpy and lopsided. I pushed away my guilt. My dragon had exploded with anger at the bruise, but Dee had hit back, giving as good as she'd gotten, though mine healed in seconds. Neither my dragon nor I would forget her strength again. And she still looked so beautiful.

I brushed my lips over Dee's cheek. I wanted to do more than just hold her hand under the stars, and she wanted the same. I could feel that desire through our Cara, especially as she slept. But she still hid from us. She needed her secrets. I understood that too well.

Dee stirred. "Don't let me sleep through our morning stuff." Her hair fell back into her eyes.

I pulled back and took a deep breath. "I overslept. Late start today."

Instead of rolling over and going back to sleep, she sat up and stretched. The hem of her shirt pulled away from her pants, exposing a strip of creamy skin. My cock twitched.

Dee mumbled something before crawling over Teyr to exit the tent. The ember grunted and cursed. He reached for her, but far too slowly. Teyr sat up and rubbed the sleep out of his eyes.

Guilt warred inside me. I knew Dee's secret, and I treated her differently because of it. She'd fundamentally changed me by awakening my dragon. Would she do something similar for Teyr? I stared at him, a fae I'd shared everything with, whom I'd never once lied to.

After what felt like hours, I sucked in a breath. "I need to tell you something."

"Coffee first, you maniac." Teyr scowled. "I don't understand how you're even functioning after finishing the cider last night, much less sprouting the boner from hell. Good luck peeing."

I took a deep breath, then a second, willing my dragon and cock to relax. The last three days had been perfect. I wouldn't shatter that.

14

ZELIMIR

I FLIPPED A PAGE IN A BOOK ABOUT RARE FAE I COULD ONLY half pay attention to, then glanced up. Shade sprawled on the leather couch across from me in his fae form. He frowned in concentration, and his outline blurred for a moment before resettling.

The last three days had been a near total repetition of this through every moment we weren't training or in class. I'd tried to talk to the necromancer on and off, but maintaining fae form took too much of his attention after six years as a wolf. Finally, our mates would arrive home in a few hours.

I sighed and glanced down at the page. *A dullahan is a shy fae that....* My attention drifted, as it had for the last three days. I couldn't stop looking at Shade. He seemed so much himself, yet so different. The trainee greens didn't help. I kept expecting him to be Light's troublesome twin, always peeking around the corner with some trick up his sleeve. The first night, after the other three left, I'd carefully opened my dresser drawer in anticipation of finding a dead fish or whatever else he might've put there as a joke, and my chest ached when I saw only clothes.

Those first few weeks and months after Light's death, I kept *pulsing* to the space where Light would have been. The message always rebounded back to me, a faint echo, and I would hurry to do whatever I had asked of him, as if following my own orders.

But being the commander mattered most in our rough spots. I had to be the one who stood tall as the Councilors sent us to the border of the fae wilds, the one who promised them everything was fine with Shade, the one Teyr grabbed for support when his knees gave out, the one sat up silently with Bash at night. The missing piece of my Cara had to matter less than maintaining the pieces I had. When I looked at Shade the fae, that missing piece became harder to ignore, like opening a book with half the pages torn out. He had kept his Cara closed since that meeting, but I wondered if he felt as I did.

I snapped my book shut. Shade picked his head up.

"Our mates return today," I said.

He nodded, his tongue lolling out. I tapped my own lips, and he closed his mouth around his tongue once more. He maintained more wolf traits than I would have guessed.

I glanced out the window. We had at least a few hours until I first expected them to arrive, and Teyr's Cara remained dark with sleep. "We've trained, but we haven't really put you to the test."

Shade's brow furrowed. I sighed. In truth, I simply wanted an excuse not to sit here and brood about Shade and Light and whether the field trip had made any difference for the other three. Still, the wolf hadn't quite figured out having two legs yet. I doubted he could handle the intricacies of the situation in which I found myself.

"Come on." I stood. "Let's walk around town a little, maybe even get a snack. That'll make sure you're all together before they return."

I added the book to my growing pile of misses and stretched. In addition to all the training, I'd been combing the library for any reference to fae with Declan's abilities. His ears had to mean something. I just had to figure out what. Maybe a trip into the little town that hung onto the side of the Academy would be good for both of us. I'd been locked within these walls for too long.

Shade sat up but didn't move any farther. He glanced out the window toward the volcanoes in the distance. Clearly, everything I said about balancing his attachment to Declan hadn't quite sunk in. I stepped between him and the window. He looked slowly up to my face.

"You can't just sit here and wait for them," I said.

He huffed.

"Doing things for yourself is important." I sounded like a first-year lecturer, but Shade had to learn everything over again. "Do you want to go get one of those robes you like?

He perked up and nodded.

"Words, Shade."

He swallowed and cocked his head to the side. "Yes."

I smiled.

Fifteen minutes later, we entered town. Over the centuries, dozens of people had tried to name the town after this hero or that Councilor, but nothing ever stuck. The collection of shops and inns that sprung up to accommodate all the fae who couldn't resist the pull toward power, but never got the call to a Cara or passed the test to be a Secca, could only be called the Academy's town. Low, spiny buildings grown from the cactuses that populated the volcanic slopes brimmed with spies, diplomats, and envoys. I'd come here more times than I could count because my father had so much business in town before I heard a whisper of the call.

Shade froze at the edge of the packed dirt that would become the main street.

I sighed and circled back. "What's going on?"

He started to dissolve into his wolf, then shifted back into fae. "People in there."

I ran a hand through my hair. "The point of the exercise is to see how you are around people before our mates get home."

"Pack is different." He shook his head. "Want to go back."

I glanced over my shoulder at the morning bustle of the Main Street Market. Food smells wafted through the air, and the low cacophony of a crowd floated toward us. With the sun warm on my shoulders, and my gaze off a book or a lecturer or a sword for the first time in nearly a week, I found I didn't want to go back just yet.

I stepped closer to him. "I promise this is going to be good for you. I will not leave your side, and I will not be offended if we have to leave a conversation abruptly."

Shade quivered but didn't begin a shift. "Pack leader talks. And I get robe."

I linked my arm through his pale, reedy one. The confusion that hummed through his Cara settled a bit.

"I'll do most of the talking," I said. "But you have to handle the robe."

Shade slumped a little, but he didn't resist when I started us forward.

Even with a partially verbal, partially solid necromancer on my arm, the Main Street Market soothed me. The proximity of the Academy meant that, in addition to local goods like cactus jams and pelts of forest creatures, many traveling merchants sold strange and beautiful luxuries. I paused to run a finger along a set of leather boots with runic purple embroidery on the sides, enchanted to toughen the wearer's feet and keep them going over long distances.

Shade leaned in, eyes bright. "For my Kitty?"

I snatched my hand back. Of course, I'd been thinking of Declan, but such a purchase would disrupt the delicate balance of the Cara. Enchanted items tended to be exorbitant. No one else could afford that sort of gift for the man. I could balance the scales by spending hundreds of gold on each of my mates, but Shade would inevitably tell the others which I picked first.

"For my sister," I said. "She has a birthday soon."

Shade deflated. I tried to regain the easy pleasure of the morning, but he'd summoned the specter of our mates. Teyr's Cara fuzzed with his normal morning irritation, but he had woken. Declan's hummed with the relaxation that followed his exercises. Bash wouldn't let them linger for long. We had perhaps three hours until they returned. Yesterday, I'd promised a pleading Shade we could meet them at the stables, carefully concealing that I would meet them halfway up the mountain if I could.

The sun drifted higher and higher in the sky, stirring more inhabitants and adding to the bustle. We passed stall after stall. Teyr should be here, leaning in to smile at that trader from across the wilds wearing nothing more than a vest and a loincloth. Bash should be at my side, keeping a weather eye for danger and pointing out little luxuries the others might like.

Declan should be here. I should've taken him already, just to watch the tinctures and baubles glimmer in his eyes. If he had asked me for the boots, or anything here, I would have been unable to refuse. The five of us would leave staggering under the weight of all the glittering treasures he'd purchased.

But he wasn't here. We'd barely passed my trial, and he had to go into the mountains to keep our Cara from tearing itself apart at the seams.

I took a deep breath. The eyes of the wilds were on us, thanks to my sister. We didn't have time for silly shopping trips, no matter how clearly I could picture the smile on Declan's face when I told him to pick out whatever he wanted. We had classes to attend, trials to train for. I needed to focus on making my mates the strongest they could be.

I steered Shade away from a stall of mummified fae beasts under glass, around a group of Secca officers bartering aggressively with a fruit seller, and toward the first pile of robes I saw. He blanched and looked at me. I pushed him forward. The necromancer would never improve if I babied him forever.

He stepped forward, and the blithe, long-eared henesh-shifter running the stall turned to him.

"What can I do ya for, dearie?" she asked.

Shade looked at me again, but this was his show now. I kept my face carefully neutral. He sent a tentative *pulse*, his first since regaining fae form, asking me to handle the shopkeeper until he picked out a robe. I sighed. The *pulse* was progress in and of itself.

"My friend is looking for a robe. He'd just like a moment to peruse your stock before he makes his decision," I said.

The shifter nodded, sending her long, green ears bobbing. "Absolutely! If you're looking for any particular colors, you can always order custom. We love to have Cara mates in our wares." She glanced at the Secca officers out of the corner of her eye.

Shade prodded at the rack with one long finger as if he expected something to jump out. When nothing moved, he began sorting through in earnest.

I could still remember the day I met the twins. They showed up last, which meant I'd spent the previous twenty-four hours fielding messengers from my father between Bash—a veteran with almost half a century on me—and Teyr—the worst fire-breathing brat I'd ever met in my life. My Cara had fizzed as two dirty, half-starved divar wandered into the Academy wearing flowing robes like I'd never seen before. One of them pulled a cadre of itzal skeletons out of the ground to herald his arrival. The other smiled sheepishly and introduced them as Light and Shade, the final members of our Cara.

I'd greeted them very cordially, walked into the other room, and screamed into a pillow. Then, all four of them had become my best friends.

As Shade plucked a deep purple robe stitched with silver designs off the rack, I couldn't help comparing him to the fae I met then. He'd lost the layer of grime and put a little meat on his bones, but something of the brightness in him had disappeared.

He studied the robe, then looked to the horizon our mates would be arriving over. A little of that brightness returned. He opened his Cara to share a brief burst of excitement. He couldn't wait to show Declan his new outfit.

My instincts warred. I wanted that brightness back for him. I missed the Shade that left tiny gisvin skeletons he'd personally attached fluffy wings to in Bash's bed. But I also knew he needed to find the brightness for himself, not in another mate he could lose.

Shade fumbled through the purchase, but each of his sentences grew a little longer and a little clearer. As we left the stall, he called, "I'll be back soon! I know someone who has to see this."

I ran a hand through my twists. I would have to keep a closer eye on him, and not just because of how dearly I wanted to see Declan's reaction to this place.

15

KINNIA

I leaned back in my saddle to help my roan balance as we made the steep, silent descent back toward the Academy. Shade's emotions drifted through our Cara. Over the last three days, his frustration and fear had turned into determination and curiosity. Now, his nervous energy matched my own.

The string connecting me to Teyr had finally thickened. So had Bash's, though, outclassing everyone else. The whole balance thing still confused me, but I'd made a little more progress. I had a basic handle on *pulses*, even if mine apparently didn't feel quite right. I'd started getting better.

I glanced at the dragon's back in front of me and brushed my hand through the space of his thick, braided rope. He turned to look over his shoulder, and I dropped my hand.

He *pulsed*, and his voice overlayed the simple communication in my thoughts. *All okay?*

What? *Pulses* didn't have a vocal component. Maybe I had come to know him well enough to lay his voice over his *pulses*? I tried to *pulse* back an affirmative and watched for his reaction. He slid his gaze down my figure, then faced forward once more.

I took a deep, calming breath in an effort to chase the heat of his eyes from my skin. Nights staring at the stars and sleeping side-by-side had only increased the brewing tension between us. But I would hold strong. I wanted his friendship more than his cock. If I told myself that enough times, maybe I could make my body believe it.

An hour later, we trotted up to the Academy stable. My Cara bubbled happily. Zelimir and Shade waited in the yard next to the low, wooden building, side-by-side in their trainee greens. The tallest of my mates, but opposite in every other way. Zelimir stood massive and dark against the late morning sky with his back ramrod straight. Worry lines from almost a century of fighting for what he believed in creased his forehead. Or maybe the lines were from the last week with me. His Cara felt like a brick wall.

Shade's pale complexion bordered on unhealthy, and he hunched his narrow shoulders to minimize his height. A long, flowing purple robe covered most of his trainee greens. He'd wormed his way into my heart as a wolf, but I didn't know the lanky necromancer. Unlike Zelimir, though, Shade's open Cara spiked with excitement and unease.

As soon as Bash stopped ahead of me, I reined in my roan and vaulted from the saddle. My Cara warned me of Shade's rapid approach. I turned and automatically adjusted my stance for one-hundred and fifty pounds of dire wolf, but Shade's fae form had nothing in common with his wolf.

His calm and confident strides ate the distance between us, sending his robe flapping. He'd braided his own hair this time. The dark locks that had slipped so silkily through my fingers the morning before we left bounced in an uneven plait against his midback, exposing more pale skin through the closely shaved sides. His long face remained unreadable, but his eyes held his wolf's excitement. Joy and desire radiated from him in equal parts. A piece of me reached out to Bash, wishing I could hide behind my dragon. No, Declan didn't hide behind anyone. I had to meet Shade. The real Shade.

His gaze locked onto my bruised face. Anger replaced joy as his last two steps brought him nearly nose-to-nose with me. He brushed long, cool fingers over the black eye, and I winced.

Blue-black power blotted out the sun. "What did they—"

"Control and trust, Shade." Zelimir wedged himself between us, facing Shade and forcing me to take a step back. "Declan is just another mate. We've all given each other black eyes and worse."

Shade snarled. Something like fear shivered down my spine. The Academy loomed over Zel's stiff shoulders.

Zelimir faced me. "We are expected in Councilor Odhrán's lecture."

I snorted before turning to unload my horse.

"Other fae will take care of that." My commander waved me to his side.

While away, Bash, Teyr, and I had walked easily together, sometimes hand in hand, sometimes just so close we brushed. Now, Zelimir walked stiffly a few inches to my left, as if doing everything he could not to touch me. Shade walked on our commander's other side, while Teyr and Bash brought up the rear.

My heart fell. Why did everything change behind these walls?

We slipped into a lecture room. Councilor Odhrán stood on a stool with pieces of Tech strewn across the floor around him, and five fae I didn't recognize in brown and cream full Cara uniforms behind him. Every fae in the room turned to us.

"You're late. Take a seat." Councilor Odhrán's rainbow robes flared around his neck.

The seats crowded with fae in trainee greens. I recognized a few faces from the cafeteria, including Leonai. A bald fae with only one massive eye on his forehead stared at me openly. A mossy fae with at least six eyes, blinking in succession, did the same from across the hall. A large, dark-skinned fae with flaming red hair waved at me. Three seats lay empty behind him, and two behind those. Before Zelimir could move, I shot toward the waving fae, desperate to not be the center of attention anymore.

"As I was saying," Councilor Odhrán said the moment our butts hit our seats. "Today, we're blessed with some fascinating Tech, as well as a few exciting guests who will be staying at the Academy to instruct for a little while. First, our guests."

One of the fae, with long, almost translucent hair flowed down his back, and matching bushy eyebrows sticking out over his small, dark-blue eyes, stepped forward. "I am Commander Lir. As always, it's an honor to return to these halls I walked so long ago."

Without even the split-second hesitation I still saw in my mates sometimes, Lir's Cara stepped forward one by one and introduced themselves. Dreng, the earth elemental, shed fine dust on the floor. Fernis, the fire elemental, had Teyr's slitted golden eyes, but his bright hair flickered like real flames. Anan, the air elemental, floated a few feet off the ground with his pale blue feet dangling down. Last of all, Myalis, who introduced himself as a magic elemental, had hair and skin that shifted through bright colors so quickly I struggled to look at him.

"They're the oldest elemental Cara," Teyr whispered with something like real awe on his face. "I think they've been together four hundred years? Maybe five?"

"Five hundred and twenty-three," Zel murmured.

Councilor Odhrán clapped his hands. "Every hundred or so years, Commander Lir and his Cara return for a brief lecture series. This, however, is just their introduction. Check your schedules for their personal lectures." He waved his hands, and the Cara turned to leave.

I couldn't help staring as they did. When I first met my mates, I thought they were a well-oiled machine. Watching this Cara was something else entirely. They moved on the same breath—the same thought. Even better, though, they smiled as they did. Dreng laughed and bumped into Myalis seemingly on purpose. Anan twirled through the air, and Lir ducked automatically out of the way like he knew the path his mate would take without having to check. My chest ached. Teyr, Bash, and I had started to feel like that on the volcano after only three days. Five hundred years....

Councilor Odhrán turned back to the class. "As I'm sure rumors are flying, a rift did indeed open just outside our valley. We were fortunate an Anam Cara...Anam Caras were near."

A small chuckle rippled through the classroom. I winced.

"A new machine, bearing the name HoldTech, emerged from the rift." Councilor Odhrán held up his hands. "Like all new Tech, we believe this is more than likely something that's been on Earth all along and simply not traveled here before." He gestured toward the dark stone wall.

Rainbow light etched the outline of a HoldTech. "Can anyone guess at the function of this device?"

Several fae raised their hands.

Teyr, seated on my left, leaned toward me and whispered, "Councilor Odhrán loves EarthTech. Rumor is, he married a goblin just to have more access to hybrid designs."

I remembered the oily smile of the goblin outside Punaky's Pub and shivered. "Why would he want something like that?"

Teyr shrugged. "Curiosity, I guess."

Councilor Odhrán bounced up and down at the front of the classroom, gesturing with a few elements of the HoldTech's arms.

"We don't really know how Tech turn magic into whatever they need. That's what the hybrid designs, items that combine magic and Tech mostly, try to figure out." Teyr shook his head. "Most fae don't bother with human bullshit. It's just Jalan, goblins, and him."

I took a deep, calming breath. I knew Caras fought Tech, but somehow, I'd thought there'd be less of it in the Academy. They even had Jalan running around. The blond Jalan, Farquin, had looked eerily familiar, but I hadn't been able to place him. He definitely wasn't any of the Jalan I'd seen briefly on Earth.

I glanced at Teyr. "Can goblins become Jalan?"

He scoffed. "Goblins aren't nearly brave enough."

"But they're smart," Zelimir murmured behind us.

Teyr nodded. "They are. Of all the fae, they're the most—"

"Thank you for volunteering, Teyr. What do you think?" Councilor Odhrán called.

I blinked, trying to guess where the short Councilor might have gone with the lecture.

Teyr leaned back in his chair and put his hands behind his head with a grin. "I choose not to think."

Councilor Odhrán took a deep, frustrated breath. "You may not think you need these lectures, but Declan does. Please, let him learn."

I swallowed a snort. I'd lived on Earth for almost five years. I doubted they could teach me anything about Tech I didn't already know.

Zelimir leaned forward, his seat creaking under his weight. "Tech is connected to either Earth or the rift itself. The longest a Tech has stayed powered after its rift closed was twelve hours."

Councilor Odhrán sighed. "Correct. In your Caras, come forward and take a moment to study the pieces of this HoldTech. Then, theorize on its power source."

The room burst into motion. In front of me, the fae who waved us over turned to face us. I was still getting the feel for the different clans of fae. Based on how he barely fit into the desk seat, I'd guess him to be at least half-titan. He offered me a bark-covered notebook.

"I'm glad you joined me." He smiled. "I'm Chrysophylax's second, Quin."

"Oh." I peeked around for my assigned partner.

"He's out today." Quin offered the notebook again. "But he had me and JoJo taking notes, so you didn't get behind."

A floating bubble of yellowish ooze in the desk to his left turned and seemed to smile as well. Probably JoJo? I risked smiling back just in case, then took the notebook, flipped it open, and blinked. The notes were organized exactly the way I organized mine, complete with little diagrams. Had the dragonkin swiped some of my scrawls from our sessions? He really didn't want me to get behind.

I raised my head to thank the fae, then froze when Shade growled. The half-titan glanced up to where I could only assume Bash and Zel leveled warning glares behind me. JoJo burbled into a new shape, and a pair of matching yellow eyes floated to the top of his...head. I scrubbed a hand across my face, then tucked the notebook into my tunic. I needed these notes, regardless of how jealous they made my mates.

I mouthed *thank you* to Quin, who chuckled and faced forward. Most of the fae in the lecture hall chatted, clearly across Cara lines. Laughter punctuated the blanket of noise.

Teyr, Bash, and I had trained a lot over the last three days, but we'd also explored, cooked, and talked about anything that came to mind. I had a lot of practice walling myself away, becoming smaller and less noticeable. In the mountains, I'd tried to be open. I looked at the door the elemental Cara had left through. Being back here didn't mean I had to become small and miserable again.

16

ZELIMIR

I sat in one of the large armchairs next to the low table in our suite and gripped the thick paper of an unopened letter with no return address. Despite his attempt at anonymity, I knew the fever-boxwood paper made at Stoneheim like I knew my own skin. My father wanted something.

Instead of opening the letter, I took a sip of the brandy I poured upon returning to our room. Shade and Teyr sat on each side of Declan, pointing at a book in his lap. Bash meditated quietly on his own bed.

Those final few hours with the necromancer had been productive. It seemed like the slow adjustment had been good for him. And, if I put down being commander for a moment, it had been good for me too. I'd gotten so used to thinking of Shade as an unhelpful mutt that I'd almost forgotten how much I liked talking to him. None of the rest of my mates wanted to analyze the world like I did.

However, the moment Declan returned, Shade's focus had snapped back to the human. In the spirit of our lecture, Shade had gotten a thick tome on hybrid Tech designs which bettered our lives out of the library and offered it to Declan. The human had accepted the book with a wary expression. Now, he sat on the couch with Teyr and Shade while they traded off pointing out descriptions and moving pictures. Teyr animatedly tried to convince our skeptical mate of the good, while Shade, like his wolf, seemed just glad to be included. A hint of jealousy leaked through Bash's Cara.

We still tilted like a poorly made scale. Bash and Teyr had clearly grown closer to Declan and easier with each other, but strengthening Bash and Declan's bond only increased the tension between the dragon and the necromancer.

I expected my own feelings to wane with distance, but I struggled to keep my hands from the human, much less my gaze. I'd put up a solid wall between our Caras and tried to maintain the same in physical space. Not the subtlest tactic, and I needed to make sure he felt closer to us than to fae like Quin, but my attachment muddied my ability to command the Cara.

I took another sip of my brandy. Years at the Academy told me communication made or broke a Cara, but communication was getting us nowhere. We needed to spend less time talking and more time training to build trust under pressure. The Council knew it too. That must be why they picked the challenge they did.

I set down my glass and opened the letter. No signature at the bottom, and only my name as a salutation. Anyone with half a brain for politics would recognize the paper. Another attempt to force my hand.

My father wrote about the weaknesses our Cara's victory exposed in the Lower Council and included praise that our performance fueled change across fae. Without using names, he referenced several groups joining his campaign and their intention to gather at some point in the future. The letter ended with his expectation that I'd return the favor, letting him know the movements of the Lower Council, and the involvement of the Upper Council in day-to-day affairs.

Treason. He wanted treason.

I crumped the letter and tossed it in the air, *pulsing* to Teyr to burn it. The ember didn't even pause his sentence to do as I asked. Ashes fluttered down around me, and my stomach sank. He should be less attached to Declan. I should be with them. I pulled out yet another library book. My mates needed balance, and we needed to keep Declan safe. The political machinations within and without these walls would only confuse those aims.

My father's words circled in my brain, even as I rebuked them. Our human did represent change, whether or not we wanted to be part of it. If I understood my father's rudimentary code correctly, significant numbers had begun to rally around Declan. Sharks circled this very room, and a power far outside magic or his *energy* reached for him.

17

______

KINNIA

T HE CLOUDY WATER OF THE HOTTEST MINERAL POOL soothed my aching skin. I dunked my head in the water in an effort to ease the pain of another day trying and failing to duck a massive log through the direction of my mates' *pulses*. The baths lay almost empty at this time of night, between the post-dinner rush and the late-night... festivities. Other than the growl of the waterfall, the pool was quiet. Although I rarely spent time alone during the years since I'd returned to Thrae, my fellow mercenaries and I had given each other space. Unlike my Cara, who now even shared my bed. My breasts ached from lack of freedom at night, and I yearned for the nights I slept curled in a pile with my Earth family, my breasts as free as birds.

I surfaced. The last few mornings in Zelimir's arms had been quite pleasant, despite the thick shirt and pants that tried to strangle me in the middle of the night. I preferred sleeping in next to nothing, but the near-burlap pajamas I'd picked up in town would keep them from discovering my true gender with minimal binding. With everything riding on me, I couldn't risk damaging my ribs.

Shade the fae hadn't shared my bed yet, but I'd started getting used to him since our return from the volcano. Unlike his wolf, he waited for others to begin most things and still lacked some coordination. Like his wolf, he always seemed to want to touch me. He placed a hand on mine or crossed our ankles under the table. If we sat on the couch, he pressed our hips together without saying a word or asking for more.

I closed my eyes and took a deep breath. I'd been dreaming of my mates again, waking every morning with desire burning between my legs. I leaned back and bumped my head against the back of the pool harder the necessary. As fucking pent up as they made me, I couldn't give into my desire. Only Declan could be the fae warrior they needed.

The sound of running water filled my ears, and the heat relaxed my sore muscles. My thoughts calmed. The low light of the fifs reflected off the surfaces around me, and my eyes slid closed.

SPLASHING WATER STARTLED ME AWAKE. MY OWN TANNED skin crested about the surface of the water, exposing my breasts. I'd fallen asleep and floated to the surface. I tucked back under the milky blue water and grimaced. How would I get out without being seen?

A feminine giggle pulled my attention to the edge of the pool as the lights of the fifs rose. Two buck-naked fae women walked up to the edge of the pool across from me and sat. The taller of the two, who had the long, pointed ears of a tinggi elf, slid gracefully into the water up to her waist. She bent her curvy, toned torso elegantly back against the wall as she studied me. The fae's long, wavy, golden hair brushed the top of the water, and a jealous pang pinched my heart as I fingered my much shorter locks.

The second fae gave me a toothy grin and reclined along the edge of the pool. The rich brown of her skin complemented the red of her hair and the even deeper red of the pointed ears. Her matching, bushy tail rested along the curve of her legs, twitching.

My heart skipped a beat. I knew that shifter. She'd offered me the cure to the Cara in the *Cross Roads*, nearly a month ago. Slavica. I crossed my arms and sank into the water up to my chin.

She giggled, her tail twitching in time with the movement. "Are all human men as feminine as you?"

I looked back and forth between the two. My heart raced. "Ah, um."

The blonde scowled at Slavica. "You're scaring the human."

Slavica grinned at me. "I don't know. He seemed pretty brave the last time I met him."

I flushed. She remembered me too.

The blonde sighed. "You like playing with your food too much."

"They don't seem to mind." Slavica slipped into the water with a giggle. "Do you, Declan?"

The two stalked toward me.

I gulped and tried to melt into the smooth stone at my back. "I don't know."

"I've heard that human men have all the right equipment. Care to show and tell?" The blonde crossed her arms under her breasts and pressed them together suggestively.

I ducked under the water and kicked off the wall. Water pushed my hair back as I darted around them and came up on the opposite side of the pool. Slavica's laughter filled the room, and the blonde pouted.

"Maybe humans need to feel more comfortable," Slavica said. "Of course, we already know each other well, but my tall friend here is Imra."

I nodded absently and looked for a way to escape without them seeing me naked. "Uh-huh. And why are you here?"

Imra giggled. "I'm visiting my brother. Slavica's one of Xerxes's puppets." She stepped closer. "And we both wanted to see what we could find down here."

I blinked, distracted from my panic for a moment. Slavica worked with Councilor Xerxes? Had the Councilors known about me even before I met my mates?

Slavica took advantage of my distraction to close the distance between us. She brushed her hand across my cheek, freezing me in place, then leaned in. My heartbeat pounded in my ears. I floated backward as fast as I could.

Imra laughed. "Aww, you made him blush."

I frantically *pulsed* to my mates as I hit another smooth wall. Esta stepped through the water to stand next to Slavica. The two had me pinned.

"Are all human mouths so small?" Slavica cocked her head to one side.

I ducked down to hide the bottom half of my face.

"Let me feel." Imra dropped into the water so her head was at the same height as mine. She ran her pink tongue over her bottom lip.

Teyr's laughter echoed around the cavern. "Really, all that panic for two of the fairer sex?"

The two fae looked in his direction. My heart rate slowed, though I didn't relax. Teyr stood naked at the edge of the pool with his hands on his hips. I should have known the ember would never resist an opportunity to show off. The last time we'd bathed together, I'd blushed so hard I couldn't see straight. This time, I had too much else to fear. And my dreams wanted to know exactly what I should be picturing.

His wiry muscles wove together under flawless olive skin in proportions too perfect to be real. Other than the fire-tinged golden locks on his head and the matching curls around his generous, half-erect cock, he was completely hairless.

Teyr winked at me and grinned. I tore my gaze away and hoped he would assume my blush came from the heat of the pool.

He smirked. "Declan's a bit shy."

I looked at two fae women, who glanced between Teyr and me as if trying to make a dessert selection.

"We noticed that." Imra bit her lower lip.

Slavica stood to her full height and stalked toward Teyr, her choice made. I let out a sigh of relief.

"We were just curious. Is he yours?" she asked.

"He's part of my Cara." Teyr gestured to me. "It might not show on his face, but he's scared witless of you two." He smirked at Slavica and slipped into the pool. "I don't know if he's even seen a female as delicious as you before."

"And me." Imra joined them so quickly the water eddied around her.

"And you." Teyr's voice dropped seductively.

Imra looked at me again. "We want to play with Declan."

Teyr grabbed the tall fae's chin and pulled her attention back to him. "He's not sure he wants to be played with."

Imra pouted but molded herself to his side. I'd escaped. Teyr sent me a wave of reassurance, then *pulsed* an offer to make the two leave. On one hand, I didn't know how else to escape. On another, I knew Teyr hadn't gotten any action in what probably seemed like years for him, and I didn't really want to be naked alone with him in that state. I *pulsed* back a simple negative.

Teyr watched me as he lifted his arms and let the two fae cuddle into his sides. He slid his hands down their backs and helped himself to a handful of each of their asses. I swallowed. Arousal grew in the pit of my stomach as the fear faded.

"Declan has no idea what to do with you." Teyr raised an eyebrow, still studying me. I flushed as I remembered he could feel my lust through our Cara.

Slavica kissed Teyr's flat stomach. "We could always give him a demonstration."

Teyr grinned, and she licked up his abs. The water directly in front of his dick swirled with what I assumed were her hand motions. He tangled his fingers in Imra's long hair and brought her mouth to his. Excitement and jealousy burned in my stomach.

"You see, Declan," Teyr pulled his mouth away and spoke in a husky voice I hadn't heard before, "Slavica's a shifter. She turns into an urander, a lithe forest predator. Her ears and tail are extra sensitive." Teyr ran his hand up the fae's back and caressed her long ears. She moaned. He kissed from her ear down to her chin.

Imra bounced, her breasts rubbing against Teyr's arm. "And what am I?"

"You're a tinggi elf." Teyr released her hair and traced her side. The fae shuddered. He ran the same gentle hand along the outside curve of her breasts. "Tinggi are especially good at manipulating reality, so their secret is light touches, just enough to spark the imagination."

Teyr cupped each of Imra's large breasts and rubbed circles around her nipples with his thumbs. Imra closed her eyes and leaned back. She let out a deep sigh as he blew across her nipples and up her neck, all while making eye contact with me. Arousal burned through my veins. The ghost of his hands cupped my aching breasts, teasing my own nipples to attention.

Teyr's eyelids fluttered as Slavica darted under the water. He groaned and held out his hand to me. "Caras share."

I squeaked, pressing myself back against the wall despite the way my core throbbed when he said that. I wished I could join him. I wished I could get myself off on this side of the pool without worrying what noises I'd make.

"It's not just us here," I mumbled.

Teyr smirked and pinched Imra's nipple. "But it will be only us sharing." He opened his bond.

My body filled with his lust, a driving need for sex wholly different from anything I'd experienced before.

"Declan," he moaned.

A spike of cold panic cut through the building warmth between my legs. If I did anything other than sit here, Declan would die. Why didn't I say yes when he offered to make them leave?

Slavica popped up from under the water. She captured the hand Teyr held out for me and guided it to her breasts. Teyr groaned but didn't look away from me. That lust flooded back in, heady and rich. I wanted to stay, to say yes, to get rid of Imra and Slavica and invite the rest of our mates. I curled my knees up to my chest and offered Teyr a weak smile. I could stay for the show. Declan would have. He grinned from ear to ear, and I squirmed.

Teyr gently kissed each of the fae. "Our human's so inquisitive." He somehow made the words sound like pure sex. "He loves to learn."

He only had two hands, but the fae touched themselves as they touched him. I imagined how his smooth, flawless skin would slide under my fingers and his tongue would coax my nipples to attention. Not that they needed much coaxing at the moment. I tucked my knees tighter into my chest and ignored the pleasure of friction. Teyr groaned, picked up the shifter, and boosted her out of the water.

"I strongly believe females should always come first." He settled

Slavica on the edge of the pool and looked at me so seriously that I almost laughed.

His eyes twinkled as he looked back to the naked fae in front of him. He slid his hands up her slick thighs, then braced on her hips and leaned forward. Their mouths met, and she moaned into the kiss.

The water rippled as Imra bounced next to him. Teyr didn't notice. He traced one hand down the shifter's chest and stomach before nudging her legs apart. She parted easily, and he slipped his hand between them.

Imra cleared her throat.

"I haven't forgotten about you." He pulled her to his front with his free hand and devoured her mouth before burying his face in her perfect breasts. He never moved his other hand from Slavica.

Teyr pulled away from Imra to look at me again. "Paying attention is key."

He lifted Imra onto the pool's edge as well. The two women reached for each other and kissed passionately as Teyr positioned himself between Imra's legs. His fingers disappeared from view, but the way the two fae arched and moaned into their kiss only added fuel to the fire between my legs.

The ember peeked at me again. I sank farther under the water, trying to hide the lust I knew burned in my eyes. He could feel my emotions through my Cara anyway.

Teyr knelt and slid Imra to the edge, then buried his face between her legs. She threw her head back with a cry. I bit my lip and laced my fingers tighter around my legs. The longer I watched, the less important staying Declan seemed.

I pinched myself. Staying Declan meant everything.

The tinggi elf's eyes rolled back in her head. She curled her hand in the long side of Teyr's hair. Imra's breathing quickened, and her eyes glazed over. Not to be forgotten, Slavica slipped into the water and started kissing along Teyr's neck. Imra sucked in her breath as her whole body arched, her thighs quivering around Teyr's head.

After a moment, Teyr pulled back and grinned at me. The lower half of his face glimmered in the low light of the fifs. I flushed as I realized why. He jumped out of the water and twisted so he landed seated on the side of the pool, his sizable erection rigid and dripping.

Teyr caught Slavica's eye and lifted the little urander-shifter onto his lap. She ground against his cock, then leaned forward and peppered his glistening pecs with kisses. Imra came up behind them and pulled both of Teyr's wrists behind his back.

"I thought I was the teacher here." He bounced Slavica up and down on his erection with his hips.

She moaned and slowly slid down his shaft. I couldn't avert my eyes as the shifter's tail wagged in time with her thrusts. I could have, but I didn't want to. The image burned down to my core, though her tail turned black in my mind's eye.

Imra released Teyr's hands and pressed him back until he lay flat on the floor. She straddled his chest. He groaned, fighting for purchase with his legs so he could regain control, but the two fae had him well and truly pinned.

He moaned and pulled Imra forward by her hips until she sat on his face. Honest-to-god sparkles twinkled over her body. The cavern filled with the sounds of skin on skin.

Slavica moaned. Her tail twitched madly as her slow ride grew into something feral. My hips began moving in time with hers. If I went to him now, he would take me without a second thought. Until the haze of lust receded, and I had to face the consequences.

I couldn't take it any longer. None of them had looked away from each other since Teyr pulled Imra onto his face. I crept out of the hot water and over to my clothes. No one even noticed.

I swallowed down the sting of rejection I'd chosen for myself and dressed quickly. The guttural grunt and wash of lust that signaled Teyr's release rang in time with Imra's and Slavica's pleasurable screams.

Heat filled my cheeks. I would never see his fingers the same way again.

18

____

SHADE

A wave of jealous rage rushed through my Cara on the heels of the lust from Teyr and my Kitty.

She belongs to all of us, my commander intoned in my mind.

Except, of course, he didn't say that. He didn't know my Kitty's gender. My Cara, my pack unthreaded before my eyes.

I tore out of my bed and flung open the door to our suite. My paws hit the hallway. The wolf's instincts became my world. My fae mind no longer disappeared into the beast, but the rage and confusion became easier to bear.

I ran.

The deep shadows of the forest surrounding the Academy whistled past me. I ran until the blood in my veins cooled, and the heat from my mates melted into sleep.

I sat abruptly. Thick, golden tree trunks. Veined, dark-blue leaves. I had reached the edge of Trollies Garden, Light's favorite place at the Academy. I howled into the night.

Balance, Zelimir kept saying, balance. How could I balance myself without him?

My Kitty's voice, sharp and disappointed. *You're not even trying.*

I flung myself back into my fae body. I didn't know how to balance myself, but I owed it to my pack to try. Sharp memories bit at my brain.

Light's hand warmed mine, practically dragging me to this Academy when the Anam Cara called us. I'd stuck out where he fit in amongst all the flashy runes and elemental powers. Most quailed when they learned I danced with death.

A smile pinched my cheeks. Not my mates. Teyr had dared me to reanimate the roast that first night, and I'd done it. I wanted to impress him, impress my pack leader, impress everyone. I learned much that night. Zelimir wasn't impressed in the slightest. Bash had a rumbling laugh. Light and Teyr would be the death of me. My heart squeezed. All the good moments had left with the pain. Wind rustled the leaves of the grove, a tight umbrella blocking out the world.

I shook my head. The leaves didn't block out the world. I always said that, but Light disagreed. Tonight, the veins of the leaves glowed with moonlight. Not enough to illuminate the glittering yellow bark holding them up, but enough to show the stars through a lattice work of shimmering silver blue.

A canal gurgled nearby. Sleep filled my Kitty's Cara. I let myself float amongst her dreams, and peace washed over me. Her waking mind battled constant doubt, but she had no wolf to grant her a reprieve. I couldn't imagine facing this world without that refuge. She had been right to yell at me.

I stepped into the very center of the clearing, gold and silver flowers crunching under my boots. Pain and sorrow flooded my gut. I dropped to the ground. The song threaded into my ears, blotting out the rest of the night sounds. My power flooded my hands, and I smashed them against the dirt. When they buried what remained of Light in the graveyard at the edge of the Academy, scant feet away from Trollies Garden, I'd sat at Zelimir's feet and howled. I couldn't look at his grave with fae eyes.

Fresh corpses and long-dead bones answered my summons, but I only wanted one answer. The song crashed and hummed. My power drained into the ground, searching for something I could never get back. I swayed with the roll of magic, letting it infuse every muscle and nerve.

My fingers tingled as if they slid through the soft soil of the valley. I hit something smooth, pliable. Familiar.

Tears, screams, and howls fought their way up my throat, all out of tune with the song. I leaned into the rhythm, wrapped my power around the bone in time, and pulled slowly until a ball of power sat on the crushed orange grass before me.

I skittered back. Even wrapped in a misty ball of my blue-black magic, gold glinted on the white shard. My tears escaped in silent streams. I had grieved so loudly and so often that faced with him I only had quiet.

A few night creatures chittered. A fish splashed in the nearby canal. The night was so alive.

Light loved life. I hadn't lived in years.

I reached out and palmed the only piece of my twin still in this world. Short, jerky breaths shook my bony frame. I brought my brother to my chest and squeezed.

"You were the brave one," I murmured. "I'm sorry."

I inhaled my first full breath since I'd watched him fall.

My Kitty's dream changed direction as my pack leader joined her in sleep. Their Caras ended inches away from each other. Fear, hurt, anger, and envy tried to swallow me.

I laid down. With the piece of Light's bones clutched to my chest, I stared at the latticework sky he loved. His voice rang in my memory. *You can't fix it unless you admit it's a problem.*

He had been talking about killing things to reanimate them, but as the bone warmed in my hand, he nodded in my memory. I was jealous of my mates because my Kitty loved them as themselves. She loved my wolf, but she feared my fae form, the power it held.

My tears flowed freely once more. I wanted to be in a pack again, with my Kitty, in this body.

That first night, the moment I rested my head against her chest in the hayloft, I'd known. A piece of my broken heart had healed. But if I wanted to keep healing, I needed more. I tucked Light's bone into my pocket and threw my head back in a half-fae, half-beast howl as I let my wolf take me.

19

―――――

KINNIA

WATER SPILLED OVER MY BREASTS. TEYR RAN HIS HANDS UP my sides, just like he had the tinggi elf. Then, he cupped my breasts and rubbed my nipples with his thumbs.

He kissed just below my ear. "Women can have two kinds of orgasms…I'm going to give you both."

An even voice cut through the dream. "Declan, a moment of your time?"

I shot up from where I'd fallen asleep over a book. My skin tingled, and my clit throbbed. Taking deep breaths, I pushed back the hair plastered to the side of my head and ran my fingers over an imprint of the corner of the book on my cheek. Early afternoon light kissed my fully clothed shoulders. I sat at a public table in one of the training yards with Shade and Zel sparring nearby.

More dreams, and this one so vivid. I swallowed.

My Cara buzzed, Bash asking me if I needed help. My imagination once again overlayed the dragon's rich voice, and heat burst across my skin. They both could have been in the baths.

I squeezed my eyes shut and *pulsed* back a frantic *no*.

Whoever had woken me cleared their throat. I whirled to find Farquin staring at me expectantly. The sun glinted off the metal plate that covered half his face. A chill ran down my spine. I'd seen him somewhere before and placing him would tell me just how scared I should be. My gut argued I should be plenty scared of anyone with that much Tech.

"How can I help you?" I asked, trying to seem polished and dangerous.

He gave me a quick onceover that told me I hadn't succeeded. Then, he lifted his blaster arm and gestured. "Walk with me."

A refusal bubbled on my tongue, but I didn't know how much pull he had with the Council. Reluctantly, I closed the book of combat diagrams Chry gave me and stood.

Farquin led me toward the far side of the yard. I walked alongside him, keeping the Tech half of his head in view.

Zel paused and shaded his eyes as I stepped away, but I *pulsed* that I was all right. He returned to the necromancer. I'd be all right as long as Farquin didn't intend to leave their eyeline.

"How goes your training?" he asked.

I relaxed slightly. Every Councilor had asked me that, though he was the first to catch me nearly alone. "Fine."

Teyr drifted off in our suite and began enjoying a dream of his own. I flushed.

Farquin looked at me sharply. "Are you feeling ill?"

I didn't like the intensity in his eyes. "I'm fine, um, Councilor?"

He chuckled, though his gaze didn't leave my face. "I'm afraid I don't rank among their number. Just Farquin is fine. Your training?"

I nodded and folded my hands behind my back, like I'd seen Zelimir do. "I'm quite good with *pulsing* now, and my lectures are going well. According to Chrysophylax, I've almost caught up on my fundamentals and mental flexibility."

Farquin missed his next step and stumbled. "Already?"

I looked at him more closely. Had I done something weird? Why did he care so much if he wasn't a Councilor? Whatever he thought, he hid it well, at least on the Tech side.

"Yep." I shrugged.

Farquin nodded. "And physically?"

I scowled, frustration briefly overcoming my distrust. "My mates are stronger and faster than me. They have to hold back when we train."

He looked at me again, his eyes lit with a frenetic energy. For a moment, it reminded me of Alex's passion, his fire, but this burned with a sharp, devouring edge.

"But I'm making it work," I said.

He looked back ahead of us, and the intensity eased. He waved his hand as if to clear the air. "How has your appetite been?"

I took a deep breath. The way the Jalan's energy shifted left me feeling almost dizzy. We came to a fork in the road, and he picked the middle path, which led toward the forest. Away from my mates.

I followed him but put my hand on the hilt of my sword. A purple rodent—an itzal, I thought—snoozed on the side of the path. Attacking Farquin would definitely destroy our chances of becoming a full Cara, but not more than dying in the woods.

"Good." I reached for my mates again. Same places. "The food here is great, though I could use more punaky and maybe something other than brandy and cider to drink."

"Noted." Farquin slowed. "Are you putting on weight?"

I blinked and matched his pace. No Councilor had asked me anything like that. "All my clothes still fit, if that's the concern."

Farquin waved his human hand casually, but he fixed me with that stare again. "I'm just concerned about your wellbeing. Are you defecating regularly?"

I halted. "Did you just ask me if I'm having regular shits?"

He grimaced.

I put both my hands up as if to ward off the answer. "I don't want to know. Look, I'm just a guy with a bit of fae in me." The lie rolled off my tongue. "Zelimir needs me. Can we continue this later?"

Without waiting, I turned and began hauling ass back toward the training field. I glanced over my shoulder to see if he was following. He could be as fast and strong as Tech with all those parts. Farquin hadn't moved from his place on the path toward the forest but stared in my direction. I could only see his human side. Thick blond hair, hanging over his ears. Black turtleneck. My stomach flipped. He'd been in the pub where I met Rydel, in one of those wild magic portals. Worse, I'd thought I'd recognized him then.

I didn't look back again.

Following the strings of my Cara bonds, I hurried to the yard. Zelimir and Shade stood shirtless, drenched in sweat, and holding wooden staffs. My commander's dark skin rippled across his every muscle, and his copper twists glistened in the sun. Although Zel dwarfed Shade, corded muscle ran along the necromancer's long arms and sculpted chest. A leather strap with a white and gold charm hung between his pectorals. I guess all that running as a wolf transitioned well. Really well. I swallowed.

Zelimir held his staff out to me. "Care to join us?"

I knew his question had nothing to do with sex, but the juncture between my legs pulsed. Whatever Farquin wanted disappeared from my mind as I accepted my commander's staff.

20

———

BASH

Cool, crisp air filled my lungs and kissed my bare, lilac chest. My mates and I stood outside the archway, waiting for the Council to finish preparing the colosseum for my trial. I stretched my arms over my head. Shade fidgeted, still uncomfortable in his fae form. He scratched the top of his head where his braid stuck slightly upward in two furry points. Ears? I filed that away for after my trial.

Teyr paced like a caged beast. The ember always had the patience of a toddler. My commander stood motionless with his hands folded behind his back, his gaze locked on the beacon that would signal we could enter.

Dee yawned. I'd shared her bed last night, and it took centuries of willpower to dwell on anything else this morning. She'd tossed and turned, pawing at her heavy sleepwear. My dragon and I wanted to tear the clothes off her, but I told myself I only wanted that for her comfort. We had both resisted, and eventually, she settled into a fitful rest against my side.

She glanced at me with a question in her eyes. I tore my gaze away and focused. Today had to be about the Cara and my trial. We were much better prepared than last time. We knew Dee's weaknesses now, much to her irritation, and she had something of a grasp on *pulses*.

Teyr kicked a rock. "It's something physical if they're not letting us in right away."

My commander nodded. "We must work as a unit and keep in constant communication."

Dee shifted uncomfortably. "Bash said the trial would be straight-forward."

"It will be." Zelimir ran a hand across his copper twists, pulled back from his face in a simple ponytail. "But when you lack balance, the simplest tasks are the hardest."

Dee grinned. "I thought you were balanced. Fire, force, mind, and adorable doggie."

Shade choked out a bark-like laugh and rubbed Dee's mop of curls.

Teyr's eyes twinkled. "Don't forget adorable human. It's not you and us. We're we now."

A hesitant smile bloomed over Dee's face before she straightened her shoulders. "But seriously, I don't understand how you—we—aren't diverse."

Zelimir shook his head. "Diverse and balanced are different."

"We have no healer." Teyr ticked off his fingers. "No damage-soak, no…spellcaster." He glanced at Shade and sighed. "We're literally, at the moment, three hard-hitters and two people who are okay at dodging."

"Hey," Dee and Shade said simultaneously.

"I'm just calling it like it is." Teyr smirked. "And that doesn't change your ability to get laid. I met another of Slavica's friends." He traced the outline of an hourglass with his hands. "Another shifter."

Dee blushed.

"I figured you were into the ears, as Shade's growing them for you." Teyr snickered.

Shade scratched his head again, shifting his hair to reveal the pink inside of what looked like a wolf ear, then he growled. Before he could lunge for Teyr, white flashed at the top of the arch.

Blood rushed through my limbs, singing with anticipation. My trial. Time to prove myself once again. I stepped through the arch, through the portal. The heat and noise of the already worked-up crowd washed over me as I appeared in the colosseum. Telekinesis danced through my mind as the archway faded away behind us. Battle-awareness sharpened every sound, every color. Piles of rock and rubble covered half the arena, while the other side sat completely empty. I couldn't guess at the challenge.

My dragon roared. The crowd surged with screams and cheers. Teyr threw his hands up in the air and covered them in fire. The crowd doubled in volume, but I could still make out a few voices calling his name.

I looked up at the five Councilors and Farquin, watching from their plush chairs in the Councils' box. Unlike the screaming crowd, they sat motionless behind a green marble railing. A purple rodent perched on the arm of Councilor Xerxes' chair, and a bright-pink pixie poured a drink for Gnuq, who waved her away without tearing his gaze from us.

The lava glinted off a dark oval hovering over the top of Ambrocio's chair. My stomach churned. None of my mates seemed to notice. Shade scratched his back, oblivious to the world. Teyr's fire show bloomed into an elaborate display of dancers above his head. My commander nodded respectfully to the Councilors while Dee scowled at them.

I looked at the dark oval again and reached out to my dragon. Together, we spun a thread of mental magic strong enough to reach the oval. As soon as the thread brushed the surface of the oval, it snapped and recoiled. No thoughts, but I could sense someone on the other side. Multiple someones. I swallowed.

Councilor Drax stood and slid to a wooden funnel glowing pink with his magic. "The challenge is brute strength! Twenty minutes to move eight tons of rubble. If even a pebble remains on the other side of the line, the trial is lost."

I rolled my shoulders and surveyed the sheer quantity of giant boulders and lava rocks. "It's going to be tight."

"To make this challenge more exciting," Councilor Drax said. "Bash will be directing instead of moving."

A clear, shimmering bubble surrounded me. It took all my self-control not to fight the magic.

"The Upper Council feels communication was an issue in the last trial and needs to be proven successful before we invest further resources."

I glanced back at the oval above Ambrocio. The Upper Council. I didn't even know they watched the trials, much less gave notes. The bubble lifted me to a point high above the action, just barely close enough that I could make out the frowns on my mates' face. I flexed my telekinesis against the barrier, but it didn't budge.

My excitement chilled, and my stomach twisted. I didn't make plans, I responded. Strategy should've been my commander's problem.

Zelimir filled my Cara with his support. I eyed him, waiting for orders. I received nothing but silence. I had to prove myself. Teyr, Shade, and Dee weren't physically strong. Their magic didn't move objects. Zelimir's titan heritage made him naturally stronger than even me, but not fast. His force magic would be the most helpful, but not like my telekinesis. He could create objects out of raw purple power, could push and pull things away from him, but only within the limitations of his physical strength. Eight tons in twenty minutes wouldn't happen.

"Ten, nine," Councilor Drax said.

Thousands of voices joined his countdown, punctuating my attempts to problem-solve. I stared at the green colosseum floor. Cheers and jeers rained down on us. Dee drew her sword, and Zelimir covered the blade in force, reinforcing its edge.

"Zero!" the crowd shouted.

A giant, floating yellow timer wound into the air at my eye level and began counting down. Dee charged one of the bigger lava rocks and began chopping it into smaller pieces while Zelimir picked up the fragments and flung them to the other side of the colosseum. Effective but slow, too slow.

Teyr melted one of the rocks, creating a mess no one could touch. Blue-black power gathered around Shade's hand as he prodded one of the stones. I blinked and rubbed my eyes. He couldn't bring objects to life. Had those years as a wolf driven him truly mad? Making the same realization, Shade snorted and placed his back against a mostly round boulder. With a grunt, he began rolling it across the chalky green floor.

I clenched my fists and threw everything I had at the barrier. It bent under the force of my will but didn't break. Shade's boulder slid another inch. Dee swept up the smaller chunks of rock that fell off during her demolition and ran them over the line before racing for a new boulder to shatter. Teyr melted another rock and looked distraught that he'd gotten the same result. His untouchable pile of lava doubled in size but still didn't flow. We needed to work together under a single functional strategy, but I'd no idea what to tell them.

Dee's voice sounded in my head. *Bash, find me!*

She could've only come from one place. I shoved my awareness into our Cara. The magic that held us together buzzed, and I suddenly remembered the first moment I'd made her smile in Punaky's Pub. With a bolt of inspiration, I stretched my hand out and grabbed, trying to touch our bond like she always did.

I swayed as my world turned upside-down. A void of white swallowed me. With a jolt, the void spit me out. My fingers gripped the force-covered katana, and I swung with all my might into the lava rock in front of me. My elbow jarred, and a chunk of stone crashed into the dusty ground.

"Shit!" My voice—Dee's voice—sounded strange to my ears, high and crackling.

Something trickled down my spine and through my Cara. The white void consumed me again and spat me out. I looked down over the stone-covered colosseum floor from above and clenched my fist around the memory of Dee's katana.

I don't understand. I forced words through our bond.

Yes, you do. Her voice sounded panicked but certain. *I've been hearing you in my head since the volcano.*

I drew my axe and placed the cherrystone head against the bottom of the bubble, then leaned on the shaft.

Shit, Bash, I don't know how to do this. Find me! Dee shouted.

My knuckles turned gray. Once again, I shoved my awareness into our bond, the bridge that connected our very souls. My dragon surged forward, demanding we dominate the well of power in front of us. Instead of trying to bend Dee to my will, I poured my magic, myself, into her.

Pain seared through my head. Pictures, memories, sounds, and smells that didn't belong to me overtook my awareness. I tumbled through sensation into a void of tingling, vibrating white. Something sliced my cheek. The void vanished and I startled at the numbness in my arms as I hacked the katana through another slab of stone. Sharp debris flew as the slab fell away. Zel hollered. Heat washed over me in waves. The metallic smell of Dee's blood made my dragon roar. I fought through the tornado of sensations.

The world looked duller than usual. My legs shook, and the muscles in my—Dee's—arms burned. I grabbed a stone that should have weighed nothing, but it slipped out of my grasp and smashed to the ground. Small, dirty hands stretched in front of me. I turned the palms to the ground and flexed my delicate fingers in and out. Dee's fingers. I'd returned to my mate's body.

Zelimir hurled small boulders with a sling of purple force magic on my left. Shade, sweat pouring down his face, pushed what I assumed was his first boulder across the middle line, then collapsed. Small rivers of lava flowed steadily across the line on my right.

I *pulsed* to stop and fall back. Had the command come from me or her?

Focus. Dee's voice sounded distant, pained.

I shuddered. If I had her body, where was she?

Magic swirled around me, warm currents over that alien buzzing I'd felt when I reached for her. I widened my stance and bent my elbows. My dragon raced forward. My fingers blurred as we reached out for every rock and boulder. Once we had them all, I raised my arms. Weight threatened to crush me into the green dust, but nothing moved. I squatted, adding my roar to my flexing muscles. My bellow morphed into a high scream, and the entire field of rock lifted into the air.

A strand of sweat-covered black hair dangled in my eyes. I braced and shoved every last rock and pebble to the other side of the colosseum floor. With another scream, I released the weight. The pile crashed to the ground, shaking the colosseum until the glowing lava surrounding the pocket dimension rippled across the marble. A cloud of green dust filled the air, along with a deafening silence.

My vision went black at the edges. I fell but didn't hit the ground.

I clutched the axe handle keeping my fae body upright. Dee lay unmoving on the colosseum floor below. The shimmering barrier still held me in the sky above my mates. I tried to shove the hair out of my eyes, but I just skimmed my bald head. Sensation rushed back in, so powerful my knees almost buckled. The crowd roared. Thoughts bounced off the inside of my skull. The brilliant fae colors I'd loved for so long threatened to blind me.

Dee didn't move. My heart raced. Our Cara throbbed between us, twisting in a way that made my skin crawl. We'd completed our task with ten minutes to spare. Would they make me wait here for those ten minutes? Another wave of vertigo swept over me. A spike of white-hot pain split my head. I fell to one knee. I wouldn't last.

"I don't believe it." Councilor Drax's voice was barely audible over the screaming crowd. "But that's it! All eighty tons!"

I let out harsh breath as the bubble lowered me to the colosseum floor but didn't drop from around me.

"Dee?" Speaking sent shooting pain along every nerve in my body.

"Here." Shade stepped into my line of sight, holding Dee's limp body against his thin chest.

I made eye contact with Zelimir and *pulsed* a blurry warning before my vision went dark.

21

TEYR

Bash collapsed, and the world around me slowed. My heartbeat thudded in my ears, drowning out the crowd. I stepped forward without a plan. My Cara still shook with Declan and Bash's combined *pulse*, strange and familiar at the same time. Another step brought me to the edge of the magical shield that still separated us from Bash. I placed my hand against it. The dragon looked weak, vulnerable. I remembered another shield I'd stood on the wrong side of, while watching my mate fall. Light had never fallen before. Bash never fell.

I spun to face Zelimir, my commander, my friend, only to find him watching the Lower Council approach, seemingly without a care for Bash or Declan. I whipped a *pulse* at him, all anger and disappointment, and he calmly pointed out that we could feel both their heartbeats. Physically, our mates were fine.

I ignited my fear into a fireball and launched it at the bubble surrounding Bash. They weren't fine. They couldn't be. I'd watched Declan settle into Bash's low stance, felt the pain rip through both their bodies. Now, they both lay unconscious, and I couldn't reach Bash to make sure that steady heartbeat wasn't some trick of the Councilors proceeding slowly toward us.

My patience evaporated. I charged forward and halted between the Councilors and my uncaring leader. "Take down the shield."

They halted and Gnuq folded his arms over his potbelly. "We came down to congratulate you—"

"Shield, now." Fire curled off my fingertips. "This game is over."

"Our trial"—Zelimir stepped forward and put a hand on my shoulder —"has been won."

I spun to my commander, *pulsing* disbelief and fury. Had he not felt the same things I did? "It doesn't matter what you call it, Declan won't wake up and Bash—" I launched another fireball at the shield. The bubble absorbed the impact without a trace and the hum continued. Bash didn't even twitch.

"We are honored that you came down here yourselves. Would you allow us to tend to our mates?" Zelimir *pulsed* a warning to remain calm.

I ground my teeth. "This is a waste of time."

He squeezed my shoulder, and I shrugged him off.

Drax made a motion with his hand, and a handful of fae wearing cream and brown Cara uniforms I hadn't noticed in the first row dropped their hands. The magical hum of the shield evaporated. I lunged toward Bash, then halted when lines of pink magic rose out of Drax's skin and pulled Bash's limp body to Zelimir's feet.

Zelimir's, not mine. Like Bash would be better off with my commander—who looked at the Councilors like they could do no wrong. I whirled to Shade for support, but the necromancer knelt beside Delcan, his body curled around the man, his now-loose hair falling like a curtain between them and the Councilors. Lucky.

"You are quite right." Gnuq shifted his attention to Declan. "My healer will see to them."

That satyr wouldn't be getting within spitting distance of my mates. I opened my mouth to argue, but a sharp *pulse* from my commander cut me off, followed by a suggestion to check on Bash.

I'd grown accustomed to being angry with Zelimir, but this sick sting of betrayal was new.

"Your offer is very generous," my commander said. "But I'm sure the trainee healers can see to him. This was a fair trial, after all. We aren't looking for special treatment."

I knelt at Zelimir's feet beside Bash. Zelimir couldn't treat me like this, but I couldn't risk our screaming match rebounding on Bash or Declan while they were unconscious. I placed a palm over his heart. Like his Cara indicated, Bash's heart thrummed strong and steady beneath his warm, lilac skin. I let my hand linger to steady my own heartbeat.

"I do insist." Gnuq stomped one of his cloven hooves.

I gritted my teeth and very politely did not fireball the satyr.

"Declan does not leave our side," Zelimir said. "But we would be grateful for your help."

I very politely did not fireball my traitorous commander either.

"Of course." Gnuq's voice oozed over me.

Odhrán cleared his throat. "What we witnessed today was both impressive and unusual."

Ambrocio scoffed. "Your next trial is set for two weeks' time, despite my recommendation."

Odhrán stepped in front of the old Councilor like his tiny body could block the auspex from view. "We feel your lack of a mentor may be holding you back. Although we still don't...have one to spare, Commander Lir will monitor you."

"Thank you for your thoughtfulness." Zelimir inclined his head. "I'm sure the expertise of a seasoned elemental will enrich our training."

I watched the scales on Bash's face move and tried to take deep breaths, unable to look at Zelimir. If Xerxes snapped his fingers, my commander would have sat and rolled over.

Zelimir said, "Now, I really must see to my mates."

Each Councilor congratulated us in turn, though the old bat Ambrocio did so with obvious disdain, then left.

Farquin stepped up to Zelimir last. "Do keep us informed of any changes to Declan's health. As I'm sure you're aware, all the wilds have become invested in your path."

Zel nodded. "Thank you for your concern. You will know what we know."

Farquin narrowed his eyes. I met his gaze, expecting concern or suspicion, like I'd seen in the Councilors. Instead, I found blazing curiosity so intense I would have stepped back if I'd been standing. I blinked and peered closer, but he'd already donned a politically neutral mask .

"Congratulations again." Farquin turned and walked off after the Councilors.

Zelimir faced Bash and me. Any concern for the Jalan's political ambitions fled my brain.

"How could you just let Gnuq have access to our mates?" I hissed. "And oversight? How will a monitor help us?"

Zelimir flattened his lips into a line. "They are not our enemy, and this isn't the place to speak openly." He bent and lifted Bash into his arms as if the muscled dragon weighed nothing.

"They are not our enemy," I repeated in a high-pitched voice. "Don't think putting off this conversation will get you out of explaining yourself."

Zelimir nodded, and I fell back to help Shade with Declan. The necromancer pulled Declan to his chest and struggled to stand. I motioned for him to let me take and Shade complied. Our human felt so light for his height. His skin remained soft under my hands, though, and no warmer than he had been in the mountains. His Cara blurred, like he was unconscious, but swirled with emotion.

My heart thudded. What the fuck just happened?

22

BASH

I stood slowly. Echoes of the pain that had knocked me unconscious in the coliseum rolled through my memory. I held my pale, petite hands up in front of my face and the long, brown sleeves of my rough cotton shirt, human in style, fell back from my wrists. I itched to rip the shirt off, but something stopped me. A thick rope of hair lay heavy along the back of my neck, and three sheathed knives were strapped to my waist.

"What are you waiting for?" a young male voice asked.

Alex, I realized, but I didn't know anyone named Alex.

He clapped my shoulder, and I flushed as I looked up at him. The tall human had gangly arms, messy brown hair, and a smile that lit up my world. My lover, my friend, my everything.

Hydraulics hissed at the very edge of my hearing in eight-beat patterns, but I didn't react. SpiderTech?

Someone laughed, and three other teenagers joined us. The rest of my family, though not by blood. We'd come here to rebuild the utopia of Earth's past. I gazed into Alex's bright green eyes, lit with the righteous fire that burned within him. That passion gave me purpose, filled my existence.

Alex cupped my cheek. "This is just step one. We're gonna make it better."

He brushed his lips across mine. Warmth filled my heart.

The sound of the SpiderTech grew louder, but nothing other than interest in the unknown entered my mind. I turned and shaded my eyes. In this grayscale world, the SpiderTech's metal components looked dull. Its human head turned this way and that before it noticed us and skittered over.

I braced to run. We'd heard rumors that Tech could be violent if provoked, but Alex thought we could communicate with them and work together. The SpiderTech stopped and swept a red beam over Elaine, from her unshod feet to her frizzy brown hair, then turned to David. I raised an eyebrow at her. She nodded with a small smile. The Tech's inspection didn't hurt.

The first step to utopia. Alex had been right.

When the thing approached me, I spread my arms and closed my eyes as if I'd spent my life waiting for this moment. Something wet and hot splattered against my face and into my mouth with a metallic taste. Alex bumped my shoulder. Elaine and Harry screamed.

I snapped my eyes open. Alex collapsed against me, red human blood pouring from a slash across his neck. I caught him and froze. He couldn't die. Not Alex. We had too many plans, too much to do. This couldn't be happening.

"Get them—" Alex choked in a wet voice.

I flinched.

"Get them out," he coughed.

The *zing* of a blaster confused me. Elaine stopped screaming. The air began to reek of charred meat.

"We gotta go!" David shouted.

I didn't look up as I crumpled to the ground under Alex's weight. The dry, white ground of Earth turned a brilliant red. I cupped his face, my hands covered in his blood. His gaze had gone unfocused, dull.

"Not like this." Tears streamed down my cheeks.

That *zing* sounded again, followed by a heavy *thud*. Harry's dark hand flopped into my peripheral vision, charred and still.

"You bastard!" David cried.

I looked up to call out to him, but my voice stuck in my throat. David charged, his glasses bouncing on his nose. One of the SpiderTech's arms shot out. The metal disappeared into David's chest and emerged through his spine. David pitched backward and onto the ground as the Tech retracted its arm. I met his gaze, pained and furious. The Spider-Tech's arm came down again and stabbed into David's brain. He went limp.

My own harsh breathing and the whir of the machine filled the air. The SpiderTech stepped back, drew its legs together, and lowered its body to the ground. It became utterly still.

Elain lay farthest away, twisted and burned. Harry lay so close I could push the curls off his face if I could get my arms to move. David's glasses hung askew in front of empty eyes. Alex—

A sob wracked my body.

I'd been abandoned, beaten, watched kids die in the streets. None of that compared to the gulf that opened in my chest. I used my *energy* to push Alex off me, then pulled my friends, my family, to me and sobbed. The ruby-red blood on my hands grew tacky. Shame cut through the pain. I'd let them die. Alex told me to get them out, and I'd frozen. I may as well have killed them.

The knowledge settled like a stone in my stomach. I had no more tears, no more rage. I looked at the still SpiderTech with cold eyes and considered charging it as David had. Some ember of Alex's fire flared to life. I had failed them. Maybe I deserved to die for that. But my family would have wanted better, and I couldn't fail them twice.

I jumped to my feet, pushed *energy* into my legs, and ran.

23

———

KINNIA

Flames filled the air around me and licked at the wood of the high cathedral ceilings. Smoke made my eyes water, and tears wove strange patterns down my face, along angled features I didn't recognize. My heavy footfalls echoed off the stone floor as I stalked toward a door I didn't recognize but that filled my gut with hurt.

Something to my left crashed. I didn't flinch. With easy grace, I faced the approaching figure, a middle-aged man draped in the silver and gold robes of the holy order. Father Isaack. He froze. I glimpsed the reflection in Father Isaack's wide eyes of a young, well-built fae with fanned ears cross his arms as I crossed mine.

Father Isaack straightened. "You should be in your room."

I looked left and right at the curtains of flames devouring the dry-rotted wood, burning alive those who hadn't escaped. The heat flickered against my back. I smiled.

Fear filled his eyes. He knew I had something to do with the fire.

"Father Isaack." I smiled wider. "It's a lovely evening. Are you coming to visit me?" Despite the confidence with which I carried myself, my hands shook with pain and the desire to throttle the man in front of me.

Father Isaack narrowed his eyes. "Son, the holy father—"

I laughed, loud and long, but felt no happiness, no pleasure. I don't know what I expected him to say, but I should have known there was nothing these men, the men who kept me and studied me and made me into a monster, could say in their defense.

I brought my fists together in front of me, my raw wrists burning, reached out with my newfound magic, and pulled. The priest groaned and wrapped his arms around his stomach.

"No, Ba—"

I would not let my name fall from his lips again. I wrenched my hands apart. He tore in two with a spray of blood that covered my tunic and face and hissed as it hit the fire. I dropped the two halves to the floor, then studied them for a moment, waiting for a rush of pleasure or vindication. I only felt the heat against my skin.

I turned and strode toward the end of the hall. Like I had for as long as I could remember, I trailed my fingers along the intricate vines carved into the wood. Gold filigree sparkled in the firelight.

I reached the door at the end of the hallway, then hesitated. The room beyond frightened me more than the others, more than even my own. This room is where my nightmare had begun. Here, I'd learned the true doctrine of the church, the taste of honey that followed their worst discoveries like a reward.

That new power seared in my veins, hot and bright as the fire itself. I tore the door off its hinges to reveal the chapel. A single candle burned on the altar, a light to guide penitents until dawn. I tipped the candle over with an easy mental command. The flame caught on the altar cloth and quickly burned down to reveal the surface beneath I knew all too well.

White marble, stained dark gray with my blood. Four leather shackles, reinforced time and again at each corner. In some ways, I was lucky the traveling priest wanted to test me in my room tonight instead of here. Moonlight streamed through stained glass depicting their god of pain and knowledge. I watched the flames chew through my worst memories.

When the fire began its crawl through the door behind me and down the aisle from the candle, when I had no option but to leave or burn to death, I spread my fingers and sank my power into the mortar between the stones in the floor. The ceiling groaned. I sprinted for the stained glass. Fire nipped at my heels.

As I leapt, I pulled, and the floor exploded outward. I covered my head as I crashed through the chest of their god, the only piece of glass large enough to escape through.

24

ZELIMIR

I RAN MY HAND ACROSS THE COPPER STUBBLE ON MY CHIN
and up through my tight twists. My eyes drooped with exhaustion. I sat
up on the couch and began digging through the piles of plans I'd drawn
up on the low table in our suite. No matter how many tactics I worked
through or historical battles I rehashed, nothing changed.

Declan still lay unconscious in his bed, as he had for the last two
days. None of us could bear to look away for long. The couch now faced
our human's bed. In front of the couch sat a low table covered in my
plans, dirty coffee cups, and a stack of books that had offered no
answers. Shade dozed in fae form at the foot of Declan's bed. Something
squeaked like an itzal, but I couldn't find a source.

Exhaustion swept over me. I scowled at Teyr, who snoozed in one of
the high-backed armchairs we'd dragged to the head of Declan's bed. I
scrubbed my hands over my eyes. I wished the Council hadn't seen Teyr
lose his temper at the end of Bash's trial. I understood his concerns. I
just didn't know how to make him understand that we needed the
Council. Their organization, their people. We weren't an army, just a
piece of a bigger puzzle. The ember turned in his sleep, his frown deep-
ening. He still struggled to realize we could do nothing by ourselves.

While Teyr slept restlessly, Declan remained perfectly still. Councilor

Gnuq's healer, a small, pink pixie without a shred of clothing, had offered no solutions to wake him. She'd only promised he wouldn't deteriorate and encased him in a parity blanket to manage his bodily functions. That had been the hour after the trial, and nothing had changed since. He still wore his grubby trainee greens from the trial, and a smudge of green dirt stood out like a bruise on his temple. The parity blanket shouldn't create this unnatural stillness.

The green wood door to our suite rolled open and crashed into the wall. I sucked in a breath as Bash stepped into the room, shirtless and dripping with sweat. A rush of raw, red anger filled my veins. The dragon had woken yesterday and disappeared without a word, ignoring all our desperate *pulses*. I'd suspected for some time that he might be keeping something from me. Now, I knew it.

Shade sat bolt upright, blue-black magic collecting around him. A good leader would have calmed the necromancer. I opened my Cara, letting my anger pour out. Bash didn't even look in my direction. He stalked to Declan's side, opposite Teyr, and pressed two fingers against the human's neck like he couldn't feel Declan's pulse through the bond. Despite my anger, my breath caught. Would Declan stir this time? Would he wake?

Nothing. A fresh wave of rage drove away my disappointment. "You would know if he worsened. Get your hands off him."

Bash pulled his hand away and faced me. I had spent nearly a century with the dragon. I knew his face like I knew my own. He tried to maintain his usual stoic mask, but guilt glimmered in his eyes. He knew, and he knew I knew.

I jumped to my feet with a stream of curses. He couldn't let Declan die for this. I knocked him back and pinned him against the wall. He tried to harden his face into neutrality, but guilt and pain still filled his eyes. He didn't try to escape.

"What do you know?" I yelled. "Why are you keeping things from me? From us?"

As my mates stared at me with wide eyes in the moment of silence that followed, I realized something deep between us had broken. I didn't trust my second. I had attacked him. I didn't know when we'd lost that trust, our connection, whether it had been Light or Declan or something else entirely, but I didn't know if we were a Cara anymore. I sank to the floor next to Declan's bed.

Bash didn't move from the wall, didn't shout back. He just rubbed his collarbone. A faint bruise where I'd gripped his neck shadowed his lilac skin.

"My Cara is something different now," he said. "Something more."

Teyr rolled his eyes. "Great details. F minus."

I didn't know when the ember woke, but I folded my arms so as not to appear that I agreed with him too heartily.

Shade stood and took the armchair next to Teyr. He rested one foot on the nightstand we'd pushed out of the way. "Do you know what's happening to my Kitty?"

Bash sighed. "I think so. Dee's dreaming, healing the mind." He hesitated, as if looking for the right words. "Our bond is thicker now, but hollow in the middle."

I shot up and stalked to the foot of Declan's bed, then clutched the footboard. I couldn't trust myself to do anything else. Bash's scales shifted anxiously around his face. We still only had some of the truth. I swallowed down a new wave of anger.

"If something's gone wrong, we need to fix it. Declan's weird enough." Teyr threw his hands up. "Is there a telepath we trust?"

Bash vaulted Declan's bed and grabbed Teyr by the neck of his tunic to hoist him into the air. Bash's pupils elongated, burning with something I'd never seen before, and his scales darkened and clustered.

"She's ours," he growled. "It doesn't feel wrong. She'll wake."

My stomach dropped to my feet. The wood of Declan's bed cracked under my hands. Bash had said "she".

Declan's need for privacy. His fear of touch. Every time he giggled before forcing the sound deeper. My heartbeat roared in my ears.

"She?" Teyr asked so softly I almost didn't recognize his voice.

Bash clenched his jaw and dropped Teyr back into his seat. "She."

Teyr stood. "She."

Shade started laughing.

"Declan is a woman, and you kept that to yourself?" Teyr shouted.

"You three are blind idiots," Shade choked out amidst his humor. "She doesn't smell human or fae, but she smells female. I knew the minute I caught her scent."

My surprise banked. Rage filled its space.

"I've seen her nude." Shade smirked. "No one feels uncomfortable around a dog."

I tuned out Teyr's demands for an explanation, Bash's growled answers, Shade's supercilious amusement. She. She. All the times I'd kissed her, wound my arms around her waist—

Bash, Declan, Shade, they'd been keeping a secret so big it could destroy us all. Whatever this did to us, our dynamic, faded into the background as I realized just how deeply fucked we would be if this got out.

I couldn't protect us from things I didn't know about.

"Enough," I barked.

My mates fell silent and looked at me.

"Bash, your display at the trial told every fae in the wilds you've found a way to increase your magic. It will be no leap to connect that to our new mate." I clenched my fist. "We will look like fools if anyone finds out we didn't know. Worse, it could make the Council watch us even more closely." I fixed my gaze on Teyr. "They might see her true value or fear her *energy*. Either outcome is bad for us."

A soft thrum of fear leaked through his Cara, and Teyr narrowed his eyes. "They wouldn't dare take her."

I sliced my hand through the air to cut off that line of thought. "We couldn't stop them if they decided to. I need you to get this through your charred skull. It's not just going to be Councilors. It's going to be everyone. We'll be destroyed if we aren't careful."

I looked at each of my mates in turn. Teyr met my gaze sullenly, Bash guiltily, and Shade...I couldn't read Shade since his return to fae form, but he faced me unflinchingly.

"We are her mates. Her place is amongst us. We all decided to put our trust in that." I took a deep breath. "Trust is built, not forced."

Teyr scowled, and tongues of flame licked over his hands. "Ironic, coming from you."

We didn't have time for these petty squabbles. We could fix them when we passed our trials, had the space and the privacy, but for now, we needed to survive.

"When she wakes, we will proceed as if nothing changed. Let the Cara grow naturally, and she'll come to trust us in time." I raked my hand through my twists.

"You've got to be kidding." Teyr stared down at his sparking fingertips. "She lied to us."

"And we'll deal with that when time comes." I crossed my arms. "For now, we have to fall in line."

Bash nodded, lending his silent support. Shade stared into the distance, fiddling with something under his shirt. Teyr opened his mouth, and Declan's Cara stirred. Everyone whipped toward her.

I'd given my orders. Time to lead by example.

25

KINNIA

"—FALL IN LINE."

Zelimir's sharp voice punctured the soft bubble of sleep around me. I tried to stay still and hear more, but only discerned light footsteps and rustling fabric. I opened my eyes. The multicolored fabric ceiling of our suite caught the late afternoon light. My mates all leaned over me. Shade tried to help me sit up, but I waved him away. The movement only made my body ache. I'd be back at training tomorrow with a little stretching. Bash put a hand on my shoulder to keep me from trying to swing my feet over the edge of the mattress.

"How are you feeling?" Teyr's cat-slit eyes glowed as he looked me over. Something burned deep within them, and it didn't look like his usual lust.

I'd missed something.

Bash's trial came back to me in a rush. I'd passed out. Images of another life assaulted my memory, and fear ate away my lingering grogginess. I shrugged Bash's hand off and scooted backward until my back hit something. Not the hard stone of the wall, as expected, but something soft and squishy. My mind muddled. Through a dark, hazy cloud, I made out the trainee greens and armor I had worn in the coliseum. They hadn't undressed me.

I took a deep breath. "Feeling like shit." My voice only shook a little. Good enough. "How long was I out? Did we win?"

Zelimir closed his eyes, his expression a mix of relief and a disappointment I didn't understand. He patted my footboard awkwardly, then dropped onto the couch behind him. They'd redecorated, apparently.

Shade cupped my cheek. "Welcome back."

The soft look in his eyes, the gentle way he held me. Shade would kiss me now, in front of everyone. Through my grogginess and confusion, I didn't quite know if I wanted that. Instead, he pulled back and sat on the floor next to my bed. I exhaled quietly. Teyr stepped to the foot of my bed. I could feel Bash on my left as clearly as if I stared at him. Just the knowledge made my heart beat a little harder.

"You don't need this anymore." Teyr grabbed the cloud at my feet and tugged. The haze made a sucking noise as it retracted into a compact ball.

My bladder screamed for relief. I pushed upright and swung my legs over the edge of the mattress. I stood and wobbled toward the washroom.

"Do that again, and you can see what a week without peeing feels like," Teyr called after me.

I rolled the washroom door shut behind me.

"You were out for two days, and we won," Bash said through the door.

I blanched. Two days?

Wood rolled against stone, and the dragon slid a fresh set of greens just inside the room before rolling the door closed once more. I closed my eyes and swiped my hand through the air in front of me. My bond with Bash had become something more than a string, more than a rope. It was a solid, hollow cable. No, I associated a cable with Earth and I didn't want anything from Earth associated with these fae, no matter how strange they were acting. I'd call this connection a bridge.

If I let my consciousness travel along the bridge, would I find myself back in his memories? I skimmed my hand through its space, and Bash's exact location rushed to me. I could have pinpointed him on a map. I rested my forehead against the cool stone wall. Bash was just Bash. I was just me. Whatever happened, we could brush it under the rug like we did everything else. Yeah, that had been working great. I turned the tap to its hottest water setting and wished we had private showers.

When I'd done all I could in the sink, I dressed and stepped out. My mates watched me cross the suite, except Bash, who'd disappeared while I washed up. A tension I didn't understand whispered through the room. Fae concern felt a lot like surveillance. A shiver ran down my back as I sat in my favorite chair, previously by the coffee table, which had somehow escaped the redecorating fury to stand alone in the middle of the room. My stomach rumbled so loud I'd swear the sound shook the chair.

I eyed Shade, still on the floor by my bed. Blue-black power oozed out of one of his hands as he watched me. Even as a fae, I'd gotten used to Shade always being near enough to touch. Of all the times to stay away, he chose distance after I'd been unconscious for days?

The door opened and Bash entered the room. He handed me a bowl of some hot stew with big chunks of soft bread. I dug in, so hungry the flavor didn't even seem to reach my tongue.

When I finished, Bash took the bowl back. Our fingers brushed. We locked gazes. The room around me dissolved. My world became his gray eyes and full lips. His memories haunted my thoughts. Our Cara didn't hum but leaned, pulling me toward my dragon.

I couldn't just pretend nothing had happened. We needed to talk. Alone. As if he heard me, Bash left the room again. My heart thudded. Would he wait for me somewhere? Should I follow? Zelimir's gaze sat heavy on my shoulders. I swallowed and remained in my seat. I had more to tell.

"Bash used my *energy*." I didn't want any more secrets between us than necessary. "I didn't know he could do that."

"We noticed when all the rocks went flying through the air. Didn't think you'd developed telepathy and forgot to tell us," Teyr said abruptly.

I blinked. Shade snickered.

Zelimir cleared his throat. "Bash caught us up. Your Cara has evolved into something more."

I swallowed. "Did Bash share any further details?"

"No," Zelimir said slowly. "He did not." He looked down at the papers in front of him.

I glanced at Shade, waiting to feel something, but no emotions came through our bond. His eyes glowed like his power had found something to reanimate. My heart pinched. The necromancer had cut me off. Before I could worry about Shade, I realized Teyr still studied me with an unnerving intensity. I fixed my hair self-consciously, and he scoffed. Had Teyr ever scoffed at me before? Surely, he had, right?

"Was the Council happy we passed?" I asked.

Zelimir didn't look up. "Mixed reactions." He frowned. "Bash's new connection to you doesn't change our goals. Teyr's trial is in two weeks, less the days you lost."

I huffed. Once again, my mates had decided my future without my input. I strummed my hand through Shade's string, trying to *pulse* a question. I knew Zel thought he'd grown too attached, and I hadn't known the real Shade long, but I needed the openness he usually showed. Without any outside sign, he opened his Cara to me. Relief mingled with concern and concentration. A hint of pain radiated throughout. He snapped his Cara shut once more, and my stomach sank. Why had I woken up so alone?

I hugged myself. "I'm going for a walk."

Zelimir barely nodded his assent. I fled.

Sunlight hit my shoulders as I exited through a side door. The bridge connecting me to Bash told me moved with me, giving me space and making sure I remained alone. My heart fluttered. We'd connected in a way I didn't know was possible. I had no idea what came next.

I found myself in a series of serene gardens on small patches of land between canal intersections, a lush paradise I'd never seen before. I'd seen so little of the Academy. I didn't even know where Zelimir got all his books. I shook my head. I needed to focus on Bash, and whatever this bridge between us meant.

One small island held nothing but a circle of navy-leafed bushes with vivid pink and red flowers. I parted the branches and settled on the orange grass inside. The water flowed quietly around me. I walked myself through the breathing exercise Teyr had taught me. In for five, hold for five, out for five. I could almost hear his voice counting for me. Slowly, the tension released from my shoulders. Closing my eyes, I brushed the bridge of swirling power. The magic binding us together no longer felt so unnatural.

I'm joining you. Bash's thoughts resounded as clearly in my head as if he'd spoken.

I opened my eyes. The bushes to my left rustled.

I want you to, I thought back.

Bash pushed through the bushes and circled me once before dropping down behind me. He lifted me half onto his lap, so my back rested against his chest. My heart raced.

He circled my waist with his muscular arms and brushed the side of my neck with a kiss. "You didn't kill them."

Bash had experienced my time on Earth. A dam of emotions I hadn't even known existed broke. Hurt, terror, and devastation cut through me like a hot knife. A sob ripped out of my throat. He held me tighter, sending me perfect images of their faces, smiling and happy. I turned my head and cried into his chest.

My hands trembled as I waited for flashbacks to steal away reality, but they never took hold. I had someone to share my terror with, someone who didn't run but pulled me into his arms. We could control our pasts together.

My tears slowed and eventually stopped. I pulled my face away from his now-damp shirt, my back aching slightly from the odd angle. I stretched before leaning back against his chest.

"No one should have gone through what you did."

I didn't know everything, from that brief glimpse, but I could tell he'd been held by those priests and experimented on throughout his childhood. For the first time, I wondered how many of his scars came from fights.

His arms tightened around me, and his breath caught against my back. I twisted to look at him. He'd closed his eyes. White and purple scales slithered along his temples, collecting in dark patches. Regret, anger, sadness, and acceptance mixed in a whirlwind as he opened his

Cara. Eventually, the storm calmed. Warmth and determination took their place.

Bash brought his head down. I tilted mine up until our lips met. I'd waited my entire life to be kissed like this. He molded his mouth to mine as he slid his hands my hips. I swiveled on his lap to brace myself against his lilac pecs. He licked the crease of my mouth, and I parted for him. His tongue filled me with love and need. He grabbed my ass and pulled me closer, pinning his firm erection between us. I rocked forward, desire gathering between my legs, and he groaned. He slipped his other hand under my tunic, up my side. My skin tingled.

He traced the edges of my chest bindings until he found the knot keeping them tight, like I always wore them when I didn't have my cuirass. Reality rushed back to me. He knew.

I pulled away. "Bash."

My dragon's eyes glowed. He ground his cock against my leg, and the size made my core throb with need. He released my ass to tangle his hand in my hair and pull my mouth back to his. This time, his kiss demanded more. I moaned as he wound my tongue with his before sucking my bottom lip into his mouth. Once again, he traced the edge of my chest bindings.

"Bash." Shade's voice shattered the moment. "Control your dragon."

I pulled back. Bash untangled his hand from my hair. I fought to steady my breathing as my core tightened and strained. Damn the cock-blocking wolf.

The necromancer approached us though a pathway of dead foliage. Bash's scales had doubled in number, covering his tattooed eyebrows and the bridge of his nose. His gray eyes burned as he massaged my rib cage. He shook his head as if to clear his thoughts. Some of his scales receded. He dragged his fingers down my stomach, sending spikes of lust to my already throbbing sex. As he reached my waist, he pulled his hand out from under my tunic. My pussy clenched. This type of torture should be banned.

Shade stopped so close the leg of his pants brushed my shoulder. I dragged my attention away from Bash to the necromancer. His two-colored eyes danced as he extended a hand to help me off Bash's lap. I stared at his hand. I wanted this. I wanted Bash. Not in the same raw, physical way I wanted Zelimir, but something more. I loved him. My heart stuttered. The last person I'd loved died.

Bash growled and dug his fingers into the ground. Zelimir's warnings about balance rose to the surface. I took a deep breath.

Shade wiggled his fingers. "Come, my Kitty."

The motion drew my attention to the erection tenting his pants. All my mates had just felt me lose myself in need.

I bit my bottom lip. "Shit, this is weird."

Shade smiled sadly. I took the necromancer's hand. He pulled me into his embrace and kissed the top of my head. His erection pressed into me. I struggled to keep my head clear. Bash stood as well, though he turned away from us to adjust his pants.

Shade nudged the side of my head with his chin. "My Kitty, you must focus on your training."

He trailed one of his hands up and down my arm. If he noticed his erection, he gave no sign. I took a deep breath. I didn't understand. Had Shade responded to his own lust or mine? Was I forcing him to feel something he didn't want to feel? I looked for the emotions my dire wolf usually shared with me, but I remained in the dark.

"You slept for days." Shade kissed my head again. "I was terrified we'd lost you. We need to get through this as a pack, or the Council will take you from us."

Bash's voice filled my mind. *Shade's right. I lost control. We need to focus on the Cara.*

My heart fell, but I couldn't argue. The Cara before my feelings. Always.

26

TEYR

The last few days had been some of the worst of my life. Zel's insistence that nothing changed meant everything did, but we had to tip-toe around that fact. Embers didn't do this. Anam Caras didn't do this. I certainly didn't do this.

I walked through the southernmost training yard behind our mate—Dee? Kitty? Fire, I didn't even know what to call her. How could I not have noticed the curves that begged for a hand to cup them?

She'd lied. I'd wanted her to fix everything, fill the hole that Light left, and instead, she started the trust breakdown that led us here, lying to each other in an effort to build fucking trust.

"Is there a hole in my pants or something, Teyr?" She winked at me over her shoulder, showing off yet another dark forehead bruise from failing to duck the log yesterday.

I pulled my gaze away and steadied my fire and my voice. "Your pants are fine."

She wrinkled her nose but faced forward again.

I rubbed the shaved side of my head and cringed. I kept replaying what I said about sex at the volcano, my display in the baths. What had she liked, and what had she put up with to avoid detection? Why did I care?

Anger sparked on my fingertips. I couldn't figure anything out because I still had to pretend I didn't know.

We stopped at the base of a hill of mud and rock, ringed by a low moat. Bash stopped next to me, and my anger burned into a flame. If the lizard hadn't lied for so long, I wouldn't have anything to figure out.

Lir, the commander of the most experienced elemental Cara in the wilds, stepped out from around the set-up. He'd taken on the features of his element over the years, like I might eventually.

"Shade," Zelimir barked. "Stay with us."

I eyed the necromancer through a mist of his power. He hadn't even tried to hide the second set of black-furred ears on top of his head this morning. He rubbed his lower back, his eyes glowing as he observed the living and the dead. Slowly, his power receded, and his gaze cleared. He shoved his hands into his pockets and focused on the ground.

Even when Light was alive, Shade spoke only when he had something to say, but I could count the number of words he'd said in the last three days on one hand. I *pulsed* to Shade, checking on him. He looked up and gave me a small smile before staring at the ground once more.

"We're focusing on teamwork. Our trials have been…unique, and we must be prepared for anything." Zelimir gestured to the fae standing next to him. "Today, Lir has agreed to help us with some training."

A few people muttered behind us. I glanced back to find a group of trainees and off-duty Cara mates and Secca officers had gathered to watch us. Since Bash's trial, our observers grew more plentiful every day.

"The idea's simple." Zelimir jerked his chin toward the hill. "Teyr and Lir position themselves at the top. The four of us need to join Teyr, who will be directing and helping, while Lir does everything in his power to stop us from reaching our goal. The two of you"—Zelimir pointed to Lir and me— "are not allowed direct conflict. We have two minutes. We lose if we don't accomplish our task in that time or if all four of us are knocked into the moat." He met my gaze. "This isn't about brute force. We must be smart and communicate. And don't forget they will be gunning for, ah, Declan."

I glanced over at the woman, who sighed and nodded. Unlike Bash, whose magic had dramatically increased in range and power after his trial, she hadn't changed at all. She still lacked fae reflexes and the near century of experience we had together. Man or woman, she held us back. I opened my mouth to comment but shut it. Nothing I had to say was helpful or witty. That seemed to be happening a lot these days.

Instead, I turned a circle, waving to my new fans and my mates. "See you at the top."

Instead of climbing the muddy hill, I turned around and blasted a fireball at my feet. The momentum carried me up, and I landed softly next to Lir, dirt-free. I'd learned since my last muddy hill. He raised an eyebrow. Despite deafening silence below, I bowed.

I had an unobstructed view from up here. My four mates spread out evenly around the hill. A few feet behind them, the shallow, muddy moat wound a perfect circle around the hill. Thank Fire we were preparing for my trial. I didn't want to touch that water.

"Begin!" Lir tossed a thin ribbon of water into the air that began counting down from two minutes.

I jerked. I'd completely forgotten to plan, and the elemental gave me no warning. Water bloomed at Lir's command, pelting my mates in a shower which left pink spots on their skin. I channeled my shock into fire above them to evaporate the droplets before they hit. The cloud remained, but Lir shot a jet of water at Shade's waist, then twisted with liquid grace and fired a much larger ball of water at Zelimir.

I whirled, *pulsing* to Shade as I ignited days of irritation into a firewall in front of my commander. Shade dove to the side, narrowly dodging Lir's attack, and steam filled the air as the water in front of Zel evaporated.

Lir whipped around, and before I could discern his target, a frothy wave of water crashed down the woman's side of the hill and swept her off her feet. She tumbled into the muddy canal face-first.

My heart skipped a beat. She surfaced, sputtering and coughing. All three of my mates raced to help her, and all three halted, leaving her to drag herself out of the ditch. I clenched my fists. At least one of them should have helped her.

Above my head, the water timer ran out and rained down on my shoulders.

Lir danced a little jig. "Round goes to me."

I flattened my lips. "Good distractions."

Lir's eyes sparkled.

I *pulsed* a plan to my mates, too fast for the human to understand. Zelimir responded first, followed by Shade. I took their ideas into account and adjusted. Bash could fill her in through their new mental link.

I didn't care. She wasn't special.

"Begin," I yelled in the hopes I could catch the water elemental off guard.

He triggered the timer and grinned.

The woman sprinted west to join Shade, slipping on the soaked ground. Lir whirled and started a mudslide directly in her path. I channeled my focus into a thin beam of fire and dried a path through the middle so she could slide in front of Shade. She drew her sword as the necromancer dropped to his knees, and blue-black power spilled into the earth. I poured fire onto her blade, super heating it so she could cut through water.

Lir chuckled. "Clever. Your teamwork has improved."

He chucked balls of dense water down at her. Out of the corner of my eye, I spotted Zel and Bash approaching the top of the hill. Lir didn't stand a chance. Suddenly, Shade's power glowed at my feet. I jumped back and yelped as tiny, winged gisvin skeletons emerged from the ground. Zelimir's dirt-crusted hand reached over the lip at the top of the hill.

Too late, I spotted the seething water that Lir had hidden just below the lip. The surface tension broke at my commander's touch, and a tidal wave of mud and water washed down. Bash managed to tether himself to the hill with his telekinesis, but Zelimir rolled with the torrent, coming to a stop in the water of the canal. If I'd warned my mates about the water, Bash could have kept Zelimir on the hill, and this round could have been ours.

The timer ran out, and Lir danced again. "Zelimir used Geminai's hyper-focus against him. It won't work a second time." He winked. "Though maybe it does on you."

I scowled at my commander as he dragged his massive ass out of the canal. He *pulsed* a regroup, and I carefully picked my way down, managing to keep the mud contained to my tall boots. Lir rode a small wave down triumphantly. I seethed. I hated losing, but I hated worse that he managed to keep cleaner than me.

Shade dripped mud. "I was just getting started. Necromancy isn't fast."

I barked out a bitter laugh. "What were you doing? How do gisvin skeletons help us?"

The woman clapped a hand over her mouth, smothering a giggle. I scowled.

Shade straightened to his full height and looked down his nose at me. "Distractions."

Lir grinned. "They distracted Teyr pretty good."

Shade glared at Lir. "I will ask Bodmier to bury something more interesting here. Maybe a water elemental."

"We need to focus on finding each other first." Dee stepped in front of Shade. "Distractions are great, but Bash couldn't reach us in the last trial. It's why—"

"Can Teyr use your body like Bash did?" Lir cut in.

I sucked in a breath. No one wanted to broach that topic. Bash thought what happened might be related to his dragon, but my gut told me it had been all her. I stayed up at night hoping it was, and that made me even angrier. I wanted to be done wanting her. I didn't want to be like Lir, or the huddled crowd at the base of the hill. She received piles of presents every night, like other fae could woo her to their sides. I'd thought the gifts silly before, but now every package spiked dark, bitter feelings.

When none of us spoke, Lir nodded slowly. "Well, I thought it was incredible. Councilor Odhrán was going on and on about how Councilor Ambrocio looked unreasonable in the wake of your success. If you weren't already, you're now the most interesting thing in all the wilds."

She wrapped her arms around herself. I bit back the urge to step between her and the crowd.

"Are you happy with Zelimir's Cara?" Lir met her gaze.

My stomach twisted. Bash growled. Shade pulled her to his side.

Zelimir's purple gaze flashed. "Lir, my friend, that's too bold."

She wriggled, her Cara a mess of confusion, hurt, and anger. Either she didn't try that hard to escape, or Shade held on tight.

Lir looked at my commander. "I can't be the first to ask."

I scoffed. "The dragonkin offered *our mate* an entire mountain." I pointedly didn't look at Bash. "I can't imagine them following through on that, the territorial assholes."

Before I could say something worse—or punch the water elemental in the nose like I wanted to—Shade stiffened and whirled, dragging the woman with him. He thrust his nose forward like his wolf used to. I followed his line of sight. Two goblins in leather and plate had joined the onlookers. I frowned. There'd never been a goblin in a Cara before—rumor said they didn't have the power..

"What are goblins doing here?" I asked.

Lir shrugged. "The Lower Council thought we needed extra security."

"Why?" Zel demanded.

I grimaced. I'd heard a rumor about this in the baths, that a rift opened in the colosseum after everyone left Bash's trial and the Council had been hiding the information and increasing security to prevent panic. I doubted they'd be able to hide something like that, and in the frustration of the last few days, I hadn't mentioned the whispers to my antisocial mates.

"You didn't hear?" Lir stepped closer and dropped his voice. "A rift opened in the colosseum, which should've been impossible. No Tech came through, but"—he looked at the human—"it appeared shortly after Bash's trial."

The human straightened, breaking Shade's hold. "I. Don't. Open. Rifts."

Shade blinked at his arm, still cupping the shape of her shoulders, and flushed. Fur grew along his chin before receding. He stared at her for a long moment, then dropped his gaze to the ground and began mumbling. I *pulsed* to the necromancer again. This time, he opened his Cara. Regret and hope filtered into me with an undercurrent of pretty intense pain from somewhere on his back. Before I could ask, he *pulsed* that he'd be fine and closed his Cara again.

"Maybe you wouldn't open a rift on purpose," Lir said.

I scoffed. "That stuff about rifts is just chatter."

"You don't have to believe me." Lir clapped his hands. "My Cara has patrol this evening. Let's see how many times I can dunk your human."

Although he sounded playful, I huffed. Zelimir *pulsed*, and we resumed our exercise.

OUT OF TWENTY ATTEMPTS, LIR DEFEATED US EIGHTEEN times. I stayed clean, but my mates all looked like drowned itzals. Cleanliness made me lonelier, for once.

"Begin." Even Lir sounded tired.

My mates moved like snails compared to the first round, and we hadn't even executed the first step of my strategy before Shade slipped and fell backward. Pain lanced through our Cara, radiating clearly from his tailbone and sending spikes of agony up his back. I went down on one knee with a squelch of mud. Lir froze. Just as fast, Shade's bond went quiet once more.

The human reached Shade first and knelt at his side. From the way Shade writhed, I could tell the pain hadn't stopped, just the sharing. I was tired of hiding and lying and keeping things from people. I just wanted my mates safe and happy. I slid down the hill, covering myself in mud.

"I'm all right." Shade leaned up on one arm.

"You're not," I growled.

The woman leaned forward and whispered, "I don't understand. What's going on? Why have you shut me out?"

The color drained from Shade's face. He took a breath to speak, but the words seemed to catch in his throat. I expected him to shift. Zel appeared on his other side and held out a hand. Shade disentangled himself from her and stood as a fae. That didn't hurt my feelings either.

"We're done for today," my commander said. "Clean up. You have an hour to yourselves before dinner. We'll spend the evening on concentration exercises."

I slid to Shade's side and offered my arm to lean on, but the necromancer pushed me away. I gritted my teeth.

"What's wrong with him?" the woman murmured to me.

I leaned away from her. "I don't know. Until he lets us in, we can't help."

She frowned, then hurried forward to fall into step behind Shade and Zelimir.

27

______

SHADE

Pain radiated up my spine as I slunk inside. My packmates trailed after me, *pulsing* and asking if I was okay. I clutched Light's bone around my neck and refrained from calling up an army of whatever lived below the Academy floors to chase them away. They cared about me. That was good. My next step sent a lightning bolt of pain from my toes to my skull. I needed to get away, to lick my wounds.

"Shade," my pack leader said. "Tell us what's going on, or I'm going to haul you to healer right now."

I spun. "No!"

My packmates all froze in a cluster behind me, wide-eyed. I cast around in my memory for the right emotion to tie that expression to. Surprise? Concern? My Kitty's worry battered at me through her Cara.

I shook my head. "I am well. Merely...tired."

The lie tasted bitter on my tongue, but my Kitty had used it often enough. She seemed to recognize that before the rest of my mates did and nodded slowly.

Teyr crossed his arms. "I felt—"

My Kitty elbowed him, and I smiled at her. She would always take my side.

"Do you need the suite for a little while?" she asked.

Teyr put his hands up. "We can't just—"

She whirled on him and swiped a muddy hand across his fairly clean cheek. "Don't you need to take a bath?"

Teyr gaped. I laughed until the vibrations reached my tailbone, and a new wave of hurt turned to nausea.

"I guess," he grumbled finally. "But you're all coming with me."

My Kitty paled. "I wanted to train a little more."

Teyr scoffed. "Typical."

She narrowed her eyes. The air turned sour with a brewing argument. Everyone fought these days.

I faded into my wolf as they turned on each other and sighed into the release. Whatever else happened, I knew my Kitty would keep my mates away from the suite. I crept there, hiding from the echoes of pain this body didn't feel.

Of course, the door to the suite needed fae hands, which meant I had to shift into fae form. Shifting that direction sparked pain all along my skin that eventually settled into the ache at my back that I'd been living with since Bash's trial. I grumbled and pressed a hand to the green wood. The door rolled into the wall, and I stepped into the quiet of the suite.

The circular room smelled like all my mates, with none of the sour upset. I took a step toward the nearest bed, Teyr's, with the intention of rubbing my face over the pillow. The pine and cardamom smell would remind me how much I loved them when I didn't hurt. One of my pack leader's many lectures about delaying gratification and quashing impulses ran through my mind. I stomped to the washroom. This latest pain had been sharper than the rest. I needed to check.

In the dark stone room, I dropped my pants and pulled the neck of my tunic over my head. My spine throbbed. With a deep breath, I twisted to see my back in the mirror. I yelped. Twisting made the dense lump at the base of my spine hurt the worst. Bigger, but still intact. A thin membrane of my pale skin stretched over a stringy mat of thick, black fur.

With a hiss, I twisted back. Just like the last time I checked, and the time before, my tail remained curled in a pocket of skin too small to hold it, ready to burst. At any other moment, this would have been a cause for marvel. When it hurt less, I'd spent quiet hours staring at the whorls of fur, wondering what this meant for mages, for divar, for magic…for me.

I pulled my tunic back down and hoisted my pants up just below the lump, then crept to my bed. I didn't deserve the comfort of their smells. I should have told my packmates when this strangeness started last week. But they would want to do something, and I didn't know what I wanted done yet. I dropped onto my bed with another spike of pain.

Councilor Xerxes had stared at me when my ears came in. I didn't like being looked at. I would bear some scrutiny for my Kitty, but a tail would confirm I'd become something more than I was. I wrapped my arms around myself. Light and I moved into Bittermist Thicket when we got kicked out for reasons beyond our ability to manipulate the corpse-rich land. The sallow swamp granted us privacy, which I treasured. I liked to handle my problems on my own, or sometimes with him.

Everything changed when we joined the Cara. I expanded my family, happy to bicker with Teyr and stretch with Bash and prank Zelimir. But they all expected me to share. Even Light didn't like it when I said necromancers need secrets.

I huffed and rolled onto my stomach to wait out the wave of pain. If I wanted my secrets, I would just have to bear them without the comfort of my wolf. I needed to try, like my Kitty said.

Someone knocked softly on the door. My heart raced. Academy doors couldn't be locked to Cara mates, and my Cara said my Kitty stood just outside. I flung myself onto the floor with a starburst of pain and slid under my bed before the door rolled into the wall.

"Shade?" my Kitty said quietly.

I bit my tongue and tried to pull the darkness around me. A single shaft of light poked under the mattress. I wanted her to leave. I wanted everyone to leave.

"Shade, I know you're here." She sighed. "I got rid of everyone, but I need to know that you're actually safe."

Disappointment and worry wobbled through her Cara. If I wanted her to leave, I need only lie to her.

"I'm safe." Even that technical truth soured on my tongue. My tail wouldn't kill me.

"Are you under the bed?" she asked.

I remained silent, staring at the single shaft of light. I'd done what she asked. She had to leave now. Instead, with a bit of rustling and a sigh, she laid on her side next to my bed. I slithered deeper into the shadows. She gleamed in the late afternoon sunlight. Her dark hair shone faintly red, and the chapped flakes of skin on her lips turned translucent.

She frowned. "This is not doing a lot to convince me you're okay."

"You said safe," I replied. "I am safe. It is safe here for me. You may go."

She rolled onto her back. "You want your space. I get that. But I can't just leave you like this."

"Like what?"

"Hiding under the bed from your mates?" She sighed. "If we're counting me as one of those."

I wriggled a little closer, heedless of the one ray of sun. I couldn't let my Kitty talk like that. "Of course, you're my mate. You are pack."

She chuckled. "It doesn't really seem like it these days. Even you pulled back." She rolled onto her side.

I flinched. She looked along the whole length of the bed but didn't seem to see me.

"Why did you close your Cara?" she asked.

The silence between us drooped with the weight of accusation, but I had no defense to offer. I didn't want her to suffer the pain I'd grown accustomed to the long hours of the day, and I hadn't yet figured out a way to make it stop hurting.

"I miss you." She dropped her head back, and the warm glow of sunlight flooded her features. Her eyes glittered, maybe with tears, and she gnawed on her lip.

I opened my mouth to say something, maybe to confess. She slid her hand under the bed along the one shaft of light that could reach me. The song roared in my ears. I scrambled backward, hit something with a starburst of pain, and pulled on whatever I could find in the stone below me. The frantic rhythm of Thrae crescendoed. A handful of small, gray worms oozed up. The music crashed, and I sent them skittering toward her hand.

She recoiled as they squirmed across her skin. "What the shit, Shade?" She bolted upright and clutched her hand to her chest. "I was trying to hold your hand."

The song died. Shame filled my cheeks as pain scorched into my awareness. I called the worms back. Of course, my Kitty had only wanted something innocent, not to tear all my secrets from me. She had reached out in a moment of emotional vulnerability, and I followed the magic rather than my heart. I set worms on her.

"I'm sorry," I whispered. "Don't come under here."

It wasn't enough, but I could manage nothing more. Power gathered around me with the itch of fur. I ached to crawl into my wolf, let the pain and mess fade away. No. I owed my Kitty better. I clung to my fae form and lapsed into penitent silence, watching the golden outline of her legs.

"Shit, fine," she muttered. "Bed's yours."

A moment passed. Would she leave? I had no more to say, but I would listen as much as she wanted.

"I saw into Bash's memories," she said finally. "And he saw mine."

I nodded, though of course she couldn't see that.

"He said that I should stop beating myself up about what he saw there, but I don't know if I can." She exhaled shakily.

I scooched a little closer. My Kitty shouldn't beat herself up for anything.

"I feel like I made such a big mistake that I can never come back from it. Like, I couldn't love somebody who did what I did, so how could anybody love me?" Her voice cracked on the final word.

I had to go to her. I slithered a bit closer. Light's bone caught on a raised chip of stone. The leather band I strung it on snapped, and the bone shot forward. I dove for the last piece of my brother with an animal cry. The music rose in my ears once more.

"Shade?" She sounded far away.

My fingers closed around the small, white bone and I clutched it against my chest, ignoring the searing pain in my back. Blue-black power billowed around me. I reached deeper into the dirt, calling more distant tiny animal bodies up through the stone to me. The song pounded into me. Of course, no one could love someone who killed their brother, much less who couldn't even protect a single bone. My Kitty had reached out to me, and I attacked her. My mates tried to help me, and I drove them away. I belonged here, in the dark, away from everyone. Otherwise, I would hurt them just like I had Light. Bones and tendons clattered out of the ground in rhythm.

If loving Light as much as I did hadn't protected him from me, only my solitude could protect those around me. I folded the animal materials together with deft hands. Here, alone, working my magic, I made sense. Only this way. The song crashed over me and faded. Panting, I peered at my handiwork in the dim light. Thin, animal-bone chains linked by ropes of rubbery tendon wove into a sturdy necklace. Light's bone gleamed in the middle.

"Shade? What's going on? Please talk to me." My Kitty leaned forward, bracing her hands on the bed but not quite encroaching on my space.

She couldn't be here. I couldn't be here. I slipped the necklace over my head and let myself melt into the quiet of my wolf. At least like this, I could be trusted.

28

———

KINNIA

I FINISHED DRAWING A DIAGRAM OF THE MAGICAL PLANES OF the mind and put the fancy quill Chry lent me back into the clear ink pot on the thick wooden worktable with a click. The dark walls of the alchemy tower glowed with beakers and specimens I couldn't describe. An ember Chry had introduced as Oisin, another member of his Cara, watched me from where he sat next to a waterfall of lava that tumbled into a boiling basin, filling the room with bubbling and splashing sounds. Lava flowers, like those I'd seen in the mountains with Teyr and Bash, sparkled around the basin's edge. Chry had started bringing one or more of his mates to most of our sessions, claiming they would benefit from my presence as he had. Only Oisin hadn't spoken to me.

Chry pulled my parchment toward him. "Well done, little killer." He nodded, and his white hair bobbed around his red and blue horns. "I think you're starting to understand how magic works. As much as anyone can understand, at any rate."

I smiled at the dragonkin. He lavished praise over my smallest success, but after two and a half weeks together, I could mostly tell when he meant what he said. This diagram impressed him. A compliment I had actually earned felt strange. For almost a week now, my

mates had alternated between stoic silence and uncharacteristically effu-
sive praise.

Chry grinned back at me. "It's too bad you don't have a true dragon
in your Cara." He took my hand, excitement glowing in his eyes. "With
your command of the mind already, you'd be unstoppable."

"And your Cara would provide me that, right?" I tugged to free my
hand from his grasp. He held on for an extra two heartbeats before
releasing me.

He stood with a laugh. "I can't imagine a scenario where I wouldn't
pick my Cara." He put his hands on his hips.

"You are shameless." I shook my head and chuckled.

He laughed again and I leaned back in my chair with a sigh. I
couldn't remember the last time my mates and I had just laughed
together.

Chry looked me over with sharp eyes, then plucked a beaker of
glowing red goo off the wall with his mind. "Do you know what this is?"

I leaned forward, happy for a distraction. "I absolutely do not."

He waggled his eyebrows. "It's a potion."

"No! Liquid in the alchemy tower is a potion?" I put a hand to my
heart. "It can't be."

Oisin snorted. Chry nodded dramatically, then leaned close as if to
whisper a secret name. I leaned in to meet him. Alex and I used to do
jokes like this, pushing each other to ever higher heights of drama.

The door behind us crashed into the wall. I whirled to find Zelimir
stepping into the room as he coated his palms in force.

Chry sat back in his chair and put his hands up. "It's a sonic tonic. I
was just gearing up for a dramatic reveal."

Zel stalked forward and reached for the hilt of his two-hander. Chry
stared him down. Oisin leaned off the wall and braced.

I wouldn't let my stubborn commander steal what little joy I had. I
stood abruptly and saluted Chry. "Until next time, coach." I nodded at
the ember. "Oisin."

Chry grinned, but his gaze remained locked on Zelimir. Oisin didn't
even respond. Smart. I skirted around my angry commander and

marched out the door, knowing he'd rather stay by my side than pummel my tutor. Well, I hoped he would. We'd been so far from the same page lately that I couldn't bet on anything. I breathed a sigh of relief as he caught up to me before I'd turned my first corner in the hallway. Not enough time for anything more than a threat in Chry's direction.

"What did you learn today?" he asked.

I answered dutifully. He asked after every one-on-one, but he never seemed to listen to the answer.

What happened to us? Teyr hadn't made me laugh since I woke up after Bash's trial. Zelimir hadn't made me smile since we arrived at the Academy. Bash kept me at arm's length, training and exploring our bond without touching. And Shade....

I sighed. I had no idea what was going on with Shade, but I knew he didn't want anyone to discover what was wrong. I doubted it could be any worse than the backpack of secrets I carried around.

We arrived back at the suite. Zel opened the door, then pushed me through.

"You're not coming in?" I looked at him.

My commander shook his head. "Stay here. Keep the door closed. Bash will be along shortly."

I gritted my teeth, but he just rolled the door closed in my face. I turned. The couch still sat at the foot of my bed, and all the emotion of this last week hit me at once. I whirled and smashed my fist against the green wood.

I could open the door, but where would I go? I barely knew how to get to the main training yard or the cafeteria with any reliability. I could wander the halls until one of the fae who'd been watching us train decided to kidnap me and see if the grass really was greener on the other side, I supposed.

Bash's and Zelimir's military-sharp beds shamed my messy blankets. I threw myself down on them anyway. At least Teyr wouldn't know a made bed if it bit him on the ass, and Shade built a nest of pillows and blankets in the middle of his mattress. But I didn't care. These fae had kidnapped me. They drew me into a world I didn't want, only to show me I could belong here. Then, as soon as I decided I wanted to belong, they pushed me away. What the fuck?

I ran my hand through my hair, and the three silvery dots on the inside of my wrist caught my eye. Eons had passed since I met the little elf bard, but her orange eyes burned in my memory. Unlike my mates, she'd answered my questions. She wanted me to have information, told me my choices would matter. *My* choices, not the men controlling my life. A sliver of doubt tinted with Zelimir's many warnings tried to stop me, but I rubbed at the dots before I could hesitate. If my choices were going to matter, I would have to make some.

"I don't know how to do this, but I need you, Rydel." I sat up. The suite in front of me remained empty. Had I forgotten a trigger word? I flopped onto my back and rubbed the dots harder.

Rydel chuckled. "I'm not a genie."

The room took on a faint glow. I shot upright. A ghostly, pastel image of the wrinkled bard faded into the suite, her dress billowing behind her. I shivered, trying to remember why I'd agreed to a deal that ended with her prying my story out of me on my deathbed. Everything about that night remained hazy but her eyes.

I ran a finger over my tender wrist, now with only two silvery dots. "I didn't think it would work."

Rydel's smile didn't look kind. "Believe it or not, this is a timed thing. It takes up quite a bit of magic, and I had to abandon my body on a windy mountain top." She spun her fingers around each other.

I dropped my wrist. "Um, right. Just the one question, then?"

"It depends on what you ask." Rydel floated closer. "I collect stories, remember?"

I shook myself and twisted on the couch to face her over the back. "I need to know if I'm on the right path. Is magic always right?"

"Right and wrong are two sides of the same coin." She shrugged. "The path you're on is always the right path. It's the future that's unknown."

I wrinkled my nose. "I was hoping for something more tangible."

"And I was hoping for an actual question, not a philosophy discussion with a mortal a fraction of my age." She frowned.

I rubbed my temples.

"Zel—my Anam Cara is pushing me away." I gritted my teeth. "They say one thing and do another." My anger rushed out of me in a wave, leaving me hollow. "I want to know if I should stay with them, or if the magic is wrong."

Rydel narrowed her eyes and leaned toward me. "I have lived for over eight hundred years. I can tell you the secrets of kings and Councilors. I can pinpoint the general direction of every open rift in the wilds and teach you the battle strategies of our greatest heroes—and you use your first question for relationship advice?"

I flushed.

"Look, child." Rydel sighed. "The Anam Cara's not sentient. It's *need*. I don't know why it chose you, but I know it chose Zelimir's Cara because they were the strongest. They could be again, with your help, and I think they're going to need to be to face whatever's coming." She put up a hand to stop my question. "No, I don't know what that is. I just feel it shaking the ground." Her gaze became distant, then snapped back to me. "If Zelimir's Cara isn't to your liking, find one that is. You're the linchpin."

I clenched my fist. "I don't want to be some fated hero. I just want to belong somewhere without losing myself again."

Rydel raised an eyebrow. "Again? Interesting." Her image flickered. "A story for another time. If it's your independence you're worried about, I'll give you the tools you lack. Though you should know I'm still sorely disappointed."

I flattened my lips. "It's important to me."

She scowled. "I'm sure. But you have to start thinking about the bigger picture." She cracked her neck. "EarthTech slaughtered Drax's wife and daughter. He's the only Councilor worthy of your trust. Give him a yellow lava flower. And close your eyes."

I closed my eyes. Light burst behind my eyelids and a headache bloomed in the back of my skull.

"This is a map of the Academy, the town, and the surrounding valley." Rydel said.

I opened my eyes to find an overlay of blue and yellow lines in front of me. I blinked again, and they disappeared. The color leached from her image.

"You'll need to explore to find out what things are, but it should give you the freedom you lack." Her legs disappeared completely.

"What if I just leave?" I asked softly.

"Then you doom us all, human and fae alike." Her body faded out, leaving just those burning orange eyes. "You can never outrun the past. At some point, you must turn and face it."

Her eyes disappeared, and the light in our suite returned to normal.

I slumped against the couch. Headache and emotion blurred into fatigue. I wanted to curl up and sleep. I wanted to ignore everything Rydel said. I didn't need to look into my past, and that meant I didn't need Councilor Drax. I reached for the decanter of brandy on the table.

The smooth skin of my other wrist caught my attention. At Stoneheim Castle, Teyr had mentioned my lack of scars, but I'd never really thought about it. Despite my life of violence, every inch of my body remained unscarred, even the places where cables had lodged in my skin for weeks at a time during my longer captivities on Earth. A slick, cold feeling crawled across my stomach. The largest of the cables had anchored there, right where my Cara wobbled unhappily now.

I poured myself a glass of brandy and knocked it back as the last of the sunset light vanished from the suite. Fifs glowed to life, and the pink ball from my initial meeting with the Lower Council exploded in my mind's eye. Maybe I should at least meet with Councilor Drax.

The door rolled back, and my dragon stepped into the suite with a small smile. Maybe tomorrow.

29

BASH

I leaned back, steadied my breathing, and unleashed another series of attacks against the dummy in the middle of the field. A few other Caras and Seccas trained around me, but their thoughts told me all of them struggled to ignore me.

Teyr's trial was tomorrow, and my mates still hovered in the same holding pattern we'd entered when Zelimir forced Dee's secret out of me. I grunted and shook out my hand. I'd picked one of Bodmier's standard-issue short swords to train with today. The cherrystone blade felt unbalanced, and I couldn't figure out what to do with my other hand, but I had to learn. Reasonably, if I became disarmed, the ability to use her sword—since she was my only mate who wielded real weapons—could be beneficial. She relied on her bow so often anyway.

Less reasonably, the feeling of walking in her body remained a vivid memory. I dreamt of stretching her hands out in front of me and the litheness of her steps. If I learned her sword, felt it in my own hands, maybe I could keep that memory from consuming me. At the very least, the exercise kept me from dwelling on how she would react when she found out I'd revealed her secret.

I reached out along our new, wider Cara. She stalked back and forth in our suite, determination and purpose clouding her thoughts. My dragon roared. I could go to her, claim her as Shade had stopped me from doing over a week ago, fog her mind until purpose disappeared. I took a deep breath, pulled back, and passed the sword to my other hand to test the weight. No better.

Like the Cara, Dee had no ability to limit what I could see across what she called our bridge. Only two centuries of honing my willpower kept me from plunging down the bridge to discover every piece of her. I had already taken her most precious secret, even if I hadn't chosen to, even if it needed to be done to save the Cara. I would protect whatever privacy she had left with my life.

I shifted into a fighting stance and whirled through a combination with my off hand. As the final slash landed, I channeled my telekinesis through my free hand and tore the head off the dummy. It dissipated into a patter of cool water and reformed, like all Academy dummies did when destroyed. That felt a little better.

The training grounds fell silent. I straightened and scanned the minds behind me, another thing that came easier since the bridge. My fellow trainees weren't reacting to my display, as I'd feared. No, the trainees had frozen at the approach of Councilors Odhrán and Gnuq.

The Councilors shielded their mind too well for my scrape to pick up anything beyond nonviolent intentions. I kept my back to them, head bent to study the sword in my grasp. Councilors rarely came to the training grounds in our first time at the Academy. The trainees' thoughts indicated that hadn't changed. Perhaps they sought another group. Quiet footfalls on grass stopped behind me. The other trainees murmured amongst themselves.

"Bashu?" Councilor Odhrán said. "We were wondering if you might take a walk with us."

Zelimir expected me in the suite in an hour's time to discuss what he called "the girl problem," along with the rest of our mates. Teyr kept complaining that we had to tell Dee, but my commander insisted we could more easily maintain the ruse if she didn't know.

I huffed and *pulsed* a warning that I'd been approached by the Councilors. Zelimir responded instantly, urging me to be cordial but not give anything away. I snorted. I'd never been cordial before, and I didn't expect to start now. I turned and nodded.

"Wonderful." Councilor Odhrán clapped his hands together. "We spoke with a number of your mates after your trial, but your unfortunate…indisposition meant we couldn't ask the mates at the center of the event, you and Declan. With your superior understanding of magic, Caras, and the fae, you seemed a natural choice."

Over the last week, Zelimir had informed me that, having no answers, he offered the Lower Council none while I lay unconscious. Now, the Councilors were here to collect.

Gnuq raked his gaze over my shirtless chest appraisingly. Teyr once complained they only let the satyr run the Academy because he had no attraction to the male form, and the density of males allowed him to focus. With Gnuq's impenetrable mind, I couldn't discern his intentions, but I didn't like the way his attention lingered on the sword I gripped.

"Branching out?" he asked.

I dropped the blade to the grass. "I am needed elsewhere in an hour."

Councilor Odhrán's whole body bobbed in a nod. "We'll do our best. If we don't get through everything, well, you're not difficult to find."

The short elf took off down the path they entered from, and the satyr followed. I clenched my fists and trailed behind. Bodmier would find the sword eventually. As we exited the eastmost training yard, the trainees' murmurs burst into excited chatter. The news would be around the Academy before I returned to my suite. I ground my teeth. I didn't miss the politics of this place.

Councilor Odhrán led the way toward an indulgently beautiful walking path that spanned a few smaller islands. Teyr favored the place, claiming its high, flowering grasses provided the perfect amount of privacy. I allowed myself a small smirk. At least I could always sprint ahead of them or out through the grasses if I needed an escape.

The Councilors split so I had to walk between them, instead of behind, and they slowed to a pace that suited Councilor Odhrán's short legs. I stepped between them with a frown.

"I suppose we should start with the first question: What happened at your trial, from your point of view?" Councilor Odhrán asked.

The searing pain, Dee's slim fingers bending at my command, the slick, red blood of her memory. I swallowed. "I remember it poorly."

Gnuq licked his lips. "I often find physical sensations stick with a person better than anything else. How did it *feel*?"

The way the Councilor lingered on the word "feel" sent an old, familiar shiver up my spine.

"I woke in no pain." I shrugged. "Beyond that, it is fuzzy."

Councilor Odhrán hummed thoughtfully and ran his fingers along the top of the high grass. "Any lingering marks? Other permanent changes?"

Dee's bridge shifted direction. With Teyr at her side, then heading for the late lecture Zelimir assigned her so the four of us could talk alone. She reached the lecture room, paused, and strode away. Teyr headed back to the suite. My dragon roared, demanding we find where she was going and follow in case of danger. I squashed the instinct. She could fend for herself.

Gnuq leaned in. "Your scales reacted to that question. You wouldn't keep something from us, would you, Bashu?"

"Bash." I didn't like hearing my full name in his mouth, the way his too-wet lips wrapped around the letters.

The satyr inclined his head.

"I withhold nothing," I said. "My dragon recently emerged, and it still escapes my control sometimes."

Councilor Odhrán made a small, affirmative noise in the back of his throat. I looked from one to the other of them. To let fae this powerful out of my sight for longer than a moment would be disastrous.

"Do you think your dragon triggered the occurrence at your trial? Mental magic can be a strange thing." Odhrán conjured a small ball of rainbow light out of nothingness and passed it from hand to hand.

I tore my gaze quickly from the light. The short elf could conjure anything, and that could be a trap as easily as it could be a toy. Odhrán gave no sign of notice or care. My dragon battered against the block in their minds, searching for any clue of what they expected from me.

I rolled my shoulders. "It's possible."

Gnuq laid a clammy hand on my shoulder.

I stopped and whirled on him, reaching for the axe on my back.

He put his hands up. "Peace, Bash. I simply thought I saw the sort of permanent mark Councilor Odhrán sought."

Amusement sparkled in the satyr's eyes. My chest heaved. I didn't believe him. He touched me to watch my response, and he'd gotten exactly what he hoped.

I resumed Odhrán's achingly slow pace through the grasses. Something rustled, and I glimpsed purple in the high grass before the Councilors walked up alongside me.

"You still believe Declan should be trained to be a member of your Cara?" Odhrán asked.

"Yes," I answered quickly.

Too quickly. The short elf nodded blithely.

"So, the experience must not have been too unpleasant." Odhrán tossed his ball of light into the air.

I tracked the projectile instinctively. The ball landed in his chubby hands once more, and he returned to passing it from hand to hand. Out of the corner of my eye, I watched a smirk crawl across Gnuq's face.

"I know your memory wavers," Odhrán said, "but did the feeling put you in mind of anything you'd experienced before?"

Orange and purple foliage floated through my memory, unconnected to anything but a soft familiarity. I couldn't even be certain if what I felt had been similar or just similarly strange. The ball of light flew from one hand to the next. It glowed pleasantly bright, illuminating Odhrán's smooth palms.

"I...can't be certain," I said. "Perhaps. But only once."

The short Councilor leaned in, eyes glimmering. "Yes? Where was that?"

Memory filtered back. "On the road—"

A burst of barking, not unlike in Punaky's Pub, broke my focus. I whipped my head up and caught sight of Shade past the tall grass and on the other side of the canal, winding up to throw himself into the water. The sun had dropped much lower in the sky. My fingers ached from fisting them so tight. When I looked back at Odhrán, the ball of light had disappeared. Gnuq rested his hands on his lower stomach and leveled a glare at my mate.

Odhrán shifted his gaze to me and smiled. "It seems you are needed elsewhere."

I swallowed against the certainty these councilors had done some magic on me. "Am I given leave?"

Odhrán spread his arms wide. "I would never stop a warrior such as you."

I shoved past him into the high grass. The path would have been easier to walk, but I needed as much distance from them as I could get.

"We'll give your report to the other Councilors, Bash," Gnuq called. "That you understand little, remember less, but still stand by your mate's side."

"And that the feeling was familiar," Odhrán muttered.

My stomach sank as I vaulted the canal away from them.

30
———

KINNIA

IT TOOK A WEEK, BUT FINALLY, I FOUND THE MOMENT I'D been waiting for on the eve of Teyr's trial. Councilor Ambrocio offered an evening lecture on the basics of the Cara bond, and Zel said he thought I should attend by myself, so their opinions didn't color my understanding. As much as I hated the way he dictated my schedule, I'd barely been able to suppress a grin. Sure, they could still feel me through the Cara, but I had an hour when my mates wouldn't be close enough to stop me from doing whatever I wanted. Harry would've called it a golden lining, even better than silver.

I allowed Teyr to drop me off at the lecture hall in the same pissy mood he'd been in for weeks, then walked right through, out the other door, and into yet another dark stone hallway with colorful cloth draping from the ceiling. But for the first time since I'd arrived at the Academy, I stood alone. I took a deep breath and willed Rydel's map to life. The lines flickered over my vision. The headache rose, but only burned softly in the back of my skull. I hadn't had a chance to follow the map yet. Stumbling around staring at something no one else could see seemed like a great way to get sent to the trainee healer.

Blue turned out to mean main halls, and I followed those to the alchemy tower easily enough. It took me another moment to find the room I'd used with Chry last week.

The round, pale door rolled into the wall at my touch, and I slipped inside. I couldn't control the fifs without magic, but the lava in the corner lit my way. The lava flowers sparkling in the dim red glow looked like those I'd seen on the volcano. A yellow one glimmered at the edge. I flicked it, and the rigid surface seared my finger. I wrapped my sleeve around my hand and snapped the flower off.

Now, I just needed to find Councilor Drax. The weapons master, Bodmier, seemed to know where everyone was and he surveyed the day's equipment usage with an army of ittles in weapons hall every evening, something I'd learned when I'd been late turning in a shield Zel suggested I experiment with.

The map turned finding my way to the weapons hall into child's play. When I asked for Councilor Drax, the centaur put up his hands.

"Don't tell me why, I don't want to know," he said. "He's well known for his cactus garden. Blooms best at night." He directed me to the left and away from the wettest part of the canal system.

Zelimir *pulsed* a demand to know my location. Two weeks of my mates peering over my shoulder and treating me like glass and barely cracking a smile roiled in my gut. I tried to *pulse* a middle finger, but he gave no response. I rolled my eyes and *pulsed* that I was okay before stomping out onto the sunset-drenched grounds.

Dee, Bash said in my head. *Zelimir wants to know what you're doing.*

Now seemed like as good a time as any to figure out if I could lie in my mind.

I'm pissed. I need to clear my head.

Bash lingered at the edge of our bridge. *I know you're upset. Just a little longer here.* He paused. *If you're gone too long, Zelimir will come for you. I cannot stop him.*

I kicked a rock and didn't answer. Bash hit the nail on the head. I'd let these fae walk all over me, and I couldn't stop them now. I wanted to be furious with them, but I just kept circling back to being angry with myself. Just like I'd followed Alex into a rift without thinking, I'd followed every suggestion of these ridiculous fae until I had to sneak out of a lecture to get a little privacy. I wasn't Kinnia anymore. I couldn't keep making her mistakes. I needed to be Declan, and Declan only. He made decisions. Took action. He carried the searing yellow lava flower over the darkening grounds of the Academy in the direction Bodmier had indicated.

The soft dirt of the yards dried up the farther I got from the canals. Magic intensified the sunset, turning it to sparkling gold that showered down on a tight circle of large stones that came into view up ahead. A waft of pink magic issued from inside. Two leaning stones formed a ramshackle doorway, and I poked my head inside what turned out to be a garden. Councilor Drax stood with his back to me, waving a gust of pink magic over the browning stem of a blue and yellow cactus potted in rich, red clay. The plant brightened, and I realized I recognized the material the plant had been potted in.

"Is that from Saltair?" I blurted.

"It is." Councilor Drax grabbed two pots and faced me, unperturbed.

I winced. Not my smoothest introduction.

"Sorry, I'm not sure if we've officially met. Declan, of course." I entered and stuck out a hand.

"No, I suppose not." Councilor Drax chuckled and gestured with the cacti he held in each hand. "I know those things are important to humans, but my hands are full. I am Drax."

I jammed my hand into my pocket. "I guess humans like things said a little more clearly."

Drax set down the cacti on the other side of the small garden and eyed me. "I'm assuming you came here for a reason."

"Yes, um"—I fished out the lava flower I'd put in my inside pocket when it cooled down—"this is for you."

Drax took the flower and raised an eyebrow. I bit my lip and nodded. Silence stretched out between us. Maybe I should've asked Rydel more questions.

"You've no idea why you just gave that to me, do you?" Drax asked.

"No, I don't." I smiled and prayed I seemed charming.

Drax's grunt sounded too much like a laugh. He turned and walked to the other side of the garden. I trailed after him, hoping that hadn't been a dismissal.

"Rydel's more than a bard, but less than a seer." Drax spoke as if talking to himself.

"She considers herself an instrument of fate." He glanced at me. "Did you know Bash fought under my command during the most recent civil war?"

Bash's focus, his love of order, the crisp way he walked, snapped into perspective. "I didn't."

"Rydel's the one who brought him to me." Drax smiled at the flower. "And this is her calling card. Bash didn't understand what it meant to be fae. He hated himself, blamed himself for the world's problems. He had to relearn how to live. How to love."

Tears gathered suddenly in my eyes. Monsters had stolen Bash's childhood, but he still smiled at me during our morning exercises. Drax lingered on the flower for a moment. I cleared my throat and straightened.

He pocketed the flower and nodded toward a little, deep green cactus studded with black flowers in a pot. "Help me with this. He's a prickly one."

I reached out to grab the pot. Two of the limbs sprang to life and jabbed at my hands.

"Shit!" I stumbled backward.

The cactus swung its tiny, prickly fists wildly. Drax swooped up the distracted cactus and moved it to a large planter. It thrashed like a boxer trying to knock out an invisible foe. Drax removed the pot with bright-pink magic and folded fresh soil over its roots.

"Do you love life?" he asked.

Rydel asked me the same question. Maybe they were friends. "Parts of it."

He grunted and rotated his wrists oddly. The pink lines on his hands and along his fingers glowed brightly. A cylindrical crystal a third the size of my pinky finger grew out of nothing between his palms. He flicked a hand, and a small leather harness wrapped itself around the crystal, then dangled off a gold chain.

He beckoned me forward. "Remember that love when you look at this."

I hesitated. Rydel may have sent me here but getting within arm's reach of one of the most powerful fae in the wilds seemed seriously dangerous. The cactus over his shoulder still swung wildly. He'd moved it carefully, but without regard for how it might have hurt him. I stepped forward, and he fastened the chain around my neck.

"Can I ask you some questions?" I fingered the necklace.

"Lessons learned through trial-and-error stay with a student longer than any lecture." Drax returned his attention to his plants.

I looked once more at the cactus in its new spot, slowly giving up its attack. Zelimir *pulsed* another question. I turned from the pink and purple Councilor and left the small garden.

The grounds of the Academy spread out before me, glistening in sunset light, and I intended to enjoy them as I walked back to my suite. I *pulsed* to Zel not to expect me back soon. I used the walk to get my thoughts in order. Too much had been wrong lately, and all of it came down to how I let them treat me. I had to take control of my own future.

Too soon, I reached our door, took a deep breath, and pressed my hand to the green wood. I had to stand up for myself. The door glided smoothly into the wall.

"*Dee* is a woman." Teyr poked Bash's bare chest. "I'm—"

My mates turned to me as one. My face went hot, then cold.

They knew.

31

————

TEYR

THE BLOOD DRAINED FROM HER FACE. I WANTED TO BE
relieved, but panic and shame overwhelmed her Cara and sank into me.

"How long have you known?" she murmured.

Despite her tone, anger began to take over her other emotions in our
bond.

Zelimir crossed his arms. "How long were you planning on keeping
it from us?"

She glanced over her shoulder, at the empty hall behind her. Would
she run? My heart thumped out of time at the thought of losing her. I
squashed the feeling. It would be simpler if she did run. She didn't, of
course. Declan never would have.

She took a deep breath, straightened, and stepped into the room.
"Forever, if I could."

The door slammed shut, echoing like the start bell in Emberhold's
dueling arena. Somehow, I never expected her to be hurt.

"Forever?" Zelimir lifted his eyebrows. "Did you really think we
would never figure it out?"

She bit her lower lip. A wave of sorrow washed through her anger.
"Why does it matter? Declan is who you met. Declan is who you know."
She balled her fists. "I *want* to be Declan."

I couldn't keep up with her emotions. I couldn't do anything.

Zelimir threw his arms up. "But you're not him. You're hiding behind him." He ran a hand through his twists. "And I know it's not just something you invented for us. Your friends at the *Cross Roads* had no idea either. I can't even imagine how long you've kept this up. What was the point?"

Her lower lip trembled, and she swiped angrily at her eyes. "So, you found out while I was unconscious. How? Did you look?"

Shade slid forward, his arms out and his wolf ears drooping. "My Kitty, it doesn't matter—"

"It does, Shade!" She glared at the necromancer. "Everyone's been treating me differently. You cut me off. Teyr doesn't joke with me. Bash doesn't touch me."

The dragon flinched. I didn't react. How could I joke with her when I didn't really know her?

She swung her gaze onto Zelimir. "You lost interest in me the moment we hit these halls, so I guess nothing's really different there."

His mouth fell slightly open, but he snapped it shut. "How can you say that? Everything I've done revolves around you, around bringing us closer."

I snorted. People in the borderlands could tell he'd been denying himself time with her. Zelly's self-deception, at least, still made sense to me.

My commander whipped a glare in my direction, but she nodded.

"Even if I believe you, you're terrible at it." She threw her hands in the air. "All you've done is push me away. I'm not one of you, I'm the useless fifth wheel."

Bitter sincerity leaked through her Cara. I faltered back a step. I knew she'd been disappointed when she failed, but every time, determination replaced the feeling. At the volcano, she'd told me I could only sense her emotions, not what she thought about them.

Zelimir took a step forward, bringing them within arms' reach of each other. "Stop saying you're useless."

She took a step backward and glared at him. "You all know it's true."

I wanted to throttle all of us, me included. The hurt, the certainty in her Cara made me desperate to fix this. I pushed Zelly back before he could make anything worse.

"We want you here." I smiled. Of course, I still wanted her. Of course. "Trust is a big deal when you're building a Cara bond, but we can get past your lie if—"

She laughed bitterly. "Trust? I can't even have a study-buddy without babysitters. Who are you to talk about trust?"

Her laughter roared in my ears. Contempt threaded through her Cara. My vision went red.

"At least I know who I am! You've tricked yourself more thoroughly than you ever could to us." Humiliation kindled into fire on my fingertips. "I can try to get over this because at least you're lying to all of us."

"We've been together for a month and a half. That's nothing to me, so I can't imagine how little it is to you." Her face reddened. "*I* will tell you about myself, when you need to know, because that's how actual fucking relationships work, not this stupid fae bullshit."

My fire burned hotter and brighter. "You wanted so desperately to be part of this stupid fae bullshit we could all feel it. And I can still feel you. All the time." I curled the fire into weapons, barely restrained the urge to hurl them against the wall just to get someone to listen to me. "You know, until we found you, our stupid fae bullshit worked. We didn't keep secrets from each other. We didn't lie. Now look at us. We can barely get through a conversation."

"How is that my fault? I don't have any control over what you say or do." A painful laugh ripped from her throat. "I don't really control what I say and do these days." She looked at the fireballs in my hands and took a single step closer with her chin high, her chest out. Daring me to do something.

Bash and Zelimir sent me waves of calm. Shade growled. I gritted my teeth.

"I told them." The dragon's pronouncement rumbled over the room.

I looked at him, but he kept his Cara closed behind a neutral expression. He hadn't even moved from where he'd been standing when she first walked in.

Denial rushed through her Cara.

What had been twinges of jealousy about how much better my mates seemed to know her, how much more she seemed to like them, coalesced into a roiling ball of bright green fire in my palm.

I spun back to her. "That's right, your beloved dragon spilled all while you were unconscious in this very room. And he figured it out before we even got to the Academy." I laughed. "Forever? Whatever game this was, you knew it had a time limit. What did you expect when we found out? Kisses and sunshine?"

She glared. I expected her to charge, tackle, take me to the ground and pin me there to kiss me senseless. I expected the warrior I saw in her every day to rise up.

Instead of boiling over, her white-hot anger evaporated. She sagged and stumbled past me, past us, to her bed.

Shade stepped toward her with a hand out. "My Kitty?"

She sat heavily on her bed and stared at us. Her eyes filled with grief. "Why is it so important to you that I'm a woman?"

"Because you need to be honest with yourself," Zelimir said evenly.

I swallowed the urge to wrestle my commander to the ground and keep him there until he just admitted he wanted to fuck her, and we could all actually have a conversation.

She looked at him for a long moment, then shook her head. She turned to Bash, and something passed between them the rest of us couldn't sense. She studied Shade's outstretched hand, then knocked it away. She didn't look at me. Envy scorched the back of my throat.

"Just leave me the fuck alone." She kicked off her shoes and pulled the covers over her, dirty trainee greens and all. Her Cara filled with bitter anger and loss.

Bash stepped closer to me, nostrils flaring. "Your beloved dragon spilled all?"

"You lied to us just as much as she did." I dropped my fireballs and glared.

Zel turned slowly away from her and opened his mouth.

"I don't want to hear from our brilliant commander either," I said. "None of this would have happened if you didn't make us keep our mouths shut." I pointed at Shade. "Or if you talked to us about anything."

Shade flinched and fidgeted with that new necklace he'd been wearing. Fire, I didn't even know where he'd gotten it. Did she? Did anyone?

"She wasn't ready." Zel said.

"Ready or not, my trial is tomorrow." I threw my hands in the air. "We don't even need the Council to set us impossible tasks. We're sinking this goddamn ship ourselves." I shut the fifs off with a gesture, plunging the room into darkness, then shucked my clothes and climbed into bed.

By the rustling, my mates did the same without a word. I stared at the ceiling, feeling her devastation like it was my own, until sleep finally stole me away.

32

———————

ZELIMIR

I WOKE EARLY FROM A RESTLESS NIGHT, PLAGUED BY VISIONS of the world falling apart around me. My mates still lay in bed. Judging by the soft gray light seeping in through the window, Teyr's trial started in about four hours.

Sleep wouldn't return. I dressed and walked over to the coffee contraption Teyr had stolen from a supply closet. I had no idea what the morning would hold, but I needed to set us up for success as much as possible.

I'd never had a screaming match with my mates before. Fights, disagreements, sure, but screaming? I tugged on one copper twist. The hair frizzed up instantly. A good leader would have managed his own reaction to the deception before addressing everyone else's. I'd stuffed my hurt down until I couldn't anymore. Until I had no choice but to explode.

I sifted coffee grounds and added water from the tap. I'd been half-pleased when Teyr stepped in with his silver tongue, but I should have known better. The ember had been taking our communication issues personally, and Declan pushed his already dramatic reactions over the top.

I'd failed to track Declan's progress back to the suite as my civilized conversation spiraled out of control. If I'd been more careful, we could have maintained the status quo for another day, at least.

A frustrated yell built in my chest. The Academy hadn't been this hard last time, even with the twins' antics and Teyr's attitude problem. People had listened to me, had wanted to make the group work. These days, all my mates seemed to be running in different directions. I pushed my hands into my ropey twists and pulled. I had commanded this Cara for seventy-five years. I could handle this. I had to. The contraption dinged, and the warm scent of roasted coffee floated into the air. I couldn't change the past.

Declan stirred but didn't rise. The moment the sun peeked through the window, my second sat up and stretched. I poured myself a coffee and *pulsed* for him to follow, then headed into the hall. After a moment, he joined me with his own mug.

"You could have told Declan I forced the secret out of you." I sipped my coffee.

My second pushed the heel of his hand against his eye. "It makes no difference. I could have ignored your orders. I could have fought for her."

My second had rarely sounded so pained outside of battle. When I met his gaze, a gulf of hurt I could barely begin to comprehend opened behind them. Another strike against me.

I clasped his shoulder. "I shouldn't have put you in the position."

"But you did." He sipped his drink. "Dee brings out unexpected emotions."

I let go of my second, trying to absorb his words as constructive criticism, maybe even a path forward, rather than a blow. He rarely told me I was wrong.

"Will she join you for your morning exercises?" I asked.

Bash shrugged. "She knows she's welcome. She didn't speak to me last night, even across our bridge."

I opened my mouth to ask what he meant but hesitated. I didn't want to demand answers from my mates. As commander, I had certain additional powers, but I wanted them to feel they were my equals. Interrogations twisted the power dynamic. I didn't want to feel like I had to interrogate them either. Trust is earned. Despite nearly a century together, I still seemed to have some earning to do. I shut my mouth.

Bash downed the rest of his coffee, winced against the burn, and handed me the mug before taking off down the hall. I watched him go, no closer to fixing my Cara than before we'd spoken. The air in front of me shimmered. With a gust of blue-green sparkles, a dark-haired pixie I recognized from home appeared clothed in a plain gray shift. She lugged a communication bowl with her, her little wings beating fast. I took the bowl before she could fall to the ground. She smiled thanks and winked out of the hall.

On the surface of the bowl, my father's miniature figure sat in his office chair, tapping fingers against a desk I couldn't see. "Zelimir, are you alone?"

His voice landed like chains around my neck. I didn't respond to his letter, so he sent me something I couldn't ignore. The Academy hallway lay silent around me, other than a purple itzal squirming from one hole to the next.

I slid down the wall outside our suite and sat. "Close enough."

"Wonderful." He smiled. "Now, we discussed exchanging some information. I offered you what I knew, but I'm afraid your response got lost in transit."

"My letter didn't get lost." I sounded tired even to my own ears.

He frowned and a hot flash of shame seared into my gut. My father had a way of making his disapproval known across any distance.

"The Lower Council shut us out." I averted my gaze. "Shut everyone out. It seems a rift appeared in the colosseum after Bash's trial, and we found out through secondhand rumors. We still can't confirm for sure. Goblin guards walk the halls in ostensible reaction. I'd guess that's Councilor Odhrán's handiwork."

He sighed. "Son, you look exhausted. What's going on? You know you can always rely on your father."

I stared at the bowl in my hand. His little image juddered, then grew until his wrinkled face spread across the whole surface. He studied me like he wanted to know.

I'd always been told I had my father's eyes. I let my head thump back against the wall and lifted the bowl so I could still look at him. "My mates and I had a fight."

He nodded. "Relationships are tricky. What are you fighting about? I haven't caused you strife, have I?"

I looked in his eyes. The concern remained, but a small, self-interested gleam appeared. I needed advice from someone, even my father, but I had to remember he would use whatever he learned.

"We disagreed on how to forge a sword," I said. "I want to heat it slowly, give it time, and ensure it's strong. Some of my mates think expediency is most important. Others have no plan at all but insist on standing in front of the anvil."

"I see." He frowned. "Well, it seems to me that the key to a good sword is a strong...head blacksmith. There are many ways to forge a blade, but you'll never create anything worthwhile if you try them all at once." He smiled. "If you're asking for more concrete advice, I'll say the same thing I've always said. Swords are best forged in the heat of battle. It's true of sons, so it must be true of Caras as well."

I nodded slowly. I knew he meant for us to join his fight and find ourselves there, but under all his blatant political maneuvering, my father might have provided some half-reasonable advice.

"Thank you, Father. I will consider your point."

He grinned. "That heat made you strong enough to handle this. I know you'll make the right choice."

A warm glow bloomed in my chest. Lively conversation started at the end of the hall and grew louder. Approaching trainees.

"I have to go. We'll speak soon." I dragged my hand through the herb mixture, and his face winked out. I took a deep breath as I stood, and the chains loosened around my neck.

I couldn't just keep letting things unfold however and whenever they chose. I needed to drive the situation, set the scene for the healing that needed to come next. Declan obviously still needed time to figure herself out, and I could give her that once everyone fell in line.

33

KINNIA

I LAY IN BED, PRETENDING TO BE ASLEEP AND WAITING FOR everyone to leave. I couldn't face them. I'd lain awake half the night, thinking about disappearing back to human lands and remembering my time with the fae as nothing more than a bad dream. I might have done it if I didn't think they'd find me.

The second they discovered I was a woman, everything changed. My worst fears had come true. I didn't even have to be Kinnia for them to drop what little friendship we'd managed to cling to, just female.

Zel came back in. I steadied my breathing, trying to keep the furious tears inside. He might know I'd woken up, but that didn't mean he got to know anything else. He roused Teyr and Shade. They complained sleepily but headed for the cafeteria at his command.

His command. Bash told my secret—a fact I couldn't consider without a lance of pain—but I knew how the Cara worked. They wouldn't have kept their revelation from me if Zelimir hadn't told them to. Hurt and anger swirled into a hazy mash of upset in my chest.

Zel lingered, fiddling with his books. I squeezed my eyes shut and tried to will him to go.

He sighed. "I know you're awake."

I cracked open an eye. He had his back to me.

"Let's go down to the baths." Exhaustion weighed down his words, but he didn't sound angry.

I cuddled deeper into my blankets. My dirty uniform clung and scratched, and my breasts ached because I'd fallen into bed in my cuirass. The leather didn't compress them nearly as much as the bindings, but without my nightly breaks, they were sensitive. After the fight, I couldn't imagine getting naked in front of Zelimir.

He underscored his request with a *pulse*. Attendance wasn't optional. I hauled myself out of bed.

We walked to the baths in silence. Every time I glanced at him, he wore an expression way too close to the mask he took on for the Councilors. What did he have to hide?

I tried to match the easy way he strode down the halls, his blank confidence, but I fidgeted more the closer we got. The halls transitioned into the natural rock formations of the baths. My breath caught. The fifs hovered low, emitting a soft blue light that cast the ceiling and walls in shadow. This early, the place lay empty. I had no excuse but my desire not to face him.

I took a breath. Declan had the same body as Kinnia, he just tucked it away. Declan wore my body. I could wear this body without changing anything. With trembling fingers, I began peeling off my dirty clothes. Zelimir turned away.

My stomach sank. Stupid. I already knew he didn't want to fuck me. I could barely think about fucking him right now. He probably didn't look at Bash or Teyr or Shade in the baths either.

I unwrapped my chest with a sigh of relief, now wearing nothing but the necklace Drax had given me, and stepped into one of the showers at the edge of the pool. Hot water soothed my muscles and eased my nerves. I closed my eyes and tried to relax.

"Teyr's trial today?" I knew the answer, of course, but I had to say something to get him to explain.

"Yes." Zelimir's voice came from far closer than I would have guessed, like mere inches separated us.

I struggled to hold onto my frustration and confusion as a fire kindled between my legs. My libido had gone untended too long. I picked up a bar of soap and started scrubbing.

"May I?" Zelimir asked from so close, his warm breath washed over my shoulder.

My pulse quickened. I could scream at him about mixed signals later. I held the soap over my shoulder. He took it without brushing my hand. A single beat passed. A moment where I could run for the pools and maintain my anger above all else.

The moment passed. I stayed. I wanted him to know he hurt me, but more than that, I wanted to know what he was thinking.

He wrapped an arm around me and drew my back out of the running water. His hand spanned from just above my pubic hair to just below my breasts. My pulse raced, and he snatched his hand away. He began gently washing my back. Once, he grazed my ass. A shiver of pleasure raced through me, but he retreated to knead the muscles of my lower back. Two knots popped under his hands.

I moaned, half-desire and half-relief. Zel paused, but I didn't want him to stop. I leaned into his hands. He continued his massage. Another knot popped, and I lost myself in his attention. My entire body tingled by the time he pushed me gently under the shower again. I spun to get the last of the soap off my skin and got my first glimpse of my naked commander.

I couldn't have dreamed him better. A wall of bulky muscles and dark skin, he stood with easy confidence as water from my shower beaded on his chest hair and misted the copper bush around his intimidatingly large cock. I lifted my gaze to find his purple eyes blazing with heat. Inch by inch, he took in my body, memorizing every curve.

Instead of pulling me into his arms, he tilted his head toward the hottest pool and walked away. I followed, heart racing. My commander used words for politics. Maybe, when it came to his real emotions, he preferred action.

We slipped into the water together and floated to the far side, where no one would be able to see us from the entrance. Zelimir took one of the seats carved into the side of the basin and made sure his twists lay on the dry stone behind him. I straddled his waist with my knees. When he didn't move, I lowered my head and pressed my lips to his.

Magic and need rushed through me in a wave of heat. Zelimir grabbed handfuls of my ass before sliding his hands up my sides to my breasts. I thrust my tongue into his mouth. His vanilla and dark liquor taste overwhelmed me. My moan echoed through the dark cavern.

Zelimir pulled back. "Tell me your name."

My stomach dropped. I didn't want to bring all the baggage that came with the answer here. But the stubborn set of his shoulders told me they wouldn't let me go back to being Declan.

Maybe if I could lose myself in him, this wouldn't hurt so bad. "Kinnia."

He nodded.

I leaned in for another searing kiss.

He turned away. "Kinnia, we're not ready."

I stared at him as he wrapped an arm around my waist and hoisted me off his lap. His erection brushed my leg. He released me into the water in front of him.

"What?" I said dumbly.

I found footing on the slick stone floor and stood. The tops of my breasts just peeked out of the water.

"I didn't come down here for sex." Zelimir stared at me, the heat in his eyes disagreeing. His voice took on the even tone I recognized from our meetings with the Council. "We need to talk."

"You don't just get to tell me what to do, *Commander*. What changes if I'm a woman, really?"

"It's not just that you're a woman." He ran a hand over his hair. "You've been lying to us. I had to learn your gender from my second, who learned it against your will." He looked away. "You don't trust m— us."

My stomach twisted. "I trust you."

Zelimir met my gaze. "If you did, you wouldn't have lied."

"One lie. And I've been more honest with you than anyone since —" I grimaced. "The day you found out I was a woman, what happened?" I began ticking things off on my fingers. "Teyr stopped having fun. Bash backed away from me—on your orders, I'm sure. Every training exercise we did became 'protect the human'. You stopped viewing me as an equal, as much as you barely did before that."

Zel shook his head. "Kinnia, it's not because—"

"Don't use her name!" I shouted.

My voice echoed off the walls. When it came back to me, I couldn't remember the last time I'd sounded so young, so desperate. So much like Kinnia.

I folded myself into the seat next to him and pulled my knees to my chest.

"I was happy as Declan," I murmured. "Declan knew what to do. You kissed Declan. Until we arrived here. Then *you* changed."

I took a few deep breaths as the silence grew thick around us.

"Change is immaterial," Zelimir said finally. "I've lived nearly two hundred years, and I can promise you everything changes in time. If we want to survive that as a Cara, we must trust each other. And ourselves."

I flinched. I didn't trust Kinnia. How could I? Kinnia let everyone die. Kinnia woke up in a white room, sweating and trying to pull cables out of her body.

"You're my mate." He met my eyes. "Your heart, your mind, your curiosity, they're treasures beyond value. They're who you are, not any name."

Something inside me snapped. I wanted to believe. Tears poured down my cheeks. Zel surged forward and wrapped me in a hug. I buried my face in his chest.

"I don't want to be Kinnia," I whispered amidst sobs.

"You can be whoever you want to be." He kissed the top of my head. "But you must accept that person before we can accept you."

Could I be someone new?

Seconds or hours might have passed before my tears slowed. My limbs grew heavy with exhaustion. The sound of the falling water replaced my thoughts. I trailed a finger between Zel's pecs, then under one. His heart rate steadily increased as my fingers wandered, though the titan didn't move. I traced up to his shoulders and across his collarbone.

Cupping the side of his face, I forced my commander to look down at me. "Whoever I want?"

His purple gaze glowed. "Whoever."

"Kiss me?"

Zelimir pulled me to him and enveloped my mouth with his. My commander traced my hip with his finger. I pulled his hand up to my breast.

He broke the kiss with a groan. "You're killing me."

I grinned.

Sharp voices cut through the waterfall noise. At the entrance to the baths, Bash, axe drawn, stood outlined in Shade's shimmering blue-black power.

I chuckled and turned back to Zelimir. "I can wait a little." I floated to his side and wrapped myself around one of his massive biceps. "I'm taking lessons from Teyr."

Zelimir shook his head and straightened. "I brought you down here for a reason."

My stomach sank. Abrupt topic change and posture shift? That meant he had a duty to fulfill.

He eyed me. "We need some new rules."

I released his arm. Of course. They always had rules for me.

Zelimir caught my gaze and held it. "Unless you're in private with us, you're still Declan." His voice took on that smooth, political tone.

I frowned. I just grieved Declan. I didn't know how to be Kinnia, and I really didn't want to stick out any more. But I couldn't become someone new while staying someone old.

"The Council must believe we're united and honest in everything." My commander looked away, as though he didn't want to say this next part. "We're all to give you space, so the Councils don't notice the... hiccups in our bonding."

That seemed like going backward. "I—"

Zelimir shook his head. I closed my mouth. I didn't want to be treated differently, didn't need to be. How would we ever achieve balance when he kept singling me out?

"The five of us must present ourselves as equals in all things. We must not fight. And our rules from the journey here still apply. Stay away from other fae. Don't give us any reason to react. The Council is searching for a reason to tear us apart." He met my gaze again. "Once we pass the trials, we will focus on our personal feelings. Your relationships with the four of us are developing unevenly, and Shade especially needs order."

I sank into the water up to my nose to hide my grimace. Once again, they'd already talked, already made the decisions. Equal in all things? Ha. And everyone else had fallen in line. They always would. I liked to think of Bash as my dragon, but he belonged to his commander. Teyr wanted to be a part of things too badly, and Shade would follow his pack leader to the end of the world.

"No friends, no flirting, no connections." Zelimir sighed. "We don't know who the Lower Council has under their control. You belong to my Anam Cara, to us. You're our problem. We need to figure this out internally, without distraction."

I flinched. Zelimir was so caught up in his prepared speech he didn't even notice. Had he kissed me out of pity? Because I'd thrown myself at him?

He met my gaze. Cold logic dulled his purple eyes. My chest ached.

I ducked under the water and pushed off the edge. The water seared against my skin, a weak salve for the burning inside. I popped out of the water on the opposite side and gulped down air.

He gave me a hard look. "Kinnia, do you understand what I've said?"

I *pulsed* an affirmative, not trusting my voice.

My commander rose from the pool. I didn't even want to look at how the water cascaded off his body.

"Teyr's trial is in an hour. Prepare yourself. I'll let the others know that last night has been resolved."

I clenched my jaw and nodded like the good little girl he wanted me to be. It had been the four of them against me since the beginning. I'd been a fool to think otherwise.

34

TEYR

I HUFFED A FRUSTRATED BREATH. I COULD BARELY HEAR over the simmering white noise of the colosseum and leapt to another level of this jungle gym for the suicidal. The Lower Council had built a six-story monstrosity of magic, wood, and ropes in the middle of the colosseum floor just for me. I'd originally thought we were facing an obstacle course. We should be so lucky.

We'd wasted our training. Every day, we practiced teamwork, communication, keeping her near us. This trial immediately split us up. The Council had handed each of my mates a totem they needed to get from one location to another and started them at opposite points in this maze of death.

I, on the other hand, had to find targets scattered throughout and blow them up. Perfect for my fire magic. At first, I'd had fun. Then, I realized the targets reappeared if I took too long between them. I'd found at least a hundred little yellow triangles already.

Once again, they'd set us an impossible task. It had been frustrating in Bash's and Zel's trials, but now the heat fell on me.

Fire, this sucked.

The woman's Cara thrummed with pain but calmed for at least the tenth time. Before I could look in her direction, a wall of jagged ice almost took my nose off. I quickly found the fae responsible, a trainee tasked with being as annoying as possible to slow me down.

I grinned and charged him with a fireball in one hand and a fire whip in the other. The trainee actually pissed himself before he dove off the side, plummeting three stories instead of facing me.

"Coward!" I shouted, *pulsing* my frustration to my mates.

Nothing. Magic shields trapped my mates where they'd dropped the totems. They couldn't help, and no amount of conciliatory bullshit would have made me feel any better. Only the human hadn't gotten her totem into position.

Cara trials were supposed to test you as a unit, not as individuals. I had almost forgotten what having no one to rely on felt like.

Her Cara spiked with fear, but when the fear cleared, she seethed with frustration. Her odd *pulse* for *stuck* vibrated across our bond. I didn't have time to rescue her. I didn't have time not to. If all the pieces didn't get placed, we'd fail the trial and lose our Cara. The bond would dissolve, and we'd either drift in numb agony for the rest of our days or destroy ourselves.

She'd lied to us. She'd gotten Bash to lie to us. Every lie we told each other, every time we didn't share when we should have, all began with her. My body shook with rage as I ran, jumped, and climbed through the hellish obstacles to find the human woman who held my future in her hands.

When I found her, I couldn't help but laugh. She dangled by one arm above a three-story pit from a set of climbing bars. Between her thighs, she clutched a surprisingly phallic chunk of cherrystone.

"It's not funny!" She swiped away a multicolored swirl of air magic away with her free hand. The totem between her legs slipped, but she managed to wrap her ankles around its base before it fell to the mud below.

The muscles in my core strained with hers as she worked her legs to gain a better grip. My cock hardened, and I seethed.

"Get ready to catch," she shouted.

She swung her legs back and forth, building momentum. I scrambled to a thin, precarious landing, the only place she could possibly reach, just as she released the totem. The stone hit me in the chest. I grunted as I fell back onto a soft platform that wobbled under my weight. I would have a bruise for at least the next two hours.

"Shiiiit!"

I caught my breath as she launched herself toward the same platform and barely managed to tighten my grip on the totem before she crashed into me. We slid to the far side of the platform which, of course, tipped just enough to slide us into the pit of deep green mud below with a *squelch*.

The crowd laughed. Furious fire billowed out of me, drying some of the mud instantly. She groaned. My anger cooled when I realized she lay on her back, pinned beneath me. The flames lapped back into my skin.

"Don't move." I adjusted my weight so I wouldn't crush her. I needed her to finish the trial. "We don't know what kind of trap this is yet."

She froze, her wide, blue gaze locked on my face. The crystal necklace she wore poked into my chest.

I ground my teeth and glanced around. I could barely make out the green stone of the colosseum through the mess of obstacles, and the mud dimmed the noise of the crowd. It felt like we were alone.

Her firm, strong waist tensed between my legs. I fought to keep my attention on the trap rather than the woman beneath me. As I shifted my stance wider to avoid the sensation, my thoughts drifted to her smile, her curiosity, the way she depended on me for answers and trusted me to provide them. But she didn't trust me. Not really. We'd given her every opportunity. I'd told her truths no one but my mates knew, and she'd still lied.

I knew what to do alone with a woman. I knew all the right things to say, the moves to drive her crazy. I learned most of them before I even left Emberhold. I'd spent the last two weeks looking at her like I would any woman. Like I'd been trained to. I'd always fancied myself a rebel. I'd cut my hair and claimed I didn't believe in the priests' teachings. But would I have left Emberhold if the Cara hadn't called me? Two weeks ago, I would have yes without thinking. Now? I'd fallen in line unflinchingly when Zel told me to because she was just some woman. I didn't even give her the basic personhood of a name.

When I looked at her now, I didn't see a woman. I saw the person I knew.

"I think it's just mud." Blush stained her cheeks. "I'm slowing you down. Just help me get back on—"

"Stop that," I snapped. My hands in the mud next to her head flamed, pure yellow fire spilling out. I'd let my temper, my jealousy, my fear of being left out, get the better of me. "You're not slowing me down. You're not slowing any of us down. You bring out the best in us." I remembered the long years of silence on the road after Light's death, and before that, the quiet nights letting Light convince me Zelly didn't actually think I was a ridiculous waste of the uniform. We'd stopped communicating long before we found her. "Even if we're not handling it well." I took a deep breath and forced the flames out.

She raised an eyebrow. "The best in us? Zel just—"

I slammed one of my hands deeper into the green mud. "Zelimir isn't the only fae in our Cara." I met her gaze. "I grew up in a world with no teams, no camaraderie, where you and you alone mattered. I excelled there. And then I came here, and I hated the Anam Cara. But my mates showed me a better world. A world where we make space for each other's strengths and cover each other's weaknesses. A world we let you tear apart." I sucked in a breath. "But that's just it. We let you. And you let us. We are all failing each other."

Her breath caught, pressing our chests together. In the quiet, with her kissable lips just inches from my own, I took a steadying breath and rested my forehead against hers.

"You either need to join us or leave."

The truth rang off the mud around us. I had her here, trapped underneath me in a nearly private place, and instead of feeling her up or making jokes, I asked her to leave. I barely recognized myself.

I rolled off her and eyed the mud trap. It would be difficult to get out, but manageable—if we worked together. I laughed bitterly.

She looked at me as if weighing my words. "Zel's new rules—"

"Fuck our commander and his control issues." I'd almost knocked the titan out when he told me. Only my impending trial had stopped me.

She chewed on her lower lip.

I held out my hand. "Teyr."

She looked at my hand with a wary expression, and I remembered her refusing me that first day. My pulse thundered in my ears. If she didn't take my hand, my heart would break. I'd given this woman my heart without realizing.

"My name's Kinnia." She clasped my hand and smiled.

Green mud slipped between our fingers, but I didn't let go until she made me.

She bit her lower lip. "We're on the fourth floor, and I have to make it to six. Could you help me?"

I grinned, tracing her lips with my gaze. "It's a bit muddy and open here."

Kinnia blushed. The way she moved lit a fire in me, but we had a job to finish.

I ignited that desire into flame in my hand and dried the mud caking our bodies. Once we had enough traction, we positioned ourselves back-to-back with our feet braced against the wall and the totem balanced on our shoulders.

We slowly shimmied up the wall as one body. Her back muscles moving against mine would have been sexy if everything else about the situation wasn't so awful. We tumbled up and over the edge of the hole. A few weak claps echoed through the colosseum. I seethed. Kinnia didn't seem to notice as she hoisted the totem and strode forward.

The trainees assigned to torment my mate scattered at my approach. We scaled, leapt, and ducked, passing the totem back and forth as needed. Working together, we quickly reached the top.

Zel nodded from his spot on the otherwise featureless top of the maze. The barrier holding him in place shimmered red and brown. My Cara pointed me toward Shade and Bash, somewhere on the bottom. Kinnia eyed the indent for her totem, encircled with runes, then turned to me. As soon as she put the totem in, I would be left alone to complete the trial. Really, truly alone.

"Now what?" she asked.

I huffed. "I don't know. Fire, I don't even know how many targets there are. I can't keep count when they reappear."

"What if you don't have to hit each one individually?" Kinnia walked toward the indent. The runes glowed slightly yellow at her approach.

I frowned. "What?"

She waved her arms vaguely. "What if you just destroy the entire thing?"

I snorted. "I'm beyond flattered you think I'm powerful enough for that, but there's no guarantee every target would get hit. Mass destruction is never the answer, especially when we're on top of it."

She wrinkled her nose. "I meant just the targets."

"Yeah, I'm not following."

She looked down and to the right. "I amplified Bash's magic."

"Yeah, you did." I grinned.

Kinnia rolled her eyes, but her matching smile let me know she'd missed my teasing. "Can you latch onto the magic powering the targets and blow them up from the source with enough power?"

"We've talked about this. Magic isn't a physical thing. It's—"

Ambrocio's voice quaked through the colosseum. "The Upper Council finds it short-sighted this trial did not contain a timed component. As such, I am imposing a time limit right now."

The same huge, yellow numbers from Bash's trial scrolled across the sky. A five loomed over the colosseum, and the crowd roared as the countdown began.

She grabbed my hand and pulled me close. "Trust goes two ways."

I licked my lips. Could I trust her? I wanted to. And I could understand wanting to keep pieces of yourself for yourself.

"Four!" the crowd bellowed.

I placed her hand on my chest. My Cara hummed with her excitement. "Guide us."

"Three!"

Her smile lit up my world. She balanced her totem over the notch so she could drop it at the right moment.

"Two!"

Kinnia ran her hand down my chest to my gut. Blood rushed to my cock, and I wished she'd keep sliding. Instead, she closed her eyes.

"O—"

Time slowed. Magic and something I'd never felt before tingled through my stomach before shooting into my Cara. Mineral-rich water flowed over my tongue. My head seared. I screamed. My fire left my heart and leapt through my Cara as the bond stretched and widened. That damnable string Kinnia always talked about became a physical sensation in my gut.

I suddenly found myself sitting on a fountain in a large human city. My chubby, dirty fingers dangled into the water behind me, and I clutched a warm loaf of bread in my other hand. A human baker leapt out of the crowd, looking like every baker stereotype I'd ever seen. My mouth didn't form the laugh I felt. I cowered. Sharp, anticipatory fear shot through me as the baker turned red with anger and raised his fist. As I braced for pain, the image froze. I tried to blink, to rub my eyes, but my hands wouldn't obey. Heartbeats passed.

Time picked up just as suddenly as it had stopped. The baker slammed me into the edge of the fountain, and pain darkened my vision. Hot tears stung the cut under my eye. The baker hit me again, and I curled into a ball, cradling my bread. The man paused to shout for the authorities. I tried to crawl out of his view with the bread while he was distracted, but he whipped back, and trapped me against the low stone edge of the fountain. I cuddled the bread to my cheek and prayed I would survive. Its flaky crust dented my skin, and it warmed my hands. I sucked in a deep breath but smelled nothing.

The reek of body odor, cooked foods, and livestock abruptly filled my senses. This human city with fresh bread inches from my face couldn't smell of nothing. Panic overtook my thoughts. A current of *energy* buzzed under my skin, sharp and cold.

I charged forward, *energy* filling my small fists, and I hit the baker in the back of the knee. He cried out and crumpled. I had to protect the bread at all costs, or this would be for nothing. I darted for the relatively safety of the alleys. An army of discordant footsteps followed.

A network of color filled my vision—yellow dots connected to hundreds, thousands of other yellow dots. Kinnia's map of my targets. I opened my arms wide and summoned my trust into a massive fireball, larger than I'd ever seen before. It splintered into pieces, spinning after every target. With a ground-shaking explosion, every target shattered.

"—ne!"

Screaming pain consumed my thoughts, darkening the edges of my vision. Kinnia's chubby, childlike hands appeared before me again. Something hit me hard. Kinnia's memories vanished. The pain in my head doubled, and I swayed.

I forced my eyes open and grabbed hold of Kinnia to keep from falling. The world shook, or maybe I did. Her eyes rolled up in her head. Together, we crumpled to the top deck of the course. The crowd roared, but for the first time, I didn't care.

Kinnia, my mate, our mate. I pulled her to my chest, tentatively feeling around my Cara. A solid, hollow bridge connected us. Fire, I loved her.

A familiar *pop* sounded lower in the course as the air pressure dropped. The cheers turned to shrieks of fear.

35

KINNIA

I stood as tall as I could in front of the gate to Inferno's Heart, Emberhold's most prestigious academy. Clean, straight lines of silver accented the dark wood. I inhaled the scent of dust, papers, and chemicals from the tannery next door. It smelled like hope.

I raised a long, tawny arm to open the gate. Blotchy, dull ink stained my left hand and wrist. I quickly stuffed my hand back into my pocket. For some reason, I couldn't allow anyone to see the stains. Two older embers appeared in my mind's eye and smiled down at me. My parents. They'd given up everything to send me here. I wouldn't let them down.

When I pushed the massive gate open with my other hand, life burst out. A courtyard full of teenage embers laughed and played. I lifted my chin and stepped in.

The first step toward a better life for me and my family. The headmaster expected me, but I studied the chaos for a moment. My test scores had broken the gauge the proctors used to measure them. This granted me a measure of prestige at a school like Inferno's Heart. I just needed to figure out how to use that social power.

My peers eyed me. Many of them frowned. Games dissolved into whispers. I struggled to maintain my confident smile. Near the wall, a team of embers, their golden hair shining in the morning light, beat sticks on the ground in patterns, while a second group jumped around and over those patterns until their feet tangled or they reached the end of the sequence. I'd watched this game through the workroom window often enough to know it. When they began a new pattern, I jumped in. The moment my feet hit the playing field, the embers holding the sticks froze.

"Who invited the coal?" A boy a few years older than me dropped his end of the stick and tossed a perfectly gathered ponytail over his shoulder. He smoothed wrinkles out of a pair of gray trousers that fit him like a glove. Gold glinted at his ears and neck, and even shone on his leather shoes.

I grinned. "The proctors. My fire melted their gauge."

Another boy scoffed. "If they wanted you, why'd they leave you in rags?"

I picked at the edge of my undyed cotton tunic and smoothed back the hair that had come loose from my ponytail during my walk here. I wore only a single, dull red earring. My loose twill pants covered the sandals I called shoes. These were first new clothes I'd gotten in years.

A boy about my age—and much better dressed—pressed his finger to my chin. "Is that dirt, or a massive pimple?"

I batted his hand away and rubbed my chin. Several students laughed.

"It's not coming off." He grinned.

I flushed. More ink, somehow.

The first boy eyed me with distaste and stepped back. "Careful, or some coal dust might rub off on you."

The rest of them copied him. My heart sank.

"It's just ink." I turned in a circle, trying to explain myself to everyone at once. "It's my family business. It's not a big deal."

The edges of the day, the memory, turned white as the yard echoed with laughter, then faded.

I opened my eyes to the bright light of noon in our suite at our Academy. Anger churned my gut. Those kids had no right to treat Teyr that way. I sucked in a breath and let it out. His behavior made a lot more sense now.

Zelimir cleared his throat, and I looked up to find my commander sitting with another book on the couch at the end of my bed. I tried to grab my blankets, but my hands met the hazy gray of the stasis blanket. I'd lost days again. He grunted and pulled off the magic keeping my bodily functions in check. Unlike last time, I didn't need to rush to the bathroom, though I would have to go soon.

"How long?" I asked.

"Just a day this time." Zel pursed his lips. "We've been summoned to the Lower Council upon your wakening."

I nodded and waited for more. Did he know why? Did we even succeed? We did. His tunic held three circles. Mine, two.

He *pulsed* a command to get moving as he turned back to his beloved books.

The anger I'd felt for the kids who had been cruel to Teyr quickly combined with my own. I didn't know "no friends, no flirting, no connections" included my own mates. These stupid fae kept assuming a physical and emotional barometer could replace talking to each other. I might be uninjured and not mad enough to hit him, but he had no idea what I thought, what I wanted.

Teyr's bitter words about the new rules when we'd spoken in the mud came back to me. They might not all agree with Zel's rules.

I sat up in bed to check myself over. My clothes, my body, even Drax's necklace remained coated in mud. Dark blood stained my front. My heart pounded, but nothing hurt. I hadn't been stabbed, and creating the bridge with Bash hadn't injured me. Something else happened after I went unconscious, and instead of telling me about it, Zel sat with his schematics and textbooks.

We didn't have time for me to start another fight. I swallowed down the anger and cleaned up as well as I could in the sink before changing out my muddy greens for a new set.

When I emerged, Zelimir stood without a word, and I followed him to the Council's audience chamber. The rest of our mates stood outside. Teyr smiled shyly, his presence peeking down our bridge. I started to smile back, but Zelimir *pulsed* to both of us that we needed to present a united front. The door rolled open as our faces fell.

We entered as one and stood in a line, like always. The fifs' brilliant light reflected off the dark stone walls. The Lower Council sat in their usual seats with no Farquin in sight, but over Councilor Ambrocio's head floated an oval of shimmering, darkly rainbowed magic. Power and tension crackled through the room.

Upper Council, Teyr whispered in my head.

I smiled. *Thank you.*

The ember had seen my past, as I'd seen his, and it hadn't broken whatever tenuous peace we'd reached in the mud. I wanted to tell him I was ready to figure out what joining them actually meant, but I didn't want him to hear that with this feeling in the air.

The thick, inky magic of the Upper Council throbbed with its own life. It pressed into me like a thick quilt, smothering the air from my lungs. I swallowed hard and reached for my commander's hand before remembering his rules. With a stab of frustration, I pulled back.

Shade shifted uncomfortably from foot to foot. Was he still in pain? It had been over a week since his fall, while training with Lir. I sent a burst of something soothing to him and swore to get to the bottom of that once we got out of here, regardless of how many worms he threw at me.

Straightening my shoulders, I faced the Councils who so blatantly set us up to fail. The five-second countdown told all. I'd been so focused on myself, on staying Declan and keeping up with my mates, that I hadn't looked at the bigger picture Rydel had mentioned.

"We've called you here because we can no longer deny your Cara is particularly unique." Councilor Odhrán frowned. "Do you agree, Commander Zelimir?"

Zelimir nodded.

Gnuq ran his hands over his furred belly. "And unique things get special attention."

My stomach turned.

"The Upper Council agrees that attention is best given at the Academy." Councilor Ambrocio grimaced and crumpled the edges of a piece of paper in his hands. One of his bushy eyebrows twitched as he stood. "For the rest of your training, Declan will reside under the watchful eye of Councilor Drax in his apartments."

Shade growled. Teyr stepped forward, mouth open to reply, then he glanced at Zel and stopped. My heart thudded out of time.

"One rift in the colosseum, despite its near impossibility, could be a fluke. Two is a pattern." Councilor Odhrán eyed me with interest.

Another rift? And confirmation of the first one. Based on the blood on my tunic, there must have been a fight while I lay unconscious. I looked at Zelimir for some reason as to why he'd kept this from me, but his gaze remained steadily trained on the Councilors.

"It's clear," he said, "by the surprise on my mate's face that Declan knew nothing of a rift opening in the colosseum."

He'd kept that information from me on purpose. He used me like a pawn, displayed my emotions to prove his points.

"Nothing is clear." Gnuq's bald head flushed, and he turned to Councilor Ambrocio. "I suggested Declan reside with me. As headmaster, I'm most fit to oversee his education."

I shuddered. Shade growled. Councilor Xerxes raised an eyebrow. He hadn't looked away from the necromancer since we walked in.

Councilor Ambrocio glanced at the dark oval. "The Upper Council felt otherwise."

The oval throbbed. Everyone in the room whipped around to face it. After a moment, all five Councilors bowed their heads.

My hands shook. Tears pressed against the backs of my eyes. The one thing we still had, our suite, our quiet time together, was being ripped away by a mysterious group that seemed to frighten the scariest people I'd ever met.

"You'll still train to complete the Cara," Councilor Ambrocio spat through gritted teeth. "Lectures and physical training will go unchanged." He glanced back up to the oval and smiled a sickly smile. "In the evenings, we will privately tutor Declan—with a strict curfew. The rest of you can do whatever you see fit without him."

Shade snarled and took a step forward. Bash hauled the necromancer back by the collar of his uniform.

We'll figure this out, Teyr said in my mind.

I sent him a wave of gratitude and clasped my hands behind me.

Zel clenched his jaw. The grip he had on his own hands behind his back made veins stand out against his dark skin. Whatever was happening between us, whatever he had said or allowed, he would put his foot down here. He wouldn't let the Councils take me. I allowed myself a small smile and waited.

He took a deep breath. "Respectfully, it seems to me that distance will harm the natural development of the Cara."

Councilor Xerxes cocked his head to one side. "My reports say you spent no more time together than this restriction will impose, and that you were implementing further restrictions soon. Are you challenging the Upper Council on a regime you yourself imposed?"

I couldn't *pulse* without moving my hands, but I tried to project the word *yes* to Zelimir anyway. I needed him to say something. If he couldn't say it to me, for me, he needed to say it for the Cara. If he really did everything for the group, he would have to act now.

"No," he said.

I flinched.

"I would never challenge the wisdom of the Upper Council." He flexed his back. "Swords are best forged in the heat of battle, and our Anam Cara will be stronger for your direction."

My face flushed, caught somewhere between embarrassment and rage. How could he keep falling into this trap? How could he give up on me like this?

Zelimir stood perfectly straight, chin up just enough to show confidence, and didn't meet my eye. Teyr claimed he disagreed, but he wouldn't look at me either. Bash focused on Shade, who quivered in his grip, barely holding back his shift.

Drax cleared his throat. "We're glad to hear you say that."

I pulled my gaze away from my mates and schooled my expression. The quivering emotions inside me—which I knew they could feel, the cowards—would have to wait until we were out from under the eyes of these fae.

"Yes, very glad." Gnuq looked me over and rubbed the thin, golden hair below his belly button. "Before we give you your next trial, is there anything else we should know? In the wake of the reveal of Declan's true power, it seems…imprudent not to ask."

Silence fell over the chamber. Zelimir *pulsed* a simple apology to me. My heart thundered in my ears. Time seemed to slow.

"Declan is not a male," he said.

I clapped a hand over my mouth to contain the bile surging up into my throat. My only rock in the storm, my only concession from the commander whose care I seemed to have imagined, the last scrap of who I was before them, was gone.

"Her name is Kinnia." Zelimir spoke in that awful, even-handed, political tone he used when he knew somebody wouldn't like what he said, a tone I'd grown to hate over the last few days.

The room spun around me. Bash's betrayal paled in comparison to this. The Councils knew. The whole Academy would know before this meeting let out. Gnuq said something about his healer being a woman. Ambrocio began babbling to himself or the oval behind him.

I looked at Drax, barely containing my tears, my nausea, my shame. I couldn't look at my mates. Nothing they could do or say now would help.

Drax's pink gaze softened. "It seems to me our part of this meeting is adjourned."

Amidst the protests of the other Councilors, he reached out a tendril of pink magic and lifted me to him. I slumped into his magical grip.

"Wait, Kinnia!" Zelimir grabbed for me as I floated away.

Drax hesitated. I shook my head, and he placed me at his side. Zelimir had taken all my choices away. He didn't get to unmake this one.

Drax gestured to a smaller pale wood door I hadn't noticed at the shadowed back of the chamber. I strode toward it with him close behind, between me and my mates. The bulk of the pink Councilor comforted me despite everything. He walked with me out of the chamber and through the winding Academy halls into red-lined Secca halls, as tears filled my eyes.

Zelimir had stripped me down to nothing. I couldn't be Declan. I couldn't be a Cara mate. He wouldn't let me be his friend, much less his lover. He made me Kinnia, his subordinate, and once more, alone.

Drax placed his hand on a round door made of golden wood rather than the red that lined the rest of the hall. "Don't be afraid to cry."

The door rolled to the side as I swiped at my eyes, revealing a sparse, windowless living room.

"My daughter had a set of lungs on her." Drax placed a hand on my shoulder. "When she was upset, even as an adult, you could hear her across the wilds. It didn't make her any less a warrior."

I shook my head, blinking rapidly. I didn't want to be Kinnia. Kinnia would cry.

Drax guided me to a dark bedroom. He pushed the two fifs as bright as they would go, but the dresser and desk on each side of the bed remained in shadow.

He winced. "I'll get that fixed. I wasn't expecting company."

I stared at my new room. I had a private space for the first time in almost two months, and I couldn't stand it.

He cleared his throat. "The Upper Council set Shade's trial a month from now. We have to understand how a rift opened in our colosseum."

A heavy silence fell over us. He didn't need to make the accusation.

I shook my head. "I hate Tech."

Drax squeezed my shoulder. "I have heard this of you."

My conversation with Rydel floated back to the top of my mind. "Tech killed your family, right?" I crossed my arms, suddenly desperate to have someone, anyone on my side. "That's how your daughter died?"

He smiled a soft, sad smile. "She was about your age when it happened."

"They killed mine too," I murmured. "I would never let them hurt anyone else."

Drax looked at me for a long moment. "I believe you."

Despite everything, I smiled.

He removed his hand and stepped out of the room. "I'm closing this door, but you can open it, and all my doors, at will. This is not your prison."

My face fell. "How long is it not my prison for?"

"At least until Shade's trial, so the month." He smiled ruefully. "Hopefully we don't make too bad of roommates."

I nodded and offered him another small smile.

"My walls are thick," he said. "I'll give you time to adjust."

Before I could respond, a door made of the same golden wood as his front door rolled shut between us. I tried to restrain my tears, to become the fae warrior everyone wanted me to be.

No such luck.

I flung myself onto the bed and sobbed ugly tears. Declan was gone, stripped from me by my mates.

Kinnia, Teyr said across our bridge.

I ripped myself off the tear-soaked pillow as my self-pity burned into anger. I crammed *energy* into my bridges with Teyr and Bash. Layers of my essence filled the tubes, sealing my mates away from me. I was done being pushed around, done waiting for Zelimir to include me.

For years, I'd been a lone mercenary, relying on my skills and wits. I'd lost that somewhere. In my desperation to be one of them, I'd stopped being myself.

I gripped Drax's necklace. He still missed his family, still mourned them, but it didn't look like he was beating himself up anymore. He'd thrown himself into eradicating Tech in their memory.

No flashback tore me away. I was no longer the seventeen-year-old girl who froze before the battle even began. I had become a warrior, even if that warrior wasn't good enough for my mates. I could become somebody who honored my family's memory, just like Drax. I could take control of my life back.

36

———

ZELIMIR

I PRESSED MY HAND AGAINST THE DOOR TO OUR SUITE, AND it rolled back at its normal, leisurely pace. Not fast enough. I shouldered the door out of the way and the wood slammed into its slot with a *crack*.

I'd failed us. Not only had I failed us, but Councilor Gnuq forced me to betray Kinnia like I'd forced Bash.

It couldn't be a coincidence that the satyr had asked that fateful question. His healer had handled Kinnia. I didn't know whether he knew or just suspected, but I knew he would never back off the scent. A long, dragged-out interrogation would have worsened the result. The Councils would trust us less and pay attention to her more. I had no choice but to offer up the information willingly.

Or so I told myself. The excuse didn't soften the fact that her Cara had gone white with pain, that she'd ignored me when I called out to her, and that she hadn't looked at any of us as our old mentor physically pulled her away.

And the Councils had still interrogated us for an hour after she left with Drax. I barely remembered my answers or their questions. Kinnia's agony made focus nearly impossible.

Teyr opened his mouth, clearly to make some smartass comment about the door, and I whipped my Cara open. He copied my gesture.

Similar anger, fear, and disappointment chased my own. The ember dropped onto Kinnia's favorite chair without a word.

Shade whined, then slunk across the room to her bed. He lay down on his side and clutched one of her pillows to his chest. Bash stalked into the room, his mouth pinched, and the door rolled crookedly shut behind him. Like Kinnia, he didn't look at me as he stepped to his bed. In one smooth motion, he pulled off his shirt and sat, shutting his eyes as if to meditate.

I clenched my fist. The dragon could read minds now. In addition to feeling everything we did, he'd heard Kinnia's thoughts as I told the world her secret. Some perverse part of me wanted to know her thoughts.

Before I could ask, Bash and Teyr shot up with matching expressions of horror.

"No, Kinnia, don't!" Teyr shouted.

I turned a circle, looking for whatever they were seeing, but found only Shade, still cuddling Kinnia's pillow while eyeing our strange mates. Kinnia's Cara shifted from pain to determination, a change we'd felt all too often. I loved the way she bounced back from every failure, every argument, every loss, but this time, a worrying current of rage underpinned that determination.

Teyr moaned. "I literally just got that."

"She's protecting herself." Bash glared at me before schooling his face. "Kinnia has blocked our new bridges, much like she blocked the Cara on our trip here."

I swallowed down frustration. She knew that only made things worse. "Can it be undone?"

Bash shrugged. "Only she knows."

Someone knocked brightly on our door. The broken thing slid halfway into the wall before stuttering to a stop. I turned. Shade jumped to his feet with a soft whimper.

Chrysophylax grinned at us, his hand poised to knock a second time. Shade snarled. Teyr called a ball of fire to his hands and started tossing it into the air.

"I can come back. But I will come back." He stepped inside, flanked by his second, Quin, and Leonai, who sneered with all of his father's disdain.

"I just heard." Chrysophylax pressed a hand to his face in an imitation of shock. "How interesting that the first human to ever join a Cara is also a woman. Even more interesting that she's been taken from you." He grinned.

I clenched my hands. My second wrapped my bicep in telekinetic pressure and filled our Cara with calm he barely felt himself.

"What are you here for?" I demanded.

Chrysophylax cocked his red and blue head to the side. Bash's grasp on my bicep tightened. The two dragons could communicate telepathically.

"Go." Chrysophylax shooed Bash. "Pack her things so I can deliver them into her perfect little hands."

My vision went red. Bash's hold fell away. I bellowed and charged the dragonkin, who'd too many times been too close to my mate. I slammed into him, but that didn't dull the red. I wrapped my hands around his neck, drove him backward and up until he hit the wall. He made a satisfying *thud*, the breath driving out of his body. Fire streaked behind me, followed by a shout from Shade and a crash.

Chrysophylax's tendons snapped in my grip. Plant shoots grew out of the walls and wormed beneath my fingers. His body knitted back together. I roared again before dropping Chrysophylax and turning to the troll healing him.

Before I could swing, Leonai scowled and held up his meaty hands, palms out. "We're here on Council orders, not to pick a fight."

The dragonkin wheezed. Leonai had waited to fully heal his commander until I called truce, no matter how much that seemed to irritate him. Behind him, Teyr sat on Quin's chest, while Bash held the titan mutt's arms above his head. Shade's power billowed across the ground, dancing with excitement. I wasn't sure I wanted to know what the necromancer found.

"You are here on Council orders," I repeated.

The Council had Kinnia. If we wanted her back, we needed to listen. I took a deep breath and forced down my rage. I *pulsed* to end the fight.

With reluctance, my mates let Quin up. He scowled but shuffled behind the troll. Healing magic soaked out of the ground in spirals of clinging vines, and Chrysophylax rose. He glared at his mates before smiling like he hadn't just been suffocating on my floor.

"Bashu, if you don't mind?" The dragonkin dramatically swept his arm.

I *pulsed* to my second to obey, and he crossed to Kinnia's bed. We watched in silence as he stuffed her paltry belongings into her pack.

My gut twisted. Teyr had burned every bribe she refused to open, which was all of them, but we hadn't gotten her a single thing. She'd lost all her belongings in Saltair, even her coin. We'd replaced her basics in Stoneheim, nothing more. The only sort of fae thing she had was that rune she always wore on her belt, and I had no idea who gave it to her.

Bash tied off her pack strangely before handing it to Chrysophylax. "She knows exactly what that knot looks like."

The dragonkin grinned. "So, she has telepathic gifts as well. I'll work on those with her tomorrow."

Bash growled and took a step forward. I joined him. Before either of us could take a second step, Shade's power coated the floor around Chrysophylax and his mates. Blobs of gray bubbled up and squirmed up their legs. One slipped between the laces of the dragonkin's leather boots. He yelped. Shade cackled. Chrysophylax's mates pulled him out, and the door juddered closed behind them.

"I didn't know there were so many of you." Shade knelt in the mess he made to let one of the little gray things crawl up his finger. "Welcome. My Kitty's gone." He glanced at me. "Taken while I watched."

"While we all watched," Teyr said.

I turned away from Shade, praying he banished whatever he'd found.

"She is with our old mentor." I rubbed my chest. "I trust him. It could be worse."

"How?" Teyr asked. "She's not here. The Council—who's screwed us every time we turn around, by the way—has taken complete control of her. They run her day, her schedule. Fire, they're tutoring her themselves."

"The Lower Council is full of old and powerful fae." I leaned toward the ember. "She will benefit from their knowledge. They see the imbalance in our Cara and believe this will help."

Teyr's eyes bugged out. "That satyr is trying to take her from us. Ambrocio wants us all dead. My trial was so obviously a set-up that they aren't even denying it." He gestured wildly. "Your precious Council is driving us apart."

I stepped back. "We are driving ourselves apart. Every test the Council put in front of us forced us to grow." I sucked in a deep breath to keep my temper. "You envisioned a massive number of small targets and precisely burned them away in second. That is a kind of control you've never had before."

"But I got it *in spite of* the Council." Teyr threw his hands in the air. "Not because of them. Zel, what is wrong with your brain?"

Shade laughed softly. "What is wrong with your brain?" The necromancer had collected a pile of the little worms into his palm. Without the glow of his power, rotting holes stood out against the dull gray of their bodies.

"You don't have brains to have anything wrong with," he whispered. "But we do."

A chill ran down my spine. I looked back at Teyr. "We will build on what we have. We know we all have feelings for her, but we need the world to believe that our Anam Cara is balanced and strong." I stared down at the ember, making sure he could feel the foot difference in our height. "Platonic, productive activities only."

Teyr sucked in a breath, fire sparking in his palms, then he spun to face Shade. "Let's get those things outside before they start smelling."

My second slid back to his bed and sank into his meditations. I dropped onto the couch and poured myself a brandy. This would work. We just needed a strong blacksmith.

37

————

KINNIA

A week came and went in monotonous routine. I woke, went to lectures, trained, and returned to Drax's apartment in the Secca tower for dinner and tutoring. Falling into bed alone reminded me of what I'd lost. Waking to empty sheets meant I never forgot.

When I saw them, my mates moved about me in perfect formation, exchanging nothing more than the barest small talk. Bash and I still performed our morning warm-up at the same time, but no longer together. Teyr kept trying to start conversations during training, but Zelimir always pinned him with a glare. Shade had barely said a word to anyone, but his hands always glimmered with magic, as though he could fix everything with one spell.

I didn't watch Zelimir, didn't hope for anything. He maintained perfect poise, gave crisp orders, and never looked at me for more than a second. To the outside observer, we looked perfectly balanced.

The alone time had some upsides, though. The transition from Declan to Kinnia went far smoother than I expected because I talked to almost no one who might react. Chry leered a few times, and he seemed to be getting more possessive, but he backed off when I told him to. I'd started letting my hair grow out. Drax handed me a box of light, less compressive chest supports one day and left without a word. They let me breathe easier, but wearing them, I showed a little cleavage at the bottom of the trainee tunic's neck lacing. I tied it tight enough to hide that when I saw my mates.

In what little free time the Councils allowed, I'd started exploring the Academy according to Rydel's map, assigning my own labels to the twisting network of lines. I had a month to learn, but even after just a week, I finally felt like I understood the labyrinth I'd been dropped into. I'd separated all the Cara areas from the Secca ones and knew Councilor Ambrocio's patterns already.

I walked past the baths on my way home from training at the beginning of the second week and paused. Drax's apartment had the luxury of a private shower, but I missed the sting of the mineral water.

A voice in my head which sounded suspiciously like Zelimir nagged me about the dangers of being naked and alone in public. I didn't care what he thought anymore. But I didn't want the weight of hundreds of eyes on my body. I turned and continued to Drax's apartment.

The warm smell of spices and meat filled my nose as I walked through the golden wood door. I followed the smell to find Drax in the kitchen, already sitting at his little two-seat table with a full plate of roast padena and mashed punaky at each place. He had a cook surface, but he only ever summoned food from the Academy kitchen.

"How were classes today?" Drax cut into his padena as I took the chair across from him.

I smiled. He'd asked every day so far, and he listened to my answers. I'd grown to enjoy the ritual. He could be pumping me for information for the Council, but it felt like he actually cared.

"They were okay. It's still hard to be around Zelimir after he—" I swallowed.

Drax cocked his head to one side. "Did you know that Councilor Gnuq already suspected?"

All the times the satyr leered at me, licking his lips and rubbing his stomach. He might have known? I shook my head.

"He was...unfortunately liberal with details about what he's calling his discovery. In short, his healer noticed some inconsistencies after Bash's trial." Drax savored a bite of his punaky. "One of Zelimir's greatest skills as a leader is his ability to read people— when he's not letting his head cloud with assumptions." Drax smiled. "He likes to expect the best, especially of leadership. But if he noticed this in Councilor Gnuq, it may be worth considering that the way he revealed the information removed the Councilor's power over you." Drax speared a bite of padena. "Which would prevent him from doing something worse."

I fiddled with the crystal necklace Drax had given me. Churning nausea threatened to ruin my dinner. Betrayal still seared in my veins, as much from the barebones apology Zel offered and the way he let the Council take me. Was Drax right? Had Zelimir been trying to protect me —or at least, his Anam Cara?

Drax let me stew for a little, then asked, "What were lectures about today?"

"Odhrán told us about the pack tactics programmed into DogTech." I didn't need the lesson. I'd been hunted by enough packs to know their moves by heart. "And Farquin—" I couldn't keep the grimace off my face when I thought about the Jalan.

Drax put his fork down and looked at me. "You're uncomfortable with him."

I shrugged and pushed my punaky around on my plate. Despite the ease I'd found with the Councilor, I couldn't imagine telling him about my years on Earth and the clusters of Jalan I'd run from occasionally.

"In human lands, Jalan are a ghost story," I said. "Because it's so unimaginable that any of us would want anything to do with Tech. It's hard to get over feeling like he's...unnatural."

He nodded. "You feel like he is Tech."

I nodded. Everybody else seemed willing to treat him like a man, but every glint of light off the metal plates of his face made my stomach flip.

Drax sighed. "I understand the impulse, but I assure you he is something else. He's been our liaison to the Jalan community for at least twenty years now, and while he did make me a little nervous in the beginning as well—all Jalan do—he has proven himself nothing but cordial."

Even if Farquin wasn't Tech, I couldn't shake the sneaking suspicion

I'd seen him before I reentered the wilds. "So, you were here before him?"

Drax sighed but smiled. "I only spent a few months on my own after Tech leveled my village. I knew only Caras fought Tech, but I applied to join an Anam Secca because I needed something to do. I worked my way up the ranks slowly, through blood and sweat. Still, I've never heard the call. My fight remains here, on Thrae, as it has for many long centuries."

My heart broke a little for the pink-and-purple fae who had treated me with more kindness than I'd known since I lost my family. Even this past week, I'd ached every time I saw belonging and knew I didn't belong myself. Whatever Secca he'd been a part of had obviously left or died. I couldn't imagine centuries on the outside.

I patted the hand he'd laid on the table "Thank you for letting me stay here."

Drax smiled. "Council orders or not, you're always welcome, Kinnia. You help me remember what I'm protecting."

After dinner, I decided to spend the hour I had until tutoring in my room. Gnuq showed up every night with a little naked pixie, and with how he leered at me, I doubted being naked had been her choice. I picked up the fabric and needle Drax had gotten me without too many questions and began sewing in the low light. The tiny, half-finished dress looked jagged and uneven. Sewing clothes was nothing like stitching wounds, it turned out. But I'd whispered the idea of the dress to the pixie as he left last time, and she'd glowed.

I had been hurt by my mates, but as I pushed the needle into the fabric, my chest warmed. I missed them. I loved them. Was that enough? Could there be life and love outside of them. If I didn't want to give up the beauty of the fae wilds, maybe I could find a life like Drax had found. I just had to make that life for myself.

38

————

KINNIA

THE BEAM SWUNG. ZEL *pulsed.* I DUCKED. AND FOR THE FIRST time after over a month of training, the massive chunk of wood passed soundlessly over my head.

I ducked. I fucking ducked!

Bash caught the beam before it could swing back and hit the line of us standing in its path. My heart sang. I turned to share my joy and found four stoic expressions.

I froze. My stomach sank lower and lower. None of my mates would share in my excitement. Bash wouldn't smile his rare smile. Shade wouldn't hug me. Teyr wouldn't jump up and down with me, nor would Zelimir ruffle my hair. None of them had touched me since Zel let me move into Drax's apartment.

Anger sparked in my gut. I clung to the emotion. Anything beat the sinking devastation. So what if he'd outed me to undercut Gnuq? That didn't make up for any of his asshole rules, or the way he folded like a house of cards when the Council so much as gestured.

"Excellent work, all." Zelimir glanced at the setting sun. "We're out of light. Let's call it a day on a high note."

A high note? I looked over their stoic expressions, hoping for even a spark of my joy. Nothing.

"See you tomorrow, then." I jogged away before they could hurt me again. No. Before I could hurt me again by expecting something I knew I couldn't have.

People who wanted you around behaved like they wanted you around. Drax always had a smile for me, always made sure I had enough to eat, enough time to myself, enough of anything else I wanted. My mates only ever kept me alive. They wanted a body. They wanted to be complete again. I couldn't keep tricking myself into thinking what they were doing passed as fae affection. I could have better. I deserved better.

Every time I repeated my logic, it made more sense and eased the hurt a little more.

As I approached the main tower, I released a breath and my anger with it. At least I could tell Drax about ducking tonight. He'd be excited for me.

A black blur shot out of a copse of trees on my left. I shrieked as Shade barreled me over. He lapped at my face with his pink tongue, and my scream turned to laughter.

"Shade!" I giggled, half trying to push the dire wolf off and half trying to hug him.

His tail beat madly against my legs. I managed to push him off enough that I could sit up. He turned around to stick his butt in my face so I would scratch it. His tail whacked the side of my head. I dug my fingers into his fur, savoring the warmth and softness. Against all my logic, all my better instincts, tears welled in my eyes. I pushed him to the side until I could bury my face in the fur on his back.

"I know you're secretly a big, scary necromancer," I murmured. "And we both have magic pulling us together and orders to follow and our own emotions to sort. But I really, really miss you."

A few tears dripped into his fur. He twisted to lap at my face before bolting for the woods once more.

My heart sank. He left. They'd all leave.

He burst from the trees with a massive stick clenched in his jaws. Emotion tore through my chest. This doomed journey had started the same way, back at the *Cross Roads*.

I smiled sadly. "I can't win this game, Shade."

Shade poked me with the stick anyway, and I soon found myself in tug-of-war match that knocked me on my ass and made me laugh louder than I had in weeks. The sun set around us. By the time I looked up, slobber covered my hands and stars twinkled in the night sky. It had started like this in the *Cross Roads*, but maybe I could rewrite the story. I wrapped my arms around his neck.

"Don't get in trouble for this." I squeezed. "I don't like staying away from you, but I can't keep making the first move."

Shade nodded, a gesture that looked strange on his wolf, then barked softly as if he were sharing a secret. I giggled. He turned and raced away.

I headed back to Drax's apartment. I'd been out with Shade so long that I had to eat and shower in record time so as not to be late for my tutor, Councilor Ambrocio this evening. Gnuq's sessions made me feel like I needed another shower, but Councilor Ambrocio seemed to genuinely resent even being in the same room with me.

As I put my plate on the counter, Drax raised an eyebrow from where he sat on the chair in his living room. "You seem happy."

I put a hand to my cheek, still stretched in a smile. "I ducked."

He pursed his lips. "Are you sure ducking is all you did?"

I blinked, then flushed. "Yes."

Before Drax could reply, someone knocked on the door. I whipped around. I still had five minutes until tutoring started, and Councilor Ambrocio usually showed up obscenely late. Better get it over with. I hurried to the door and rolled it open. Instead of finding Councilor Ambrocio, I came face-to-face with Farquin.

"Kinnia." Farquin nodded, a small smile on his lips. "Ambrocio is busy tonight."

My skin turned clammy. It took all my willpower to step back instead of shutting the door in his face. The dim light of Drax's fifs turned the metal of his face sickly and threatening. Teyr's voice rang in my memory. *In for five. Hold for five. Out for five.*

The last time I'd been alone with Farquin, he'd been pushy and strange, but he hadn't attacked me. When I'd run, he'd let me go. I couldn't run this time.

Drax nodded as he gathered his papers to adjourn to his bedroom. I couldn't run, but I wasn't alone either.

I led the Jalan into the living room. My skin crawled with him at my back. I closed my eyes, thinking of Bash. I missed his touches, our silent connection. He would understand my discomfort and accept it without a word, making it easier to accept myself. I had to figure out how to be comfortable without him.

The fifs glowed brighter as Drax left, a spell he'd figured out to account for how much brighter I preferred my spaces. Despite the warmth of summer, the pink Councilor always had a fire going in his hearth on the far wall. Two high-backed chairs sat in front of the fireplace, with a low table between them. A golden desk with two chairs stood along the wall to the kitchen.

"Um, where would you like to work?" I gestured vaguely.

Farquin nodded at the desk, and we took our places next to each other. I repeated the breathing exercise as he put a bag on the table.

"I'd like to focus on your unique...magic today." He pulled out objects ranging from normal rocks to chunks of metal that looked like something I'd avoid on Earth.

"I don't have magic," I said automatically.

Farquin nodded almost approvingly. "But you have something." He flicked a cable in his blonde hair, which sparked.

I followed the gesture with my eyes. When I looked back at his face, he wore that intensity which unnerved me last time.

"Humans, of course, cannot connect with magic. Earth is Thrae's opposite. Where we distanced ourselves from the natural world, built machines and technologies to better our lives, fae dug their heels in, laid down roots, and created many of the same things with magic." He blinked, and his face shuttered. "But that's not why we're here."

I crossed my arms and leaned back.

"Do you want to tell me what you call your something, or may I continue referring to it as magic?" Farquin asked.

I pursed my lips. As much as I wanted to blame Zelimir for everything, I'd shown my cards to every fae in the colosseum during Bash's trial. "I just call it *energy.*"

He smiled just a little, and a shiver ran down my spine. If I wanted to be paranoid, I would call that smile *knowing*. But I didn't know him, and he certainly didn't know me.

"I don't suppose you'd be willing to give me a scope of what you're able to do?" he asked.

I shook my head. I'd been trying to be attentive and helpful during these tutoring sessions, to make a good impression on the Council so they'd at least loosen up on my curfew, but Farquin made that plan fly right out the window.

"You've always been stubborn, I suppose," he murmured.

"Always?" I repeated.

He hesitated a second too long. "Since you've been here. Don't worry, I think stubbornness is a wonderful trait." He smiled, but the expression looked small and awkward. "Now, since you won't tell me what you can do, would you show me? Just try to manipulate these objects here."

I tugged on Drax's necklace. If I screamed, he would be here in a moment.

I took a deep breath. I needed to rely on myself. Maybe some Jalan had seen me without my knowledge. Maybe all Jalan talked, and they'd passed on stories of a human teenager on Earth. That would explain a little of the intense way he looked at me.

"I don't have magic. I'm not going to be able to do anything with those." I glanced at the items on the table.

He sighed, finally sounding a little aggrieved. "Kinnia, I'd like for us to be friends, but unfortunately, if you refuse another request, I'm going to have to report your insubordination to the Lower Council. Perhaps they'll decide Councilor Drax isn't the best guardian for you, after all."

Panic seeped into my veins. I didn't want my fate back in their hands. I kept my face as steady as I could and threw my hands in the air. "Fine. What do you want me to do?"

Farquin talked me through a series of exercises with each of the objects, writing down notes every time. Like I predicted, nothing reacted.

Finally, we reached the last object in the line, the chunk of Earth metal I'd been eyeing all evening. He plucked it off the table and held it out. Fine lines marred the sheer surface of the cube about half the size of my fist, but they seemed intentional, like the thing could pop open and start shooting lasers any moment. A bead of sweat ran down my back.

"Kinnia," Farquin tried to meet my gaze, but I couldn't look away from the cube. "Take a deep breath. You're better than this fear."

The sincerity in his voice startled me into laughter. "Better than this? Who the hell are you to say you know that?"

He set his human hand over mine and squeezed. I met his gaze, finding that furious intensity once more.

"I'm someone who knows you could be more powerful than all of us," he said.

I yanked my hand from his grasp. He lifted the cube again, forcing it toward me.

"You can prove me wrong right now." Farquin sounded desperate and strange. "Just touch this, try to spark it. If nothing happens, I'm wrong, and I'll apologize. If not...."

His voice, his desperation whispered down my spine. Long-hidden memories of metal and blood clawed at me. I grabbed for the edge of the desk to steady myself. The golden wood bit into my palm, and I relished the sting. My world whirled back into focus, but his gaze remained on me. I wanted him to go away. He'd offered me a way to make him leave. Before I could think it through any further, I reached out and pressed my finger to a corner of the cube.

Metal chilled my skin. I shoved my reluctant *energy* forward. A little spark fizzed at my fingertip. Like I feared, panels slid back, but instead of lasers, the square morphed into a star covered in tiny mirrors with some sort of clear ball in the middle that reflected rainbows.

Farquin tossed the star into the air with a victorious laugh. A string tumbled out, and he snagged it, making the rainbows dance around the room as the star swung.

"I knew it," he whispered. "You're something special, Kinnia, but you're never going to figure out what that is if you don't push yourself." He grabbed my hand, then placed the star in my palm and closed my fingers around it. "Fear makes fools of even the most powerful. Don't make yourself a fool."

He swept the rest of the items back into his bag, stood, and let himself out without another word. I opened my fingers and stared at the star.

What did Farquin know?

39

———

TEYR

I PACED ACROSS OUR DARK, KINNIA-LESS SUITE. SHADE SAT on the floor, his legs outstretched in front of him. Zelimir had permanently commandeered the couch at the foot of her bed—her old bed—by covering the leather surface in his ever-growing stacks of papers and books so nobody could share. Bash sat with his legs crossed as though meditating in the chair next to the cask of brandy, though he filled his cup with liquor at regular intervals. Each of them tracked my progress across the room with varying levels of frustration.

We'd been doing this, letting the tension boil ever closer to the breaking point, for almost two weeks now. At this point, even the fifs blared an unhappy yellow.

"I said all of this was a bad idea." I didn't look at Zelimir. I hadn't in days.

Although she'd blocked our new bridge, the Cara let us feel every single one of her emotions. She'd spent the first week as mopey as us, but lately, spikes of joy and laughter filtered through.

They'd given us her schedule, so I knew Chrysophylax made her laugh during their one-on-one sessions. Her Cara bubbled happily during dinner. I loved feeling her happiness, but all of it came without me. Without us. Or so it seemed.

I scowled at the necromancer on the floor. When he met my eye, he widened his legs so his feet faced nearly his left and right, then flattened his chest to the floor and reached for his toes as if stretching. Shade had been sulking furiously, summoning more of those worms and cooing at them whenever he got a chance. Until a couple days ago, when he went silent. At the same time, Kinnia started experiencing these random heights of pure joy I couldn't track to anything on her schedule. In fact, they were usually when she had free time. And when Shade was suspiciously absent.

I should be breaking Zelly's stupid rules too.

"Kinnia's ours," Zelimir said finally. He turned a page in his book. "We just need to give her time to feel it too."

"More time? You're blind as a fucking bat!"

Shade glanced up at me, and I remembered with a small shiver the time he'd reanimated one of the red-spotted Earth migrants and tried to keep it as a pet.

Zelimir slowly looked up from his page and pushed calm across our Cara.

Not for the first time, I considered burning his whole pile of books just to make him look at me. "She's not 'ours,' as you keep saying. She isn't something any of us can possess," I said. "And the fact that you don't get that is the fucking problem." Irritation sparked on my fingers. "We brought her into the wilds as a prisoner and we're still treating her like that."

Bash shifted in his seat. "I'm not treating her like that."

I stared at the dragon in disbelief. "Then why aren't you with her right now?"

He looked at the cask, but I caught the second in between when his gaze flickered to Zelimir.

"We're no better than ember priests." I paused to let my words sink in. "It's not right."

She's not right, I couldn't keep myself from thinking. The fractured memory I'd seen pushed itself to the front of my mind. I wanted to talk to her about it first, but she'd been pulled right out from under me. She'd even blocked our mental bridge.

Bash's gaze bore into me.

Stop eavesdropping! I screamed in my thoughts.

He narrowed his eyes. "You shouldn't be keeping secrets from your mates."

I spat at the dragon's feet. "Hypocrite."

"Stop, both of you," Zelimir bellowed.

The tension in my hands bloomed into a dancing flame on my fingertips. The fire twisted and reshaped, becoming Kinnia's smiling eyes. I snuffed the flame.

Zel stepped into my space, forcing me to meet his gaze. "Teyr, this is not the time for your dramatic flair. She's not chained to a bed for us to use. She's free to make whatever choices she wants."

Smoke curled into my vision. "Your words don't match your actions, Commander." I put a hand on his chest and found the sleeve of my tunic on fire. I shoved him anyway. "For one moment, I connected to another person in a way I'd never experienced before. It was beautiful. She's beautiful. She could bring us, our magic, our bodies, together in a way none of us have even imagined." I stalked toward the door. I needed to start backing up my words with action. "I won't stand here and watch us throw that away because of the Council's manipulation and your fear."

I flung the broken door to the side, scorching a dark handprint into the already damaged green wood, and tore out of the suite. Fuck balance. Fuck all of it.

My Cara guided me toward Kinnia but didn't pinpoint her location. She'd been awake for less than half a day before she blocked me. Cut me off from something so perfect it literally changed my world. And I'd let her. I'd been so angry that she left me out. That she focused on Zelimir like he was the only fae that made decisions. And then what did I do? Despite disagreeing with Zelimir, I'd backed him up. Cowered in his shadow and ignored my instincts when she needed me the most.

Fuck Zelimir and fuck me. I blasted an itzal out of my way.

I reached the door of the library and bit back a groan before storming inside. The librarian's eyes went wide as my smoldering sleeves threatened the room of delicate paper and dried leather. I let fire bloom in my eyes, and her blue skin turned almost white as she let me pass without comment.

My last time at the Academy, I'd avoided this place like the plague, except on the rare occasion I needed a new location to entertain a partner. Life should be lived, not read about. So, I quickly lost myself in the uneven, natural spirals of shelves. Magic-bound books floated past my head, making me curse and dodge, and bookshelves of every imaginable wood made finding my path impossible.

I rounded into a dead end. "Fire!"

I could feel Kinnia right on the other side. I turned and began praying for a way around.

The oily voice of that Fire-damned dragonkin echoed off the wall of shelves. "Please let Leo heal you."

I slowed, not as surprised as I'd like to hear Chrysophylax's voice.

"No," Kinnia said. "I'll see the trainee healer like everyone else in the morning."

My heart leapt to my throat. Her voice sounded clear and even.

"I've never been anything but honest with you." Chrysophylax sounded desperately sincere. "Don't you trust me?"

Kinnia sighed. "Chry, it's not about trusting you."

I smiled. She didn't trust him.

"Your Cara doesn't want you," the dragonkin hissed. "They let you go. Even before this mess with the Council, did they bring you to the library?"

Kinnia's silence answered more clearly than any words could have. My face burned. Of course, we should have taken her to the library. Of course, she would love it here.

"They don't take care of you," Chrysophylax said.

I clenched my fist to smother an angry flame. I hadn't been trying to keep her in the dark. My old hatred of the place just colored my decisions. Right?

A book slammed shut.

"I don't need to be taken care of," Kinnia spat. "I'm not talking about this anymore. Bring it up a third time, and that'll be the end of whatever friendship we have."

I found a small hole in a dense shelf and peeked through.

"I just want you to be happy." Chrysophylax prowled the small, round space encircled by curved bookcases.

She looked small in an overstuffed armchair with him looming over her. She'd tucked her legs under her, and a closed book lay in her lap. Her curly hair brushed her cheekbones, longer than I'd ever seen it. A lumpy, double-eared head poked up from another chair to my left. Leonai, Chrysophylax's healer. I noted the entrance to the circle, just a few shelves back.

Kinnia rolled her eyes. "That's a lovely sentiment, if not a blatant lie."

Chrysophylax stopped pacing and looked at her. "I do want you to be happy. We can protect you from all that makes you unhappy. My family has lairs all through the wilds. We see your value. You're an uncut diamond."

She narrowed her eyes. "I don't need protection, and I certainly don't want to be hidden away in a dragon's lair."

"That's not what I meant." Chrysophylax grasped the arms of her chair and boxed her in when he leaned close. "I've spent weeks working with you. You're brilliant, brash, and creative. It's your ideas, not mine, that have merged our very thoughts. If we keep working together, I'm sure we can do even more." He leaned forward. "Killer, the feel of your hip beneath my fingers stokes my dragonfire and makes me sick with need. When I brush your bruises, I see red. I don't understand how your mates can do that to you. Let. Leo. Heal. You."

Kinnia leaned back. "My training is the same training you go through. I'd rather have bruises and be an equal than be hidden away in a cave."

My gut twisted. We didn't deserve her loyalty.

Chrysophylax snarled, "They should cherish you."

I hated agreeing with the dragonkin. Fire after fire sparked and died in my clenched fists.

Unlike me, Kinnia stayed calm. "Look, I get that I owe you," she said.

I grimaced. What deal had she made?

"My Cara thinks I'm an idiot. In their defense, I've been caught up in...my own matters. But I know someone on the Council owns you, and I know I wouldn't still have the freedoms I do if you reported everything." She shrugged. "So, thank you."

Chrysophylax straightened away from her, and I remembered how to breathe. An informal deal like that couldn't be enforced unless Kinnia thought it could.

"But I'm not joining your Cara." She crossed her arms. "The last thing I need is to end up in the same place I started. Thanks, but no thanks."

Chrysophylax latched onto her chair again. "I may work for the Council, but what I feel comes from me alone." The dragonkin leaned forward and angled his mouth toward hers.

Fire bloomed in my chest. I lunged into the entrance of the cul-de-sac of shelves and launched a compact fireball into the side of Chrysophylax's face. Heat and light burst, filling the air with acrid burnt skin and scales. I charged forward and slammed my fist into his face before the skin even cooled. He stumbled back into one of the bookshelves, and a pile of tomes tumbled onto his head, adding insult to injury.

I shook out my fist. How did Bash manage this? My knuckles would bruise.

Leonai's healing magic streaked toward his commander in a crawling line of plant life. I stepped back and faced Kinnia instead of watching my hard work healed in seconds. She stared at me, eyes wide and mouth open. A tumult of emotions flowed through her Cara, difficult to pick apart. Maybe a little pleased, maybe a little scared. Definitely angry. I placed myself between her and the dragonkin. I needed to address her anger, but the overgrown snake came first. If he came at me again, I'd hit him with something that would stymie the troll for at least a minute.

Chrysophylax emerged from the pile of books, blue and red scales spreading across his entire body. His face elongated as smoke curled out a mouth filled with wicked teeth. We stared at each other. I wouldn't be the first to blink. If not for the pile of kindling—uh, books—surrounding Kinnia, I would light him up again. I didn't want to ruin anything she might be fond of. He seemed to come to the same conclusion. Slowly, his scales receded as he returned to his more friendly shape.

"No matter." He smirked. "Zelimir is playing by the Councils' rules. Your actions here do nothing but demonstrate the instability in your Anam Cara. How can he be trusted with once-in-a-lifetime power if he can't even control his mates?"

I clenched my jaw. True or not, coming for Kinnia had been the right thing to do.

"No Cara is stable on day one." I pinned my gaze on the faded level-four symbol on his shoulder. "Some don't leave for years. That's the point of the Academy."

I took a step back with the realization, and the backs of my legs brushed Kinnia's in the chair. A shiver of pleasure rippled through my body, not just from touching my mate, but from the bond-deep feeling of rightness that coursed through me. All of us had forgotten that. We needed to worry less about what we looked like and more about who we were. Zelimir was wrong.

Chrysophylax slid to the side so he could see Kinnia. Despite Leon-ai's healing, a scorch mark remained on his perfect white hair. I smirked as I stepped into his path. I wouldn't let him any closer.

"I'll see you tomorrow, little killer." He scowled at me. "And my offer stands, no matter anything else. I want those bruises off your body. You can trust that's all I want. For now. Leo?"

The troll tipped his lumpy head in Kinnia's direction but stepped to his commander's side. The two stalked off. Once they rounded the corner, I turned to her. A heavy blanket of emotions lay over her Cara, and I didn't dare try to interpret them this time.

"Why did you block our connection?" I demanded.

That shouldn't have been my first question, but I couldn't stop myself. We'd worked together flawlessly to get her totem to the finish line during my trial. I'd made her laugh right before she connected us, fusing us closer than I knew two souls could get. I didn't just want to sleep with her, I wanted to wake up with her at my side every morning.

"Because you don't actually want me." She studied my face, as if she was as desperate as me to understand.

I opened my mouth to interrupt, and she put a hand up to stop me.

"I get what it feels like to lose someone. It sucks without this soul connection, so I can't imagine what your life was like without Light. But I'm not just a body to plug into an equation." She blew out a harsh breath. "You can say whatever you want, but when push comes to shove, you always side with them. It's me versus the rest of you. It has been from the beginning." Her posture wilted, and she crossed her arms over her chest. "I was just too blind to see it."

I reeled. Fire, if I thought I was lonely....

"That's not what I— I love Light, but I don't want you to be him." I took a step forward. "I'm glad you're not. I don't want a replacement, and I don't want to fix our Cara at your expense. You're as entertaining as you are infuriating, but I've enjoyed every minute you've been in my life."

Kinnia narrowed her eyes. "That's not how you've treated me."

I paced back and forth. "I shouldn't have followed Zelimir's orders. I knew he was wrong, but following orders is what Caras do." I closed the distance between us and knelt on the floor in front of her chair. "I told you we were four different fae, but I didn't put action where my words were. And I should have. I'm sorry."

Kinnia sat up straighter and pressed her lips into a line. Despite her posture, hope ghosted through our Cara. I clung to that. Maybe I had a chance.

"You don't like me, Teyr, you're just a good liar. Why bother?"

I blinked. "I'm not...." How could I convince her? All my clever words, my silver tongue, none of it counted for anything if she thought I was lying. "Where did this come from? What have I done?"

"Stop." Kinnia unfolded herself from the chair and stood. I realized she was trembling. "Just stop. I'm doing as asked. I'm keeping my distance. I'm...."

I only had one card to play. I stood, closed the distance between us, and slid my warm hand around the back of her neck. Our foreheads touched like they had in the mud.

Kinnia's lips quivered. I closed my eyes and opened my Cara to show her my regret and love. I could offer no better proof.

"I like you, Kinnia," I whispered. "More than like you." I cupped her cheek with my other hand and kissed her forehead. "I want a second chance, a do-over, where I'm not following anyone else's orders."

Her honey and leather scent enfolded me. This close, I had a clear view down her shirt. Blood rushed to my cock, but I couldn't deflect into sex.

I closed my Cara, took a step back, and held out my hand. "Walk with me?"

She looked me up and down, piecing me together like a puzzle she wasn't sure she wanted to solve. My reflection wavered in her big, blue eyes. Her confusion poured into me, but she couldn't tamp down the building fire of hope.

She dropped her gaze to my hand. "I guess I can let the ittles shelve my books."

Relief flooded me. I released a sharp breath, closing my Cara before the overwhelming feeling could reach her. She picked up a piece of crystal from the tall stack of books next to her. I raised an eyebrow as she tucked the crystal into a pouch on her waist.

"Quin made it for me," she said. "It lets me read books in languages I don't understand."

I hated the warmth that rose in her Cara when she spoke about Chrysophylax's second.

"Did you read all of these?" I eyed the pile, at least a dozen books high.

Kinnia shrugged. "Most of them."

She couldn't have read that whole stack. I'd trained with her just this afternoon. But she also had no reason to lie. A problem for later. I came here to win her back, not push her further away.

I gestured to the pouch at her waist. "Is it bad that I want to break your new toy because Quin made it?"

Kinnia rolled her eyes. "Yes. Why does he bother you so much?"

"Because we should've given it to you." I huffed. "I should've."

She smiled a brilliant smile I wanted to see over and over.

"You soaked up my words on our journey here. You ask questions like the world would disappear if you didn't get the answers fast enough." I sighed. "I should have known you'd love it here."

I grasped her hand. She rolled her eyes when I tucked it into the crook of my arm, but she didn't pull away.

"We were focused on getting out as quickly as possible," I said. "We forgot it was your first time. We should have let you do more. See more."

Kinnia squeezed my arm. I guided us into the network of halls with no destination in mind. Colorful cloth covered our path. An ittle floated slowly along, sucking up dust. Just having her near me poured cool water on a burn I didn't know I had. We walked in silence for a while. Confusion and frustration still swirled through her Cara. I'd made progress, but she still didn't quite believe me.

"I want you." I hated the words the moment I said them.

She eyed me. "Do you? Or do you want to be whole and important again?"

I grimaced. "I want you, Kinnia. I would rather nobody looked at me, nobody spoke of my exploits, nobody ever offered me a scrap of adulation again, if you're not at my side."

She stared at the floor, distrust flooding her Cara. Shame flushed my cheeks. Too big of a promise. She didn't want my pretty words. Maybe she knew I'd only shown her pretty emotions. I took a deep breath and opened my Cara properly. Frustration, weeks of loneliness, and the desperation from years of being the outcast poured out.

Kinnia looked up at me with wide blue eyes. "You've never shared anything but lust before tonight."

A goblin patrol rounded the corner. I pursed my lips and veered to the right, down a different hall.

"Emotions are honest." I shrugged, trying to seem casual instead of desperately vulnerable. "I know I sound dramatic, but I have big emotions that like to show themselves in big ways. This...makes it a little more real. Makes everything more real." I bumped her hip with mine and sent a healthy dose of lust her way.

Color rose to her cheeks. Fire, I could do fantastic things with that response. I grinned and released her from the crook of my arm to pull her to my side. She didn't exactly mold herself to me, but she didn't pull away. Progress.

"I'm not good at this. I've not really courted anyone before, as Zel would say."

Kinnia slowed. "You're courting me?"

Sex would be so much easier than this. Why couldn't Zel have just gone for my orgy idea?

"I would like to be." I glanced at her, hoping for a smile or a blush or anything encouraging.

She refused to meet my eye. "I'm not the sort of person people court. We can be friends. I enjoy our friendship."

I didn't hide my hurt and disappointment, nor the hint of playfulness that her challenge sparked in me. "I am happy to be your first."

She grimaced, her gaze still on the ground.

I needed to break her out of this sulk. I traced up her side to her armpit and tickled. Kinnia jerked away with a laugh. I chased her until I had her backed against the wall. Her gaze looked open, honest. Like she was actually trying to hear me for the first time.

"I want *you*." I placed a hand on her hip and tried to force my emotions stronger through the Cara. "And by the time I'm between your legs, you'll believe me."

40

BASH

I LET MY ARMS HANG LOOSELY AT MY SIDES, TAKING DEEP breaths as I faced Councilor Drax's golden door. In another life, I'd fought under General Drax's command, guarded his sleeping body, and drank him under the table. But when I showed up here and found him a Councilor overseeing my Cara's development, the rules had to change. We'd once shared a drink and reminisced about the old days. Since then, we'd been nothing but mentor and mentee. I'd never approached his home. And now, I knew he and Dee sat on the other side of that door.

My heart thrummed as if preparing for battle. I hadn't told Zelimir where I was going, but he could figure that out in an instant. After Teyr floated back into the suite, flush with Kinnia's praises, I could no longer contain myself. I didn't know why I was here, what I expected, but I knew I couldn't be without her any longer.

My dragon bellowed that she belonged to us.

Teyr had argued she belonged to no one and, despite my dragon, I had to agree. My heart broke every time she achieved something new in training and, under our commander's watchful eye, we all turned away. I felt her aching loneliness, her frustration, her shame. And I missed her. Perhaps things could be that simple if I let them.

In the months and years after I left the church in flames, an emptiness had driven me to destruction. Drink and drugs and whatever pain I could lay hands upon filled my days and nights. Without her, that emptiness yawned before me once more, deep enough that no training or meditation could pull me free.

I took a final calming breath and knocked. Councilor Drax opened the door. I snapped to attention out of instinct.

He inclined his head, unsurprised to see me. "At ease."

I relaxed slightly. "I—"

He shook his head but stepped out of the doorway. "She wasn't expecting visitors, so she's in the bath." He grimaced. "I'd forgotten how long women take in there. I only have the one."

I stepped inside at his unspoken invitation. I would wait however long I needed to. A fire crackled merrily in a hearth bookended by two chairs. No windows, but a few doors leading deeper into the apartment. My only way out was the door I entered from. Out of courtesy, I had brought no weapon, but the fireplace pokers would do in a pinch.

Councilor Drax paused, then twisted his wrist and one of the chairs shimmered faintly pink before stretching into a three-seat couch with round, golden pillows at either end. I nodded gratefully and sat.

"Women love a throw pillow." The Councilor shrugged.

"Does Dee?" The question spilled from my mouth before I could catch them back.

I had been trying to give Dee her space, to keep from using my newfound power to pry too deeply into whatever secrets she might be keeping now, but I ached for whatever scrap of information I could glean.

Councilor Drax took the chair and studied me. "In truth, I don't know. Stereotypes never get us quite as far as we hope, it seems. No human or fae is quite like any other."

I nodded as two cherrystone mugs floated out of what looked like the kitchen on another current of pink magic.

My mates and I had never truly thought with the same mind, but our differences felt starker than ever. Shade saw her in wolf form only, as though that diminished the slight. Teyr went about proudly, defending her from my commander's less generous comments, not that Zelimir spoke about her often. He seemed to be disappearing into command, handing down orders but helpless to see them followed. I couldn't remember how we'd worked together for seventy-five years.

One of the mugs settled on my palm, shining with the soft orange glow of melony, a drink Councilor Drax and I had long shared. He took a sip, and I discovered having Dee in his life brought out his sentimental side. He spoke softly of his wife and daughter, names he'd only murmured in the depths of drink during the war. Here, in his home, they seemed to bring him peace.

I tried to listen, but even with our blocked bridge, I could feel Dee directly through the wall in front of me. My dragon twisted happy circles, and my blood heated to think of her naked in that bath. I sipped the melony, letting the sweet herbs and fruits hit my tongue and tangle with my magic, but that only encouraged my dragon's lustful thoughts.

Finally, she emerged, wearing the leggings we'd bought her in Stoneheim, one of my tunics that I'd packed from her drawers with shaking hands, and a crystal necklace I hadn't seen her without since the fight. I choked on a sip and fought for breath as I struggled to keep enough blood in my brain to have the conversation I knew we needed.

"Ah." Councilor Drax set his cup on the small table to his left and gestured to the couch. "Bash came to see you, but I didn't want you rushed, so we've been talking. Please, join us."

She looked at me with a carefully neutral expression. Fury poured out of her Cara.

My dragon purred, encouraging me to take her in my arms. I settled for moving neither closer to the middle nor farther away. She sat slowly, so close her hip brushed mine. The heat of the bath radiated off her skin. Water dripped off her hair and rolled down my arm. I took a steadying breath. Grabbing her and crushing her into the couch with a kiss wouldn't get me any answers.

She gestured to my glass. "Your drink is glowing."

I grunted and passed her the cup. The ribbons of color on the surface swirled and twisted, reflecting in her eyes. She took a sip from a different part of the mug than where my lips had been and savored it.

Drax leaned forward. "Do you feel anything?"

Dee shrugged. "Relaxed?"

He leaned back. "The drink's called melony. It's a concoction of liquor, fruits, and liquid magic. But the magic only mixes with other magic."

Dee scrunched up her nose and passed the drink back to me. "Right."

I took a slow sip, pressing my lips to where hers had been. The liquor had never tasted sweeter.

"How was your tutoring session with Councilor Xerxes?" Councilor Drax asked.

Her hip brushed mine, and she leaned away. I fought my dragon not to chase the contact. I needed to move at her pace.

"Um." Dee looked at me, then away. "Good. I didn't realize this valley used to be a giant volcano, or that it became center of magic after the volcano dried up. Though I should have guessed that because the Councils are here." She frowned. "Honestly, Councilor Xerxes seemed more interested in Shade than my geography lesson."

Drax nodded and took another sip.

Dee glanced at me out of the corner of her eye. Suddenly, I felt out of place. I'd interrupted some ritual of theirs. Dee had a life without us, perhaps even a happy one. I should have listened to my commander and stayed in the suite, no matter what my emotions urged me to do.

I braced to stand. Dee and Councilor Drax turned to look at me as one. A whip of hurt lashed through Dee's Cara. Councilor Drax pinned me with his eyes, daring me to do something to bring that unhappy look to her face once more. Between my general and my commander, I had no good choices. Selfishly, I chose the one my heart preferred and settled back on the couch.

"Bash was just telling me about your journey here," Councilor Drax said. "How long did it take you to understand your mates' *pulses*?"

His lie covered the awkward silence I created and made Dee relax a little.

She blew out a breath. "I still don't, really. I've got vague ideas, but I'm just not compatible."

I flinched. "Until you are."

She nodded but kept her gaze on Councilor Drax. "I've been doing a lot of reading." She tucked the overlong hem of the tunic into her waistband. "And my experimentation with Chry is limited, but I'm starting to see patterns."

I growled. "You shouldn't have anything to do with Chrysophylax."

She scowled. "Then you shouldn't have shut me out."

I twisted to face her, anger rising in my own chest. "You. Blocked. Me."

You told Zelimir about me!" Dee leaned into my face. "You took away the only thing I had left to myself."

I gritted my teeth against the fire in my veins. "I would still be keeping it now, but it was destroying us. Destroying me. Zelimir deserved to know, and you should have been the one to tell him." I raked my gaze over Dee, taking in the set of her shoulders, the swell of her breasts, and the heat in her gaze.

My dragon bellowed. It took all my willpower to keep my arms at my sides.

Dee balled her fists so tight they shook. "You told me I was a problem."

"Our commander told you that." I leaned forward, my nose a scant inch from hers. "And he's right."

Dee's jaw dropped, her plump, kissable lower lip close enough to lick. "How dare—"

I cut off her words with my mouth. I lacked Zelimir's fluency to explain myself, but all his words had gotten us here. I crushed her lips with mine and the understanding that we were all problems, and that the Cara was about finding the way our problems fit together. I thrust my tongue in her mouth and painted the knowledge that she was no harder to deal with than Teyr in the beginning, no weaker at training than the half-starved Light and Shade. I twisted and pressed her against the couch, grinding into her that no matter what she was, I wanted her exactly as she was.

My Cara fell open, hammering lust, pain, regret, and love into my mate. I wound my fingers into her curls. My thoughts became cloudy as blood rushed below my waist, and my dragon took control.

As if she had a dragon of her own, Dee poured her anger and frustration into our kiss. She fought me with every meeting of our lips, which only made me want her more. I claimed her mouth like I would never get the chance to again. If Zelimir got his way, I wouldn't.

The thought drove me. I leaned over her, one arm braced on the couch cushion beside her, and ran my free hand under her shirt. I skimmed the silky skin of her stomach up to one of her perfect, unbound breasts. Her nipple pebbled instantly, and I rolled it between two fingers. In return, she slid her fingers into my pants, digging her nails into my ass. My cock throbbed. I pressed it into her thigh, desperate for friction.

Dee hissed and raked her fingers up my back, anger and need filling our Cara. I pinched her nipple harder and flattened my weight against her. She moaned. I sank my teeth into the tender flesh of her neck, licking and sucking. She arched into me, pressing her sex against my thigh hard enough that I was sure I could feel her wetness. I groaned.

Ice-cold liquid splashed down on me from above, soaking my tunic. I yelped and jumped from the couch while pulling off my shirt. I couldn't let a mystery liquid remain against my skin. I spun and dropped into a fighting stance while looking for the fireplace poker. The only other fae in the room remained Councilor Drax. My old general raised a single eyebrow as the pink of his magic disappeared from the air.

"I feel the Council may have been misinformed," Councilor Drax said mildly. "Is this *energy* how you were able to amplify Teyr and Bash?"

I turned back to Dee, who now sat upright. She nodded. Through our Cara, I could tell her need raged out of control, dwarfing even her anger. She looked at me and caught me in the blaze of her lust once more. Her gaze burned down my chest, taking in every glistening muscle. She reached for my pants, where my erection proudly denied the cooling powers of water, and bit her lip.

"Kinnia," Councilor Drax said.

She pulled her gaze from me. I smirked.

"I...think so?" She shrugged. "So far, I've only let Chry work magic through me. I haven't tried to combine it or take control of it."

My dragon and I snarled as one. I shook my head. Dee did what anyone would have done. She used the tools she had to learn more about herself. It was our fault those tools included that lying, scheming—

I stepped toward the fire, shook out my wet tunic, and spread it over the grate to calm myself. After a few deep breaths, I was able to cross the room back to her, scoop up my glass of melony, and sit.

I made sure our hips touched. She didn't move away.

Councilor Drax gestured for her to continue.

"Right, um." Dee crossed her legs.

My cock ached, but more than that, I needed her in my arms. I needed to whisper my apologies into her ear, my promises to do better. Councilor Drax shot me a quelling look. I sipped my melony. All I could do was force the sentiments through our Cara, trying to use the strength of my emotion to burn through the block she placed between us.

"I was trying to understand my *energy*," Dee said. "I guess the next step would be seeing if one of my mates can work magic through me the same way, and if it reacts differently to my *energy*. Which, just to reiterate, hasn't reacted to Chr—"

I growled.

"—anyone else's," she finished.

Drax nodded. "You should test that. I'll pick a morning, have Zelimir come in as your partner instead of Chrysophylax."

I nodded as my dragon ground my teeth together. She and Zelimir needed to spend more time together. My old general stared into his drink, deep in thought, and Dee shifted next to me. I couldn't wait any longer.

I cleared my throat. "I will talk with my mate privately."

He laughed, the sound dusty but honest. "You will not."

Dee cupped my face and turned my face to her. "We can trust Drax with whatever you have to say."

I took a deep breath and stared into her eyes. She seemed determined, the embers of her anger banked but not gone. It seemed privacy would be hard to come by.

"I'm sorry." I laid my hand over hers on my face. "It should have been your secret to tell. But it was driving us apart."

Tears welled in her eyes. "I trusted you."

That emptiness yawned, beckoning me into the darkness. I couldn't defend myself. I had taken something more precious than I knew. Dee pulled her hand away to swipe the tears off her face and turned back to Councilor Drax, but I couldn't give up so quickly.

I grabbed her arm. She froze.

"I can't take back what I've done," I murmured, "but I never wanted to hurt you. I will never do something like this again. I'll never go against your wishes."

Dee nodded, but she didn't fall back into my arms. Her gaze remained guarded.

She was slipping away from me, and I didn't know how to stop her. "What can I do?"

She furrowed her eyebrows. "Honestly, I don't know. Rebuilding trust is gonna be hard." She sighed. "But let's start small. No more rules. No more keeping things from me. No more staying away to protect me." She crossed her arms. The action made her look suddenly small and very tired. "It's not working."

I nodded. My dragon searched for an opening to kiss her again, but she remained closed off. A glimmer of bright pink magic sparkled in my peripheral vision, reminding me that even if I did see an opening, Councilor Drax would put an end to it. I burned the bruise I'd left on her neck into my memory, then slumped back against the couch. I'd lost Dee's trust, but she still wanted me. I could fix this.

"I'm getting lost in you," Dee said. "Not just you, in the Cara. Time after time, it's me against the four of you. That can't keep happening."

I inched closer. "It won't."

"Not on my couch." Councilor Drax raised his hands, water half-summoned.

I leaned back and rubbed my eye with my palm, then ran my hand over my still-damp head. The spark of hope Teyr lit in my heart bloomed into a flame. Kinnia still wanted us, and she now knew that Teyr and I, at least, still wanted her. With a little work, we could still be an Anam Cara.

41

SHADE

The door to our suite rolled a few feet and ground to a halt. I jumped. The three fat grubs I'd been transferring life between collapsed into piles of dust, covering the room in a gray haze.

"Damn it, Shade," Teyr said between sneezes.

I grinned. Bash grinned back as he stepped through the door and opened his Cara to me. Joy, love, and a healthy dose of lust hit me before he shut me out and turned his attention to closing the door.

He'd been out with my Kitty. I started to stand, and a searing spike out pain lanced out from my tailbone. I splayed my legs and leaned forward to relieve the pressure. My wolf would do better, but I had to hear from Bash.

Teyr and I looked to Zelimir, who shook grub-dust off the book he'd been reading. After a long moment of quiet, he asked, "How is she?"

"In good spirts." Bash smiled softly. "We spent an hour in the archery yard, and she put most of Bodmier's magical bows to shame with that carbon-fiber of hers."

Zelimir grunted. Teyr peered at our pack leader, then shook his head. Bash and Teyr had been spending time with my Kitty under the guise of training for a week now. Always more time than Zelimir allowed, and sometimes, with Drax's help, more than the Council allowed. They didn't lie about their behavior, but nobody talked about it.

Sour tension filled the room, and I realized my stretch wasn't helping like usual. I had seen my Kitty first, but only as my wolf. I hadn't worn this face in front of her since that awful day. I sucked in a sharp breath as another stab of agony brought sweat to my brow.

My brother's bone hung against my shirt, away from my skin. I clasped it for his strength. I'd promised him I would be different this time. That I would be as brave as him and take life by the reins. Instead, I crumbled at the first hurdle.

Bash settled onto his bed with that soft smile on his face, and despite the pain, I yearned. Life had been simple as my wolf, but rarely had I been truly happy. That, I only remembered as a fae.

Voices crowded my brain. I would make the same mistakes again. I was a selfish necromancer, grasping for power despite the effect on those around me. Even now, I'd coated our room in dust to amuse myself. When I grabbed power next, I didn't know who would be on the other end of the disaster. It might be my Kitty. My breathing sped to gasps, each introducing a new wave of pain. Four ittles popped into the room and began sucking up the shambles of my necromancy.

Teyr laughed at something. Zelimir grunted as he rose from his couch. Two ittles bounced off each other with a soft *hiss*. My head seared to match the pain in my back. Too busy, too noisy. Only Light knew how to ask for help. I collapsed into myself. I felt a presence on my mind and looked up. Bash stared down at me.

Go to her, he said in my mind.

My hesitation dropped away. I called to my power, and the song swelled in my ears. I hadn't summoned a portal since before—

The old motions came easily to my hands, and a shimmering blue disk expanded in front of me. Elation filled my chest. The portal wobbled as I lost clarity. Brave. I had to be brave. The spell flowed through my head like a scroll written on water.

"Shade, don't." Zelimir took a step toward me.

I wasn't a wolf anymore. I couldn't be hauled around by the scruff of my neck. And I had to make things right with my Kitty, even if it meant she'd never speak to me again.

The portal stabilized, and I tumbled into it. The gateway through the space between sucked the heat from my skin, easing my pain for a moment. It spit me into a dimly lit hall in front of a golden door, but I was out of practice. I stumbled backward and landed hard. White-hot pain scorched up my spine. My vision went black. A vicious howl tore out of my mouth.

"Shade!" my Kitty called.

She sounded distant between my gasping breaths. In moments, she cupped warm hand around my face.

"Tail," I gasped, finally saying the word I'd been too frightened to use. "Help. Roll over."

"I don't know what to do." She sounded frightened.

I frightened her.

"My bed is right here," she said. "Can I help you lie there instead?"

I nodded. "Pressure, need release. Help."

My vision cleared. Her face swam into view. Her eyebrows knitted in concern, and her mouth flattened into a panicked slash, but she looked so beautiful. She rolled me over. I gasped as the pain abated a sliver. She wound her arms under my chest and hauled me up onto the bed.

"So strong," I groaned. "Don't deserve you. Didn't—"

"Shh." She stroked the back of my head. "I'll go get Drax."

Panic cracked through the pain. I was turning into something new. I didn't like the looks, didn't like the whispers. I wanted privacy until I understood.

"No." I turned my head to the side and met her gaze with all the blurry focus I could muster. "No Drax. No healers. Just you." Tears streaked down my face. "My fault."

My Kitty bit her lip and caressed my face. "It doesn't matter whose fault it is." She swallowed. "If you're in pain, you need help."

I reached out and gripped whatever part of her I could reach. "Your help. Only you. Please."

Uncertainty filled my Kitty's Cara, but she nodded. "Tell me what to do."

I guided the hand on my face down the line of my back. The pain remained brilliant, but her touch eased a deeper agony. "Pants."

My Kitty snorted. "If you were Teyr, I'd smack you."

I groaned as a throb of pain took me. I didn't feel my pants move, but she gasped sharply, and I knew she'd seen it.

"I need towels, bandages. None of my daggers are sterile," she mumbled.

"Fae healing," I hissed. "Just—quickly."

I must have impressed my need finally. She yanked a dagger out of its sheath on the nearby table and shoved the leather covering between my teeth.

She braced a knee higher on my back, mumbled an apology to my pained scream, and said, "On three."

Vaguely, half-mad with pain, I wrapped a hand around her calf for the comfort of touching her.

"Three."

I screamed. Something tore in my throat, my back. My vision went black.

Some time passed, but I had no sense of how much. I slowly opened my eyes. Pain radiated along my spine, but softer, more bruise-like. A familiar-unfamiliar weight rested against the backs of my legs. I curled my tail experimentally.

She tugged it back into place. "I'm still cleaning the fluid off, relax." She giggled. "It matches your ears."

I relaxed as the sensation on my tail slowly filtered into my awareness. Warm hands and a wet cloth stroked its length. I barely resisted the impulse to lean into the pressure like I would have as a wolf.

For all my hesitation, my weeks of quiet suffering, the tail felt like it had always been there. It belonged, made sense. I was more myself now than I had been as wolf or divar.

Light's bone pressed into my chest. More myself than I had been since he died.

"You should have gone to a healer," she said quietly. "I could have hurt you."

I smiled into the bedclothes. "I trust you, my Kitty."

She sighed, and I sensed the beginning of a disagreement, so I opened my Cara to her for the first time since I'd awoken to the ache in my spine. That trust flowed into her, along with love and relief and the shame of having kept such a silly secret for so long.

My Kitty gasped. "You're not cutting me off anymore?"

"My tail was very painful." I scooted to feel her folded knees against my side. I craved her presence, but the wobble in my movements told me I couldn't sit up yet. "I didn't want you to feel the pain."

"Why—?" She left the end of the sentence for me to fill in.

With the pain still echoing, I chose the cowardly question to answer. "Fae don't change clan. I think I stayed a wolf too long." I huffed. "Xerxes kept prodding me about the ears. The tail would only spur him on." I shifted my gaze to the mattress to avoid her eyes. "Everybody here looks at me with pity. I didn't want more reasons for them to look."

"Well, I like the tail," she said. "It suits you."

I wriggled in her grip, unable to contain the euphoria of hearing my thoughts in her words. She grabbed my hip to steady me, and I pressed into the contact.

Brave, I had to be brave. "Do you like me as a fae?"

"Honestly…" she said slowly.

I froze. My heart sank.

"I don't know you that well as a fae," she said. "But I want to. I want to love you as both."

I twisted to look at her. I had to see her face as she said she loved me, even just as a wolf. She stared at my tail, her brow furrowed in thought. Thoughtfulness flowed through her Cara on an ebbing current of worry. I would take her in my arms and kiss her if I could trust my body to support me.

My Kitty met my gaze with hard eyes. "But you blocked me and kept me at arm's length."

I flinched. "I'm sorry. I was protecting you from the pain and following my pack."

She shook her head. "That's not good enough. You keep boxing me—boxing everyone—out. You've been injured for weeks, and you didn't tell anyone. You didn't have to follow your pack."

I took a deep breath. When Teyr came back from his first contact with her, he'd gushed a play-by-play. Neither my pack leader nor Bash had cared to listen, but I stored every word. She was hurt. She needed to feel like an equal who got listened to.

"Being a wolf made it easy to ignore things, to pack them up in a box, like you say, and shove them to the back of my mind." I sorted through half-remembered *pulses* in years gone by that slowly became less frequent. "But...I wasn't a good packmate as a wolf. I need to remember how to be fae again, and how to be packmate."

She removed her hands from my tail. "You're all clean, whenever you're ready to get up." She sighed. "And I get that, but you chose Zelimir over me."

The pain had subsided to a dull ebb, so I pulled up my pants and rolled over to put my head in her lap. She didn't reach for me like usual.

"Has anyone told you how my brother died?" I fingered his bone under my shirt.

She shrugged. "In battle."

"I channeled my magic through him," I said simply. "I didn't mean to, but the power needed a live conduit, and I didn't think of anything more than how spectacular my work would be. I follow my pack leader now because I didn't then." I swallowed. "I was scared I would hurt you like I did Light." I pulled the bone out. "This is all I have left of him."

His face filled my memory, the peace that peeked through his pain in that last moment. I had never been able to understand it. In a moment of agonizing clarity, as I begged the same from my Kitty, I realized he had forgiven me.

Tears gathered in my eyes, and I buried my face in my Kitty's tunic. "I'm sorry," I sobbed. "I only didn't want to hurt you."

She wound her fingers through my hair, and it felt like a future I could imagine without Light, the only one I'd ever wanted. She let me cry for a while, then pressed a kiss to my forehead.

"I think you have to learn how to trust yourself," she said. "Zelimir told me that, and I didn't want to listen to him. Maybe we can learn trust together."

I twisted to look at her. Her eyes gleamed with unshed tears.

"But you are perfect. I trust you with everything I am. How could you not trust yourself?" I asked.

She laughed bitterly and looked away. "I've got plenty of reasons."

I cupped her face and forced her to look at me. "Please tell me. You let me talk to you. If we are to be equals, you must talk to me as well."

She grimaced. "You know I spent time on Earth."

I nuzzled into her lap.

"When I was there—when we were there—Tech came and—" She swallowed. "Bash said it wasn't my fault." My Kitty tried to pull away.

I put my hand over hers in my hair.

She sighed. "I went to Earth with the only people in the world I loved, convinced we would find held a better life. And Tech slaughtered them." Her bottom lip trembled, and she looked at her hands. "I didn't do anything. Alex told me to. I had my *energy* then, but I sat and watched them die." She sobbed. "And then I ran. I fucking ran. I don't even know what happened to their bodies."

I sat up and curled my arms around her so her tears could fall like mine had. I'd spent so much time worrying about my darkness, my unpredictability, that I would scare her away. Never had I considered that my Kitty could be so much like me, two souls healing from the past as we looked toward the future.

"Bash was right," I said as her tears abated. "And I would like to learn to trust myself as much as I trust you, if you would do the same."

My Kitty trembled. I held her close, letting our sorrow mingle in our Cara. Eventually, she pulled away and dried her tears.

Our night started slipping away, but I wasn't ready for it to end. "I've got something to show you, if you don't mind a walk."

"A walk would be nice." My Kitty bit her lip and petted my tail. "Do you need to go potty?"

I blinked at her. "No. Why would you ask that?"

"Because…you…." She threw her head back and laughed. "We've got to work on your sense of humor too."

I nodded. Whatever my Kitty wanted.

My second portal came easier than the first. Her eyes widened, and she whooped as she stepped into it. When I arrived after her at the edge of the archery yard, she rubbed the chill off her arms.

"How does that work?" she asked. "It's colder than the one that takes us to the colosseum."

"I'm a necromancer." I grinned. "Do you really want to know?"

Her eyes went wide in the moonlight. I caught her hand in mine and guided her through the grounds until we came to Trollies Garden.

"This was Light's favorite spot," I said as we stepped under the moonlit canopy.

Her eyes filled with wonder. We laid down in the grass together, still hand in hand.

"Can you tell me more about him?" she asked quietly.

I hesitated. Memories of Light hurt, no matter how good. But I needed to be brave. Just like my Kitty did.

I smiled. "Only if you tell me about your friends."

42

———

KINNIA

I PUSHED MY SWEATY HAIR OUT OF MY EYES BEFORE LACING my fingers with Bash's as we headed into the cafeteria after a late morning warm-up. Despite Council orders, Drax recently declared it was a waste of his time to clean up after me every meal and banned me from his apartment for breakfast and lunch. We'd still eat dinner together, of course. I'd squealed and kissed him on the cheek, which made him blush a charming violet.

Teyr and Shade waved from a table along the wall as we entered. My heart sank. Still no Zelimir. No. I would not be disappointed. I would not want to see someone who betrayed me, and who clearly didn't want to see me either.

"Pick an emotion," Teyr grumbled as I sat down.

I stuck my tongue out at him. Shade tangled his ankle with mine under the table. My smile made my cheeks ache.

"I'll take content," Bash said.

I bit my cheek. I still hadn't gotten used to the way they talked about emotions like they were as legible as facial expressions.

Teyr looked at the newest bruise on my neck, the reason our exercises ended so late. "That better be Bash's work."

I sighed and rested my chin on my hands. "It was Drax. He's such a gentle lover."

Teyr sprayed a sip of coffee all over the table. Shade froze in horror. I laughed before picking up a napkin and dabbing at my coffee-covered arms.

"Yes, it's from Bash." I tossed the napkin at Teyr. "I couldn't tell if it was for me or Chry, though."

"Both." Bash wrapped his sweaty arm around me and pulled me in for a long kiss. As much as I wanted to enjoy his touch, the gazes of our fellow trainees weighed on me. We were flaunting Zelimir's rules, the Councils' rules. Guilt panged in my gut.

"It's too early for this," Teyr grumbled.

We broke apart. Shade nodded in agreement and took a sip of his coffee. I rolled my eyes.

"I need help with something." I looked at my three mates. "Drax said I should tell Zelimir to take Chry's time with me this morning, but he's not here, so...."

Shade leaned forward. "Whatever you need."

Bash grunted agreement. Teyr sipped his coffee. My heart soared, but I permitted myself a small smile.

We finished breakfast, and Shade shifted into his wolf so he could pad at my feet. Confidence I hadn't felt since I entered the wilds filled my gait as I led my mates through the halls of the Academy.

Shade shoved past us when we reached the door to Drax's apartments. Nose to the floor, he sniffed the new environment with single-minded focus. I tugged on my necklace with a smile. He wouldn't find much. I loved Drax, but his social life left much to be desired.

"I said Zelimir would be your partner this morning. Not your entire Cara, less the only person I asked for," Drax grumbled from his favorite armchair by the fireplace.

"Zelimir and I don't have a bridge." I bit my lip. "And we haven't patched things up yet."

Drax peered at me. "Zelimir is your commander. You understand that, yes?"

I crossed my arms. "Well, my commander's too stubborn, and I have shit to do."

Drax rubbed his chin. I gave him my best puppy dog eyes.

He sighed. "You remind me too much of my daughter. Do what you will."

I nodded and plopped down on the worn area rug, motioning for Bash and Teyr to join me. We sat in a loose circle, and I took a deep breath.

Farquin's words about my *energy* mixed with Chry's recent lessons on mental control. I should've started experimenting long ago. With my mates at my side, I could do it safely.

Shade sat on the floor at Drax's side. Everyone in the room looked at me. Nerves fluttered in my stomach. I wasn't used to performing for an audience.

"Get rid of your block." Bash crossed his legs and rested his hands on his knees as if meditating.

Teyr leaned toward me.

I shook my head. "I want to try with them up first."

Teyr grabbed one of my hands with both his own. "You should try with me. I have no mental powers. Smaller focus."

Bash scowled at Teyr but gave us a begrudging nod and moved to the other chair. I scooted so Teyr and I faced each other, so close our knees brushed with every twitch. Leaning forward, I placed my fingers on his temples.

Teyr slid his gaze down my neck to my cleavage. "This is an amazing view."

I sighed. "I'm sure you've seen better."

"No, I don't think better exists for me anymore." Instead of flashing me one of his charming grins, he met my eyes and smiled shyly.

My heart leapt to my throat. I didn't want to think about what that meant. I squeezed my eyes shut and pushed my consciousness through the block. I hesitated. My mates should be working through me, but only I could navigate the bridges anymore.

"You've got this, baby," Teyr murmured. "We're just as big a part of you as you are of us." He trailed his hands up my thighs. "We tell young embers to pull their fire back into themselves. Try it."

I blew out a breath. I wasn't fae. I couldn't control magic. Teyr needed to take over.

I bristled at my own thought. No, that was the point of the block, of every choice I'd made since Zelimir pulled me off his lap in the baths. My life. My future.

My nerves settled. I inhaled slowly and reached for Teyr's magic. Like I thought, my fingers slid through his fire without even feeling the heat of the flames. I screwed up my face and tried to channel the feeling that had overtaken me at the trial. The surety, the focus. I pushed my *energy* into Teyr's heat. It warmed me, and I smiled. Carefully, I pulled that heat back into myself. Orange light bloomed beyond my closed eyelids, and my palm warmed. Every inch of me tingled with joy.

I could use magic!

The air pressure dropped. Shade barked. I snapped my eyes open to find a small, silver rift above the fireplace. I clenched my hand, destroying the flame, as fear flooded me. Bash lunged forward, Teyr on his heels. Even a rift so small took two to close.

This didn't make any sense. I didn't open rifts. I couldn't.

Bash and Teyr lined up their pinky fingers, their faces scrunched in concentration as they synchronized their movements. Goose bumps rose on my arms. The rift popped out of existence. In the quiet, everyone turned to me. Their faces all bore one message.

I opened rifts. My *energy* opened rifts. All along, back to that first rift my family and I found impossibly quick, it had been me. Bile crawled up my throat.

What was I?

"That was unexpected." Drax's voice sounded almost too calm.

Bash sat down on my left. "Breath, Dee."

Shade whined and barreled into my lap. He lapped at my face, and the shock slowly faded. Teyr lowered himself onto the carpet to my right, crushing me into Bash. The hard planes of their bodies pressed into me, supporting me, letting me know that whatever happened, everything would be okay.

"Don't focus on what you just saw." Teyr rubbed my thigh.

I finally pulled my gaze away from where the rift had hung.

"I don't open rifts," I whispered.

Teyr rubbed my back.

I forced myself to breathe and think. "My *energy* doesn't open rifts on its own. But when it interacts with magic...." I shook my head. "Chry used magic through me, and nothing happened, but he couldn't even feel my *energy*."

Drax frowned. "When was the first time you amplified your mates' magic?"

"Bash's trial." I swallowed. The first time a rift opened in the colosseum.

He narrowed his eyes. "Are you certain?"

I nodded. "Before that, every time I touched magic with my *energy*, they didn't mix. No rifts appeared. Or, not like that, anyway."

"Interesting." Drax tapped a deep purple finger against his lips. "But rifts chased you along the route here...." Anger darkened his brow, and the air around him crackled with power.

If rifts chased me here, and I didn't open them, that meant *someone else* had opened them. At the back of my mind, a voice nagged that Farquin seemed familiar.

Shade barked and thumped his tail against the floor. I sank my fingers into his fur, scratching behind his ears, and he calmed.

Drax's gaze returned to normal. "Lectures and training with your mates. We can discuss the implications of this later."

Teyr stood, offering me a hand. I clasped his fingers, and he pulled me to my feet. Though he smiled, the emotion didn't reach his eyes.

"Kinnia." Drax's voice caught my attention. "Zelimir was raised in a world of impossible standards. He's a titan prince, pulled from his duties and thrown into the politics of the Councils. He is a leader in a system his father wants to destroy. On top of that, he's a commander balancing what could well be the most powerful Cara the wilds have ever seen. It's no excuse, but it's a pretty good reason."

I clenched my fist. "And I spawned the rift that killed my only family, trapping me on Earth for five years." Emotions vibrated through my body, too strong to notice anyone's reaction to my bald confession. "I don't even know what I am. How many fae died to Tech in the colosseum after I tore an opening between our worlds?" I pulled away from Teyr. "I don't want to know. I shouldn't even be here. Zelimir's right to keep me at arm's length. There's something fundamentally wrong with me. There always has been."

Bash and Teyr reached for me. Shade's blue-black magic swirled around his wolf. It was all too much. I shoved *energy* into my legs and rushed across the room, then turned to pin my mates with a hard look. They froze.

"I'm sorry Zelimir has so much to deal with, I really am, but the entire point of the Cara is to not bear your burdens alone. Zelimir's said some version of that to me over and over, yet what's he doing right now?" I gestured to us. "Shit if I know, but whatever it is, he's alone." I swung my gaze to Drax. "And if he can't see his hypocrisy, then nothing I do will change it." I turned. "I need some space. Don't come after me."

$$43$$

ZELIMIR

The door of our suite shattered into green splinters. I stood, grabbing the hilt of my two-hander. A cloud of Shade's blue-black necromancy bloomed in the doorway. I dismissed the blade as the necromancer stepped through, flanked by Bash and Teyr. Agitated sparks bounced around the ember, and my second's gaze looked hard.

Shade met my eyes and leapt. I could only watch as he slammed his fist into my cheek with all the force of a gentle slap. The crunch of his hand and pain in his Cara told a different story. Three broken bones, if I had to guess. Shade swore and jumped back, clasping his hand to his chest. Rage billowed through our Cara.

"She thinks there is something wrong with her." The fur on his ears and tail stood on end. "I am challenging you for command of the Cara!"

I took a deep breath. I'd been marshaling my arguments in their absence. Their all-too-frequent absence. At least Shade had challenged me. The necromancer was most likely to stand alone.

"I reject your challenge. And there *is* something wrong. Several somethings, in fact, but she must trust us before we can help her."

Shade flung his arms wide. "She trusts *us* now." He winced and cradled his hand back to his chest.

"She doesn't. It's too soon. We should be trying to help her, not coddle her." I gestured to the books and papers covering the table. "In over a month of reading, I haven't found even a passing reference to fae with magic like hers. I've moved onto human tomes, but I haven't found any mention of a creature called 'sister', either."

"Sister?" Bash said. "What are you talking about?"

"When we followed her to Earth, and the Tech called for sister."

They all stared blankly at me, then recognition dawned on Bash's face. "I'd forgotten that."

"Well, I didn't," I shot back.

"Fire, you'll do anything to avoid her," Teyr snarled.

Frustration ripped through me, but I forced calm. "We need to know who she is to help her be herself,"

Bash stepped to Shade's side. His arms hung loosely, no sign of imminent violence, but I knew the battle-sharp look on his face. "No, we don't need to know who she is."

I narrowed my eyes. "How else can we possibly help?"

Teyr joined the two of them with flames licking up his fingers. "I don't think you can reject a challenge out of hand like that."

The bottom fell out of my stomach. They were aligned against me. I searched along Kinnia's Cara to find a well of anger and confusion in the northernmost training yard. She wasn't here, but she certainly wasn't happy. My world tilted on its axis. For the first time in seventy-five years, I stood well and truly alone.

"A challenge won't solve anything. Kinnia needs a heavy hand to guide her. You didn't see her in the baths." I raked a hand through my twists and tried not to remember the warmth of her body against mine. "She's not as strong as we want to believe. We can't treat her like just another fae. We must cover for her weaknesses, physically and mentally."

Power dripped out of Shade's eye in blue-black tears. "Why are you so blind?"

The world pulled away from me. I grabbed the back of the couch for balance. Layers of blue and black shrouded my vision. My skin grew cold. I tried to take a breath, but the thin, frigid air wouldn't fill my lungs. Strength drained from my body, leaving my arms too heavy to lift.

I looked at my other mates behind Shade. Perhaps the magic warped them, but wide grins pulled at their faces. I twitched my fingers, calling on my force. Shade's raw, undeniable power ripped the magic away.

"No, no, no!" The magic around me muffled Shade's scream.

I shut my eyes. With a sound like shattering glass, I exploded back from the couch and hit the wall with enough force to send whatever breath I had left in my chest whooshing out. I landed on my hands and knees, eyes open, sucking in lung-fulls of air.

Shade's magic rushed back into him and vanished. He stood in the center of a perfect ring of demolished furniture. Bash and Teyr both had their arms across his skinny chest, and he trembled. Fear, pain, and guilt poured through his Cara. He howled and wrapped his arms around himself.

A few heartbeats passed before he straightened and growled. He whipped his tail against his legs as he moved uneasily to the brandy and poured himself a finger. The glass shook in his trembling fingers. My second *pulsed* to check on me. I finally caught my breath and pushed off the floor, weak as a child.

"Fine," I muttered.

Teyr joined Shade and murmured something I couldn't discern. Shade offered his hand, and Teyr set the knuckles with the pop of bone.

Bash stepped to my side. "I've dedicated my life to this Cara, stood behind every decision you've made. I cannot stand behind this."

I closed my eyes and let out a weak breath. When I opened them once again, he had moved to block my view of Teyr and Shade.

He put a hand on my shoulder. "You're better than this."

Bash opened his Cara, filling me with his support, belief, and love for Kinnia. I opened mine as well. Determination, disappointment in myself, and frustration. He winced at the physical pain and took a step back.

"I will be better than this," I said to the room.

Now, I just needed to figure out when I had stopped being good enough.

44

KINNIA

I LAY IN THE BED OF MY WINDOWLESS NOT-PRISON AND watched one of the fifs shift from purple, to blue, to green, and back. The last week of training came easier, but having three of my mates back in my life might have just made it seem like that.

Zel and I still hadn't spoken outside of training and technical questions. The more time I spent with the other three, the more I couldn't ignore the ache in my chest when I looked to him to share a joke or victory and got nothing. I couldn't adjust to the fact that he would only ever be my commander.

At least the others had returned to normal. Bash worked out with me in the mornings. Shade spent as much time with me as a fae as his wolf, finding a balance between them. Teyr took me on evening walks, talking love and commitment, but I'd finally managed to reel him into one of his crude jokes. We were finding a new normal. It came so easily I sometimes forgot to miss Declan. Old habits had fallen away, and I found myself more like him than I expected.

The clock chimed midnight in the living room. I flipped my pillow over to find the cool side.

"Shade's trial is tomorrow. You've got to sleep," I told myself sternly.

After Teyr's trial, Zel hadn't wanted to train for anything specific. He and Lir simply kept us on our toes. *Most* of us were better at working together than ever before. I groaned and rolled over. My wall split with the dark shimmer of one of Shade's portals, and I sat up, ready to welcome the wolf into my arms.

Bash stepped through, with Shade on his heels. Both wore only soft sleeping pants.

The portal closed behind them. I raised a brow. Shade had snuck in a few times to cuddle as his wolf, but he'd never brought anyone else.

"Zelimir is upset," Shade said.

I bit my lower lip, unsure if I wanted to laugh or cry. I'd heard all about Shade's bid for control a few days ago, and Zel's promise to do better. Nothing had come of either.

I sighed. "You may as well be here. I can't sleep for shit."

Bash snorted.

Shade rounded the bed and sat down, then leaned his back against the headboard. He looked everywhere but at me, like he didn't know if I would let him stay. Sometimes he reminded me so much of his wolf I couldn't help but laugh. He looked at me, and when I smiled around my laughter, he settled.

Bash ran a finger along one strap of the little night shirt Drax had rounded up for me, along with thin, matching shorts. They were a little big, but I preferred big to too small. If I never had to constrict my breasts again, it would be too soon.

"I liked seeing you in my tunic," he murmured.

I grinned and scooted next to Shade. The necromancer wrapped an arm around my waist. I jerked my head, inviting Bash to join us.

"Maybe you two can help me sleep."

The dragon sat next to me. "Our commander's heart is in the right place. He wants to protect you and the Anam Cara."

I huffed. "He wants to control everything, and he can't."

"He has watched Caras fall apart." Bash slid a hand onto my thigh and stroked up and down, sending bolts of heat to my core.

Shade nuzzled his face in my hair, which now hung past my cheekbones.

"But that won't happen to us." I laid a hand on Shade's thigh. "Balance is...." I placed the tip of my finger on Bash's collarbone. "Think about standing on a skinny ledge." I let my finger teeter before standing it upright again. "Until you actually fall, it might not be pretty, but you're still on the ledge, right?"

Bash smiled.

I let my finger fall, dragging along every delicious muscle of his lilac chest. The air in the room grew thick with tension. I finally, finally had nothing to lose.

"And what if we fall only to find ourselves balancing differently?" I dipped my finger below the waistband of his pants for a moment before returning to his collarbone again. Nothing in the seemingly billion lectures I'd sat through matched my bridges.

Bash ran his other hand up my back. With soft pressure, he turned me toward him and pressed my back against Shade.

"You lost me when you put your hand in my pants." My dragon crushed his lips to mine.

I kissed him back greedily, parting so our tongues danced between us. Bash released my mouth to kiss down my neck, laving attention over the bruises he had left. I leaned back into Shade and looked up at him. His pupils had grown so wide his white eye almost looked black.

A shiver ran down my back. In my memory, I sat in Bash's lap under the afternoon sun, and how Shade had pulled me away. I shook my head. This time, I wouldn't end up alone. The necromancer's eyes glowed. He studied my face, then his gaze followed the path Bash had blazed with his lips. Shade's mouth fell slightly open. A frisson of heat burst through me.

"My Kitty." Shade lowered his head toward mine. "May I?"

"You don't need to ask," I murmured. "I want you too."

Shade kissed me tentatively. I tasted the difference between his mouth and Bash's in peppery gasps and herbal sighs. He had thinner, wider lips, and unlike my dragon's furious claiming, Shade seemed to be testing what I liked. When I parted for him, he sucked on my lower lip. When that made me moan, he nibbled.

He pulled back with a radiant smile. "You amaze me, my Kitty."

Bash *pulsed* the same sentiment from my neck, then pushed me farther into Shade's lap. The necromancer's erection pressed against my ass, and I ground down. He moaned and pulled me into another kiss, this one deeper, slower. His love radiated through every movement.

Bash slid his lilac hands under my shirt and cupped my breasts in his calloused palms. I pushed into the contact, keeping my mouth on Shade's. Bash rubbed my nipples in alternating circles. My hips rose and fell in a frantic rhythm, and Shade's kiss picked up speed.

Desire turned me into a living torch. Fuck sleep. Fuck the trial. I loved these men, and I trusted them not to let this change anything between us.

I ripped my mouth from Shade's. "I need you, both of you."

Growls ripped from their chests in unison. Bash grabbed my shorts, Shade my shirt, and they pulled. Bash must have used telekinesis because the garments spilled off my body like water. I lay bare before them.

My mates stared. Another Kinnia might have blushed or fidgeted. I remained still and let them look. They found me beautiful. They found me desirable.

Shade skimmed my breasts, ignoring the whine that escaped my mouth as he moved on and down my ribs. Bash watched. I twitched my hips, and Shade continued his path downward. He left one hand on my hip and tangled the other in my pubic hair. I moaned and jerked into his palm, but Shade didn't move.

Bash claimed my mouth with the same fire I'd come to expect from him and set his hand next to Shade's, between my legs. When I thrust into his touch, he placed two insistent fingers on my clit.

Sparks filled my mind. I rocked between them. Shade laid kisses along the line of my neck and stroked up and down my ribs. I moaned into Bash's lips. As my pleasure began to peak, he gave up my mouth and shifted down my body. Shade wrapped both his long-fingered hands around my hips. I ached to feel them inside me. Bash flattened himself on the bed and pressed his face between my legs.

My achingly close orgasm rushed back to the surface as my dragon ran his hot tongue in circles over me. Shade's gentle kisses turned sharper as he realized how I responded, then he peppered my neck with bites. He moved his hands to my inner thighs and pulled apart my legs so Bash had better access. Bash shoved his tongue into me, and my mind went white with pleasure.

I blinked back to consciousness. Shade's hands rested comfortably on my ribs while Bash sat in front of me, the lower half of his face glimmering in the low light. I looked up at the necromancer. Before I could read his expression, he leaned in and kissed me. His still-clothed cock shifted rhythmically against my back, and I matched his rhythm as warmth blossomed between my legs again. I wanted more.

As if Bash could hear me, he pressed two fingers into my slit. I rocked into the pressure, trying to time it with Shade's movements. As soon as I found the rhythm, Bash dove back between my legs and applied his talented tongue to my clit while he fucked into me. Shade slid a hand up to my breast and played with my nipple in the same experimental way he kissed. I moaned, trying not to lose the rhythm as pleasure threatened to overwhelm my body.

"Come with me, my Kitty." Shade pressed me closer to his chest. "You are our mate, our world, our everything."

Bash added a third finger, plunged deep, and sucked. I cried out as another orgasm took my body with the force of a thunderstorm, sending me spasming between my mates. Shade grunted. His cock twitched against my back with a burst of liquid. I rocked into the warm wetness as I came down.

I reached for Bash. "Please—"

He took my face in both hands and kissed my forehead. "We are not yet fixed. When you forgive me, take down your block, and we won't leave bed for a week." He smirked. "My dragon won't allow it."

The need between my legs started to dim, and exhaustion clouded my mind. I nodded. We cleaned up in easy quiet and fell back into bed completely nude.

I pillowed my head on my wolf's warm chest. My dragon curled around me and wrapped an arm around my waist. The moment I closed my eyes, a deep, dreamless sleep took me.

45

———

ZELIMIR

KINNIA'S LUST FILLED MY CARA. MY COCK ROSE TO attention under the book I read. I squeezed my eyes shut. My second warned me. He'd said he and Shade would spend the night with Kinnia. I doubted even then he would be able to restrain himself in such private quarters. I could have told him no, but he wouldn't have listened. Orders seemed like a waste of breath these days.

Until Light died, my Cara had been the strongest. I'd led us to that title. We found Kinnia under my watch. We grew to love her because of what we endured on the road, good and bad.

"Swords need a strong head blacksmith," I muttered.

My father's words still held true. I wouldn't be the fae I was today if I hadn't jumped through his hoops and been burned by politics and battles. Experience lent me knowledge and strength. I would impart that to Kinnia until I molded her into the fae I knew she could be. I exhaled through my teeth and didn't feel jealous.

"Fire, they are working her over." Teyr lay in his bed.

I opened my eyes to see his hand resting on his tented pants.

"Bash and I drew straws. That could be me right now." The ember groaned, and my cock stiffened further.

I stood, slamming my book down on the table. "I need to clear my head."

If Teyr acknowledged me, I didn't hear it. I dropped the shield of force I maintained every hour of the day to replace our door and stormed down the hall. A patrol of goblins scurried out of my way.

Kinnia's pleasure grew until her climax crested in a wave of emotion that forced me to lean against a wall to keep my feet. My erection throbbed. Walking became nearly impossible. I cursed and ducked into the nearest pale door. While three of my mates had what felt like spectacular sex, I pleasured myself alone in a public washroom.

I caught my breath and scowled. There was a right way to do things. Kinnia would be worth the wait, if my mates didn't ruin our chances of ever becoming a Cara first. When Kinnia and I indulged our carnal desires, we wouldn't be hidden, wouldn't be in the dirt or the dark. Everything would be perfect, balanced, and as beautiful as her.

She relaxed into sleep, and I stumbled down the hall like a drunk. I hoped, for a moment, that my errant mates might return to our suite, but Shade passed out almost as quickly. Bash resisted a few moments longer to *pulse* me a reminder that I wanted to be better. I punched the wall. I wanted to have a functional Cara. I wanted stable bonds I could rely on. How much I wanted to fuck Kinnia had to rank lower than that.

A familiar golden door stopped my pointless wandering. I hadn't entered Councilor Drax's apartments in seventy-five years. That first week, I sought out our mentor to ask if I was really best suited to be commander when my Cara contained a veteran with about forty years on me. He told me then leadership had less to do with experience and more to do with your ability to keep track of everything on the field. I'd taken that to heart. So why wouldn't anybody let me do that?

Councilor Drax opened the door, though I didn't remember knocking, a glass in his hand. I looked at the spot where I could feel my mates sleeping.

"Zelimir," he said. "I didn't expect you. Come in."

I took a deep breath and pulled myself together. My Cara had led me here. Perhaps, on the eve of our penultimate trial, I could listen to its edicts. I stepped across the threshold.

His apartment looked just as sparse as the last time I'd seen it. He sat in a chair and sipped his drink. The fireplace flickered, and a mug of glowing orange melony floated into my hands. I accepted the cup and took the high-backed chair across from his. My mates slept through the wall behind him. I studied the dark stone as I gathered my thoughts.

Councilor Drax broke the silence. "I thought you might visit sooner."

"I thought you'd mentor my Cara." I frowned at my drink.

"Truly, your highness?" He raised an eyebrow. "With all your experience in politics, you thought I would officially hop into the middle of your shitstorm?"

I grimaced. "I'm no prince here."

"Then stop acting like one." He stared at the fire.

I took a sip of melony. The warm magic soothed Councilor Drax's words. I didn't come here to fight.

"Have you figured out what Kinnia is?" I asked.

"In the month that she's lived with me, I've chased Shade out a dozen times. I've warded my door against fire magic to keep Teyr from busting in at all hours to retrieve her for dates. I've dumped water on a centuries-old dragon who saved my life more times than I can count." He met my gaze. "But I have not seen you until this night, and you ask me *what* she is?"

I straightened. "We need to know. All of us. Me. The Councils." I ran a hand through my hair. "Bash tells me her *energy* spawns rifts. But she lies to herself. She needs to know who she really is."

Councilor Drax pursed his lips. "Does she?"

I blinked. "How can we know her if she doesn't know herself?"

He nodded. "And this knowing herself, it happens on your timeline?"

I clenched my fist. "No. Just…not before she's ready."

"Which you alone know," he said.

I glared at the wall over his shoulder. "I know she's not ready yet."

Councilor Drax chuckled. "This is what I mean by acting like a prince."

Heat flashed through my veins. Perhaps the Councilor didn't mentor us because he had nothing else to teach. I knocked back the last of my melony and clung to the arm of the chair. Our old mentor had sway with the Council. I couldn't irritate him, no matter how I wanted to storm out.

"What do I always say?" he asked.

I squeezed the cherrystone handle of my empty cup. "Lessons learned through trial-and-error stay with a student longer than any lecture."

He smiled. "What does that tell you here?"

"It tells me to maintain the Council's rulings, and my own which sprung from theirs." I exhaled sharply. "Our trials have been grueling, but they push Kinnia to discover new parts of herself."

Councilor Drax looked at me with an expression I'd never seen in his eyes before. Disappointment. "Do you know how we discovered Kinnia spawned rifts?"

I shook my head. That had ended in Shade almost killing me, so I hadn't asked many follow-up questions. My second only remembered to tell me about the rifts the next day.

"Bash and Teyr fought over who would help her. Your spitfire of an ember won. He sat in front of her, holding her, guiding her to his fire." Councilor Drax smiled softly. "They tried something, and it failed, and we learned from that." He looked at me, and his gaze grew hard. "Kinnia discovered a part of herself because of the love and support of her mates. Not in spite of the hardships thrust upon her." He stood. "It is a subtle difference I thought you understood."

I rose to face him. I was a seasoned Cara commander, not a child he could speak down to. "The Council's trials or her own experimentation, both prove my point. She needs time and space to learn."

"Time, perhaps. But I think the last thing that girl needs right now is space." He sighed. "We spoke once about a leader seeing the whole field. I'm worried you didn't understand how much of that is listening." My old mentor shook his head. "Come talk to me when you're ready to listen, Zelimir."

I opened my mouth to argue, but he gestured to the door. I looked at the wall one last time, as if I could pierce it with my eyes, and left without another word.

I'd barely made it down the hall before a blue pixie popped up next to me, lugging a communication bowl. I eyed her. I could just let her drop the damn thing. But my father would merely send another. I accepted the bowl, and his image appeared on the surface. He smiled.

"I'm not in a good location. Give me a moment." I covered him with my hand and hurried down the corridor.

The lust in Teyr's Cara told me he would almost certainly be engaged in something untoward in the suite, so I headed for the nearest lecture hall. As expected, the space was dark and quiet this late in the night. I found a corner desk where I could watch both entrances and removed my hand from the top of the bowl.

"Well, son, I must say I was pleased to receive your letter." My father smiled. "The Upper Council's focus on your Cara intrigues me, but I'll admit I'm more interested in Councilor Odhrán and the goblins."

My heart thudded unevenly and a warmth filled my chest. I'd pleased him.

"I'm glad to hear that," I murmured.

He leaned forward. "Goblins are a weak response. They suggest an untoward interest in Tech from our beloved liaison. Whether or not the threat is real, their very presence undermines faith in the Councils."

I nodded. The other trainees seemed to regard the goblins as little more than an irritation.

He clicked his tongue. "I did, however, find your letter missing a measure of detail. How many goblins are in each patrol? How many patrols run at once? What weaponry do they carry?"

Answers sprang to my tongue, but realization came faster. I'd declared my loyalty to the Councils moments ago, but I fed their information to my father. How could Kinnia—any of my mates—trust me when I said one thing and did another?

I dropped the bowl onto the desk, ignoring my father's shout. He'd lured me in again. A few smiles, a bit of paternal concern, and I'd fallen right into his trap. When Cordelia and I were young, we would joke that you knew which way something unpleasant headed based solely on who Father spoke to most at dinner. I scooped up the bowl.

"Ah, so they bear blasters. Interesting," he said.

He had been filling in answers to see my reaction. Just like he did that day in the hall. Just like he always did when I put up a wall. I barely resisted the urge to scatter the bowl against the floor to get him out of my head. This time, I needed him to hear me.

"I grew up learning your lessons," I said. "I am a sword forged in the heat of battle. But I didn't need to be." I swallowed. "I shouldn't have listened to you."

He frowned. "Well, son, maybe if you told me what this sword thing was really about—"

"No." I shook my head. "It doesn't matter what it's really about because I'm not doing this anymore. I will not be strung along on scraps of attention to betray what I hold dear." I held the bowl close to my face. "You raised a political monster who prefers tentative allyship over enemies, but I am my own man now."

His eyes, my eyes, stared up at me.

"I don't care if this makes us enemies, Father. I belong to my mates, and my mates alone. Not you, not the Councils, not even the wilds." I tapped my chest. "I belong to the magic running through my veins."

My father opened his mouth, but I covered my hand in purple force and crushed the bowl in my fist.

Bash was right. Teyr was right. Even Shade was right. Magic called Kinnia to us, and magic didn't need a guiding hand.

46

KINNIA

I slowed to a halt as I entered the smallest training yard in the dawn light. I'd awoken with a pang of loneliness in an empty bed, so I assumed Bash would meet me here for our morning exercises. Instead, all my mates stood in the middle of the field with horses at the ready. I rubbed goose bumps from my arms in the cool morning air.

"My Kitty!" Shade gestured me over as if I hadn't seen them.

I studied Zelimir, but his impassive face gave me no hint of what he might be thinking. I rubbed my arms once more before hurrying forward and coming to a halt just out of my commander's reach.

"A little early, isn't it?" My traitorous Cara hummed, thrilled to be in everyone's presence outside of training.

Teyr yawned and tipped the last sip of a mug of coffee into his mouth.

Zelimir took a step toward me. "I'm sorry."

My throat tightened.

He leaned forward but didn't crowd me. "I could give you excuses, but they wouldn't change anything. I was wrong. I shouldn't have tried to control everything. I shouldn't have sided with the Councils. And I shouldn't have pushed you away."

My heart raced. I forced myself to breathe.

"Would you join us for a surprise?" Zelimir extended a hand to me.

Behind him, my mates each stood by a horse, though my roan was absent. Teyr looked utterly unhappy to be out of bed. Shade yawned next to a dark mount I didn't recognize, but he whipped his tail so fast it made its own whistling breeze. Bash stood with his arms crossed and his Cara wide open, radiating trust and hope.

I turned back to my commander. The fine lines around his eyes looked deeper than I remembered, but his usual guarded expression slipped into something almost shy. No, not shy. Concerned. He didn't think I would say yes.

"Yes." I crossed my arms. "But I'm riding your horse."

Zel inclined his head. "Everything I have is at your disposal."

I strode to his huge bay Shire horse and put my hand out. The horse sniffed me before snorting and slamming one of his hooves on the orange grass. I glanced at Zelimir before gathering my nerve. I said I wanted the horse. Bash stepped forward and laced his fingers together to give me a leg up. I stepped into his hands, then swung my leg up and over the massive saddle. The horse skidded to the side, his every motion exaggerated by his size. I managed to hang on without losing too much dignity.

"He gets along best with Teyr's mare. Keep him there, and he'll stay in line." Zelimir shortened the stirrups for me.

I gripped the pommel tightly. Zel whispered to the beast before mounting the dark horse next to Shade. The necromancer grinned and shrank into his wolf. With a few happy barks that made all the horses prance, he darted into the forest. Teyr and Bash vaulted onto their mounts, and we thundered away from the Academy's grounds.

Unlike my roan, Zelimir's Shire horse itched to run. His gait rocked me like a toy, bouncing my necklace against my chest. I fell into his rhythm and grinned as my mates urged their horses faster and faster to match. Wind whipped through my curls. I clung to the pommel and prayed the beast between my legs followed its friends better than its owner did.

We reached the edge of the valley and slowed. My horse followed the others down a small game track that ended at a cave opening. All four horses breathed hard, especially the one Zel rode. A bit of foam dripped off its lips.

"Is he okay?" I dismounted and stretched my legs.

"They're all a bit out of shape." Zelimir reached under his saddle to loosen the girth. "Especially Shade's."

They must've left the horse here when they realized Shade wouldn't be riding after Light's death.

"And he had to carry your titanic ass." Teyr grinned.

Zelimir sighed, but still smiled. I studied the two as they tethered their horses. The tension I'd felt for weeks had disappeared. They'd talked behind my back again. A small, hopeful part of me believed it might have been for good this time.

Zel walked up to me and started to put his hand on my lower back. I slid out of reach. I appreciated the apology, but I couldn't offer anything more than a ride until I understood what was going on.

He frowned but stepped back. "Your surprise is in the cave."

I wrinkled my nose. Zel turned and walked ahead. After a moment, I followed him inside the cave with the rest of our mates. The passage narrowed the farther we walked, twisting and turning until the light of day vanished from sight. Bash helped himself to a handful of my ass. I batted him away and scampered to Teyr's side. The ember stuck his tongue out at Bash before resting his hand on my ass. I couldn't win. Shade loped up to my free side, back in his fae body, and took my hand when I offered it.

After a few more minutes of walking, the walls ahead of us took on a soft, golden glow. We rounded a final bend and entered a massive cavern covered in twinkling gold stars. I spun to see everything and laughed. My life hadn't felt magical since we arrived at the Academy, but this blew most of the things I'd seen on the journey here out of the water. Excitement thrilled in my veins. I drifted toward one of the walls to see if the stars felt as spiky as they looked.

My mates opened their Caras. Love, support, and worry mixed into my excitement. Shade wrapped an arm around my shoulder and guided me forward. The stars turned out to be tiny fae, no bigger than my pinky nail. They dodged through holes in the cave wall, winking in and out of light. Shade pointed to one that didn't glow as brightly as the rest. The air around it shimmered, engulfing it in light. It exploded outward into glittering crystals, and I barely made out a little face before it scampered back into a hole. I grinned wildly. Shade brought my hand to his lips and kissed each of my fingers.

"They're called aurum fairies." Teyr traced the shell of my ear down to the top of my tunic.

I shivered.

Bash wrapped rough hands around my waist and lifted me off my feet. The fairies turned back into twinkling stars as he carried me to the center of the cave, where Zel had spread a blanket. The dragon sat, then settled me on his lap and kissed the back of my neck. Memories of last night rose to the surface. Heat filled my core.

At our commander's grunt, Bash slid out from under me. I landed on the pillowy blanket. When my mates stayed quiet, I lay back. I'd let them have their show. The cave fell nearly silent. My mates shuffled around behind me as they exchanged rapid-fire *pulses* I couldn't quite make out.

Were they undressing? My heart pounded in my ears. Nerves buzzed in my chest. Why had they brought me here? Before nerves could completely replace my curiosity, Shade pressed his head under my arm. He buried himself into my side, his ears tickling my nose as he rested his fae head on my chest. Still dressed, I noticed.

"Shade." Zelimir sighed.

I giggled and trailed one of my fingers up his fuzzy wolf ears.

Shade trapped my hand with his. "Not now, my Kitty. Our pack leader has a plan that doesn't involve sex."

I forced my pulse to slow. Teyr's warning about shifter ears being extra sensitive echoed through my mind.

I dropped my hand to Shade's hair. "Why did you bring me here?"

"To make amends," Zel said. "Teyr said watching your eyes fill with stars in the mountains made him realize he was in love."

Teyr lay down on my other side and pillowed his head on my shoulder. He slid his hand under my shirt and rubbed small circles on my stomach. My skin fluttered under his touch, matching the quiet pace of his heartbeat.

"I forgot that balance is learned, not forged." Zelimir's voice came from just above my head. "I didn't listen to my mates. I didn't act like I was part of a Cara, much less its leader." He brushed his fingers across my cheek. "I forced Bash to give up your secret."

Tears pooled in my eyes. My chest grew tight. Bash stood a few feet away, and I tried to whisper acceptance through the block. He hadn't used our commander as an excuse. He knew he'd made the choice.

Zel took a deep breath. "What do you want?"

I unfocused my gaze, blurring the twinkling lights together. I wanted this, exactly this, only this. No rules. No complications. No EarthTech.

"I don't think I can get what I want." My stomach clenched around phantom cables. "Life is too complicated."

Teyr chuckled. "It's taken you this long to figure that out?"

I wrinkled my nose and swatted a body.

Shade grunted. "I didn't say that."

Teyr cuddled me closer, pinning my arm to my side. Sneaky ember.

"We aren't leaving this cave until the five of us are on the same page." He kissed just below my ear. "We're here to free you."

"Free me?" I frowned. This didn't feel like a breakup.

"Metaphorically," Shade said.

Bash lifted my legs and draped them over his lap. "No more decisions behind your back." He massaged my calves.

"We'll be honest with you, always," Teyr said.

Zelimir lifted my head and rested it on his lap. "I want you by my side. I want to trust you, and you to trust me." He massaged my shoulders with his warm, large hands.

I trusted my mates, but Zelimir specifically? He'd pushed me away in the baths like I meant nothing. He'd made Bash tell my secret. Even if it had been to protect all of us, he'd given me up in front of the Council. Trust meant nothing without action.

"Honesty goes two ways," Zelimir said.

I tensed.

"You haven't talked about it. And, on my orders, we haven't

broached the subject." He squeezed my shoulders. "We know you fear the rifts because of your time on Earth, that you want nothing to do with Tech." He met my gaze, passion lighting his purple eyes. "But we're an Anam Cara. Protecting our world from EarthTech is what we do. It's what I want you to do at our side."

I squeezed my eyes shut. Alex's green gaze burned down into mine, lit with that same fire. I wanted to live in Zel's passion, make it my own, and fight for it. But I'd already tried following other people's dreams. I had to choose this for myself, like Drax had.

Bash, Teyr, and Shade all stood at the same time. Zelimir wiggled out from under me and straddled me. His bulk blocked my view of the fairies.

He caressed my hips, ghosted over my breasts, and cupped my face. "I want you with us."

Zel's warm breath heated my cheeks. Vanilla filled my nose. My core warmed.

He opened his Cara, letting me feel the simple truth of his words. "I wanted to give you, us, time to trust, but we just don't have time."

I didn't want to fight Tech, didn't even want to see them. Phantom cables in my belly, arms, neck ached. Metallic voices rang in my brain. Earth's white dirt packed under my fingernails. I buried my fingers in Zelimir's copper twists and pulled my commander's face down. He brushed his mouth against mine, then leaned back.

My heart broke. What happened to us?

He shifted back to straddle my legs and smiled at me like the kiss had been everything he wanted before pulling me up to sit. "Kinnia, will you stay with us?"

Shade and Teyr ran their hands up my arms, making me squeak with surprise. Bash brushed possessive lips against the back of my neck, promising all the heat my commander denied me.

Staying couldn't be about love, or lust. It had to be about facing my fears. About accepting the role Rydel thrust upon me. About becoming someone who honored my family's memory.

I turned my head to steal a kiss from Bash's lips. He poured passion into me, and I reveled in the roiling emotion. Teyr pressed into me from the side, and when I broke the kiss with Bash, I found him waiting. His kiss started off sweet but burned into pure hunger. Fire seared across my lips. Whatever part of me still thought of Teyr as more of a friend turned to ash and vanished in his flame. He ran his hands down my sides, caressing my hips and Bash's.

Heat flooded my limbs as I opened my lips, and my already-excited sex clenched. Teyr explored my mouth, his tongue twisting and curling. Pleasure began to peak in my veins. I didn't know who ran their hand down my stomach to rest on my clit, but I bucked into it. Someone peppered my neck with kisses. Bash clutched me tighter.

"That's enough," Zelimir growled.

Teyr kissed me one final time. Bash leaned back and pulled his hand out of my pants. Shade removed his lips from my neck. I glared at Zelimir, panting.

My commander adjusted his pants. "We didn't come here for this. Shade's trial is in a few hours. We need to rest, eat, and prepare."

I grabbed Shade's hand. "You're going to do great."

"I will be brilliant." Shade squeezed my hand. "You'll see."

I closed my eyes and strummed the air for the bridges that connected me to Bash and Teyr. If I joined the Cara, I needed to be all in. I pulled the *energy* I'd blocked them with back into me. Teyr's presence intruded into my thoughts.

Bash shoved Teyr back into his own mind. "Manners."

I laughed. Lightness filled my chest. Teyr's hands rested on my hips, overlapping Bash's. It wouldn't be easy, but this Anam Cara was my home. My heart sang. I could feel almost all my mates, finally. Zel truly wanted me to be a part of his unit, but for whatever reason, he didn't want more.

I smiled at him. "I have some rules."

47

SHADE

"Is the crowd larger than usual?" my Kitty asked.

The thick, iron-and-moss scent of goblins crawled into my nose. My stomach turned. More fae were gathered here in the pocket dimension of the colosseum than had even been at the Academy. I sniffed again. Something else lay under the goblin smell, something I'd smelled before. I leaned into the stiff, sulfuric breeze and took another lungful. Jalan. And not just Farquin.

"I'd say you're right," Teyr said.

I froze. Had he responded to my thoughts? No, Bash read minds. Someone must have asked a question.

Teyr wrapped an arm around my Kitty. "You're going to be amazing."

"We're going to be amazing." She squeezed Teyr back. "All of us together."

She looked at me, and my heart raced. I pulled her away from Teyr to my side. Today was my day. I puffed out my chest as my mates took position on my flanks. The song of Thrae rose to a quiet hum. Necromancy pooled in my eyes, opening my vision to the space between. A howl of pure joy ripped from my chest as I led us to the center of the colosseum floor. The Jalan could wait.

Zelimir *pulsed*. I looked around for my task. He *pulsed* again, this time lacing he response with my Kitty's discomfort. He wanted me to let go. I loosened my grip on her shoulders and brushed Light's bone with my fingers. I needed to focus, to listen. Spreading my arms, I turned in a circle, but found nothing more than flat, green sand. No bodies answered my call.

"Why is there nothing for me to reanimate?" I asked. "Or obstacles, or enemies…there is nothing here."

Odhrán's voice boomed through the colosseum. "An Anam Cara must not only be strong in body and mind, but in control. True strength is not the power in one's limbs or the amount of magic one can channel, but finesse." He paused. "Finesse under pressure."

Teyr murmured, "Drax isn't announcing."

My Kitty's scream pierced the air as an invisible force ripped her from my grasp. My heart slammed against my ribs. The Council tossed her into a transparent bubble far above our heads. She banged off the sides. Her terror ripped through our bond, just as it had when the clear tube of that Earth monstrosity had imprisoned her. My blood boiled. The song of Thrae grew louder, coaxing me into its rhythm.

Three full Anam Caras stepped out from behind a door on our level of the colosseum. Behind them stood at least two dozen Seccas, some on foot, others riding impressively large beasts. They pounded out in waves of bright colors and discordant music. A juggler tossed fireballs high into the air while a water spirit twirled a hoop around her shapely hips. Overly cheerful music plinked from my left as a trio of tall, gem-toned sirens beat melodies onto crystalline bars with their fingers. My head screamed.

My mates closed ranks, putting their backs to mine. My Kitty pounded against the bubble, but her terror faded into a mix of fear and determination.

"When I'm done with this explanation, your time will begin," Odhrán said. "Finesse under pressure, surrounded by distraction. I, personally, along with Councilor Xerxes, designed this puzzle. It shall test Shade's concentration and endurance, the Cara's communication, and the human's observation skills."

A knot of colorful ropes appeared before me, impossibly tangled and almost the size of a horse. Five bright ends floated at waist level. Magic flowed through each colored length. Golden sparkles burst in my peripheral vision. The crowd gasped. Something made them roar with laughter.

Odhrán chuckled. "We've outdone ourselves this time." He cleared his throat. "The task is simple. Separate the orange string...before Kinnia drowns."

A fat bead of water gathered at the top of the bubble and dropped onto my Kitty's hair. My heart skipped a beat. The water rolled down her body, leaving a dark line on her trainee greens. She beat her fists against the wall and mouthed my name.

My world narrowed onto her. I shook. My wolf threatened.

"Kinnia can see the pattern from above." Teyr sounded distant.

Light's death kissed the edges of my memory.

Zelimir gripped my arm as my Cara *pulsed* madly. "She's fine right now."

I needed to act, but what if I made the wrong choice again? She would die, just like Light.

"Shade." My pack leader stepped in front of me and put a hand on my trembling shoulder. "We're a team. A pack. If we work together, we can do anything. Right?"

I took a breath and met his gaze. "I cannot fail again."

"You won't. Because we're an Anam Cara." Zelimir jerked his chin up. "She needs you. You can do this."

My tail twitched with agitation. I *pulsed* a promise to my pack. Zelimir squeezed my shoulder, then stepped back.

"Bash, try to identify the pattern and see if we can isolate the magic by their types," he said. "It's a slim chance, but we should explore every option. Teyr, see if you can trace any of the lines with fire. If that doesn't work, use firewalls to keep distractions out of Shade's view. Shade, let me know where you need barriers to keep it from reknotting behind us."

Relief filled me. Zelimir knew what to do. I trusted my pack leader. And my Kitty trusted me. I rushed forward, brushing his shoulder with the side of my face, and *pulsed* that I understood.

I sank my hands into the magic.

WHAT SEEMED LIKE EONS LATER, SWEAT POURED OFF ME, making my uniform cling to my skin uncomfortably. I coaxed more of the hated orange rope away from the others and *pulsed* to Zelimir to block those strands from returning. Nothing I did had anything to do with necromancy or my pack. My concentration wavered. I glanced up at my Kitty. Just her head remained above the waterline. My stomach twisted. I wasn't going fast enough.

Part of the orange string inched back to its original position. I howled.

"Focus." Zelimir emphasized his command with a *pulse*.

I growled at the knot again, then took hold of the orange and began easing it free once more. A firewall flared up on my right, blocking whatever inane nonsense the Council designed to torture me. The upbeat, repetitive music intensified. Another few inches of the orange rope spooled out of the knot. I *pulsed* to Zelimir and looked up just as my Kitty's head slipped under the water.

No. This couldn't happen to me. To us. To her.

I shook. Terror and rage screamed through my limbs. The world faded to shades of gray, the space in between life and death, and I spun to the Councils' box and waved my hands in defeat. The trial ended. I'd lost. I had to admit defeat, or she would drown. Our bond had broken every other rule. I didn't believe this test could break us.

A heartbeat passed, followed by another. They didn't move. They didn't care. Fear coated my stomach. Her panic filled my Cara. The edges of my vision went black.

Zelimir *pulsed* to save her.

Bash's scales shimmered in my muted vision as he leaped onto Zelimir's shoulders with his axe out. My pack leader launched him into the air, but the ball remained out of reach. My Kitty's struggles grew weaker. My world spun around her. She couldn't die. I wouldn't let her.

The song intensified. Power bled out of my every pore, electrifying my muscles and sending shooting pain down my limbs in rhythm. The crowd roared for blood. The music plinked maddeningly. Still not enough of Thrae's song.

"You dare threaten my Kitty?" I murmured.

I thrust my hand into the mess of twisted rope magic and pulled their fae power into me. The very essence of the fae leapt to my call, and I sucked in a breath as the song rebounded, doubled over itself, and became deafening. I combed the dust beneath me for a worthy vessel with half my mind.

They still didn't release my Kitty. She floated to the bottom and splayed her fingers against the clear case. Her emotions poured through my Cara. Panic, regret. Relief.

Relief? She couldn't feel relief at her own death.

I ripped the remaining magic from the fae powering the mess of tangled strings. A cloud of black billowed around me, power bursting against my too-frail body. The song screamed. This would destroy me if I let it. Perhaps I would.

Ancient bones answered my call, steeped in unimaginable magic, and I laughed.

The cloud fled me, pushing deep into Thrae's core. The colosseum rumbled and shook. The shield that protected the place ruptured, and small rivers of lava poured in to consume the unfortunate. I danced to the beat. They would pay for what they had done.

Ancient, bare bones burst through the ground beneath my feet. I stumbled back to avoid the debris. Fae scattered, screaming. As the dead rose, they remembered their former life, snapping together into something unmistakable. Something that would keep my Kitty safe.

My bone dragon landed on the green dust. His eyes burned with blue-black power. I turned a circle, whipping my tail back and forth so hard I thought it might snap. My mates *pulsed.* I reached for my bond with my Kitty to show her what I'd created.

No emotion. Just emptiness. I'd felt this only once before.

The world spun and bled. I let out a blood-curdling howl which turned into furious laughter. The song beat a frantic rhythm against the seams of my skin. My new pet bowed to its creator.

48

ZELIMIR

The colosseum roared. Some yelled for us to save Kinnia. Others shouted for the Council to intervene. I should've kept a closer eye on Shade. Kinnia remained trapped in the ball of water, and he couldn't look anywhere but at his dragon.

My chest constricted as I lifted my gaze up to Kinnia. She looked so young, her brow uncreased for once. Her dark hair, longer this morning than I'd ever seen it, floated in a soft halo around her face. Her Cara went abruptly silent. I took a step toward her. She slumped against the bottom of the bubble. My knees gave out, and I dropped to the fine, green dirt.

Not again.

Raw power exploded across the arena with a force that nearly knocked me on my back. I snapped my head in the direction of the stands. The magical barrier that usually prevented audience interference shattered. Shade had already failed his trial. They were going to kill him.

Then the spectators' magic began to force the bubble downward. My heart thundered. They were on our side!

I leapt to my feet, looked at Bash, and knitted my hands to give him another boost. A dark grin cracked his face, and he got into position. As the ball dropped low enough, I flung my second through the air. His glistening red axe bit into the transparent shell. Kinnia rushed out in a gush of water.

I whooped in unison with the crowd as Teyr sprinted forward to catch our mate, then I raced after him. A thunderous *boom* split the air as the dragon's skeletal tail whipped into the wall of the colosseum. The wave of cheers morphed into screams. I halted.

Shade balanced atop the skull of his dragon, laughing wildly as chunks of the colosseum's green marble scattered around him. The tinkling music from his trial cut off with a sour note. His Cara swirled with a darkness I couldn't fathom. Rage obliterated all other emotions. I *pulsed*, but he only kicked up his heels and wagged his tail madly.

Water crashed down on Kinnia and Teyr as she landed in his arms. An explosive *crack* reverberated, and a flash of brilliant white light blinded me for an instant. Kinnia's emotions flared to life in our Cara, but when the smoke cleared, a dark crater separated me from my mates.

"How dare you?" Shade's words boomed across the colosseum. "I'm going to hang you with your own entrails."

The dragon charged toward the Councils' box. Shade continued to issue threats.

A few feet from where Teyr pushed into a sitting position, Kinnia lay unmoving amidst mud and cinders. My heart leapt to my throat. She was alive. That should have been all that mattered.

We had to reach Shade.

I threw a bridge of force over the crater and raced for Kinnia, his Kitty, our girl, then dropped to my knees and slid through the muck to her side. She blinked up at me.

"Whatever you did with Bash and Teyr, we need that now," I said.

"You can't ask that of her." My second skidded to a halt beside us, axe at the ready, panting heavily. "Shade's lost his mind."

I took her face in my hands. "You must. He's going to hurt so many before he's brought down. They will kill him."

She coughed a strange, racking cough, and looked at Bash. My second knelt on her other side, his mouth set in a hard line. Kinnia reached a shaky hand toward him, then clutched a dark burn on her side that leaked blood. I released her and swallowed. Bash glared at me. Shade bellowed his threats and nonsense.

She shook her head. "I'll be fine. Bash, you'll be with me." Her gaze hardened. "We can't let our wolf die."

"Fuck." The scales on Bash's face whirled, and his knuckles went gray, but he holstered his axe. "I love you, Dee. Be strong."

He pressed a gentle kiss to her lips, grabbed her free hand, then held his other hand out as Teyr stumbled to a stop beside us. The confused ember clasped Bash's fingers. I stood and stepped back. I chose to slow things down. I wanted my relationship with Kinnia to grow without magic. I wanted her love for me to be true and honest. I swallowed against rising bile.

"Forgive me." Bash closed his eyes.

A pocket of magic powerful enough to make my hair stand on end enveloped the three of them. Kinnia whimpered. The crowd shrieked as the dragon destroyed the railing of the Councils' box. Some Secca officers tried to defend them, but their magic bounced off the creature's ancient bones. A swarm of goblins beat at the dragon's feet and ankles, but the beast crushed dozens with every step.

My mates went still. White-hot joy engulfed my Cara. Shade stopped shouting and cocked his head to the side. He whipped his tail once, twice. He crumpled, hit one of the bone dragon's horns, rolled, and plummeted toward the ground.

I sprinted toward him and launched a cushion of force in front of me. He plunged through layers of my purple magic, but his fall slowed, and he settled softly to the ground. With a purple battering ram, I sent an approaching pack of goblins flying. Councilors screamed orders and pointed at us. The sounds of fighting rang around me.

I reached Shade, and my world narrowed onto his face. His eyes flickered under closed lids, and his pulse jumped in his neck. I approached with my hands out, like I would a wild animal. He looked so pale. When he didn't move, I slid my arms under his shoulders and legs to lift him.

His eyes snapped open. He stared without seeing, his pupils a swirl of Kinnia's blue, Bash's gray, and Teyr's molten gold. On the other side of the colosseum, Bash shouted, and Shade's eyes slammed shut. The dragon lifted its head into the air as if to roar, then froze. The last few chunks of green marble from its assault crashed to the arena floor.

I cursed. Bash and Teyr skidded to a halt next to me. The ember held Kinnia close to his chest. A curl of smoke spiraled out from under his left hand. I looked between the bone dragon, still upright, unlike Shade's usual undead pets after he fell, and the Councils' box. Amidst the chaos, the dark oval of the Upper Council gleamed.

The air pressure in the colosseum dropped with a familiar *pop*.

No. Not now.

I snapped my head in the direction of the forty-foot-high rift tearing into our world. Tech poured out. Armored fae turned their weapons onto the alien machines. Others screamed and surged toward the portals that would take them back to Thrae's surface. Magic of every kind shot through the air.

My mates looked at me.

I looked at Kinnia.

And I knew what to do.

I hefted Shade and handed him to Bash. My second took him without question. I spun and scrambled onto the bone dragon's head. The screams of dying fae took me back to the Battle of Light. There, I fought until we won the day. This time, my Cara came first.

I spread my magic between my fingers and stretched the delicate sheets of force across the fans of bone on the dragon's back. The creature shivered with delight. My mates scaled onto the dragon and settled between two massive spikes on its neck. The battle raged around us.

The dragon tested its new wings with a flap, knocking me to my knees on the bony ridge of its brow. I latched onto a horn and prayed I hadn't made a huge mistake. After a few massive wingbeats, the creature rose into the air.

I twisted and looked at Kinnia, still crushed against Teyr's chest. She mumbled in Shade's necromantic language, her hands pressed into the dragon's shoulder blade, shaking with effort. The burn in the side of her armor oozed red blood and a thin stream of smoke. A brief, bright light flickered inside the gash.

The dragon dove for the hole Shade had torn in the ground when he animated the creature. The dry, sulfuric heat overwhelmed me. As we rocketed toward the depths, Teyr flung up a shield of flames that only barely dampened the intensity. I closed my eyes and clung to the dragon with all my remaining strength. Kinnia howled.

After a few interminable moments, we lost momentum. I cracked an eye open as the dragon landed in bubbling lava like a duck on water. We had survived, whatever that meant. Shade sprawled, unconscious in Bash's grip. Teyr's skin looked raw and red for the first time since I'd met him. Kinnia....

I picked my way down the dragon's spine to her. Her eyes swirled black-and-white. With her fingers pressed to the bone, I had a clear view of the wound in her side. The gash spanned the left side of her ribs, wider than my hand. She leaned forward, and her features crumpled into a grimace. Deep and painful, but hopefully not lethal. The wound lit up again. Recognition crashed over me.

Sparks.

"Kinnia?" I asked.

The bones beneath her fingers glowed blue-black, and a small stream of sparks spat out of her side. I inched closer and discovered a few broken strands of cable peeking past bone, skin, and leather.

My stomach roiled. I cleared my throat and tried to steady my voice. "Kinnia, come back to me. There's something you need to see. *Please.*"

Her eyes cleared, though the swirling colors still threatened at the edges of her pupils. Her brow pinched as the pain broke over her anew. I opened my mouth to explain, but no words came. Instead, I took her right hand, still clammy from the water. I didn't want this to be the first time we held hands. Together, we touched the wound. The cables sparked again at the pressure.

Kinnia stared up at me with wide, wild eyes. Her panic exploded across the Cara, dwarfing even the heat of the lava.

"But I'm bleeding," she whispered.

SNEAK PEEK OF BOOK THREE IN THE ANAM CARA SERIES

THE CRYSTALLINE HEART

Can her mates love the woman beneath the machine?

On the run and stunned that the woman Thrae magic has called to their Cara isn't who they thought, her four fae mates try to understand what's gone wrong. She, the magic…the Tech, are all tearing them apart. But when they are captured, they must make a choice.

The old magic or the new magic. Kill Tech. Embrace Tech.

If she has her way, they will have to face a fate worse than death and live with the death of their newest mate.

Her.

1

—————

KINNIA

Dark blues, greens, and purples whipped past me so quickly I couldn't identify the foliage, but my feet—my four paws—pounded across the ground with practiced ease. A flash of sunlight mixed with shadow, and another wolf yipped excitedly. I turned my head from the path to see the gold and white wolf darting through the forest alongside me. My heart filled with warmth. He dove for me and sank his teeth into my shoulder. I slowed and squirmed to bite at his back leg.

We tumbled out of the tree line together, and blue-black haze overtook my view as a wild song rose in my ears. Heat seared across my skin, then aching cold with the strength of gale force winds. Finally, I dissolved into itchiness.

I blinked and stared at the lakeshore where we'd landed. A terrible homesickness overtook me. We could never go back. A hand lightly gripped my shoulder, and I looked up into the young face I knew so well. Laughing black and white eyes that mirrored my own, and a head topped with curling golden hair, underlined by a brilliant smile. My brother. The very center of my universe.

"We no longer have a home, Light." My voice cracked on the final word, a recent development.

He laughed. "We don't need to stay somewhere we're not wanted. Plus, you were out of things to reanimate there anyway."

I slowly closed my hand into a fist, and the world around me turned gray. The ground lit with a network of corpses as a haunting melody I recognized as the song of Thrae hummed in my ears.

He sat down next to me, swaying with the rhythm. "We'll build our own home here. We'll keep each other safe, beat the odds." He shook his head and met my gaze. "I won't let the magic burn you out."

I grinned. "I won't let the magic burn *you* out."

The ground beneath me rocked, and my brother—Shade's brother—exploded into nothingness in front of me.

There you go, Bash said in my mind. *You're not Shade. Separate your thoughts.*

I sucked in a breath. Pain blossomed across my abdomen. Before I could scream, I floated away from the agony.

Whatever I sat on fell away. I forced my eyes open to the darkness around me as Zelimir roared. He clung to a large, white spike, a jut of bone on the top of the ancient skull of the dragon we rode. His copper twists streamed through in the night air as I fought to contextualize the flying dragon skeleton in my memory. I jostled back onto the bone in our steep descent, and someone wrapped an arm around my ribs. Another spike of pain burst through my body, so sharp I almost blacked out. Droplets of moisture whipped through the air, stinging my skin like bees. Where was I?

I remembered Shade's trial, the agony of banging helplessly against what felt increasingly like a death trap. I remembered my mates turning to me as one when my head slipped beneath the water. I remembered the pressure of the water, my lungs screaming for air. I remembered a single moment of peace before I inhaled what I thought would be my last breath.

Teyr clutched my waist, the long side of his fiery hair flapping in the wind. Bash clasped a lilac hand around him. My stomach churned. I wanted to be done running, done fighting, but I never wanted to be done with my mates.

After that, my memory fell to flashes of pain, bright lights, and screaming. A kiss. Bash's hand in mine. Or Teyr's? My Cara with Shade had widened into a bridge, so clearly, I had done something to create that.

Our steep descent suddenly evened out. I bit back a scream. More pieces of memory fell into place. Somewhere deep within myself, I knew I'd forgotten on purpose. But now, I couldn't stop the memories. Zelimir's panicked voice, his dark hand on mine. I'd shaken out of a trance. He'd pressed my hand to the searing pain in my side. Then, sparks. Coming out of me.

The bone dragon hit the ground with a *boom*. The sounds of insects and frogs rushed in as the wind died down. I fought Teyr's grip, clawing and scratching. I might have remembered wrong. My memories were fragmented. Chunks had disappeared. Some of them could be wrong.

"Please," Teyr whispered in my ear. "Please relax."

I sank my teeth into his arm. He swore and released me. I slid down the cold bone of the skeletal dragon. Bash caught me with his telekinesis and lowered me onto the grass of a small clearing. Teyr lit two fireballs behind me. The world took on a soft, orange glow. My body screamed in agony as I struggled against Bash's hold, but I had to know. My dragon landed in front of me, Shade cradled in his arms.

"Let me go," I spat. "You promised."

Don't do this, Bash said across our bridge. But, true to his word, he did not disobey my wishes. His telekinetic hold loosened.

I'd been injured before, even seriously. I'd stood on death's door more than once during my five years on Earth. Nothing should have changed. I took a deep breath and looked down. On my left side, along the seam of my cuirass, a deep, angry wound oozed a trickle of blood. I touched the edge experimentally. Charred leather crumbled, but I couldn't see anything with the armor in the way. My mates stood in a half-circle around me. I pulled off my cuirass, ignoring the blazing pain the action triggered in my side. I had to know.

I tugged the blood-soaked, burnt edges of my trainee greens away from the gash and stared. Angry red and black curls of skin peeled away from the wound, blistered and bleeding. Beneath that, I saw flesh and bone. Beneath that—

I retched.

"Kinnia," Teyr murmured.

He had clearly seen what I had. Metal gleaming under my own flesh.

It could be a trick, an illusion, a hallucination. I wiped my mouth with the back of my hand and straightened. I had to be sure. I pressed a finger into the wound, swallowing down a scream and another round of vomiting as agony darkened my vision. Wet flesh. The jagged scrape of bone. And smooth, warm metal. A frayed cable that ached dully when I tugged at it.

The wound ran deep enough that it should have hit my heart. I should be dead. If I were human. If I were ever alive in the first place. Zelimir took a step forward with his hands up. I looked up into his purple eyes. His Cara stuttered open. Worry, confusion, fear, and underneath it all, hate.

I had to get the Tech out. I plunged more of my hand into the wound, grabbing for the cable, intent to yank it out of my body. With a scream, I blacked out before I hit the ground.

2

———

ZELIMIR

Teyr's fire flickered on Kinnia's unconscious face, glinted off the blood and metal inside her. My instincts warred with my heart. Force magic coated my fingers, and I itched to shape a weapon. What *thing* had tethered itself to my Cara—to my mates' very souls?

"Inside." Shade clambered out of Bash's arms. "Before my own defense spells attack us."

I didn't know when the necromancer had woken, if he even knew about the Tech, but he met my gaze resolutely with his black-and-white eyes and tottered toward me.

Bash rushed to Kinnia. Shame joined the revulsion in my stomach. I should be at her side. I should convince my mates to leave her and let the defenses work. Before she'd fallen unconscious, I'd lost control of my Cara. Everyone knew I held as much hate and disgust for the metal in her side as she did. A perverse desire to laugh climbed up my throat. I'd demanded she accept her true self.

"Teyr, your tunic, now," Bash called.

Teyr stripped, and my second bound her injury. She became our Kinnia again, crumpled on the dirt, her dark curls splayed around her face. She wheezed but gave no sign of waking.

Shade tugged on my arm, *pulsing* his urgency. When I remained in place, he took a step away and crumpled. I caught him around the waist and pulled him back to my side. Instead of concern for his mind or body, anger flooded me. Shade had pushed beyond his limits, used up every scrap of magic he could reach. He'd forced me to choose between him and my chain of command. For what?

"You tried to kill the Council," I hissed.

"They tried to kill my Kitty," Shade growled. "They tried to break us. She needs help, now. I will crawl inside my tower and let my spells suck the life out of you if you don't begin walking."

I flinched. Whatever he knew, he still claimed her as his own, and he was willing to let me burn for that. Teyr's firelight tangled in Shade's loose, black braid, highlighting the pale skin under his shaved sides, and I remembered how he cackled in the colosseum. The shame and revulsion in my gut intensified.

Bash stood with Kinnia in his arms. Teyr hovered nearby, fluttering his hands uselessly. The Councils had tried to kill Kinnia, but the Lower Council couldn't have known about the Tech inside her. Their response would have been swift and punitive. The Upper Council, however....

Teyr stroked a lock of hair back from her face, and I winced. He knew the truth about her. How could he touch her? How could I turn my back on her? I swallowed hard and opened my Cara to Shade carefully. Discomfort, worry, no more. The necromancer opened his, all frantic anger and fear. He didn't know anything more than me, except that we would be killed if we stayed out here.

"Where are we?" I took most of Shade's weight and let him guide me forward.

"Bittermist Thicket." Shade nodded at a tall, crooked tower I hadn't noticed in the clearing ahead of us. "My home, before the Cara called." He swallowed. "Light and I built it together."

Teyr caught up with us quickly and fell into step beside Shade, his fireball turning his slit-pupiled eyes molten gold. "And you picked the creepiest, most unstable part of the wilds because...?"

"There are lots of toys to entertain me here." Shade shrugged.

The ember frowned. "Did Light like it here?"

I forced myself not to check if Bash was following. I didn't even listen for his footsteps. He would bring her, or he wouldn't. Both options made my heart pound unevenly.

I cast through my memories for any sign I missed, any clue I ignored. Her eyes sparkled with pleasure, deepened with rage, shifted with all her wild emotions just like Tech eyes did not. She moved fluidly, but she lacked their inhuman grace. Some of her mannerisms might have been awkward or uncouth, but I chalked that up to her years as a mercenary.

"I never thought to ask if he liked it here," Shade said. "My twin chose this spot. That was enough for me."

Teyr just nodded.

We reached a wooden double-door at the base of the deep-blue stone tower. The necromancer wobbled forward, traced a finger over the door, and murmured something. His blue-black power inked the wood. Something clicked behind the door, and it swung open with a whine.

Shade wobbled, and I caught him to my side as we entered a large, empty, dirt-floored room. A round, stone well sat in the center next to a fire pit. A bucket hung on by a single thread above the well. I held him close as we walked past the well and climbed a spiral staircase to the second floor. Shade murmured at another door, which burned light blue and left glowing lines in its wake. This door opened into a space the same size but divided into three rooms with open doorways between each. A large fireplace and a rotting couch lay ahead of me. Faded tapestries and paintings hung askew on the walls.

I walked Shade to a desk and pulled out the high-backed chair. He collapsed onto the hard wood, sending up a puff of dust. When I turned, Bash and Teyr stood behind me. Kinnia still lay in Bash's lilac arms. I breathed a sigh of relief and choked down the feeling I was a traitor to all I'd ever stood for.

"This place needs to be secured." Scales swirled over Bash's face, collecting and breaking apart again. "But Dee needs my help, and I...I don't...." He hugged her tighter to his chest.

Shade stood and stumbled to Bash's side. "Go do what you're good at." He squeezed his eyes shut. "My defense runes are on the lower floor."

I stared at my mates, all clustered around something that shouldn't be. Bash's helpless confusion made more sense than anything else that had happened in the last few minutes.

Shade turned to me. "Zelimir?"

He wanted me to take her—it—her. My stomach squirmed. Like this, she just looked like Kinnia, the woman I'd spent the last couple months with, had maybe even come to love. But I knew. I had seen. A few curls tumbled off her forehead, and my stomach churned. Even her hair gave her away. She'd only been growing it out for a month, and already, the curls brushed her chin.

Shade crossed his arms. "She's ours. She always has been."

Bash nodded.

Teyr scowled. "Like I would think anything else."

I leveled a stare back at him, and he dropped his gaze. We'd spent most of our lives fighting Tech, and what time we hadn't been fighting, we'd heard stories about their horrors. This woman, whatever else she was, had Tech inside her. Not tech like Jalan, with their strangeness displayed for all to see like a poisonous creature's colors. She hid whatever machinery she had inside, like a secret, to blend into our world. We couldn't ignore that because just we loved her.

Shade stared at me. His strength seemed to be returning. Drops of his power spilled down his cheeks. "I just brought a dragon back from the dead. With my Kitty now a part of me, I hesitate to think what I am capable of."

I had felt Shade's wrath. I didn't want to face him in a place like this.

"She's our mate." I held up my hands, searched Teyr's gaze, then Bash's. "But we have to be smart. We can't allow emotion to blind us."

Teyr kicked a clump of dust. Bash frowned but nodded sharply. Shade let out a pitiful howl and leaned against the wall as though he hadn't just threatened my life.

My second held her out, and I swallowed. Despite everything, I was the leader. I had to lead. I took her into my arms, struggling to repress a shiver.

She hung limply, and I remembered the moment in the arena when I had been certain she was dead. I missed Light every day. When he died, a piece of me died with him. But nothing in my life had broken my heart like the moment I thought I lost her. I cradled her gently against my chest.

"My Kitty can curl up in my old bedroom, through the left door," Shade said.

Bash began to head downstairs, and Teyr drifted toward the window.

"Wait," I said. "Secure the location, destroy the trainee greens because the Councils can track them and then"—I swallowed—"and then we'll talk through everything when she wakes up. Together."

Shade grinned. Teyr hesitated, then offered a soft smile. Bash patted me on the shoulder as he passed.

I knew you could be the leader we needed, he thought to me.

I almost smiled.

ANAM CARA BOOKS

A Flash of Silver
Behind Stone Walls
The Crystalline Heart